THE
LAST GOOD
SAMARITAN

THE
LAST GOOD
SAMARITAN

A NOVEL

CHRIS THOMAS

ISBN: 978-0-9965607-3-3

Acknowledgements

My heartfelt thanks go to the following people for taking the time to read drafts of the manuscript and providing me their valued opinions and support; Mic Gumb, Art Cudworth, Scott Guetz, Karen Gumina, Sue McIlvennan and my story editor Madison. Also to my brother Dan, and my sisters Kathy and Tere, for not only reading the manuscripts, but also for having the honesty to tell me what they really thought. Lastly, to my wife Nan, and our three kids, Sarah, Wil, and Sam, for their belief in me and the dream.

Everyone who has ever built anywhere a "new heaven" first found the power thereto in his own hell.

—*Friedrich Nietzsche*

Prologue

Seattle, Washington
Mid-March

Ray was confused. The sun was shining, and the elegant terrace surrounding the equally impressive pool he was standing near was shaded by a canopy of palms swaying before a soft, cooling breeze. He couldn't remember how he had gotten there or why. There were important men on the terrace, sitting around a large linen-covered table talking, but their faces weren't identifiable, their words unintelligible. Other men like him were standing behind those at the table—serious, hard-looking men; something about these faces he seemed to remember. Suddenly, the man in the black suit to his left lunged for the one Ray now remembered was called the Condor, but for reasons not clear to him. Ray was ready, and he jumped toward the assassin to protect his patron, his knife already clear of the concealed sheath. The knife plunged deeply into the man's chest in the ensuing chaos, and he felt the blade glancing off bone as it sank to the hilt. They were on the ground; he was on top of the man and felt more than heard the last breath escape from the dying assailant.

The chaos ended, and the images blurred, dissolving from the shaded terrace to a cool, dark, damp place. Now he was on the bottom, and the man over him wasn't the assailant in the black suit but, rather, a kind face—a friend, he thought. The man appeared sad, and he was the one who had hurt him, it seemed—just how, or in what way, Ray could not recall, but he knew he had betrayed his friend somehow, and the hurt feelings were justified. The bad dream turned to a nightmare when his friend pointed the dull chrome nine-millimeter Glock in his hand at him, and he had no choice; he struck upward with the knife in his hand, still bloody, it seemed, from the assailant in the black suit, even though he knew that was impossible somehow.

The electrical impulses of the brain's synaptic action can do that—jump around from one recess of your memory to another, linking disparate thoughts as if they were one. Somewhere in those same recesses, a part of him seemed to understand, and it reminded him that dreams are like that.

The image of the scene and his friend's face returned as it changed from sadness to shock, and then to a lifeless, empty stare; this was what stayed with him. The pain he felt in his gut at his friend's death dulled an aching in his side he was now aware of, where a bullet from an earlier shooting he couldn't quite place had smashed his rib.

As his friend took his last breath and collapsed on him and he realized what he had done, he shattered the silence in the dark, musty space with an anguished scream. As his scream echoed down the dark tunnel he found himself in, the echoes were slowly replaced by a growing, annoying ringing that wouldn't stop. And then that place in his brain that always seemed to question events and sort them out overrode the darkness and said *alarm*, and he was suddenly awake and reaching for the persistent iPhone on the nightstand.

Ray turned off his phone and lay back down; his breathing was shallow and ragged, and he was in a cold sweat. He hated waking with this feeling; this wasn't the first time. He swung his legs out of bed and sat there for a second trying to control his breathing, and then he stood and walked unsteadily to his bathroom and turned on the shower. He stepped in without waiting. The water was cold, but he didn't care; he needed the cold to get fully awake. As the water warmed and his breathing slowly returned to near normal, his mind started analyzing the situation. He couldn't help it. It was habit; that was what he had been trained to do. Most of the nightmares had stopped months ago, and last night's was the only one that occasionally reoccurred. But even then, it still had been several months. Why now? What had set it off? That was what he focused on.

Nothing in his personal life or at work had changed in the last several months. Both were pretty dull, he admitted. The only event, if you could even call it that, was Bennie's call out of the blue yesterday from DC to tell him he was coming to town and it was necessary they meet. When he pressed his boss as to the reason, Bennie cut him off and said any further discussion would have to wait until they were face to face. That meant whatever was on his mind was need to know. He could read Bennie, even over a cell phone. Need to know meant this had to be about a mission, either the one last year he was trying so hard to forget and put behind him, or possibly a new one. That was both a scary thought and an exciting one, for exactly the same reasons.

The problem was his doc had told him last Monday they were nearly done with his therapy. He hadn't had nightmares for months, and the agency was asking for a final report on his condition. It was either back to undercover work or out on a medical report that would effectively end the only aspect of his law enforcement career he really cared about. That he couldn't accept. Bennie would probably put him to work in Washington shuffling high-level paper for him, but that would be as bad as carrying the stigma of an emotionally damaged field agent around with him the rest of his career. He knew Dr. Mercer was finishing his report, and today's session was only going to be a general review of the past year and his official exit interview. Knowing Doc Mercer as he did, the doc would say something simple but profound and send him on his way, most likely telling him once again that sometimes bad shit just happens, so move on, get over it, and live his life.

He dressed and left his apartment. The Seattle DEA office was in the Federal Building right downtown on Marion Street, but it was Monday morning, and he was due at Dr. Mercer's at nine at his office in the psychiatric annex near the UW Med Center on Portage Bay. He wasn't a liar, but as he drove toward the UW campus, he knew this morning he would lie to his shrink. Maybe he'd get lucky and wouldn't have to actually lie. If the doc didn't ask him directly, he simply wasn't going to tell him about last night. But he was smart enough to know there wasn't much difference between the two.

He had always been a pragmatist. If a cryptic phone call from Bennie could bring the dream back, how on earth could he handle a mission? He knew it probably made no sense, but a part of him deep inside said he needed another mission, in part *to help* put the past behind him. In another example of dishonesty, he had to admit he had never really explored that part with Doc Mercer, not liking where those thoughts led.

He parked his car in the patients' lot and walked slowly to the front door of the annex, composing himself. There was the typical light rain falling, but he paused anyway, the moisture beginning to trickle down his face, and he looked across the bay toward the high rises of downtown. Then he took a deep breath, turned, and walked in. Doc Mercer would be a tough guy to fool. If he could do it this morning, then as far as he was concerned, that meant he still had his game face and could put it on when the situation demanded it. The miserable shits he'd have to deceive if Bennie was giving him another crack at undercover work down south were certainly a ruthless and dangerous lot, but by and large they weren't all that smart. No matter his weaknesses, he'd take his chances. He had to.

1

The white cargo van came out of nowhere and startled Jack as it blew by him. With the occasional hairpin curves and short straightaways on the highway descending the eastern slopes of the Continental Divide, he simply had not seen it coming out of the darkness in his rearview mirrors. That, and as usually was the case late at night when he was alone, he was thinking about his two daughters and everything that had happened to him recently, not focusing on his driving as he should.

Normally Jack loved this part of his drive no matter the hour, and he was only a mile or two beyond the lookout and monument that announced the pass's summit at 10,857 feet above sea level when the speeding van surprised him. US Highway 160 had been snaking its way over this part of the Continental Divide for nearly a hundred years, through the natural cleavage in the high, intimidating southern end of the Rocky Mountains. Pavement eventually supplanted the early dirt-and-gravel road, and more projects widened the route and burrowed through other obstacles, resulting in the safe mountain highway that existed today. "Safe" was a relative term, of course, for despite all the improvements, there was no making shallower the constant 7 and 8 percent slopes of the highway, nor could the occasional tight curves be straightened. And the steep and rugged drop-offs on the valley side were a deadly hazard to the careless or stupid.

Driving the large panel truck between his employer's computer-drive factory in the north Denver suburbs and their customers in the Greater Los Angeles basin would probably be boring and too mind dullingly repetitive for most others; for Jack it was a salve. Since his wife had divorced him and unfairly won primary custody of his daughters and moved them out of state, driving to and from California twice a month for his job made it possible to see his girls as regularly as the court would allow. He took the interstates on his way down—better to get there as fast as possible—but after the two days he was allowed to see them every two weeks, he always took more scenic and longer routes back, to allow him the time he needed to deal with the great melancholy that leaving his daughters behind always brought on.

As the red taillights of the speeding van pulled away at an ever-increasing rate, the now-wide-awake Jack muttered, "Asshole. Just where in the living hell you think you're going that fast?" Jack knew this road as well as or better than most, and the straightaway they were on, while one of the longer on this part of the mountain, still was only measured in hundreds of yards and ended at a very tight left-hand curve designed for thirty or forty miles per hour, not the near seventy or eighty he judged the van accelerating away from him was doing.

Then, of course, there was the black ice to be considered. Anyone driving this road as carelessly as the van's driver was had to be unfamiliar with high-altitude roads, which meant he was also probably ignorant of black ice. The midday temperatures of mid-March were getting plenty warm enough, even at these high altitudes, to melt some of the snow pack. Despite the highway engineers' best efforts to see that the runoff flowed in the borrow pits adjacent to the pavement or crossed under the highway in culverts, the grading of roads was an imperfect endeavor, and occasionally trickles of water found their way across the pavement. The cold nighttime temperatures of March froze the thin films of water after dark, and many of these slick patches were undetectable to even a careful driver like Jack. Where the small slick patches occurred in a straightaway, they went mostly unnoticed as you drove over them, your tires and momentum all aligned straight down the center of the road as they were; but where they occurred in and near curves, Isaac Newton's first law of motion unfortunately came into play.

The object in a state of motion that was the speeding white van continued unaltered in its accelerating path as the road curved sharply left, and the front tires encountered the black ice and failed to do their job. Dry tires on dry pavement might have had a slight chance at altering the motion of the van, perhaps keeping it on the pavement, but the van's momentum was simply too great, and this part of the road was too slick.

Jack watched with shock as the red taillights of the van simply disappeared in front of him, never wavering from the centerline of the straightaway as the van hurtled into space and was lost in the darkness. Recent construction had widened the highway and the shoulders, making the overall drive far safer than it had once been, and the highway engineers' plans called for new low native stone walls to be constructed as esthetic guardrails in the tighter curves. The work had been finished on the west side of the pass but was still in progress on the east. Many of the curves, including the one he was approaching, were absent this last small but important safety detail.

Jack had his truck down to a safe speed long before his headlights picked up the dull, glinting reflections of the icy patch in the curve. A sudden sick feeling in the pit of his stomach came over him, and he knew time was critical if he was going to be able to help the unfortunate passengers of the van. Past the curve was another straightaway, but he had to go several hundred feet down the road before he found a shoulder wide enough to get his truck mostly out of the eastbound lane. He turned off his engine, put his emergency flashers on, and then glanced at his cell phone, knowing before he did there would be little or no coverage on this part of the pass. He quickly grabbed his jacket, his large flashlight, and the first-aid kit from under his seat and ran back uphill to the curve. He glanced up and down the pass, hoping to see another late-night traveler who could help him, but he appeared to have the pass to himself. Disappointed, he pointed the powerful beam of light over the edge, and a feeling of dread came over him. As he expected, the steep rocky slope seemed to go on forever, disappearing into the darkness beyond the range of his flashlight. He carefully went over the side and picked his way down over the rocks as quickly as he could without losing control.

He was in excellent shape, and that was a good thing because the air at this altitude was thin and the energy required to climb down considerable. He had no idea how long he'd been climbing—two or three minutes certainly—before he encountered the tall leading trees of the Ponderosa pine forest that covered this part of the Divide. Jack stopped to get his wind and to get his bearings. He was certain that his path down the steep rocky slope was pretty much on the bearing of the van's path, but after shining his light toward the trees, he did not see the van, nor did he see any evidence of a van having barreled into the pristine pines. He looked back up the slope, the edge of the road above barely visible as a silhouette against the star-filled sky, and tried to visualize the arc of the van's path at the speed it was going and decided it was possible, maybe even likely, that the van had arced over the initial tree line of the forest. Whoever was driving the van was insanely stupid, he thought, to have been going that fast. But he quickly dismissed the negative thought, knowing he had to get to the driver and any passengers quickly if he was to help them. After a last look up the slope, he descended into the trees and the enveloping darkness.

He picked his way through the dense pines, deep snow, and deadwood from the natural decay of the forest on the rocky slope, which slowed him even more. He climbed perhaps another fifty feet down before he finally saw the emerging spectral shape of the van through the trees. The slope he was descending continued farther down into the darkness, but the van was smashed into a granite outcropping that grew out of the side of the steep slope like some terrible unsightly growth. The windowless cargo van had sheared a number of trees off as its ballistic path through the darkness finally intersected with the steeply sloping ground, and then the largest and most unmovable of the granite boulders of the outcropping had violently ended the van's short flight.

Jack made his way up the left side of the van as quickly as he could. His heart sank as he got even with what was remaining of the driver-side door and he could see the totally smashed front end. The van was wedged into a natural cleft between the two largest boulders, and the driver, who evidently had not been wearing a seat belt, had been catapulted through the windshield at impact and was clearly dead on the boulders. Jack went to him to confirm his initial instinct, but he was certain; he had seen more than his fair share of death in his time, the two principal occupations of his adult life having made comfort with or indifference to violent death a prerequisite.

He shined his light toward the passenger side and could see another man, half in and half out of the mangled opening that was once the windshield. The passenger-side air bag was still in place partially inflated, and that had evidently kept the man in his seat, where the driver's air bag had failed somehow. Jack worked his way around the back of the van until he got to where the passenger door had been. Somehow with the force of the impact, the door had been thrown open and sheared off. Several medium-sized packing boxes bearing the name and logo of a plastics company out of Las Vegas were covering the passenger, with yet more boxes piled up against the back of the two front seats as a result of the collision. The boxes were very light, to his surprise, and he was able to clear them from the front and managed to get himself into a position where he could lean the passenger back into his seat. His lower body was crushed by the collapsed and mangled front end, which was pinning him in place from the knees down. Given his appearance, Jack was certain he also was dead, but nevertheless he gently started to move him back into his seat. To his surprise, there was a low moan. He could now see that the man had a catastrophic head wound, and he was determined to help him as best he could.

"Hang in there, buddy," he said as he opened his first-aid kit and found the largest of the gauze pads and some tape to try to stem the bleeding, knowing from experience they'd be terribly insufficient.

The injured man coughed and seemed to be aware of his presence, and he slowly turned his battered face toward Jack, trying to speak. Jack leaned in close, and through troubled wheezing and gasping, the man said, "Diaz. Debe decirle a Diaz…Matamoros." The man then turned away, making a terrible groaning sound, and Jack knew he was gone.

"Goddammit!" he angrily spit out loud. "If only I'd been quicker."

In the terrible moment of the unknown man's death, he felt bad that he wasn't able to help him, but after standing in the door opening for a few seconds thinking about it, he knew it wouldn't have mattered; his injuries were too severe. The intellectual side of him knew the passenger was lucky to have survived as long as he did, but the emotional side still wished he'd climbed the slope quicker.

He had a decent grasp of Spanish and mulled over what the dying man had said. "Diaz. Must tell Diaz Matamoros." He would deal with that later, he thought.

He shined the flashlight into the back of the van to check for more passengers, but what he saw illuminated by the light stunned him. He did a double take at first, for he could not believe what he was seeing. There were no other passengers in the mostly intact rear of the van; what Jack saw instead were neatly stacked packages of what looked like plastic-wrapped American currency, partially concealed beneath a jumbled top layer of boxes marked as plastic products, all half covered by a plastic tarp.

He backed out of the passenger door and went to the side door; after considerable effort he managed to force it open. From just behind the two front seats to the rear doors, stacked two high, were large neat packages of American cash. Evidently, the layer of benign boxes was camouflage of sorts in case someone looked in one of the front windows. The impact had sent the unsecured boxes flying forward, along with the tarp, but the packages of currency remained mostly jammed where they had been initially loaded. Jack reached out and touched the nearest wrapped package and confirmed what he saw—stacks on stacks of bundled currency vacuum wrapped together with a clear plastic. He reached into his pants pocket for the Swiss Army knife he always carried. He carefully slit the plastic of the top package and took out a pack of bills. The neat paper-banded pack appeared to be all hundreds; he did a quick count and determined he was holding ten thousand dollars.

Good lord, he thought. *There must be millions here. Has to be drug money.*

Jack knew what he was talking about. From his police and Marine Corps experiences, he knew the van and its cargo had to be a collection run by some

Mexican cartel. The illegal drug business was very lucrative to the criminals who ran it, but it was a cash-only business. At some point in the distribution process, someone trusted by the leaders in Mexico had to go and collect all the money accumulating in the north. The van's two occupants obviously were trusted collectors for someone, probably the Diaz guy the passenger had tried to tell him about.

He went back to where the passenger was still sitting and out of professional habit began looking the van and the body over for evidence. In the glove box, he quickly found some folded maps and other papers that confirmed his first intuitions. There were carefully detailed notations on the state maps indicating an exacting schedule for the van's occupants to call in verifying their location and progress. They had started in Las Vegas, taken I-15 east until reaching St. George, Utah; then followed smaller, less traveled state roads to Flagstaff; and there they picked up Highway 160, ending up here.

Between the front seats, Jack found a leather duffel bag concealing several automatic weapons lying on the floor. He recognized the assault rifles as being the very popular Belgian-made FAL 50.63, the variant with the folding stock and the shorter barrel length commonly used by paratroopers.

Nasty, he thought. *If these guys knew how to use these, taking the money from them would have been a dangerous proposition.*

He unzipped the duffel and examined the contents, which turned out to be nothing more than a change of clothes for one of the two dead men, several expensive new handguns with extra clips, and a handful of prepaid cell phones. He took the clothes out and then put into the bag all the papers and maps he could find. He went through the pockets of both victims, finding two sets of identification on each body—another curious fact—put them in the bag as well, and zipped it up. He stepped back to a nearby rock, sat down facing the van, and turned off his flashlight as a new, mostly disturbing thought started to enter his mind.

The night was clear, with enough light from a descending quartering moon filtering through the trees that as his eyes adjusted to the darkness, he could make out the wrecked van in front of him and the silhouetted shape of the dead passenger in his seat. As Jack sat there, the realization came to him that had he not been immediately behind the van as it plunged off the pass, he'd have never found it. Because it had literally flown over the first rank of tall pine trees before crashing into this rock outcropping, there was no way to see the wreck from above. Nor was it likely that hikers or fishermen would discover the wreck from the valley floor below.

He turned on the flashlight and pointed it down the slope; there was nothing but heavy pine forest continuing down as far as he could see. The van was wedged into the boulders on the well-concealed uphill side, and the rock outcropping was definitely concealed from view from below, he judged. It seemed likely there were would be no hiking trails between the valley below and the road. Why would there be? He knew the ski area he'd passed a mile up the pass was a trailhead for hikers and fishermen, but any trails would lead down into the valley paralleling the highway, not anywhere near the rocky slopes such as this one.

He pointed the flashlight back up the slope, checking out the forest he had climbed through to get to the wreck, and then he closed his eyes and visualized the highway above. It struck him that he was the only man on earth who knew where this particular van had ended up, and as such he was the only one who knew about this money—or, more precisely, some trafficker's dirty money. That was both a troubling thought and a rather interesting one. He'd never done anything close to illegal in his life, his recent troubles with the Denver DA and Police Department notwithstanding. Yet as he sat in the dark thinking about his current life situation and the van in front of him, the idea of not reporting the wreck started to creep into the back of his mind. The two Mexicans were dead despite his best efforts, he couldn't do a thing for them, and there was no doubt the cash was illegal, the currency forfeited by the fools wanting the poison the cartels sold. His years in Vice had exposed him to a bellyful of the type, and they mostly sickened him. Whoever this Diaz character in Matamoros was, he'd no doubt wonder where his money had gone, but where could he look? Nope, Jack thought. There was no finding this wreck unless whoever owned it had a real good idea where the van might be and then knowledgeable experienced people started looking; but to look here, in this exact place on the highway? Not likely, nor was it likely that Mr. Diaz would be contacting the proper authorities anytime soon for help.

He wanted to think about this some more, but for the time being, he'd keep silent about the wreck, take what money he could carry, and then deal with his troubling thoughts further when he got home.

He went back to the van and the package of currency he'd opened and started taking out bound packs of cash, putting as much as he could stuff into the small duffel bag. Done, he forced the side door closed, took a last look around, and then started working his way back through the deadfall, angling his way east up the difficult slope toward the section of highway where he had parked his truck.

⊷⊷ ⊶⊷

Colorado State Patrol trooper Larry McDermott left Lucy's Diner in Pagosa Springs around three with the thermos of coffee he'd stopped for and made his way east up and over the pass. Every third week he had the overnight grave-yard shift, mostly patrolling this section of US Highway 160, which connected the Four Corners area of southwest Colorado with Interstate 25 to the east in Walsenburg. Along with his fellow troopers out of Durango and Alamosa, he covered the few state and federal highways that crossed through District 5, the southern- and westernmost designated area covered by the state patrol. There wasn't a lot of traffic or action on the graveyard shift typically, which suited Trooper McDermott just fine. Graveyard during the winter could be brutal, but now that spring was here, he'd have seven or eight months of nice weather before the heavy winter storms so common to southwest Colorado again required real work.

He made his way past the summit and the ski area located there and was a little surprised a few minutes later to come upon the twenty-foot panel truck parked on the side of the road, its emergency flashers going. He slowly pulled up behind the truck, stopped, and turned his rooftop-mounted emergency lights on. Then he punched in the license plate number on his computer keyboard and hit Enter. Unlike the commercial cell networks, the state police

9

had their own system of dedicated shortwave radio and data relay stations all along the mountain pass. It took the system only a few seconds to process his request and give him the registration and ownership information he was looking for and let him know there were no outstanding warrants or issues. He clicked on his radio mike and said curtly and professionally in the radio shorthand all troopers were trained in, "T-48; 10-46; 10-20 at mile 169."

Fifty miles away down the east side of the pass, the bored graveyard radio dispatcher working out of the division office in Alamosa instantly translated the codes in his head as they came in and understood that *Trooper McDermott, badge number T48, was assisting a stopped vehicle about two miles east of the summit of Wolf Creek Pass.* "Ten-four" was his succinct reply. *I understand and acknowledge.* The tired and bored dispatcher then routinely entered the contact information into his computer.

The trooper grabbed his flashlight, got out, and walked up to the driver-side door. He climbed up on the running board and peered in, but the cab was empty. This got his attention as he had expected to find the dozing driver; one did not normally find delivery trucks of this type abandoned on the side of the road in the middle of the night. He stepped down off the running board, touched the engine hood, which was still warm, and then did a quick walk around the vehicle checking the tires, noting that they looked all right. *OK, where's the driver?* he thought, now a little concerned. He knew he'd passed no pedestrians coming over the pass, and a quick look down the decently long straightaway to the east also revealed nothing. Concerned, he was starting back toward his cruiser when he heard something to his left and then saw some movement out of the corner of his eye, momentarily startling him. He turned and pointed his flashlight toward the road's edge just as Jack climbed up.

"Evening officer", Jack said. "Sorry if I surprised you."

Trooper McDermott, sensing there was no threat from the friendly-looking stranger, said, "Good evening, sir. That's OK. This your truck?"

"Yes, sir. I mean I'm the driver. The truck belongs to my boss's company."

"Want to tell me why you're stopped here? Not the safest place in the world to be parked, especially in the middle of the night."

Jack smiled and shook his head. "Sorry. Yeah, I know. A helluva big bull elk came off the mountain in front of me, took two strides, and went over the side. I'm pretty sure I clipped him as he went by, so out of curiosity I stopped to check."

Trooper McDermott smiled back. He'd been tracking and hunting elk in Colorado and the West since he was fifteen and knew from experience that unless this guy had really nailed the elk, he'd be long gone, as tough and agile as they were. "Couldn't find him, I'll bet."

"Nope, no trace. No blood trail I could see, but it's darker than the hubs of hell over the side and real rocky."

The trooper chuckled. "Amazing, isn't it, that an animal that large can move the way they do across slopes like that. Why don't you get your license and the registration and we have a seat in my car. Just routine, but I do have to make a contact report."

"Sure, officer. Here," Jack said as he reached into his back pocket for his wallet and handed his license over. "The insurance and registration papers are in the glove box. Be right back."

The trooper walked back to his car thinking that there was something familiar about the truck driver. It was just an odd feeling, as if he'd seen his face before. Jack came back to the parked cruiser and opened the passenger door and got in; the trooper was drinking some coffee and entering Jack's driver's license number into his computer.

"Here you go," Jack said to the trooper as he slid into the seat.

"Thanks. This will just take a second."

When Jack's name and photo came up on his screen, Trooper McDermott remembered instantly where he'd seen this driver's face and the name Jack Williams before. He was the Denver cop—a well-regarded detective, he recalled—who had shot and killed a child molester caught in the act, only to be indicted for police brutality and manslaughter by an ambitious district attorney with eyes on a higher political office. There wasn't a law enforcement officer in the state—or a father, for that matter—who didn't think this guy was a hero, not a criminal. He recalled the basic story. His young daughter had been snatched by the pervert a couple of months before the shooting, but the perv apparently had second thoughts and dumped the little girl after going only a couple of blocks, due to the presence of too many witnesses to the grab. Two Denver traffic cops who responded to a description of his car and stopped the molester for questioning were a little too emotional in their arrest procedures, and the pervert walked on some technicalities in the law intended to safeguard law-abiding citizens from illegal search and seizure. In this case, unfortunately, the law released a dangerous pedophile back into the public.

Detective Williams apparently spent every off hour after his daughter's attack stalking the man, was warned by his department to cease and desist after the pedophile registered a complaint, and eventually was served with a restraining order. The detective ignored the order and because of his diligence caught the man red-handed several months later dragging an eight-year-old boy into his run-down rented house. According to the news stories in the paper and online, this Jack Williams had jumped out of his car, ran across the street, and literally kicked in the front door, catching the guy in his living room with his pants down cutting the clothes off the hysterical young boy with a pair of shears. According to the detective's own testimony, the surprised pedophile turned when he burst in and then, recognizing him from his earlier court appearances in his daughter's case, simply started to laugh before turning back toward the boy. According to the DA, Detective Williams then calmly, and with malice aforethought, shot the pedophile right square in the head without a word of warning.

Trooper McDermott remembered thinking, when he had followed the story in the news last year, that the shooting seemed entirely justified, and he hoped he would have done the same thing if it had been his daughter. The Denver DA, however, didn't see it that way. The detective was suspended, and then the ambitious DA tried to convict him on felony counts of manslaughter and excessive use of force. Surprisingly, a sympathetic jury wound up convicting him of a lesser charge involving no jail time. Nevertheless, despite saving the young boy from a horrible crime, he was booted off the force—a real screwing, the trooper thought at the time.

"You wouldn't be the Jack Williams from the Denver Police, would you?" the trooper asked.

Jack's normal friendly look turned to a frown. The last thing he wanted right now was to get into a casual conversation with the trooper, but under the circumstances, he didn't have a choice. Looking the trooper straight in the eye, he said, "Yes, I was once with the Denver Police."

"I thought so. Mr. Williams, I want you to know that me and every trooper I work with think you got railroaded. It's a privilege to meet you sir," he said as he extended his hand.

"Thanks, Trooper."

"I can't believe they ran you off the force, Mr. Williams. It's just not right, if you don't mind me saying."

"Nah, that's OK," Jack said, a small forced smile on his face. "Just between the two of us, the only real regret I have is that I couldn't kill the sick bastard twice."

Trooper McDermott smiled back and chuckled. "My sentiments exactly. Everything checks out fine, as I knew it would. I'm sorry if I've delayed you."

"No delay, Trooper. Just headed for Denver and to bed as soon as I get there. Thanks for the kind words."

The two men shook hands again, and then Jack went back to his cab as the state trooper pulled around him and started down the pass. Jack waited until he had disappeared around the next curve before he quickly jumped out of his truck and retrieved the first-aid kit and the stuffed duffel bag. Earlier, he had been climbing for a hard ten minutes and was glad to finally see the shape of the edge of the road above when he realized there were flashing lights and a state trooper's cruiser parked behind his truck. He had ducked back down into the darkness and tucked the bag and the first-aid kit between two large rocks, and only then did he climb up on the road as the officer was walking back to his car. The entire bullshit story about the elk had just come to him, and as unaccustomed to lying as he was, in retrospect, he was surprised how easy it had been to lie to the polite and decent young officer. He shook his head at the thought and quickly got into his cab and started down the pass after the trooper, not wanting to give him anything more to question.

It would not have been surprising to anyone who knew Jack why the young state patrol trooper sensed there was no real danger after Jack had startled him from out of the darkness. He was a powerful-looking man physically—tall, broad shouldered, very fit—but there was nothing intimidating about his presence to those first meeting him. He had kind eyes, people said, and an engaging smile to go with his easygoing mannerisms. Anyone who spent any time around him ended up liking him. Jack had many such admirers, mostly because of the person he was, but also because of what he had done. It simply did not matter to any of the many people who knew and liked him what his former wife; or his former employer, the City of Denver Police Department; or the Denver DA's office thought. All knew without a doubt that what he had done had been right, and the law in his case was simply wrong and unjust.

Until the recent events over the last year that had so drastically changed his life, Jack had considered himself a lucky man. Always had. Life did have its ups and downs, but for as long as he could remember, he had been upbeat and optimistic; it was his nature. But now, he had to admit, there were a lot of exes in his life—ex-Marine, ex-cop, ex-husband. If forced to think about things, especially when alone with his thoughts during his twice-monthly long drive, he could admit his luck had changed for the worse. In his mind, the measure of a person, whether good or bad, was how one dealt with the inevitable events that seemingly blindsided a person from time to time, and he was determined to get past all his troubles.

He'd made his choices on those occasions where he could exercise some control, and he would live with the consequences; all his decisions were made with the firm conviction at the time that they were the good and right thing to do. As to the actions of others, such as his ex-wife or the Denver DA, he would do as he always had—adjust and make the best of the situation. In his ex-wife's case, so much of what she had done during their marriage was wrong, even cruel; nevertheless, he still had feelings for her, and only time would heal that particular wound.

He could admit to himself that he *had* stalked the pedophile, knowing intuitively the sick bastard would strike again, but that one such experience constituted a "history," as his ex-wife's attorney had argued during the divorce hearing, was unfair and simply wasn't true. It still hurt that his wife let her attorney paint that terrible picture of him to the judge to gain custody of their daughters. That the stalking and subsequent killing of the pedophile had saved the boy from molestation and probably a premature death had fallen on deaf ears, it seemed, as she got everything she wanted, including some monthly child support that left him little. Not that he cared about the payments. He didn't; he wanted his girls to have everything they needed and then some and did not need a judge's order to do what was right.

The last six hours of the drive were uneventful, and he collapsed on the beat-up couch in his living room around nine. Usually, after returning the truck to the company and retrieving his pickup, he'd have stopped and had breakfast at one of the local restaurants and then gone right to bed, but there was no eating or sleeping after the night's events. After a few minutes, he struggled up and grabbed a quick shower, and then he did what he had wanted to do for hours. It took fifteen minutes to carefully count and recount the cash from the duffel bag, until he was sure he had it right. There was no mistake; sitting on his small kitchen table was exactly $280,000 in one-hundred-dollar bills. He'd never seen that much cash in one place at one time in his life, even when he had worked Vice. It was unbelievable; he'd simply grabbed as many packs of bills as he could get into the duffel with the papers and other evidence, as he still thought of it, and that had ended up being twenty-eight carefully banded $10,000 packs. It had been dark, but his sense was that he'd barely made a dent in the plastic-wrapped package he'd opened, and there was so much more. He hadn't really thought about it at the time. He had simply closed the van's side door and started climbing the slope.

He had to think this through, but he was exhausted and needed sleep. Given all that had happened in the last year—the trial, his dismissal from the force, his wife divorcing him and taking his girls—he knew he needed a fresh start in life, and he had been struggling with the idea not knowing how to begin again. Until now. Now, as he thought about the money and the potential it held, new, previously unimaginable possibilities were taking shape. He fell into bed and tried to sleep. He had some decisions to make—life-changing decisions, he realized—and he couldn't do that in the shape he was in. Only thoughts of his little girls slowed his mind down enough to finally drift off, but his sleep was fitful as his subconscious kept playing and replaying scenes of the van going off the road mixed with the images of the crash site, dead Mexicans, and stacks of money.

2

Jack tossed and turned for six hours but must have managed some sleep, because he awoke with a start and sat up. He glanced at his watch; it was five in the afternoon, and he was still depressingly tired. Dressed only in the gym shorts he had worn to bed, he got up and went into the small dining room of his apartment. The neat stacks of hundred-dollar bills were still there, and he sat down and stared at them.

"What in the hell am I'm going to do?" he said quietly to himself. The right thing to do, the lawful thing, was to contact one of the many friends he still had on the force, explain what had happened, and then turn the money in. It would be impounded—that was a certainty—and the papers, maps, and cell phones would be turned over to the DEA or the FBI and scrutinized for whatever evidence could be had. The information might even find its way down to the proper authorities in Mexico, where it might do some good. The quantities of illegal drugs being shipped into the country had decreased, if you believed the talking heads on television. Still, he knew from what he read that illegal trafficking still accounted for billions of dollars' worth of business; the mostly destroyed van full of cash he knew about was evidence enough of that.

He had been too tired this morning to think about how much might really be in the van. Now that he was a little rested and *was* thinking about it, he tried to make an educated guess as to how much the van was holding. He willed himself to remember how many wrapped packages he had seen from the passenger door; at least two rows stacked two high, he was sure, each package about twelve inches square and about twice that long. How many were there from front to back? He had cut into a middle package, he thought, so at least one to the right toward the front seats and two, he thought, to the rear. He had never been more than an average student in math, but it didn't take much math to figure there were at least sixteen wrapped packages of money. More if there were more rows; he wasn't sure and was too tired to recall any more detail. How much had he taken from the one? His sense was maybe a fourth, certainly no more. If that was the case and his guesses were right, that would mean there really was millions of dollars still sitting in the van. He was flabbergasted at the thought.

Could he keep the money even if he wanted to? That was a more complex question to answer than he thought it would be when he first started thinking about it. If he did keep the money—and not just the piles on his table, but if he went back and somehow carried out all that was in the van—what could he do with it and not attract attention? Jack had been a good cop for many years and was all too familiar with the kinds of footprints dumb criminals left in their paths as they committed whatever offense it was they were committing. By and large, criminals were the dumbest group of people he had ever seen. Very few really ever thought through their crimes in any detail. He'd come across a few sharp criminal operators while working Vice who had stayed under the radar for a long time, either in prostitution or gambling, but eventually, even they were caught.

To simply show up at his bank and start depositing huge sums of cash into his account was out of the question. He could keep the cash locked up, he thought, say in flameproof containers stashed in a typical storage business, and then go there from time to time and take what little cash he needed to live on. This could go unnoticed but seemed like a nuisance. He could pay a lot of his normal living expenses with cash, but the world had evolved beyond cash, really, and was mostly electronic these days. So that was a potentially thorny issue without resolution. Big purchases were also out of the question. Walking into a car dealership and picking out a new pickup and then plunking, say, $25,000 cash down on the sales associate's desk would surely draw attention from someone. If he decided to keep the money, he'd need a plan on how to hide it and then somehow launder it to legal funds, as he understood the cartels themselves had been doing for years.

Jack was a smart guy and knew it, but he wasn't that smart. He knew nothing about offshore accounts and the intricacies of international banking that would somehow allow bringing explainable money back into the country, paying taxes on it even, and then living a normal life somehow after that. If he was going to keep the money, he'd need real smart help that he could trust. As ironic as it was, had it not been for the pedophile he'd blown away who had so significantly changed his life for the worse, he wouldn't have known whom to safely approach about all the questions he had. But as it happened, he did.

Henry Berman, Attorney at Law, name principal and lead counsel in the prestigious Denver law firm of Berman, Greenberg, and Levine, had defended him in his legal proceedings with the City of Denver and the State of Colorado, and he'd done it for free. He had steered the jury away from the felony manslaughter charge and made the ambitious DA looking to make a big name for himself politically by nailing a so-called brutal cop look like a self-promoting fool. Henry's skills in defending him at trial resulted in the jury arriving at the far lesser conviction of nonfelony excessive use of force. This meant his getting sacked from the department but kept him out of jail. He did his year of community service and was on a suspended sentence for another year, but that just necessitated he stay out of trouble, and he wasn't a troublemaker anyway.

Henry Berman's son had been the hysterical eight-year-old about to have the last of his innocence ripped from him when Jack shot the fully erect pedophile dead. After he had the boy safe and out of the house and called in the shooting, the deeply distraught Henry Berman and his wife arrived to reclaim their physically unharmed child. A tearful Henry embraced Jack, thanked him, and told him he had a friend for life.

From most people, that would have been hyperbole, something said in the emotion of the moment and soon forgotten, but not from Henry Berman. When the shit hit the fan over the shooting and it became clear he would need an attorney to help him, Henry came to him, not the other way around, and offered his services. From that service, a true friendship grew. Henry also intervened in his divorce on his behalf, but Jack handcuffed him and wouldn't allow him to go after his wife. Jack told him he would agree to anything as long as he had joint custody. His now-ex-wife agreed to this in their private talks and then unleashed her lawyer at the settlement hearing, and the stunned Jack sat there, with no defense for the awful picture her lawyer painted of him other than what Henry could say extemporaneously in his defense. Henry's eloquence got him visitation rights twice monthly, but it was a profoundly sad day for him.

Money had been real tight since the divorce. The city settled with him on his retirement account, and between that and his share of their home sale, he had a few dollars in the bank, but not much. Following the divorce and his wife's move, he knew he needed a cheap place to live and a job that would allow him to see his girls as often as he could. He addressed his need for cheap housing first, responding to an ad for an on-site apartment manager position and getting the job and his small one-bedroom apartment in the deal. The property owner met him personally at his interview. When going through the stack of applications and seeing Jack's name and former employers listed in his history, he knew immediately who he was because of all the recent local press coverage of his trial. Like most people who followed the case, the landlord also thought Jack had gotten screwed. That, and twenty-five years earlier, the landlord had also done some time in the green machine and was only too happy to have a fellow marine as his building manager; semper fidelis still meant something to him.

Jack was lucky with a new job as well. He needed to get to California as often as possible, and he researched local job postings on the internet, looking for anything that required travel to California. It was a long shot at best to focus on such a parameter, but his due diligence paid off. A Lafayette-based specialty computer-drive company near Boulder had need for help in their shipping department. Given the special packaging required for their delicate drives, the company had their own trucks and delivered their products to their customers themselves. The human resources director for the company had been polite at his interview, but Jack could tell she was uncomfortable with his background. No matter how righteous the killing had been in his mind, the HR director for Hammond Computer Drives was having nothing to do with him.

He could get very single minded and focused when he wanted something, and he wanted the driving job bad. It would get him to Southern California twice a month on someone else's nickel, and that was something he desperately needed. The next day he got into his best suit and drove back to the company and approached the young woman manning the security desk in the lobby of the building and identified himself, adding that he was with the Denver Police and had business with David Hammond. The young woman quickly passed him through security and to the elevators. At the top floor, the elevator opened onto a very nicely furnished and finished reception area, and he identified himself to the older, competent-looking woman who approached him. She said she was Hammond's executive assistant but appeared to not recognize him from his recent trial, and she announced him straight in to the president's office.

David Hammond was not only a very smart businessman but was also up on his current events and recognized Jack immediately as he entered his office. After thanking and excusing his assistant, the smiling Hammond stood up and came around his desk, his hand extended, and said, "Well Mr. Williams, to what do I owe the privilege? I think we both know you're not here to talk with me in any official capacity, so how can I help you?"

Jack apologized for the masquerade and for just showing up, and after shaking hands with the very direct but pleasant man, he explained in some detail his failed interview with the woman from HR and why he badly wanted the job. Hammond listened quietly until Jack was done with his contrite explanation. Then he got on his phone, called his HR manager, and told her he had personally filled the open shipping-and-driving position and was sending their new employee down to her office to take care of the paperwork.

As a grateful Jack was walking out of his office, Hammond stopped him in front of a family portrait hanging on the wall; the picture showed a smiling and proud David Hammond with his wife and their six children. He looked at the picture and then turned to Jack and said, "From one grateful father of six, thank you, Jack, for getting that son of a bitch off the streets." And that had been that.

In spite of his intellect and great common sense, it was lost on Jack that people like his new boss, and most others who knew and liked him, secretly thought he was the unluckiest man they had ever met. His life story seemed to be cluttered with a collection of unfortunate and even disastrous events or decisions—his marriage, his decision to leave the corps, his decision to defy the court order—but all had been made with the best of intentions. He'd married for all the right reasons, true love being the most important, but had married the wrong woman. He had acquiesced to his new wife and transferred out of his beloved Marine Force Recon and his sniper unit to pursue a career in the Criminal Investigation Division when his new wife drew the line at any more overseas deployments. He had hoped that his wife could be happy with him in CID, but the arrival of two kids and the modest living he made as a marine cop changed that.

He acquiesced again out of love and left the corps at her insistence and returned to his native Denver, taking the detective position with the Denver Police. Sherry was the one who researched and discovered the government-funded program that placed well-trained ex-military police into the public-sector police departments without necessarily having to start at the bottom. Four years as one of the marine's elite snipers and another eight as an investigating sergeant in CID had proved his personal character and his abilities as a police officer to the Denver PD. The city was only too happy to have a new detective of his caliber on their force and to have the feds paying a chunk of his salary. Be that as it may, after he followed his intuition and saved the young boy when no one else could, his actions were deemed criminal, and that same city instead tried to punish him for his good deed.

But that was now in his past. Truth be known, leaving the corps was hard, but leaving the snipers was not. He was a crack shot long before he enlisted, but once the corps discovered his ability, he was quickly slotted to Recon and then the snipers. He was gung ho at first with the assignment, but he was also just eighteen at the time and didn't know any better. He had a conscience, and however justified his orders or the cause may have been, after three tours in the Middle East, he'd seen the pink mist far too often through his high-powered scope and knew he needed out. Sherry simply accelerated it. He learned it wasn't in his makeup to kill, and you could only witness death by your hand so many times before it began to weigh heavily on you. The terrible irony was that without his time in the snipers, the likelihood that he would have been able to pull the trigger against his daughter's abductor was probably nil. But he had the time in, and he pulled on the bastard without a second thought. The killing wasn't the hard part, he discovered. Living with it was.

He had hoped his wife would be happy in Denver; he knew he could be. But she had been born and raised in the warm coastal climates of Jacksonville, North Carolina, where the daily high temperatures in December and January were near sixty and tolerably acceptable interludes into the otherwise hot and humid year-round climate. She hated Denver. He never stopped trying to make her happy and keep everything together, but the chain of events the kidnapping of their daughter started ended that and broke his tenuous, almost desperate grip on their marriage and his family.

As he sat at the table staring at the stack of cash, he knew he wasn't ready to make any decisions. You couldn't go against a lifetime of settled behavior without a lot of thought—and good reason also, he admitted to himself. He wasn't sure keeping the money just because it was dirty was reason enough, and he'd only consider keeping it if there was a way to safely launder it and live a normal life, which seemed like a fantasy in his present frame of mind. He realized that the kind of money sitting in the van was life changing. And he knew he needed a change, a big change, but there was so much that it was dangerous and unsettling. He had to talk with Hank—for advice, certainly, but he also needed perspective.

He was hungry and needed some dinner. As he sat at the small table, he slowly smiled, perhaps for the first time since saying goodbye to the girls two days earlier, as he thought about buying dinner while staring at the piles of bills. He decided to treat himself to a decent steak; he hadn't done that for a very long time. Money, as it were, would not be a problem. He slowly peeled off five C-notes from the nearest stack, thinking as he did so that in this small way, the money was already changing him. He got dressed, left the apartment, and treated himself to the first fancy meal he'd had in over a year. He was back at his apartment by nine. He sat at the table, scrolled down through his cell phone directory until he found Henry's private number, and called.

Henry answered on the second ring. "Hey, Jack. What's up?"

"Hi, Hank," Jack said soberly. "Sorry to call so late and at home, but I was wondering if you'd have a few minutes for me tomorrow. Something's come up, and I would really appreciate your advice."

"What is it, Jack?" a clearly concerned Henry asked.

"Not over the phone, Hank. It's real personal."

There were a few seconds of silence before Henry said, "OK, Jack. Eleven at my office. We can talk, and then I'll buy you some lunch."

"Thanks. Eleven it is. Sorry for all the mystery, but you'll understand. See you tomorrow."

"Sure," Henry said. "No problem. See you tomorrow."

3

The offices of Berman, Greenberg, and Levine
Lower downtown Denver
Tuesday morning; week one

Jack stepped off the elevator and walked into the rustic, high-ceilinged lobby of Henry's law firm ten minutes early. Henry was smart in all things, it seemed to Jack, and had bought the historic old brick building near Coors Field in lower downtown Denver before the real estate values in the area around Twentieth and Blake Streets had taken off because of the new ballpark. His firm occupied the top three floors of the small four-story brick building. The tall ground-floor retail space he leased out to an art gallery he liked and had supported over the years.

Henry's private secretary stood and smiled as Jack walked in, telling him how good it was to see him again, and then she took him down the hall to Henry's fourth-floor corner office. She quietly knocked, opened the door, and stood to one side to allow him to enter, and then then she closed the door behind him. Henry was standing at his large antique desk talking on the phone and waved Jack in, rolling his eyes at the same time as if to say, "You wouldn't believe the moron I'm talking with." Henry pointed to his couch in the corner and then held up one finger, indicating he'd be but another minute. When Henry politely ended the conversation, he said, "Just a sec, Jack," and then continued jotting a few notes on a pad while mumbling to himself.

Finished, he smiled and walked over as Jack stood, and they shared a quick man hug. "OK, pal," Henry said, "I've been concerned and a little curious since last night. What's on your mind?"

Jack had a grim look on his face and said, "Hank, you won't believe it."

Jack told him the entire story, right down to the gruesome details of the wreck and the two dead Mexicans. Before driving down to meet with his friend and lawyer, he spent the morning alone in his apartment going through all the evidence he had collected at the scene, so he passed on this information as well. He had translated the documents he found with his decent knowledge of Spanish and was able to determine that despite the obvious false identification he had found on the bodies, the two dead Mexicans were brothers named Aguilar and that they worked for a man named Cesar Diaz. He ran a Google search on Cesar Diaz Matamoros and came up with some hits, but they were for a decorated senior Federal Police colonel who, from the various articles Jack scanned, had gained quite a reputation for the courageous battle he'd fought for many years against the cartels. Diaz had arrested and killed many, had been wounded himself several times in various attacks on him and his office over the years, and was well thought of. In the most recent attack on him, his wife of many years was apparently killed. Jack knew that it must be coincidental that the probable drug leader the Aguilar brothers were delivering a pile of cash to was also named Cesar Diaz. He decided the name was probably as common down there as Smith or Jones was up here and thought nothing more about it.

He didn't have an address where the cash was to be delivered, but he did have an end location near the Gulf of Mexico south of Matamoros circled on a map, with a notation saying "Beach house, noon, Tuesday." The notation was similar to many others dotting the various maps. Either the Aguilar brothers had never done this pickup run before, or security was such that whoever this Diaz character was, he wanted to know every four hours where the brothers were and, apparently, if they were on schedule. According to crude notations on one of the maps, they had last checked in from Durango in southern Colorado at midnight on Sunday and were scheduled to call in again from Walsenburg, where Highway 160 ended at Interstate 25. Jack had checked through the cell phones and had identified the last one used, which still retained the last number called. Once Jack thought about it, why the van was speeding became clear to him. While it was only four hours from Durango to Walsenburg, where the van had passed him was only an hour and a half out of Durango and some two and a half hours out of Walsenburg. The Aguilar brothers were evidently behind schedule for whatever reason and were trying to make it up over Wolf Creek when their carelessness and a patch of black ice ended the attempt.

As was his custom, Henry sat silently as Jack told his story, his poker face not revealing anything. When Jack finished, Henry looked at him and said, "Well...that's a hell of a story. I won't bother you with my standard advice to simply turn the money in. Clearly, Jack, you wouldn't be sitting here if you weren't thinking about trying to keep it. I know you; you'd have called it in by now. So, what are we talking about here? What's on your mind?"

"I'm ashamed to admit it, but I *am* thinking about keeping it, Hank. I mean, think about it. This is truly found money. It's certainly dirty, no doubt about that, and if I'm going to steal for the first time in my life, who better to steal from than some unlucky drug trafficker in Mexico? It's not like this Diaz character can come look for it, and even if he could and did somehow, where could he look? Its two hundred miles from Durango to Walsenburg, where, if my reading of the maps is correct, these guys called in and where they were to do so again. That's a shitload of miles. And it's not like anyone is going to be contacting the state patrol for help. I'm telling you, if I hadn't watched the poor dumb bastards go over the side, no one—I mean no one— would know where that van is. They couldn't have concealed themselves better if they had deliberately tried."

Jack leaned forward, his elbows on his knees, and quietly went on. "Hank, you more than anyone knows how bad things have gone this last year. It's dumb, but I used to think I could walk through raindrops. But getting prosecuted, and then Sherry taking the kids, was a real eye-opener. With the kind of money that's sitting there in those rocks, if I could turn it into legal dollars somehow, I could move closer to the kids and start over in a place like LA, where there's lots of people, none of whom would know me from Adam. I need a fresh start. You know as well as I do that with my conviction, my long-term job prospects are pretty dim. Henry, this is an opportunity to make it possible to be around my girls more, start my life over, and maybe set them up for life."

Henry stared long and hard at Jack and then slowly smiled, shaking his head. "You know, this is really a breath of fresh air for you. I love you like a brother, so don't take this the wrong way, but until I met you, I used to think there was a little larceny in each of us. Welcome to the human race, Jack."

And with that Henry held out his hand, and Jack took it, smiling back but slightly confused.

"OK, Hank, what gives here? What are you saying really?"

Henry chuckled. "Nothing offensive, Jack, believe me. But you are without a doubt the most straightlaced guy I have ever met. You're decent and deserve a break is all I really mean, and thinking about lifting some unreportable missing cash is not only understandably tempting but a typically human thought, is all. You've suffered what I believe to be some harsh injustices in your life. Maybe this money helps even that out some. Anything I can help you with I will, especially if it helps you get closer to your girls. So if you're thinking about keeping the cash, I'd suggest you start by figuring out how you're going to get it all back up here, and soon, without getting caught. While technically not a prosecutable theft—this Diaz character would have to appear in court and document the money was in fact his to make a theft case—getting caught with that kind of money opens several cans of worms we want no part of, especially with a bunch of dangerous, likely cartel-related Mexicans running around pissed off about their missing cash. In the meantime, I'll start working on a laundering plan for you that's mostly legal."

Jack didn't trust himself to speak for a few seconds, and when he finally did, he thanked Henry. The two friends left his offices and enjoyed a fine lunch together, which Jack bought, paying with cash.

After lunch, Jack drove to work and told the shipping supervisor he needed to take some personal time off until the next California run in two weeks. The supervisor knew of Jack's special relationship with the owner of the company and told him no problem; take all the time he needed. Jack had been thinking about little over the last twenty-four hours other than how he would get the money back to Denver unnoticed if Henry agreed to help him and he made the fateful decision to try to keep it. To keep the drug money would be forever stepping over a moral line he believed in. Because of his attitudes, over the years he'd received a lot of teasing about being a real Boy Scout, but other than the criminals he'd arrested over the years, he never considered himself better than other people because he chose to conduct his life the way he did. He accepted people for who and what they were, with all their imperfections, and found the good in most everyone; it was his nature. It also explained how he had stayed married to his ex-wife for as long as he did.

Finding a southern beauty like Sherry and getting married as fast as they did was, at the time, the greatest surprise of his life. They couldn't have come from more different backgrounds; she from the old southern moneyed class and he a simple marine staff sergeant. Meeting at the college near Camp Lejeune where each was taking some night classes had been chance. Marrying as quickly as they did was based mostly on unabashed passion, as they each had thought the other was the most physically beautiful person they had ever laid eyes on. Jack didn't know it at the time, but there also existed a rebellious streak in her to push back against the years of continual pressure she'd always felt from her parents to live her life as they had, in a grand and socially acceptable southern fashion. Marrying a tall, handsome marine sergeant, no matter how bright and well-thought-of he was by all who knew him, was the worst thing she could have done to strike back at her parents, and she had happily and impulsively gone through with it.

No matter how good Jack looked in his dress blues, her parents and their friends were all too aware that he wore a number of medals for heroism that attested to his involvement in battles and the shoulder patches of both the Scout Sniper Platoon and Force Recon, whose motto was "Celer, Silens, Mortalis" (Swift, Silent, Deadly). Anyone who knew anything about the Marine Corps knew that meant Jack was a part of the elite within the elite that was always there when the metal of American force met the meat. Jack was a trained killer, and the genteel class of North Carolina society intellectually could appreciate such guardians at the gates, as long as they didn't marry into the family. Her parents were mortified at the turn of events, and in retrospect, Jack could see a life with Sherry was doomed from the beginning. She could only hate her parents for so long, and over time, her roots would take over and she would reconcile with them. And he would be on the outside looking in, as he now was.

That, however, could all change now. He wasn't sure what a new life would look like if he had a lot of money, nor did he know how such a life would affect his relationship with his ex-wife or his kids. He'd be able to provide them anything. That was a certainty—the best private schools, and certainly the best colleges when the time came. His ex was doing well for herself in LA working as a paralegal, but it was her father who had bought her and the girls their modest home in the hills east of downtown Burbank. He'd change that the first chance he got if he kept the money; his kids would live in a home he provided, even if he didn't live there.

He worked out his plan to retrieve the drug money to the same level of detail he had used in planning out his ops with his spotter when he was with the snipers years before. He bought a United States Geological Survey map of the Wolf Creek Pass area and located the area of the wreck on paper. The Mexican druggies had missed the first tight curve two miles east of the ski area located near the summit, and that was easily identifiable. There was a jeep trail that took off from the highway near the ski resort parking lot and provided access to a valley that contained a number of high-altitude lakes and streams. The jeep trail almost paralleled the highway about a quarter of a mile to the south and some three or four hundred feet lower in elevation as it snaked down the steep valley. Jack figured it was no more than a quarter-mile hike from a spot on the jeep trail he marked, up through the forest to the rock outcropping concealing the wrecked van. After studying the map, Jack felt certain that the rocks were as hidden from below as they were from above, as the ponderosa pines covered the slope all the way to the valley floor.

Jack located the nearest sporting goods store to his apartment and bought a cheap rod and reel. He was born and raised in Colorado but had never really fished. He had picked hunting over fishing as an outdoor recreation simply because he did not have the patience to stand quietly by a stream or sit in a boat and fish. It was the stalking of big game that appealed to him, skillfully being able to close a distance on an animal whose senses were more highly developed than any man's. It turned out that he didn't have to be all that skillful at closing distances, as he was a natural crack shot, able to take down deer or elk from four or five hundred yards. Good sport, he thought at the time, but hardly a fair match between him and the elk, he came to believe later in life.

He bought the biggest, most expensive backpack rig he could find, a small compact tent, and a new down sleeping bag. He next went by an auto-supply store and purchased a shell that covered and enclosed the bed of the older F-150 pickup he drove. The one he selected wasn't as attractive as some others, but it was solidly built, had no windows, and came with two heavy-duty locks. All his purchases were made with cash, and despite his initial nervousness at handing over so much cash, especially for the truck shell, no one seemed to notice or care.

He didn't have all the details worked out yet—that would take some on-site reconnoitering—but he'd either park at the ski area, like a lot of tourists did, or down in the valley alongside the jeep trail, depending on what his reconnoiter revealed to be normal and would not draw attention. He hoped that parking and camping alongside the jeep trail was the norm, because it would make his hike to the wreck shorter and allow him to do more round trips per day, but that was just a detail. If he had to hump it up to the ski area parking lot and back, so be it. He was in the kind of condition that made that possible.

His initial planning in place, and having all the outward appearances of a dedicated outdoorsman, Jack pocketed a thousand dollars in cash for expenses and hit the road early on Thursday morning. It was a six-hour drive back to the pass, and once in the area, he continued over Wolf Creek and drove into Pagosa Springs to the Forest Service ranger station located there. He bought a camping permit and a fishing license, and the young ranger also gave him a Forest Service map and pointed out camping sites near where he wanted to fish.

Jack thanked the young woman and drove back up and over the pass. From his thorough studying of his map, he knew where to look for the jeep trailhead. After locating the turnoff, he slowly wound his way down through the steep forest into the valley south of the highway. He noted his odometer reading at the trailhead and had a pretty good idea where he needed to stop. While he did not pass any other fishermen or campers on his short drive—it was still March, after all, and early in the season—he could see evidence of others having pulled off the trail and now camping. He found a spot he liked about the right distance from the ski area and pulled well off the jeep trail. He felt certain he was roughly a quarter mile south and a little west of the crash site, and if the topo on the map was correct, about two hundred feet below it.

He unlocked his shell, grabbed his near-empty pack, and put it on. Satisfied that he looked like your average backpacker, he folded up his USGS map and put it in his pocket in case he needed it but was sure he wouldn't. His dead-reckoning skills had been honed by the corps years before, and he had a very good idea where the wreck was. Because of the pines, he couldn't see the highway well above him, but if need be, he could always climb high enough to see the road and confirm his position. Surprisingly, the quarter-mile hike to the crash site took him forty-five minutes and not the fifteen or twenty he had thought it would take. The going was tough through the deadfall on the forest floor, and he missed the crash site the first time, walking below and past the outcropping before doubling back when he felt he was too far east, climbing higher as he did so. He came on the wreck from the east and from slightly above, and even then, it was tough to spot until he was within twenty or thirty feet. This confirmed the belief he had that the wreck would be impossible to find or even stumble upon.

Jack immediately felt bad when he finally reached the van. The cold mountain temperatures had greatly slowed decomposition, so the bodies were pretty much as he had left them. But there was evidence of feeding by something—lion probably, he thought. He set aside his well-thought-out plans and his backpacking gear and set about moving and covering the bodies as best he could—something, he thought with remorse, he should have done before leaving the van the first time, even in the dark. After struggling to free the passenger from his seat, he gently moved him and the driver to a clear and level spot near the base of the larger boulders and spent the next hour hauling smaller rocks until he had each body neatly covered. He was exhausted with the effort and dropped to one knee for a breather and to whisper a silent prayer for the two men. He had been brought up Episcopalian but wasn't going to church much by high school, and then not at all once he enlisted in the corps at eighteen. He couldn't make sense out of religion for himself, but maybe the criminals had, as twisted a thought as that seemed, so he said the short prayer anyway.

He stood up, realizing he'd been at the site for an hour and hadn't even thought to check on the money. He walked around the van to the side door, which looked exactly as it had when he'd left it, and forced it open. The money was there, untouched. He first removed the dozen boxes of plastic widgets or whatever it was the boxes contained and stacked them neatly off to one side. Now that he was seeing the currency in the light of day, he realized that the $280,000 he had taken out of the top package had barely made a dent. He shook his head; he had no idea how much was there, but it was a fortune. He opened his pack, emptied it of the few extra clothes and the prepackaged foods he had brought along as camouflage, and started filling it with the $10,000 banded packs from the opened package. His backpack was advertised as an eighty-pound Himalayan mountaineering type, complete with integral lightweight carbon-fiber frame. Its cost had shocked him at first when he bought it, but he had simply peeled off a few more of the hundreds he was carrying in his pocket at the time and handed the money over to the young sales clerk and stopped thinking about it.

He pulled cash out of the already-open first package until it was gone and his pack was about three-quarters full, then he covered the cash with the clothing and food. Satisfied, and with some effort, he hoisted the mostly full pack up onto his wide shoulders and judged it weighed ninety or a hundred pounds. He was surprised that such a small package of currency weighed so much. *Shit*, Jack thought, *this is going to take a while. How the hell much is here?*

After his steak dinner on Monday night, alone in his apartment and with the first $280,000 sitting on his kitchen table, Jack did some research online about currency, curious as to how much money he might have stumbled onto. There wasn't a lot of information that was helpful to him, but one small fact he saw he remembered: apparently, $1 million in hundred-dollar bills weighed a little over twenty-two pounds. Why anyone would have figured that out was a mystery to him, but it did give him a point of reference.

As he started down the wooded slope back toward his parked pickup with what was about a hundred pounds on his back, he did the math over and over in his head to pass the time. If what he had read was accurate, he was hauling roughly five million dollars on his back; just thinking the number astounded him. More astounding, however, was the fact that by his count, there were twenty-four such packages in the van, meaning the van held roughly $120 million. *A hundred and twenty!* Jack thought. *My God, can there really be that much there?*

The number was truly astounding if it indeed was accurate. Jack had never made more than $60,000 in a year, and with what his wife had managed to earn on average, he figured they maybe had made $100,000 a year in the best of times, and that was just in the last couple of years after the girls were born. They had lived a modest life—too modest, it turned out, for his ex—but it was an honest living, and what he did was worthwhile.

He kept dividing a hundred thousand into five million in his head as he struggled down through the forest and after several tries decided his math was right, even if it didn't seem possible: fifty years. *Can that be right?* he thought. He simply had trouble getting his head around the fact that with just what was on his back, a family of four could live a comfortable life for decades, and there were twenty-three more such packages!

Money, or the lack of it, did not drive his life; never had. He had made his decisions to be a marine and then a cop because that was what he wanted to do with his life. They were tough jobs, meaningful jobs that appealed to his sense of nobility. The fact that there wasn't much money to be made doing what he loved had never really occurred to him or mattered. He simply adjusted his lifestyle to his income and got on with his life. He had to admit to himself that his attitude changed somewhat after the department shitcanned him and Sherry divorced him. The despicable court settlement that Sherry had her lawyer engineer required him to send her $1,000 a month for child support, which he was glad to pay because it meant he was helping his girls, but it left him little. He'd been lucky with the job he'd found and lucky that David Hammond was as good a man as he was. He could live on what the job paid; nevertheless, his reduced circumstances did get him to thinking more about money, far more than he ever had before.

By the time he had hiked back to the truck, it was nearly four in the afternoon. The sun was already over the pass, and there were deep shadows in the valley. He threw the heavy pack into the back and slowly returned to the highway and drove toward Pagosa Springs. He had a reservation at High Country Lodge and Cabins, just outside Pagosa, because they advertised individual cabins and he wanted the extra privacy. He figured it would take him two more full days, maybe three, to carry the cash out, so he'd need a room for at least two nights. However tired he was after the last day of hiking back and forth from the wreck, he would take off for Denver anyway.

After checking into his cabin and showering, he was pleased he had chosen the small rustic resort to stay in.

As an ex-Marine sniper, an MP for eight years, and then a Denver police detective for three more, Jack was very sure of himself. There had been few times in his life when he had been scared or paranoid about anything. Sitting on his bed looking at his closed backpack, knowing what it contained, he now was. He wanted some dinner, and there were some nice places in town, but should he leave the pack in his room? He thought about hiding it under the bed, but it was too large. As stupid as he felt, he took the pack with him and locked it in the back of the truck and then drove into town and had his dinner, making sure he had a booth by a front window of the diner he'd picked so he could casually watch his truck the entire time. When he returned to his room with his pack, he put it on the floor between the bed and the wall, as far from the door as he could manage.

His calculations were pretty much right on, and it indeed took him two full days to get all the cash from the van back to his truck, humping the quarter mile back and forth almost nonstop from sunrise to sunset. Totally exhausted after the first full day, he still had a mostly sleepless second night in his cabin, as there was no way to haul all the cash into his room and then back out to his truck the next morning without attracting attention, so he left it all in the locked shell, except for what he could hold in his pack. He had brought several boxes of fifty-gallon heavy-duty lawn-and-trash bags with him and transferred the money from his backpack to the bags, double bagging the cash because of the weight. He made the transfers in the safety of the woods after each round trip, out of sight but near his truck, in case someone came by. Only when he was sure he was alone would he toss the tied heavy bags into the back of the truck and double lock the shell.

By late Saturday afternoon, he was back at his heavily loaded pickup, and all the cash and the plastic wrapping material was safely concealed in his shell. He'd broken down the assault rifles, making them inoperable, and left the biggest pieces in the van before hiking out the last time, depositing the trigger assemblies randomly along his path through the difficult deadwood. In the unlikely event that the van and the bodies were ever discovered, any good investigator would quickly figure out that the Mexicans were illegals and likely gun or drug runners and that mysteriously, after they had crashed, someone had covered the bodies and tampered with the crash site. However, using his crime scene experience, he carefully went over the crash site before he left for the final time and made sure there was no evidence that could tie him to the scene, including fingerprints. Anyone finding the van, if ever, would only find the van, the neatly stacked boxes of plastic whatevers, the broken-down weapons, and the two piles of stone. It had started to snow some when he left the site for the final time, and he knew the snow and other spring storms would take care of cleansing the area of his footprints and his impossible trail down through the forest.

The six-hour drive back to Denver was nerve wracking but uneventful. He passed by a half dozen state patrol cars during the drive and had never felt more self-conscious in his life. It was late and he was exhausted when he got back to the apartment. After everything he had done so far to get the money home, the next step was perhaps the most dangerous. His ground-floor corner apartment was the first you came to as you drove into the small apartment complex. His marked parking spot was right in front, which was good, but any of the other tenants or their guests coming in off the street had to drive right past him. If any of his tenants saw him lugging trash bags into his apartment, it was likely they would stop and offer to help, as he was well liked by most of them.

He backed his truck into his spot, which put his front door only six or eight feet from the rear of the truck. He carried his backpack and all his gear in first. Then, with a glance around, he went out and grabbed the first trash bag and carried it in, repeating the process until all the bags were safely inside. Only once during the hauling had someone driven by, but he was inside the apartment at the time looking out, and whoever they were took no notice, as far as he could tell. He closed and locked his front door; the drapes covering his living room window had never been opened and neither had the bedroom window blinds, so he was as secure as he was going to get.

All the bags were sitting in his bedroom, taking up most of the available floor space. He took a shower and dressed in a T-shirt and gym shorts. It was after midnight and he was exhausted, but he couldn't help himself. He went into the bedroom and brought one of the bags out to the kitchen. He had spent only a few thousand dollars of the first bit of cash he had brought back, and what was left of the original $280,000 he had stashed in his one and only suitcase in his closet before going back to Wolf Creek. He had picked this trash bag at random, and as far as he could tell, it was no different from the twenty-three others strewn about his bedroom floor; each held one of the plastic-wrapped packages.

He started pulling out the packs of tightly bound hundreds and stacked them into piles on his kitchen table. An hour later, his curiosity satisfied, he had his answer: $5,080,000. If all the other bags were like this one, he now had something close to a $120,000,000 in cash in his apartment. A panicky feeling came over him as he sat back in his chair staring at the incredible stacks of currency thinking, *A hundred and twenty million dollars. This is completely insane; this cannot be real…but it is.*

Like most people, he had always thought $1 million seemed like such a huge number, impossible to relate to, but a hundred times that? It simply was too big a number to think about, much less be comfortable with. He had taken a big step in his mind, bringing the cash here and not leaving it at the scene and reporting it, but it was still a reversible step. If he called the authorities, there would be some questions asked, but basically it was a no harm no foul at this point—the money was all accounted for. The dangerous big step across the line from right to wrong was still ahead of him. As odd as it now seemed, during the week, while preparing to go back to the pass and get the money, he had slowly started to get comfortable with the idea of keeping a couple million dollars of illegal money. But there was so very much more now that he had serious doubts; it was just so much. He would contact Henry in the morning and let him know what he had done and how much there was. He would listen to Hank. Only after talking it over with him and hearing what kind of plan he had devised would he make maybe the biggest decision of his life—turn the money in or keep it.

4

The Beach House
Near Matamoros, Mexico
Sunday morning; week one

Cesar Diaz had been staring at the map of the southwest United States for an hour, and with each passing minute his frustration and anger grew. The Aguilar brothers were now five days overdue. A thorough check of the considerable information available to him had convinced him that their going missing was not some random event. They had simply disappeared as if into thin air. That took planning and skill. They had not been arrested or detained by any American law enforcement agency; he knew that for a fact. Nor had they been involved in an accident or been admitted to an area hospital; he knew that as well. There would be a record of such information routinely entered into the data banks of the various American law enforcement agencies having jurisdiction, and he had access to most of them. Such were his capabilities.

Diaz trusted exactly two people in the trafficking side of his life, and the Aguilar brothers were not a part of that select group. Nevertheless, he had no reason to suspect them of acting unilaterally and taking his money and disappearing. They were his nephews, his worthless younger sister's sons, and were every bit as worthless as their mother had always been, but the one thing he could count on was their fear; this made them reliable. They would never cross him. They knew all too well what he was capable of, and of course, they knew he had El Lobo.

The Aguilar brothers were about as ignorant as any two people he'd ever known. That, and they had neither the courage nor the guile to try something this big on their own. About the only thing they were good at was blind obedience. Given specific instructions and a simple, firm plan, they had shown in the past they could perform. He dismissed any notion that his missing money was a planned act on their part. That left only a couple of possibilities in his sharp analytic mind: either one of his four distributors or two partners, acting alone or together, had gotten ambitious, or the Aguilars had been involved in some sort of incident that had gone unreported.

He was certain his money had been stolen, and whoever was responsible had to be close to him, which limited the possibilities. In addition to his missing nephews, only two other men were aware of the recent shipment to America and the great amount of money changing hands in this onetime event—Felix Brillo, his partner who handled distribution, and his enforcer, El Lobo. His money partner and launderer, known only as the Banker, was aware their money was missing but had no idea it was for their entire inventory. Diaz knew if he ever found out, there would be blood in the streets of Matamoros, starting with his own. If it was the Banker or Brillo behind the missing money, then it would get dangerous, because they were every bit as ruthless as he was. It was also possible the thief was one of the four distributors who were to receive the shipment, but that would be an uncharacteristically bold move on their part.

He spoke with his partners each day and had done so since last Monday, when the Aguilars failed to call in as scheduled Sunday night from southern Colorado in the US. He knew from the tone of the conversations that the Banker for sure suspected him of a double cross, just as he suspected the Banker. But the Banker would need help, and that could only mean Felix Brillo. Brillo, however, was one of the two men he actually trusted in the trafficking side of his life. Diaz did not really believe he was involved, but every possibility had to be checked out.

He had been looking forward to one last big score for more years than he could remember, and then he was going to get out. It was a miracle he had lasted as long as he had in the drug business; there was simply too much retribution to survive for very long. The double life he had been living was complicated, and he was lucky to have survived down through the years. Tragically, his wife of many years had not. With her now dead, killed two years ago by one of the rival groups in the last serious attack on him, there was no reason to stay in Matamoros—or Mexico, for that matter—for another day. But he needed his share of the money to disappear, and now that was what it had done. He would die before he would let anyone get away with this, and he would never stop until he found it.

Diaz was widely known and respected in government and police circles in the state of Tamaulipas and in Mexico City. What was not known was his close business relationship with Matamoros's longtime most powerful cartel leader, Jesus Qiuntero. He had known Qiuntero long before he ever became known as the Butcher of Brownsville; they had been friends once, many years ago when they were children. As they got older, their paths diverged as Jesus turned more and more to a life of crime, while Diaz went to school. Diaz's parents were both teachers, and education was respected in their home. After secondary school, he studied at the Tamaulipas Institute of Higher Education, took a management degree, and joined the Federal Police in their officer training program. He had been with the Federal Police for over twenty-five years now and had worked his way up the ranks, serving his entire career in Tamaulipas.

He was the Matamoros barracks commander by the time he was thirty and interceded in a brawl in the station's booking sally port late one afternoon, likely saving Jesus Qiuntero's life. His old primary school friend had a growing reputation back then as a major player in trafficking, and Diaz wanted him as badly as he wanted the others within his jurisdiction. Jesus had been booked on many occasions but had yet to be brought to trial; his police, political, and judicial connections simply ran too deep. On this occasion, Diaz's frustrated officers had arrested Jesus on the slimmest of charges and decided they'd solve the problem of Qiuntero's always getting away with it. Who could challenge them if they said they'd had to defend themselves because he chose to resist arrest? Diaz could not stand by and watch his men beat Qiuntero to death, so he stopped it. The officers were disciplined and reassigned for their own protection, and Qiuntero survived. As predictable as the sun rising in the east, the charges against him were dropped by a friendly judge, one no doubt on Jesus's payroll, and he was free to continue with his illegal trade.

Several months later he was approached by an intermediary sent by Qiuntero and invited to a private lunch in the small farming town of El Realito, thirty miles southwest of Matamoros. The handwritten note from Qiuntero struck him as sincere, and although it was risky, he drove alone out to El Realito. The small cantina was neat and clean, and as far as Diaz could see, other than about a dozen retainers belonging to Qiuntero outside on the street and inside at the bar, there appeared to be no patrons. His childhood acquaintance was sitting alone at a back table, a bottle of exceptional tequila and two glasses sitting on the table. During what was a pleasant lunch, Qiuntero thanked him for stopping his men and spelled out in great detail the realities of the trafficking business in the state of Tamaulipas, which Diaz knew all too well.

The police were being overwhelmed by the sheer numbers of gangs and cartels and dying by the dozens, and the trafficking was only growing. Qiuntero told him that in a matter of a few years, his cartel would be the strongest. Qiuntero said he did not wish to kill a childhood friend and the man who had undoubtedly saved his life, but he would be forced to do so if an accommodation could not be reached. In exchange for information and cooperation, Qiuntero promised information on his rivals and protection. Diaz knew that as Qiuntero grew stronger and dominated trafficking, he could eliminate a lot of very bad groups, to the benefit of them both. Diaz had never done a dishonest thing in his life, but the realities of the trafficking business forced his hand. There had been too many funerals, too many of his young officers gone and their families broken, all because neither he nor the government could effectively protect them. He made his deal with his devil and as a result saved lives. And with Qiuntero's help, he caught or killed many of the other traffickers. There was some solace in that. And then, of course, there was the money.

Adolfo Lobo quietly walked into Diaz's office while he was staring at his maps and stood almost at attention in front of his large, handsome desk.

Lobo was a big man, well over six feet tall, with thick arms and large, rounded shoulders. It was his eyes, though, that strangers first noticed that put the scare in them. His eyes were as black as coal at first glance and seemed life-less. Set into his rugged, darkly tanned, and scarred face, they made Adolfo appear every bit as menacing as he actually was. To everyone in the business who knew him or had heard of him, he was simply El Lobo, the Wolf. He'd earned the nickname at an early age, partly because it was his last name but also because like the wolf, he was a relentless hunter-killer and had been for a great many years. Unlike the wolf, however, who killed for survival, Adolfo killed for profit, and sometimes just for pleasure.

Adolfo should have died years ago. If not for Cesar Diaz, he would have. There had been much bad blood between the many gangs and cartels that operated out of the state of Tamaulipas, and specifically the Matamoros area, for many years. The bad blood caught up to him twenty years earlier when he was in his twenties and had been careless because of a woman. Some enemies caught him alone with her one night and without his weapons close by. They killed her and then took him out toward the Gulf, where the drinking and the beating began. They beat on him for an hour with baseball bats, laughing and taking turns, and they were about to finish him off when Cesar Diaz stopped them, killing three of the four from out of the darkness. The fourth escaped into the same darkness and lived for a while, until Adolfo hunted him down several months later and slowly finished him. It was by chance that Cesar had come down the lightly traveled beach road when he did. He had stopped at the parked trucks on the side of the road to check them out because that was his job, and then he had followed Adolfo's screams and the attacker's laugh-ter into the tall native-grass-covered sand hills. He had asked no questions or issued any demands when he came on the four drunken men beating the single man to death; he simply took out his gun and started shooting.

Afterward, Diaz took him farther down the beach road to a plain house that overlooked the low sand hills that met the Gulf of Mexico, not to the hospital in town. The house, called the Beach House by the few who knew of its existence, was owned by Diaz's business partner and had been given to him as the perfect secluded place to conduct the private business that so conflicted with his real job. The simple, flat-roofed adobe-block and stucco house looked typical for the area, old and a little run down, but the interior was surprisingly modern and had every convenience, including the latest in computer and satellite technologies.

Diaz summoned a disgraced old doctor on his payroll to treat him and the police were avoided, and that was good for both of them. Adolfo healed fast, but it still took two months, and he nearly died twice in the first week, even under the watchful care of the old addict, who stayed with him the entire time. Adolfo did not have friends, not since he was a boy, and Diaz wasn't really a friend—not in the way that most people understood the definition—but he owed Diaz his life and his loyalty. It wasn't much of a code to live by, but it was the only one Adolfo Lobo understood and believed in.

Diaz looked up at his man; if his plan had worked, El Lobo would be in Nassau in the Bahama Islands and his dangerous and intelligent banking partner there would be living the last few precious hours or minutes of his life, but that was all blown away now, like the afternoon heat on the evening offshore breezes.

"Lobo, old friend, it will be necessary for you to go to America. In spite of our planning and our care, someone has taken that which belongs to us. I will not let whoever has done this succeed. This will be dangerous for you. I know this, and so do you. I will have the protection of my office and can provide the information we will need, but it will be necessary for you to move on your own, and there is danger if you're ever detained for any reason and your credentials are questioned. I would not ask you to do this if there was any other way."

Lobo's eyes were fixed on Cesar as he spoke, yet his face revealed nothing about his feelings or thoughts. In a surprisingly soft but deep voice, El Lobo said, "I want to do this, Cesar. It is my money too. Your plan was a good one; it should have worked. Maybe Brillo knows something more. One of the watchers called; he is on his way here."

"Yes, yes, thank you," Diaz said, slowly nodding his head, and then he nearly shouted, "It *should* have worked!" Momentarily embarrassed at having lost his composure in front of Lobo, he looked at his man and said evenly,

"The fact that it did not means whoever did this is very close to us. You will need eyes in the back of your head, my friend, from this moment forward."

El Lobo simply nodded his head in agreement. He liked the danger; in a way, he needed it.

Diaz looked back down at his maps and after a second said, "You must go see our four distributors and determine their roles in this theft, if any. Use any measures you require. One way or the other, we will no longer be doing business with them. All that is important here are results and information. After you question them, they must be eliminated. If they are innocent, then it must be the Banker, perhaps in league with Brillo, who has robbed us. If that is the case, things will get very difficult for us. But first, do what you must with the distributors."

El Lobo had not moved or taken his eyes off his boss. "What cover do you wish me to use?"

"Your Federal Police cover, but as if you are on holiday to Las Vegas. Start with our distributor there. I have arranged a passport for you, a border crossing card, and a vehicle permit. It will take you longer if you drive yourself, but there will also be fewer tracks. Fly when necessary once you reach Las Vegas, but pay with cash—always cash. I have also included all the information I have on each of them—their known addresses, associates who will likely be around them, their favorite restaurants, and the vehicles and license plates they currently use. This should be enough for you to get close. If you should discover that our distributors are innocent in this matter, I then must eliminate the possibility that the Aguilars met with some kind of as-of-yet-unreported detention or accident before I take on my partners. It is possible the DEA or the American FBI discovered them and the money somehow and are keeping the information tight, and that's why there is no mention of this in the various databases I have access to. I will work on this as we go along, and you get us more information. For now, go north as quietly as possible and see what our distributors there know."

El Lobo simply nodded his head, turned, and walked out. Diaz had known twenty years ago, when he saved Adolfo from the beating he stumbled upon, that more and more he was requiring the services of men who could operate in the two completely different worlds he lived in. He knew when he loaded the nearly dead man into his car and started for the Beach House who El Lobo was. He was suspected in a number of murders, but his office had nothing on him that he could be arrested for. Because of his then-evolving relationship with the Butcher, he needed hard men he could trust; the hard part was the recruitment, then establishing that trust. Saving El Lobo's life had been by chance, but in it, he had seen the possibility of forging the kind of special relationships his new business position required. That El Lobo had turned out to be as loyal and indebted as he was had been pure luck.

As Diaz watched his man walk out, he leaned back in his chair, closed his eyes, and went over every detail of his grand plan in his head. Diaz knew his plan *had* been a good one. Business had been bad for a year, ever since Qiuntero and several of his top lieutenants were killed and his cartel and the other half dozen major ones were hit hard by the government. That and the new, improved border structure the US finally finished, manned with all the new Border Patrol agents now in place, made it more and more difficult to get product north.

Demand in the US was as high as ever, but supply from and through Mexico had been interdicted effectively by the authorities. With his principal partner, the Butcher of Brownsville, now dead, he and the Butcher's surviving lieutenant, Felix Brillo, had partnered up with the Butcher's banking partner and agreed to continue operations and again move product north. Only Brillo knew the workings of the transshipment methods and the distribution network north of the border, so his involvement was imperative. Initially, Diaz was certain that Brillo did not possess the intelligence or the skills to lead or run the operations; however, over the last six months as he worked more closely with the younger man, he realized that Brillo was far more capable than he appeared. The policeman in him wondered whether his long-held opinion of the man had been a misread on his part or clever deception on Brillo's.

The Banker was responsible for the upfront cash for their inventory and for laundering and investing the cash from the sales, but he never set foot in Mexico. He stayed in the Caribbean, where he not only lived comfortably and safely but could do the one and only thing he was good at. If the Banker was indeed involved in the theft, he would need someone local, like Brillo, to help him. When the Butcher was killed, Diaz felt it was only a matter of time before he would have to step in and lead, or nothing profitable was ever going to be accomplished again. This was troubling because it would raise his profile significantly, and that made exposure a real possibility in the face of recent government successes in fighting the cartels. He had been a leader his entire life, just not in the trafficking, and he did not want to start now. This one last unprecedented product shipment was supposed to be the one that would make leaving trafficking and the country possible.

At great risk two months ago, Diaz sat privately with Brillo over a lunch at a favorite local cantina and told him he wanted out. To his great surprise and relief, Brillo also said he wanted out but had not known how to tell him. Brillo said he hated the Banker, and now, with Qiuntero dead, he wanted to move on, perhaps returning to his hometown of Chihuahua and organizing his own small operation with his brothers, but that would require a bankroll. They shared some tequila and some private smiles over their mutually shared fears, and then Diaz told him his idea about doing one large last shipment financed by the Banker. Brillo quickly agreed. Diaz was relieved to discover that Brillo felt much the same way about their current situation. El Lobo had been out of sight but nearby during the luncheon. If the conversation had not gone as it did, Brillo would, regrettably, have been killed. Having to kill Brillo was not something he wanted to do or looked forward to, and he was privately pleased with the outcome of the meeting. It wasn't as if he and Brillo were friends—they were not—but he did respect him greatly, and in an environment where trust was a priceless commodity, he trusted Brillo. The plan meant double-crossing the Banker, and that was an irreversible step down a very dangerous path that could only lead to certain death for some, but it was the path they selected.

The Butcher's network had not sent an appreciable amount of product north for the last six months, yet their suppliers in South America and Mexico were able to deliver a great deal of cocaine to their storage facilities in and around Matamoros. The Banker fronted all the cash for this and was putting great pressure on him and Brillo to get it north. From Brillo, Diaz learned that the ruthless Butcher had been a great deal cleverer than Diaz would have ever thought, given his lack of education. Periodically, whenever his instincts told him it was time, the Butcher would relocate his distribution hub in America, sometimes to a new business, sometimes to a new city, sometimes both. This in turn required changing up the transportation methods to work seamlessly with the new cover business at the hub. The Butcher had been in the middle of such a move when the Federal Police had killed him a year ago. With Brillo's help and guidance, they finished the move and prepared their first shipment. But unlike the past, when only one or two tons of product were moved at any one time in order to protect inventories, Diaz's plan was to have it all go in one huge, risky shipment without the Banker's knowledge. They would get the money collected and then disappear after Lobo paid the Banker a visit. Brillo was to get a cut and El Lobo, of course, but the Banker was to be eliminated. Where Diaz was going after leaving Mexico, he could always find another banker.

The new distribution hub was a cartel-owned specialty plastics manufacturer outside Las Vegas, Nevada. The manufacturing of plastics requires petrochemicals, and in the state of Tamaulipas, that was a very big legitimate export business. The plastics company required tankers full of petrochemicals to keep their lines up and producing. Taking a typical petrochemical tanker and adding an outer wall placed only several inches outside the first would allow several hundred gallons of petrochemicals to be carried in the thin space trapped between the two walls. As hard as it was for Diaz to believe, according to Brillo, Jesus Qiuntero had come up with the idea of double-walled tankers. If the tanker was stopped and proof of transport was required, a sample of the chemicals could be provided from the sample port. In the meantime, high and dry in the principal tank would be one to two tons of cocaine, almost two thousand one-kilo bricks in the typical load to be transported to Las Vegas each month. At the $20,000 a kilo wholesale price to their four principal distributors, that was nearly $40 million a load for the cartel. Diaz and Brillo had agreed with the Banker that the proceeds from the first shipment of two tons would all go to him to reimburse him for the cash he'd put up for their inventory. That bought him and Brillo some goodwill with the Banker and the time they required to execute their scheme.

Diaz and Brillo had secretly met personally with the four distributors in Las Vegas two months earlier and told them what would be coming. When they finally had their completed special tanker and managed to safely substitute it for an authentic load of petrochemicals going to Las Vegas, a total of eight thousand kilos, almost nine tons of pure cocaine with a street value of almost $400 million, was jammed in the tanker. It had taken the distributors two months to quietly get their financing in order and be in a position to deliver the cash for the sale. At the $15,000 a kilo discounted price that he and Brillo had agreed to with the distributors for the risk of taking on so much product, waiting for the tanker in Las Vegas was an astounding $120 million in cash. Each of the regional distributors was already enormously successful in some other cover business. Each had access to private jet travel, and each could credibly fly to Las Vegas on a regular basis and not have it questioned, just as they had when the hub was located in Dallas or Los Angeles before that. Whatever the front business was at the time, it always dealt in products that required fleets of trucks to deliver, and the plastic company was no different. When the trucks left the factory, hidden in the beds or walls of the trucks was always a layer of kilos.

Because of the huge fortune to be collected in Las Vegas, Diaz had proposed to Brillo one last tweak in the plan that only the two of them and El Lobo would know about. The money was supposed to be loaded into the now-empty tanker and simply driven back south with a dozen of his men in additional vehicles discreetly serving as convoy guards, a very safe and reliable way to get the money south under normal conditions. Diaz, however, did not trust the distributors or put it past one of them to try to take the cash-laden tanker. So he came up with the Aguilar brothers' part of the plan. Brillo made sure that when the shipment arrived, he was there with a dozen armed soldiers. The distributors arrived in their private jets with their own retainers and suitcases of cash. With lots of very nervous people standing around the plastic company's warehouse late one night, the money was counted out and verified, then plastic wrapped and left sitting on long tables under guard in the office.

The product was unloaded from the tanker, distributed, tested for quality, and then loaded into delivery trucks and driven off by the distributor's retainers.

Back in the warehouse, with everyone but Brillo and the Aguilar brothers standing discreet guard on the outside, they had loaded the cash into the plain Chevy 1500 cargo van instead of the tanker. The van bore the logo and contact numbers for the specialty plastics company and had local plates and registration. The Aguilars had forged identity papers identifying them as legal aliens and drivers for the company, along with a forged manifest for a delivery to Corpus Christi, Texas. The tanker left the warehouse with an escort of retainers as planned, looking like a well-guarded convoy to all who were aware of the money. Thirty minutes later, the two Aguilar brothers left the now-deserted plastics factory alone in their nondescript van, drawing no interest from anyone. Diaz felt it was a certainty that someone would take a shot at hijacking the tanker, and Brillo had agreed. Ironically, it returned to Matamoros having never been touched or questioned. Instead, to his amazement, his nephews and the carefully orchestrated shipment had simply disappeared from the face of the earth.

He got up from his desk and went to one of the floor-to-ceiling windows in his office and looked out; he had a few more minutes before Brillo would arrive, and he had to think. He trusted his instincts and knew Brillo was still with him and not a traitor, but Brillo would not be able to shed light on the van's disappearance. He could help in the search; there were possibilities he could look into, risks he could take instead of Diaz, but nothing more. It would be left to him and Lobo to track the money down. Diaz knew that meant he would have to determine where to look, and that in and of itself could draw unwanted attention because to get answers, one had to ask questions. He would eliminate the possible involvement of the others first, and if Lobo discovered they were not involved, that likely meant the Banker was responsible. But not even the Banker could pull this off without leaving tracks, and he would find them, for there were few in Mexico with better investigation skills. As he stared off into the distance beyond the low dunes, a very troubling notion began to creep into his thoughts: What if the distributors and the Banker really were not involved? What then? Where was the money?

5

The Beach House
Near Matamoros, Mexico
Sunday morning; week one

Felix Brillo was as disturbed as Diaz, and about so very much more. He knew Diaz had been looking for a way to get out from under Qiuntero since his wife was killed, but that was just the last few years; he had wanted out for the last ten. The past decade had been a living hell for him, and with Qiuntero's death in the successful government raid against the Gang of Four a year ago came his salvation, or so he thought at the time, until his true sponsor was also eliminated soon after. The confusion and uncertainty within the Butcher's organization since then made each passing day in Matamoros dangerous, especially for someone wanting to just get out.

Felix had secretly been a member of the rival Vargas family cartel out of Chihuahua since he was sixteen. When he and his twin brother, Guillermo, were twenty, the leader of the Vargas family, an intelligent and powerful force known only as the Condor de Muerte, had asked each of the brothers to take on a very dangerous but important task. Each was to move to another part of the country and then, using his guile and instincts, allow himself to be recruited into one of the large rival cartels. The plan was for them to provide the Condor with information on the workings and plans of the cartels they infiltrated and, over time, work their way up the hierarchy. Felix had come to Matamoros, and his brother had gone to Tijuana. Their younger brother,

Javier, remained in Chihuahua with their mother until he was old enough to join the Vargases. There had been no guarantees they could actually get themselves into a rival cartel, nor was there any guarantee that they would have success once in, but both of the brothers had succeeded, and far beyond the Condor's expectations.

In his years as part of Qiuntero's cartel, Brillo had performed every vile act a good soldier would be expected to carry out and volunteered for every dangerous or disgusting job that came up. Qiuntero's calling card was to leave the heads of his enemies on six-foot steel spikes along some well-traveled road as a reminder to all about his ruthlessness, and he acquired the nom de guerre "the Butcher of Brownsville" as a result. Brillo had participated in a great number of the decapitations, trying not to vomit or show weakness in the early going until the repetition had numbed what little humanity he had out of him—all in the effort to be seen as the loyal and ruthless soldier. With his survival and success had come respect, followed by more and more responsibility in Qiuntero's organization. Diaz and Qiuntero had been involved together as partners for years before he was recruited into the cartel, and due to his loyalty and intelligence, in ten short years he rose to become Qiuntero's second-highest-ranking lieutenant. When Qiuntero was killed in the same government raid a year ago that caught or killed a dozen of the worst traffickers in the country, only he and Diaz remained of the old leadership. But Diaz was known to the government as a trusted and gifted Federal Police leader, whereas Brillo was a known and wanted associate of Qiuntero's.

When Diaz and the Banker approached him about continuing the business with them, he agreed, but only to buy time until he could figure out how to extricate himself from the organization and live. His brother in Tijuana had survived last year's big government raid on the northern cartels by simply not being included in the entourages for that particular meeting. Someone had to remain behind and watch over business as the other leaders met, and the twins had been lucky; their younger brother was not. Javier was still part of the Vargases' cartel and was at their Hermosillo estate when the government captured the Condor and killed off his cousins across the country in Chihuahua. Javier was young and nothing but an inconsequential driver and occasional guard for the cartel, but when the government troops swooped into the Hermosillo estate in their concurrent raids and arrested everyone, he was thrown into jail and also charged with trafficking.

Felix had quietly found and funded a defense lawyer he could control and had spent the last year trying to free his brother. It looked as though his efforts would finally pay off, as at the very least, Javier was to finally be released on bail after spending months in jail awaiting a trial. He and Guillermo had been making plans for the three of them that only required some capital and their brother's release to be implemented. Never again would any of them work for anyone else if Felix had anything to say about it.

As he drove up the sandy road to the Beach House, he was anxious. As one of the few men who was aware of the vast amount of money that had changed hands in Las Vegas, he knew he was under a cloud of suspicion, and in Matamoros and in the business he was in, that was usually a death sentence. First things first. He had to face his partner and clear his name. He and Diaz had talked almost daily on the phone about the missing Aguilar brothers but had not met face to face. The Banker was a threat to Diaz as well as to him, and they would need to meet that threat together if they were to survive the next few weeks or months. As much as it was possible in their business, he trusted the older National Police commander and knew from their conversation several months before that Diaz trusted him.

He passed the last of the small ramshackle shacks that sat just off the sandy road leading to Diaz's beach house, knowing the inhabitants were not fishermen or peasants but well-armed guards sitting in the shade observing him. He didn't give their scrutiny a second thought, for he was used to it and known to them. He pulled into the dusty parking area in front of the flat-roofed adobe-and-stucco beach house and got out of his car, knowing that his every move was being watched by someone. There were no obvious guards around, but as he approached the large covered front porch, Diaz's menacing longtime enforcer, El Lobo, came walking out, nodded recognition, and continued to the parking area. Even after ten years in the cartel, the presence of El Lobo could still raise the hair on the back of his neck. It took all the control he had to keep his eyes focused forward and not look over his shoulder and check and see if the killer had turned and drawn a weapon. He knew it wouldn't matter; if Lobo intended to kill him, there was nothing he could do about it, and he had known that when he agreed to come out here. He learned from observation over the years that there was no hiding from El Lobo. Killing was his skill, but his special talent was finding those who did not want to be found.

In many ways, the thirty-minute drive from his apartment in Matamoros to here had been the longest thirty minutes of his life, and that was saying something when considering all that had transpired in the last ten years. As he opened and closed the front door, he stole a quick glimpse, and saw with relief Lobo slowly getting into his pickup. Through the small, grime-covered window in the door he watched as Lobo drove west down the road, and he thought, *Not today, El Lobo. Not today.*

From the next room he heard "Felix? Is that you?" He turned and headed for Diaz's office. Diaz was waiting for him, and as he entered, Diaz looked up from his desk and then stood up and walked around it to greet him warmly.

"Felix, thank you for coming," he said as he took Felix's hand and also grabbed him affectionately by the shoulder. "I wish I had good news to tell you, but I have learned nothing more since we last spoke. You?"

Felix's intuition told him that Diaz's friendly greeting was genuine, and he relaxed some, although his pulse was still racing from having seen his enforcer. "Nothing, Cesar, but all I have really done is listen around town in all the places news like ours might be talked about. I have not asked questions or spoken to anyone. Is our secret still safe? Are we the only ones who know about the missing Aguilars?"

"Yes, yes, my friend. You, me, and Lobo are the only ones that know the truth. And, of course, the thieves that have stolen our money, if that is what happened."

Felix was puzzled by his partner's comment. "What else can it be, Cesar, but a theft? You've lost me."

Diaz nodded his head in understanding at the question. "Forgive me, Felix. It is my police training to always think in possibilities and contingencies. While I'm reasonably certain that we are talking a bold theft here, it is possible that the American DEA or FBI has caught my nephews and simply are holding that information tight. I can access many law enforcement databases and there is nothing that would indicate this yet, but it is a possibility that we must investigate. Also, there is the possibility, however remote, that the brothers simply met with some accident that has gone unreported thus far. Their route took them across several tribal reservations, for example, and even though the land is part of America, the native tribes there can be very autonomous. And their tribal law enforcement would likely never report our money. In either case, however, eventually there would be some word, I think. I have sent Lobo north to eliminate the most obvious of possibilities, the involvement of our distributors. The most likely scenario remains that one of them, alone or in league with others—maybe even the Banker—is our enemy here. It will take Lobo several weeks, maybe a month, but he will find out what we need to know.

"In the meantime, the Banker is getting more and more threatening about his missing money; always our conversations come back to that. Between us, given his tone, I believe his anger at the missing money is sincere. My instincts tell me he's not a part of this. I suspect there would have been attempts on our lives by now if he was involved, don't you?"

Felix nodded his head glumly.

"Before I eliminate him as a suspect, however, we must learn more. He wants us to send another shipment north with better security this time and get him some significant money. I told him we were preparing to do exactly that and would, when we felt it was safe to do so, but we were looking at about a month. He is not happy, but we have some time."

"We have nothing to send, Cesar!"

Diaz exhaled a large breath slowly. "I know, I know. But we needed time, so I said what I had to. One way or the other, we will be dealing with the Banker, and soon. We have no choice but to eliminate him, and that will not be easy. Lobo has said he will do it, but after all these years, I have no desire to send an old friend on a suicide mission. I will need time to try to devise a plan."

Felix looked at his partner for a few long seconds and then said, "I passed Lobo on my way in. You believe me, Cesar, when I say that I had nothing to do with this?"

Cesar smiled and took him by the shoulder. "Of course, of course. You need not worry; I know we are in this together."

Felix looked at his partner with a pained expression. "If the Banker is not involved and El Lobo eliminates the others as suspects, where are the Aguilars?"

Diaz shook his head. "Felix, I have no idea, but I know how to look. There is no black magic at work here. My nephews are not that clever, and they are cowards. They would never cross us. So this becomes an investigation. There will be tracks, evidence. That much money just does not vanish. Where humans are involved, there are human weaknesses; the money will not remain hidden if it currently is. That kind of money will be talked about, and there are fancy cars and villas to be purchased, women to be impressed. We will be patient, we will listen and watch, and we will never stop looking.

"We will find out who has done this, trust me. And we will get our money back, and those responsible will pay. If it turns out the American authorities have done this, I will find out in time. If that turns out to be the case, our money is just gone; there will be no getting it back. But I know the Americans' methods, their procedures. Any initial contact by them of the Aguilars would have been reported somewhere. I'm sure about that, and none has. It's not like the Americans not to announce a capture of this magnitude; their internal politics almost demands it. While we must investigate this possibility, my instincts say it's not the authorities. If not our partners or the authorities, what I suspect is that the Aguilars have had an unreported incident of some kind. As to what, I don't know. But I do know my nephews. If something unpredictable happened to them en route, they would have called—the van breaking down, a run-in with local criminals or gangs, whatever. The fact that they have not called tells me something unexpected and sudden happened. A simple traffic accident, for example."

"I don't understand, Cesar. If they did have an accident of some kind, how does it not go reported? That makes no sense, not in America."

Diaz shrugged and sighed. "Yes, my friend, that may seem the case, but we must imagine the impossible if we are to find our money. I thought long and hard about their route before I gave it to them. Most of it was through sparsely populated parts of the country on good but lesser traveled roads. The area they last reported from is very rugged; good roads, but mountainous and lightly populated. They were driving at night, when traffic is even less. While improbable, it is possible they simply met with an accident, and given the rugged area, the light population, and the time of night, the accident went unobserved. For all we know, my nephews are alive but unable to communicate with us and perhaps injured. Maybe they're dead, and our money is just sitting there, undiscovered. I know it's something we must check out."

Felix never took his eyes off his partner as he went through his explanation, and he respected greatly Diaz's intellect and experience, but he wasn't buying it. "You are the investigator here, Cesar, not me. Tell me how I can help. What is it you wish me to do?"

"Come, Felix. Look at my map."

Felix followed Diaz around the desk and looked down at the large detailed map and could see the Aguilars' route had been carefully drawn in red ink. Their prearranged route was a strange one to Felix, leading from Las Vegas northeast on Interstate15 for a short while into the state of Utah, then on local highways through small towns such as Saint George and Mount Carmel Junction, and dropping south very briefly into northern Arizona. The route turned north again into southwest Colorado, passing through more small communities with names like Durango, Walsenburg, and Trinidad. They were to head south for another brief while on Federal Interstate Highway 25, then once again return to smaller state roads as they continued south in eastern New Mexico and then east into Texas. Once in Texas, the route continued south until finally making the border near Del Rio, Texas. He knew Diaz owned a US Border Patrol captain there who had lived and worked for years in Brownsville, where Diaz had compromised him before he was promoted and moved. With the captain's help, the Aguilars would cross the Rio Grande into Ciudad Acuna. There they were to be met by a Federal Police unit Diaz controlled that knew nothing about their mission or the special cargo and would passively escort them home. It was a long, dusty drive to Matamoros but a relatively safe one.

Diaz pointed at the map and said, "Here is where they checked in last, at midnight a week ago local time. They were to call again from here at four, before they started south on this major highway. If their disappearance is nothing more than a tragic accident of some kind, it is along this small high-way somewhere. Other than the information available to us on the map, I have no idea what this route looks like or what is possible or not possible. This is where I'd like you to go—to Durango, Colorado. From there, drive the road. See if it's even possible for an accident to go unreported. Parts of the area are mountainous, but the route is well traveled. Frankly, it's hard to believe they could have gone missing here and not be discovered, but I need you to go see for us."

Diaz started going through a small stack of papers on the corner of his desk until he had the documents he wanted. "Here, I have arranged a border crossing card for you, a passport, and false police credentials in the name of Martinez. You will be nothing more than a tourist, but if stopped for any reason, you are one of my captains. Any inquiries concerning you will come to me.

"I know you are planning to go to Chihuahua to help with your brother's release; take your trip as planned. On Wednesday you'll fly to Houston; then to Denver, Colorado; and finally to the small town of Durango. I've booked you a hotel and reserved you a car; all the information is there in your docu-ments. Drive the route. Concentrate on areas where it may be possible in your judgment for an accident or event to go unseen. This all presupposes that the Aguilars were doing as they were told and staying on route, stopping only for gas, food, and to piss, but for this line of investigation, we will assume that. What choice do we have?"

Felix had a concerned look on his face. "I'll do this, Cesar, but I am not a policeman. I do not have your experience, and my English is just OK."

Diaz nodded his head sympathetically and then said, "I appreciate your concerns and understand, and I can't be there to tell you what to look for. But you are bright. I know you will figure it out. And do not worry about the language; you know enough to get by. Be courteous when situations require you to speak with people, especially the authorities. Just drive the road and look. Maybe you come up with possibilities; maybe not. But we must start somewhere, yes? I have observed you for years. You are intuitive and observant. You would have made a fine police officer in another life. Try to put yourself in that van. Drive the route at least once at night, as they did. Experience what they presumably did. I've checked the weather reports for last Sunday; all was fine. The forecast for the end of the week is similar. This is important. Take no more than a week, and call in once daily. Use only prepaid cell phones."

"Whatever you wish, Cesar. I'll go. I do not know if I will be of any use to you, but I do know it's better than sitting around here doing nothing and wondering where our money has gone. Thank you for trusting me."

Diaz had a very serious look on his face. "No thanks are necessary, my friend. We have been violated, our money stolen. All we have is each other and El Lobo. A day of judgement is coming for our banking partner that cannot be avoided. Men will die. Until then, I will get us information and be our eyes and ears into America. I will eliminate other possibilities if I can. You take care of this one."

With that, the partners shook hands and parted.

Felix left the Beach House and returned to the highway that would take him north back into town; on the way was General Servando Canales International Airport. He pulled into the long-term parking, grabbed the bag from the trunk, and took a flight to Chihuahua, where his brother Guillermo picked him up as planned. The identical twins shared a warm brotherly embrace and then, with Guillermo behind the wheel, headed into town.

At a little over eight hundred thousand people, Chihuahua is the twelfth-largest city in Mexico and one of the most industrialized. It lies on the western edge of the Chihuahuan Desert and is dominated geographically by three hills that appear in the city's coat of arms. Because of its proximity to the US to the north, many American-owned businesses had located manufacturing facilities there. The city had grown and its residents had prospered, and as a result, many new gated middle-class and upscale residential zones or subdivisions called *fraccionamientos* had developed. As Guillermo drove away from the airport, his route did not take them near any of them.

The brothers were from Hoyo del Infierno, Hell's Hole, one of the oldest and the worst of Chihuahua's more poverty-stricken *colonias*, or neighborhoods. The name Hell's Hole did not appear on any city map, and if native Chihuahuans were asked, they would deny its existence. But for decades, the run-down, dangerous neighborhood south of the city center had been the breeding ground for the worst of the criminal elements that had plagued the city over the years, and with the rise in trafficking, it was the home for the worst of that crowd as well. The old neighborhood was dangerous to any outsider, including the local police and the federal troops, who seldom patrolled its streets. To those who had been born and raised there, in addition to the familiarity and comfort of the local streets and businesses, there was also safety and security. No one entered Hoyo del Infierno without being noticed and, if unknown, without being passively watched. Hoyo del Infierno protected her own.

The Brillo family home sat in the middle of one of the dozens of dusty, run-down blocks of small houses and trashed-out commercial strips that made up Hoyo del Infierno. Faded pastel paint jobs and flat tin corrugated roofs were the norm, rusted-out cars and trucks on the streets and in the occasional dirt driveway typical, and unfenced yards full of weeds everywhere. The city's close proximity to the Chihuahuan Desert and its elevation above sea level seemed to invite the oppressing sun and constant dusty breeze that raked the neighborhood's unpaved streets. Guillermo parked in front of their mother's faded yellow house, which looked as if the cement block walls hadn't seen a new coat of paint in years. The brothers had made plenty of money over the years, but to fix up her home would only make it stand out and draw attention, and that had to be avoided.

Felix looked around as he stepped out of the car. He couldn't remember a day when the air on his street had not been filled with dirt and dust. He wrinkled his nose at the thought, but a feeling of peace also came over him. His mother was waiting on the porch wearing a simple dress with her favorite white apron over it. She was only fifty but looked far older. The neighborhood and her husband's hard life had done that to her—that and the drinking she did when alone, trying to forget. Their father was dead; once a trusted soldier for the Vargas brothers, long since a casualty in the trafficking business. She always cried when any of her three sons showed up, and today was no different, especially because it was her *dos angulos dulce*—her two sweet angels, her twins.

The brothers said they could only stay for a quick lunch but promised to take her to dinner that night. There was business to attend to downtown, and they had to go. She was aware of their efforts to get her baby out of jail and was grateful. As with her husband, she knew what they were involved with but didn't really want to know, so she never asked questions. She was grateful they were alive and for the money the twins sent her regularly. They had tried to move her out of the old neighborhood once, but that hadn't worked out. Her entire life was spent within a few miles of her dilapidated old house, and all her family and friends were there. It was the only place, she said, where she felt safe.

After lunch, she stood on the porch wringing her hands and watched them as they walked toward the end of the block and the businesses located on the main street there. The Goat's Head sat on the main drag that defined the northern edge of the Hole. The owner's family had been serving simple meals and drinks for several generations from the same two-story building, sandwiched as it was between others that looked just like it. If not for the turquoise-colored awnings and the simple wood sign over the door with the crude painting of a goat's head, the small cantina would have been indistinguishable from the other storefronts. A neighborhood friend, not much older than they were, now ran it for his family and lived in the apartment on the second floor. His father had run the place for as long as Felix could remember, but he had been arrested and jailed some years earlier for killing off a competitor in an old feud. Felix and his brothers had, each in his own time, taken their first drink in the dark, cramped bar. Their father had taken them there just as his father had before that. Neither brother knew exactly how much business had been transacted at the old round wooden tables in the dark back corner of the bar, but each knew it was measured in the tens of millions. They were on Vargas ground, or what used to be Vargas ground, but since the government crackdown and raid on the Vargas family compound west of the city a year ago, even that decades-old given was now in flux. All they knew for sure as they entered and their eyes adjusted to the darkness was that the few faces they saw were all known to them.

None of the other locals who had been a part of the Vargas brothers' cartel and were still around had any idea what the brothers had been asked to do ten years earlier or where they had gone. They had simply disappeared, moved to other parts of the country, and from time to time returned to visit their mother and take a meal or two at the Goat's Head. Whenever they returned, they were always in the company of one of the Vargas brothers and as such were afforded great respect by association.

They walked to a back table and sat down as the young owner came out from behind the bar, bringing two glasses of their favorite beer with him. After shaking their old friend's hand, Guillermo asked, "Any word, Angel?"

"Nothing yet, but I have been careful with who I've talked to, just like you instructed."

"Thank you. Keep a sharp ear, and be careful. But I want to find him if he's still alive."

"Anything you say, Guillermo."

Angel returned to his bar, and Felix watched him until he was out of earshot before turning to his brother. "What was that all about?"

"You asked me about a security chief for our new business. I found out a month ago that one of the Condor's bodyguards may have survived, the young one they called El Cuchillo."

Felix raised an eyebrow slightly with the name. "I only know the rumors about the man. What do you know of him?"

"Only what Javier has told me, but it is enough. He sounds like a young version of Diaz's El Lobo. At one time or another, he saved each of the Vargases from certain death, according to Javier. He is young and smart, but cold and ruthless when necessary. Javier says he is trustworthy, and the proof of this is that the Condor took him to his side after only months in the organization. Javier spent a lot of time with him and liked him, and he liked Javier."

"What makes Javier think he survived the attack?" Felix asked. He sipped on his beer and casually looked around the bar to make sure they were not attracting any attention.

"With the information Javier provided, I have been able to talk with not only some of the men who were at the estate and survived but also several of our contacts in the Federal Police still here in town. This El Cuchillo—his true name is Ray Espinoza—was not listed on the kill lists, nor was he jailed with the others, as far as we can tell. He simply has vanished. I sent the lawyer, Valdes, to Mexico City, and he was able to be named lawyer for one of the guard captains who was captured at the Condor's estate. This guard told Valdes two interesting things. First, that there was much chaos during the attack and therefore opportunity to escape. But more importantly, there were rumors among the guards of a secret passage out of the estate for the Condor and those close to him. We know that the Condor was captured and the Vargases all killed during the assault, but there also existed the chance for escape. As this El Cuchillo was not listed as killed or in the jails we have checked, he must be alive. If so, I want to find him. Anyone our friend and mentor would take to his side and trust is someone I want by mine."

"Well, if even some of the rumors are true, I agree. He is apparently a capable killer and able to see attacks before they come. A very valuable man if true."

"It's true. Javier says it is."

"So what have you done to find this El Cuchillo?" Felix said as he glanced over at Angel at the bar. "In trying to find him, all you may do is expose him, if he is in fact still alive."

Guillermo leaned in toward his older twin and said very quietly, but tersely, "Don't you think I know this? All I've done is speak to a few men like Angel there, who are loyal to us and work in the few cantinas here and in Hermosillo where the Vargases regularly went. All are old friends of Carlo Vargas, and according to Javier, El Cuchillo went everywhere Carlo did. I've spoken to only four, and like Angel, all would know this El Cuchillo on sight if they ever saw him again. All I asked them to do is call me if they see him and quietly tell him a friend is looking for him. They're to give him my private number to call, nothing more."

"You've done fine, brother. Do not be offended by my comment. It's just that we must be very careful. We have enough problems as it is."

With that, Felix went on to tell Guillermo about the missing money and his part in Diaz's plans to find it. A very agitated Guillermo could hardly contain himself with the news.

"Jesus Christ, Felix! This is a disaster," Guillermo hissed in a whisper. "I'm supposed to meet the Vargases' Columbians in Tapachula at the end of the May with ten million American!"

"I know, I know, Guillermo," Felix said, just as quiet. "But I can't change the fact that our money is missing. We have some time, and I trust Diaz. If our money can be found, he will find it."

"So what do I tell our Columbians in the meantime?"

"Say nothing and do nothing. We do, and we start all over with sources we do not know, and there is far too much danger down that path. I fly north tomorrow to do my part for Diaz. In the meantime, you and Javier stay out of sight. Try and find this El Cuchillo, but carefully. Stay close to Hoyo del Infierno, and stay safe."

"Easy enough for me, but what about you? I mean, you are known to the American authorities."

Felix drank down the last of his beer and stared at his brother. "I don't like this any more than you do, but what information the Americans have on me is incomplete at best and old. They have nothing from the last year, and shaving and cutting my hair has changed my appearance enough that I hardly recognized myself when I did it. Diaz has provided good papers and made me a captain in the Federal Police. That should be sufficient if anyone stops me. Anyway, I'm to travel as a tourist, so unless something really goes wrong, I should be fine. I return in a week from my part of the search and will rejoin you and Javier here before returning to Matamoros."

"You know your business and your people, Felix, but be careful. You may not know the thieves who have stolen from you, but they do know who it will be that comes looking for them. That is a great advantage for them."

Felix had a grim look on his face. "A fact, Guillermo, that is never too far from my thoughts."

The brothers looked at each other, both realizing the dangers to them and their plans without having to say more.

After their lunch, Valdes, the lawyer they had hired to get Javier out of jail, dropped in and updated them on what was to happen later in the day. When the lawyer left, they returned to their mother's to wait while he did what he had to do in court to get Javier released. When finished, he would bring him home, and the three brothers would be together for the first time in a long, terrible ten years. And when their mother could get her weeping of happiness under control, they would do as they had promised and long wanted to do and take her to dinner at her favorite restaurant. There she would enjoy the company of all three of her sons, unlike so many other mothers of the neighborhood whose sons were long since dead or in jail. The Hoyo del Infierno was like that.

6

The offices of Berman, Greenberg, and Levine
Lower downtown Denver
Sunday morning; end of week one

Henry didn't feel right. He was being glib when he made his comment to Jack about having finally joined the human race and doing something not quite honest, but that had been for his troubled friend's sake; Henry was as straight an arrow as Jack was. If he thought for a second that Jack would accept his act of generosity, he would have staked Jack financially to a new life long before now, and the dangerous act his friend was obviously contemplating could be avoided. Henry had more money than most, and his two partners and the other thirty lawyers of his firm were cranking out very profitable billable hours as fast as they could. Henry's practice was mostly corporate, contracts, and some tax, and with the success he had had with Jack's high-profile trial, he was building up a lucrative criminal practice as well. It was interesting work, and there were plenty of fees to be made defending the clients who were contacting him, but for the most part, he didn't like them. Everyone was entitled to a defense, but he had to believe in a client to defend him or her.

Helping Jack do something illegal went against every moral fiber of his being, but after listening to his friend's story, he knew Jack wanted to keep the drug money to ensure a better life for his girls. After what Jack had done for him, he'd suck it up and use his brains and experience to devise a scheme that would keep his friend out of jail; he owed him that and far more. Samuel was nine now, and the nightmares had stopped months ago. To look at him, you would never believe he had been through the trauma he had. The pedophile Jack had blown away had done nothing more than snatch Samuel out of the yard and drive him back to his house, where Jack, by fortunate happenstance, was waiting and watching in his off hours, despite the court order against him. It only took Jack seconds to realize what he was witnessing and to run across the street, kick in the door, and kill the bastard, so Samuel had not been touched. Thanks to a merciful God, Samuel didn't even witness the horrific shooting in the hysterical state he was in. It was ironic as hell, and not lost on Henry, that the evil man had snatched both his son and Jack's daughter, but each had been saved by circumstance or providence from any real devastating harm, likely a premature death. In the case of his son, however, Jack had paid dearly for his actions and lost almost everything, and he would never forget.

Henry had not heard from his friend since their lunch on Tuesday, but he knew Jack had been getting the cash back to Denver. He was glad someone like Jack was trying it and not him. Given Jack's description of the mountain crash site, he was certain he was physically unable to do what his friend was trying. He could only hope that all had gone well and that Jack hadn't gotten tripped up right out of the gate. He had a busy schedule for the week but had still managed to put the outlines of a decent laundering plan together. It would require a major lifestyle change for his friend and a real change in scenery, but that was the price Jack was going to have to pay to pull this off. Jack had finally called this morning and caught him in his office and was now on his way. They would have ample privacy to go over the broad outlines of the scheme he'd put together.

Jack arrived a little after nine, and Henry went to the lobby to let him in. There were no receptionists or secretaries working this Sunday, so the front door was locked. A few other attorneys were working, but none took particular notice of Jack. All knew of the special relationship that existed between the two men and attached no further significance to the weekend meeting. Henry thought Jack looked tired, even beat up, which was unusual for Jack. He was in superb condition for a thirty-three-year-old. Henry led him down the hall to his office, showed him in, and closed the door. "Have a seat, Jack. If you don't mind me saying, you look like shit."

Jack tried to smile. "To tell the truth, Hank, I can hardly walk. My quads are killing me. I know I only humped fourteen or fifteen miles total going back and forth from the wreck to my truck, but I'm wasted. Maybe it was the altitude, or climbing the tough terrain through the snow. Maybe even the tension. I haven't slept worth a damn since last Sunday."

"Everything go OK?"

"Yeah…OK, I guess." Jack paused, staring at Henry with an odd look about him, so Henry just sat, waiting for him to go on. "Hank, this whole thing is way more serious than I thought. I didn't do an exact count, only an estimate, but you cannot imagine how much money is back at my apartment. It's unbelievable."

Henry smiled. He was only human, and his curiosity was aroused and had been since Jack first told him about the money. "OK, Jack, don't leave me hanging. How much are we dealing with here?"

Jack slowly exhaled a deep breath. "Would you believe something in the neighborhood of a hundred and twenty million?"

The smile on Henry's face disappeared, his looked turned serious, and his eyes widened. "Holy…shit," he said very slowly as he sat back in his chair. "You're kidding me!"

"No, I'm not. It's still hard for me to believe. I don't pretend to know a damn thing about how the drug cartels operate, but it baffles the shit out of me that there would be that kind of cash sitting around waiting to be picked up and driven to Mexico by just two guys. So many things could go wrong…I mean, look what happened—a stupid car wreck. I guess I thought the cartels were more sophisticated somehow." Jack paused and shook his head. "Well, I suppose it doesn't matter. I have the money, and whatever asshole thought he was going to get it is just shit out of luck."

Henry was staring off into the distance as Jack was talking, past the windows behind his desk, which provided a great view of the Denver skyline, and then he turned and looked at him when he was finished. "OK, Jack, *now* I'm real worried."

"About what?"

Henry smirked. "About the weather. What the hell do you think I'm worried about? The money. With that kind of money in play, someone or some group is surely going to come look for it, and that someone—or some-ones—are very, very bad people. With your background, you of all people should know about the kind of people we're talking about here. These assholes would kill you for your kid's milk money. What do you think they'll do for a hundred and twenty million? Whoever's money this is will be relentless looking for it."

"Don't you think I know that, Henry?" an exasperated Jack said. "I've thought about nothing else for the last two days. But I also took a step back and looked at this coldly and objectively as a detective. Unless you saw that van go over the edge, there is no finding it, and I'm the only one who did. From the maps it's clear this Diaz character will know his van is somewhere between Durango and Walsenburg, but that's it. And that's only if he believes the van did what it did and crashed and wasn't simply driven off to Timbuktu by the two guys driving it, or maybe hijacked by some other assholes. Those are really the more logical conclusions, don't you agree? Especially when you consider all the fighting that apparently occurs between these groups.

"But the hell with it. Let's say this Diaz gets past all that and really believes his men were trustworthy and there was no hijacking and that the van really is somewhere in that two hundred miles and was involved in an unreported accident, as unlikely as that would be. And now let's say he somehow gets enough people beating the bushes to find it without drawing any attention and does find the van. What then? He still has nothing. He only confirms the basic facts: his van crashed, and the money is gone. I went over that site with a fine-tooth comb, and there is absolutely no evidence of how the money got out of there, and absolutely no evidence that gets back to me. Now you tell me where my thinking is wrong."

Henry, his lips tense and pursed, shook his head slowly. "No, Jack, I agree with you. From your description I don't for the life of me see how the van is discovered, much less see someone getting to you. But take it as gospel, Jack—someone will look for it."

"Let the bastards look," a determined Jack said. "Where in the world can they look without any leads or drawing attention? Unless you tell me it's not possible to launder the shit, Hank, I'm keeping it. Now, is it possible?"

Henry nodded his head slowly in the affirmative. "Yeah, Jack, it's possible. We have to be careful. It's complicated as hell and will take a lot of time, but it's possible. You're going to have to leave town, and you're under a court order not to for another year, but that's not insurmountable. I know a senior judge who will relook at your probation if it means you pursuing a new job. What I have in mind moves you east, a long way from the girls, but given the recent changes to your cash flow situation, you can fly instead of drive to LA whenever you want."

"Lay it out for me, Hank. What are you thinking?"

"First things first. To make this work, you need to get the cash safely in a bank offshore without drawing attention, and in this hemisphere, that means the Caribbean. I'm thinking the Bahamas, maybe Antigua or the Grenadines. Lots of banks, and not all of them are strictly on the up-and-up despite the international pressure for more transparency. You need to establish a business and the appearance of residency there, all legal and aboveboard, and you need to start generating income from this business that will result in regular deposits. Once you've established a relationship with a bank down there and we learn more about the local players, then we can start to look at large cash deposits. This will cost you. I understand the graft down there is spectacular, if not typical, but more on that later. Question: Does sailing appeal to you?"

"I sailed with the fleet, of course, as part of Force Recon, but you're not talking about that kind of sailing, are you?"

"No, I'm talking sailboats, catamarans, yachts for hire—that sort of thing."

Jack had a look on his face that seemed to say, *Are you kidding me?* "I was raised in Colorado, Hank. Not exactly the sailing hub of the world. But what the hell—considering the road I'm headed down here, I'm pretty flexible right now, and sailing sounds fine. So you're thinking I get into the sailboat renting business?"

"It's called chartering, and no. That was my first thought, but I have a better idea. No, the sailboat part is how you're going to get that boatload of cash, if you will forgive the pun, to the right island. It's also a good place to keep it, I'm thinking, in the near term. No, the business I've been research-ing for you is private charter security out of the Caribbean area. That's more in line with your background. Lots of incredibly rich people charter big-ass motor yachts, and with threats of piracy and plain old crimes against persons, most of these folks hire private security to go along with them, suitably dis-guised as other guests or deck hands. Ever scuba?"

"Again, no, but I always liked the idea of scuba diving. Looks interesting."

"Well, that's something else I would suggest you get into. More access to potential clients. Being a scuba guide is good cover for a security type."

"Not to kill this idea before it gets going, Hank, but seems to me there would be a lot of established businesses in that sort of thing already, staffed by professionals better versed in charter security than me. How in the hell can I get a business like that up and going when there's almost nothing I know about that sort of security?"

Henry smiled tolerantly at his friend. "You're missing the point, Jack. What do you care if you ever made a real dime at it? All that's important here is that you *look* like you're making money. A great many of the kind of super rich we're talking about here would require confidentiality. Your business record keeping could be general information—not a lot of details or specifics on the clients, what boats they charter, that kind of detail—and you can say their payments to you are in cash. Get it? I'll help you fabricate the records in case anyone ever wants to look into the business, something I dearly hope never happens. If you really do get clients, we include that as well. It helps us, in fact. You can then live on your boat when you're in the islands, literally sitting on your cash. Did I mention that you'll be buying a boat soon?"

"No. We passed over that little detail."

"Right. Yes, you'll need your own boat. I've already started looking into this for you, as a matter of fact. We need to get you relocated down near Miami to start. There we will get you hooked up with a real sailor, and he'll teach you the ropes. And in your spare time, you get yourself scuba certified. If anyone looks into your life, we need to convince them you're really getting into this big life change. You somehow get that pile of cash at your place down there and onto your boat without being discovered. You sail to one of the primary islands—I'll figure out which one by then—and drop anchor, as in start living a new life on your boat, all the while protecting the cash. I suggest you get creative and hide it somehow, but those kinds of details—that and getting it safely that far—I leave to you. I'm your partner for the security business, or, rather an LLC I set up will be, to front you the cash for the boat and start-up expenses. Since I'm your lawyer and a corporate director, we have attorney-client privilege. I'm aware of a Bahamian company that offers a variety of shelf companies, which come with years of regulatory filings behind them, lending a greater feeling of solidity, if I feel we need that. All legal, of course."

Jack raised his hand, as if to say stop. "Hold on, Henry. You've built a great life with Sylvia and the kids and your practice. I need your help, but I was talking just advice, deniable conversations between us in private. This could all go bad; there must be a million things that could go wrong with this scheme. And I'm so ignorant, I can't even tell you what those things are. No way do I want you compromised in this deal. Point me in the right direction, and the rest is up to me. As far as the world is concerned, we either never had this conversation, or after I came to you with this scheme, as my attorney you told me to do the right thing and turn the money in. That's the way it has to be."

Henry smiled at his friend. "Noble, Jack, and thanks, but the only way to keep this between just the two of us is to do it my way. Lest you think I'm falling on your old corps sword for you, relax. I'm going to be your financial partner in one or more legal businesses. I'm providing the seed money from cash you'll give me before you head south, and there will be partnership agreements between us, all proper, notarized, and filed with the appropriate government agencies here and in the Bahamas. After a while, once the bulk of the money is safe, we'll amicably dissolve our partnership and go our separate ways. Do this my way, Jack, and I won't get touched if something goes wrong. I can always say I never knew about all the illegal cash if it ever comes to that."

"Henry, unless you swear to me that's exactly what you will do, I don't think I can go forward with this. And you know how much I need it."

Henry paused and sat back in his chair before going on. "OK, Jack, I swear. If this scheme goes south, I cut you loose. I'll feel like an unmitigated shit, but I understand." He slowly leaned forward again and looked intently at Jack for a long moment before going on. "Listen, I can get you an offshore business organized on paper, a website announcing you to the world, and help you set up legal accounts onshore and off for the business. That's all pretty simple and straightforward. You're the one who will be running the risks, and they're considerable."

"Such as, Hank?"

Henry shook his head slowly and ran his hand through his prematurely graying hair. "Jesus, Jack, I'd like to think that I'm not as ignorant on this as you are, to use your words, but there are so many possible ways for this to blow up, I don't really know where to start. Assuming you do as I say and follow the plan I've outlined, you still have to get the cash to Florida and not draw the attention of traffic cops in about twenty states. You'll have to keep it hidden until you get a boat and learn how to sail it. You'll then have to keep the cash hidden somehow in your boat in an area that's rife with crime—I'm talking the entire Caribbean area here. Smuggling and drug and gunrunning are big-time concerns down there, so you need to make sure that if you're boarded, say by the Coast Guard in a routine inspection, for example, for whatever reason, they find nothing. The same goes for what passes for the Coast Guard or customs from the other countries in the area, and who knows how honest and law-abiding those groups are? Maybe someone confiscates your boat on general principals; they don't like blonds that week—who the fuck knows.

"But let's get beyond the simple transport and concealment details of a hundred and twenty million in dirty US currency. Once you've established residency down there and a presence, we need to find you a bank that likes large deposits and cares little where the money comes from. This is where things get dangerous. I can help some here, but it's tricky. The best possible scenario is that you manage to establish a very friendly personal relationship with a senior-level banker who in turn has connections in customs, if that's needed, that allows you to bring in lots of cash all at once and get it deposited.

We're talking at least two well-placed individuals who, for a fee, will pass you from the dock to the bank manager's office without questions. This will likely cost you a quarter of what you bring in, maybe less if you're lucky. But even at a quarter, you're still talking something in the neighborhood of ninety million safely stashed in a bank and now making money on your money, and that's not a bad neighborhood.

"Once in a Bahamian bank, you can then make regular transfers to your Florida business account as if you're getting fees from rich vacationers from your offshore registered business. Because you will be spending a lot of time in the US seeing your girls, you will still be classified as a US resident regardless of all the offshore bullshit I set up, so you'll be taxed to death. That will cost you another thirty percent. I'll handle the tax prep for you, so that will all be aboveboard. You're fucking with a lot of unknowns here; we will not include the Internal Revenue Service on that list. Next, I think we can safely get about sixty percent of the cash back here over time, both in business deposits and in investments here at home funded from your offshore account. I can set you up with some investment partners when the time comes, and also a financial planner I know who's honest and sharp as a tack. You and the girls should be set for life, and a few more generations beyond that."

Jack was amazed, and his face could not hide it. "Jesus, Hank, that all sounds pretty good to me. I think I can safely handle all the moving around and then the boat stuff. And I'm friendly enough; I'll hook up someone so it doesn't seem that high risk."

Henry shook his head. "No, Jack, it is risky. The second you get someone other than me involved, you're out of the shadows. Best case, we get one crooked bank official with one crooked customs official involved. Two crooks, Jack, at least, and that's the best scenario. There's a reason these people are called crooks. Maybe you get lucky and they remain discreet. In that case, no problem; you're home free. But if they're not, you'll never know until someone blindsides you with a threat of some kind, and any threat will be dangerous, maybe even fatal. The biggest unanswered question in this scheme is whom to approach for the banking. If you can't find a banker on your own just living and working in the islands, I'm representing some characters who could probably help you, but that's a last resort. Because of your case last year, the criminal side of the practice has really taken off. I have a number of pending cases with some real successful lowlifes in Southern Florida who I strongly suspect are already doing what we're talking about here. What I'll do is learn what I can that could help you. Then I violate my oath and divulge to you privileged information from one or more of them. I owe you that, and I know such a violation goes no further than you. I can live with that.

"But let's not get too dark here. If you can get your money into the Bahamas, then we can start to wire it back to your business account in Florida and into legitimate investment partnerships. I even have a name for your new business: Caribbean Aqua Security. I've already registered the name, and it's yours. I'll retain a web page designer and make you look great. The key here, Jack, is going slow and keeping the money hidden as you slowly get it transferred. After we get you a business up and running on paper, you make small cash deposits on a regular basis to your offshore account—nothing larger than, say, ten or twenty thousand at a time. That shouldn't raise any flags. Over a year, that's a half million or more. With your sniper-like patience, you could do that for years and get no one else involved. You can live a cash existence in the islands from your stash. That's not unusual in the tropics, and you slowly transfer the money to the mainland, now clean for your girls' futures.

"The downside, of course, with the slow and easy approach is that you have millions of dollars hidden away on your boat for years, and that's liable never to be all that comfortable. Hell, accidents happen. Look no further than your two dead Mexicans for evidence of that. And you will be living on a boat in an area that has an annual hurricane season. Nothing like a little hurricane to wreck or sink your boat and the money.

"But having said all that, I'm thinking if anyone can make the right kind of friends and be able to get large sums deposited without becoming exposed, you can. You're good with people, Jack; I've got to believe you'll make the right connections. Start small. Get known and get comfortable, an expatriate starting a new life. Anyone really checking up on you will find out why you're starting over, and you can live with that, right?"

"Yeah, I can. Truth be told, the more we talk about it, the more I realize how much I need a new start. I didn't understand it this past year living it, but I've been depressed, I think. A guy doesn't like to admit this to another guy, but while thinking about the possibilities the last several days that having money could help with, I can see now how unhappy I've been, and I hate that feeling. Any future has to be better than my current situation. I don't know how to thank you, Henry."

Henry leaned forward and grabbed Jack by the arm, an outward show of friendship. "Forget it, Jack. I owe you, not the other way around. It will take two weeks to get your probation changed or dropped and get all the organizational paperwork done."

Henry sat back, pulled out his Blackberry, and looked at it intently. "I have some depositions scheduled in the Miami area around the first week in April. You need to take care of business up here. Let people know you're leaving, and then we meet down there.

"Oh, incidentally, I don't want to seem all paranoid here, but just tell people you're leaving town to get closer to your daughters. Everyone will assume you're headed to California. It's no one's business for now that you're going to Florida. I think you're probably right about that crash site going undiscovered, but just in case you're wrong, I'd suggest you keep your movements quiet. Let's go back to your place, and you give me, say, five hundred thousand dollars. I'll transfer that amount from my investment portfolio to the new company account I open in Florida. From that account we'll have the funds to buy a boat and take care of any other expenses. You will be identified as the managing partner; we'll get you a company bank card to use for charges, and I want you to use it."

Jack had a concerned look on his face. "Henry, how will you get five hundred thousand dollars into your bank without drawing attention?"

"Don't worry about that. I'll get a second safe deposit box, one that Sylvia will know nothing about. I'll make cash deposits to my business account over a long period—a little here, a little there; no one will be the wiser.

"Oh, one more thing. Cancel any credit cards you have. Get off the grid as much as possible. Travel to Florida on cash. The only real family you have left are your parents and the girls; you make contact with them. I assume you have a bank account here, so set up some kind of automatic monthly transfers for your child support. Set it up so you have something like two years' worth covered. Let me know if you need some cash for that. If you go through with this, I want you to truly get lost for a while."

Jack sat quietly as Henry finished up. He had a look on his face that Henry could not exactly read. "Well, Jack?"

Jack said slowly and quietly, "Hank, I have a big decision to make, and it's a hard one. Until this past week, I never could have imagined any of this; it's just too off the wall. But it's happened, and there's a once-in-a-lifetime opportunity here, even if it is illegal. But before I cross that line, I need to know how you really feel about this, and more importantly, I need to know how you'll feel about me. Losing your respect and friendship is something I would not want to do. I'll solve my problems some other way if I have to, however hard."

Henry said, also in a soft voice, even though the two friends were alone, "You know, like you, I've never done a sideways thing in my life, if you don't count the Econ 100 final I took for one of the dumber football players my first year at Stanford. I was young and dumb and broke and hungry, and he was offering a hundred bucks. That's an expulsion offense at Stanford, and I swore, when I got away with it, it would be my last act of larceny. And I swear to you, Jack, it has been. I've never told a soul about that sad event, not even Syl, until now. It would have never occurred to me that I could ever counsel you, or anyone else for that matter, to break the law. But then, like you, I've never imagined a set of circumstances as has occurred. And I don't mean just this past week. I'm talking about the last year and a half. I know I'm emotionally invested here, and that's surely coloring my judgment, but when I leave you today, I'm going home, and when I get there, I know I'll end up tossing the ball around the backyard with Sam. The idea of him not being there when I get home, of him being taken from us…well, ah…that's something I don't think I could have survived as a parent. I was an only child, Jack. I don't know what it's like to have a brother, but I swear, after what you have done for me, that's how I feel about you. There is nothing I will not do for you, and I'll be grateful to you until the day they plant me."

Henry paused and cleared his throat, trying to conceal the lump of emotion that had come to him at the thought of his son, and then he went on. "If ever there was a human being who needed a break in life, you're it. You risked everything for my son and got kicked in the teeth for your efforts. I refuse to believe that God, or destiny—whatever it is you believe in—is that cruel. We can pull this off. I want to pull this off, for your sake and for your girls."

Jack had also become emotional just listening to him, and he didn't trust himself to say anything for a few seconds. When he regained his composure, he looked at his friend. "Well...I guess this is it then, isn't it, Henry?"

"If you mean as in it's time to shit or get off the pot, then yes it is, Jack."

Jack stood up, so Henry did likewise. He stuck out his hand, Henry took it, and the two friends shook hands. Then Jack said, "Let's go to my place and get you the seed money for our new company."

7

DEA Agent Ray Cruz walked briskly out of the Starbucks near his office with his morning coffee in hand, turned left on Second Street, and headed toward the Federal Building across the street. Bennie Santiago, his boss and mentor from DC, was in town, and he was meeting with him this morning on an unspecified subject and was anxious to get to work. He had been in the Seattle office for almost a year now, involved in the routine operations and investigations that came with the interdiction of illegal drugs into the US from Canada. For those in the know, this meant he had been involved in very little for most of that time. All the real action in the interdiction business was at the country's southern border. He had spent a lot of time in the south his first six months in the DEA, and in Mexico specifically as an undercover operative. Bennie was head of covert operations for the agency and after his first mission had reassigned him to Seattle and put him in therapy. The agency shrink brought in to talk with him agreed with Bennie that it was best he "chill out" for a while, given all that had gone down on his first operation. So he'd been shuttled off against his wishes. Truth be known, however, even he realized he needed some help dealing emotionally with parts of his last assignment. The time he spent in deep undercover had been rough. Living and working in beautiful Seattle was good, but he was antsy to get back in the game. With the able help of his government therapist, he had processed the killings he had been a party to during his first assignment as much as he ever would. It was time to move on.

He was lucky in that unlike the other rank-and-file agents, he had a direct pipeline to his boss. Benjamin Santiago had been with the agency for going on thirty-five years and could be in Washington if he chose, heading up all field operations for the DEA. Bennie's two closest friends were the director of the agency and the deputy director for intelligence, the number-one and number-two men in the leadership. But Bennie had turned down the number-three posting to head a sensitive intelligence-gathering and operations unit run directly out of the director's office. As such, Bennie was free to remain in the field and really solve problems, which was something he had been doing with brilliance for many years. Ray didn't have to bother calling Bennie, even though he had his private number and could do so, for he knew Bennie would call him. He often did. The last time was a week ago; Bennie informed him he was coming to Seattle and wanted to meet. Ray was tired of shuffling paper in Seattle and took the opportunity to bluntly tell Bennie it was time they talked about him getting back to work.

To his surprise, Bennie agreed, saying that some interesting new intelligence had come in that might require his attention. This got his juices pumping, but when he asked Bennie for details, he had said simply they would discuss it face to face when he was in Seattle next. Ray's recent bout with boredom made concentrating each day at work tough enough, but the past week had been even worse, wondering what Bennie had in mind and knowing he was coming to town. They talked often on the phone, but Ray had not seen his old boss for several months. After the last trip, he had driven him to the airport, and as Bennie was getting out of the car, he'd said cryptically, "Incidentally, Ray, grow a beard. Next time I see you, I don't want to see that baby face of yours." And he had turned and walked into the terminal. So despite the fact that he hated facial hair on himself, Ray did as ordered.

After clearing the lobby security screening, he took the elevator to the twenty-fifth floor and passed through a second screening and made his way to his indistinguishable cubicle, one of many sitting in the middle of the large, modern, open office layout. He sat his coffee down on his desk and then saw the small yellow note stuck to his computer monitor: "In SAC's office. Join me when you get in. B."

Ray knew the special agent in charge for Seattle, his immediate boss for the last year, was out of town on other business, so he was probably not involved with whatever Bennie had in mind for him. Ray was quietly grateful for this. The SAC was old school like Bennie but seemed to have a bee up his ass about having a well-connected, decorated young agent on his team and then having to put up with his time spent out of the office with the shrink. Ray would be glad to get out of Seattle, despite the fact it was a nice place to live.

He quickly grabbed his coffee and walked to the SAC's large corner office. Of the few private offices on the floor, the SAC had the nicest. Located at the southwest corner of the building, it provided a great view down Marion Street to Puget Sound and the waterfront with Bainbridge Island in the distance, when the typical fog or rains of March didn't obscure the fabulous view. The door was open, and Ray walked right in and found Bennie at the small conference table adjacent to the tall exterior windows, his back to the view, going through red-tabbed files marked "Eyes Only."

Bennie heard him walk in and looked up, a neutral expression on his face that revealed nothing about what he was reading or thinking. But then he smiled and said, "The beard looks good, Ray. And the longer hair—that short prison-style cut just wasn't you."

He stood up, and they shook hands. "Sit yourself down and tell me how you're feeling. And Ray, no bullshit."

Ray smiled and chuckled. One of the things he really liked about his boss was his down-to-earth, no-nonsense personality. A person always understood where he or she stood with Bennie. If you had any doubts, ever, all you had to do was ask, and you'd get a straight answer right between the eyes.

"Couldn't be better boss, really. But itching to get back in the game."

Bennie nodded his head, watching Ray closely, and then he grabbed the nearest of the red-tabbed files. "I've got Dr. Mercer's final report on you here; he seems to agree. Says here that you haven't had nightmares for some months now and that you have, quote, processed the trauma satisfactorily, end quote."

"Come on, Bennie," Ray said soberly. "They were bad dreams, and then only occasionally. Not nightmares. I'm fine, really. Slept like a baby last night," he said, flashing a quick smile to mask the lie.

"Sure, there are aspects that I'll always remember, but who wouldn't? I know now I did my duty and what was right, and in the end, that's what matters to me. I can live with the things I did or didn't do. I'd like to move on."

Bennie was watching his prized covert agent carefully as he spoke. He had been reading and intuiting people his entire career. After a few long seconds, he decided he believed Ray.

"OK, Ray. Jump up and shut the door. What we discuss from this point forward is need to know."

Ray did as he was asked, sat back down, leaned back in his chair, and sipped his coffee. Bennie grabbed a different red-tabbed file folder and started flipping through the pages before finding whatever it was he was looking for. "Remember in your report on the Vargas cartel from last year—the part where you said that the Condor had the other major cartels as penetrated as he had the government?"

"Yes, right. No question about it. He got people in with them years before. It was his great gift, I think—intelligence gathering. That and convincing men to do the dangerous and impossible for him."

"Did you ever have any names? None are mentioned specifically in the report, and I don't recall discussing this with you in the debrief."

Ray thought for a second. "No, Bennie, no names. Eduardo Vargas was doing the legwork for his cousin and would report with information on the other cartels. When I asked Carlo Vargas about it one time, he would only say that loyal men were at work doing very dangerous jobs and had been for a great many years."

"Well, I think we can safely put a few names to some faces. Does the name Javier Brillo ring a bell?"

Ray's face showed immediate recognition. "Sure. Javier—he was a young driver-enforcer type from a local Chihuahua family, as I recall. He was either in Hermosillo or Monterrey when we busted the cartel. I worked with him quite a bit. He was my driver a lot of the time."

"Hermosillo was where he was busted, swept up in the concurrent estate raids. He was returned to Chihuahua pending trial and has been held for the last year in the federal prison there as the government works its way down to him. They had lots of big fish to fry, so the wheels of justice have moved a little slowly in Brillo's case, even with our good friend now running everything."

The reference to "good friend" was a personal code between Bennie and Ray whenever they referred to the former commander of the Federal Police, Alberto Rodriguez, who acceded to the presidency of Mexico following the exposure of the then president as the leader of the Vargas family cartel.

"So he hasn't even been tried yet?"

"No. As a matter of fact, he just made bail and was released, which in and of itself isn't news. But he was seen last week in Chihuahua with two older men, a set of twins who, I'm told, are his older brothers. Ever hear of Guillermo or Felix Brillo?"

Ray had a very interested look on his face, but he shook his head no. "Never heard of them. You're asking if this Javier ever mentioned older brothers, right? And the answer to that one, best as I can recall, is again no."

"Right. Well, a special group of feds down there has managed to get some electronic eavesdropping and some human assets in place, in a few of the popular hangouts in Chihuahua and Hermosillo that folks like you and the Vargases used to frequent. The intelligence take seems to indicate that these two brothers spent a lot of time in two of the other important cartels we busted up, one in Tijuana, the other in Matamoros. Knowing what we do based upon your intelligence that the Condor had the other cartels infiltrated, and knowing that this Javier Brillo was in your group, these are very interesting characters to us. Does the Goat's Head Cantina sound familiar?"

Ray smiled and chuckled. "Yeah, it does. It was one of Carlo's favorite places to go in Chihuahua. With all the upscale places the Vargases controlled uptown, we would more often than not go to the Goat's Head, down in a real tough neighborhood called the Hoyo del Infierno, to drink and have their version of green chili—the best I've ever had, incidentally. Shitty, run-down cantina, by the look of it. You'd simply pass by if you didn't know the place, a real dump. It was run by old family friends, which was typical for the cartel. And, of course, the Vargases were raised in the same neighborhood. Pretty impressive about the eavesdropping, but is it really secure? Frankly, that strikes me as pure fantasy in the Hoyo del Infierno; little goes on in that neighborhood that doesn't get seen or heard."

"Well, that's what our friend tells me his intelligence team is telling him. Anyway, the real news here, beyond your old acquaintance having two older brothers you were unaware of, is that your name came up in a conversation between them a week ago."

Ray sat up, wide eyed and startled. "My name! How's that possible?"

Bennie smiled and held up his hand. "Whoa there. Sorry, relax. Not your real name, but, rather, your old El Cuchillo nom de guerre."

Ray sat back but was still concerned. The fact that he was known in Mexico as "the Knife" was something he had spent a year trying to forget. "Not many people even knew that name, Bennie. What gives here?"

"Well, it seems that the one older brother, Guillermo, has been spreading the word to a few people he must trust in select places like this Goat's Head for folks to keep an eye out for the one who was known as El Cuchillo. Appears he wants to talk with you. What the Mexicans got from their surveillance at the Goat's Head is that the older Brillo brothers want to get the band back together with just the family in charge and run their own operation out of Chihuahua now that the Vargases are all gone and Javier is out of jail. Ten million US was discussed and a buy with the Columbians, so we are talking some serious weight. They want you for head of security or enforcement, I gather. So I got with Alberto privately, and between us, we agreed maybe it's time you got off your dead ass and went back to work down there."

Ray smirked at his boss's comment, because he had been pestering Bennie for months about getting involved again with covert operations.

Bennie had a small smile on his face, pleased with his friendly teasing, but then he became more serious once again. "Ray, I'm convinced this is genuine and not a setup of some kind. I still believe absolutely that no one is the wiser to you down there. Given their surveillance, the Mexican authorities can prob-ably bust up this Brillo thing before it gets started without our help, but both of the twins were very deep in some very bad places we still have concerns about, specifically Matamoros and Tijuana. I suggested, and our friend agreed, that with you in with them for a bit, we may gain an insight into those two dens of iniquity that we currently don't have. We are particularly interested in the distribution network of the recently deceased Butcher of Brownsville out of Matamoros. Two snitches we have, one in Las Vegas and another in New Jersey, of all places, have both reported recently about a very large coke ship-ment that came north. This was news to us. We've had zip advance intelligence on anything like that in the works, and because we know so little, we think it's the Matamoros distribution network that's delivered it. But that's guessing, and I'm goddamned sick and tired of guessing about that network. The one brother, Felix Brillo, was apparently involved with the Butcher, and it stands to reason that he would know about his distribution network and maybe even be think-ing of using it in his new family enterprise. Any intelligence on that network you could develop gives us a helluva step up into that investigation."

Ray followed along with great interest and was excited by the possibilities. "I'm game. Without tooting my own horn, there was a bit of hero worship for me from Javier."

"Well, that's good for us, because whatever these older brothers have heard on the grapevine about you, they also have the kid brother singing your praises, and you're their pick as a security chief. That's way too great an open-ing not to exploit. So if you volunteer, I'll make it happen."

Ray smiled as he put his coffee down. "Since when are we a volunteer agency? As I recall, Bennie, you give the orders, and we common folk jump to."

Bennie smiled back but then turned serious. "Since your last mission, if you want to know. Change of procedure I talked over with the boys in DC, and they agreed. Anytime we send someone covert where there is even a remote possibility that we cannot keep them closely backed up, it's strictly volunteer. Call me a pussy, but losing track of you for all those weeks and knowing I had ordered you into that mess when you had no choice…well, it's something I don't want ever to repeat. No one has the right to order someone else to do that."

"Come on, Bennie. I wanted the mission. I would have volunteered for that one, just as I will volunteer for this one. So now that I'm in, what's the plan?"

Bennie nodded his head, quietly grateful but not surprised. "Thanks, Ray." He put down the one file he'd been skimming and grabbed a different one.

"We're calling this operation Walsingham—a meaningful title to the few of us in the know but meaningless to all others."

"Well, you've got me if I'm one of the few in the know. What the hell does it mean?"

Bennie chuckled. "Not up on your history, I see. As you know, I came up with the clever Trojan Horse op name for your first mission because of the way you went in last time, getting a bad guy to personally take you into the cartel. It was, I'm sure you agree, very appropriate, and the same is true with this operation. You return to Mexico this time as the experienced master spy, much like Sir Francis Walsingham did five hundred years ago when he returned to England from exile in France and helped the first Queen Elizabeth against the Catholics after the death of her half sister, Queen Mary of Bloody Mary fame. So as the Brillo brothers take over for the now-departed Condor, you return and help them in their rise. Clever, eh?"

"If you say so, boss," Ray said, shaking his head and smiling again at Bennie's obvious delight with his new mission code name. "So, how do you see me doing this one?"

Bennie became more serious again. "Well, for starters, you head south and get to this Goat's Head place without attracting attention. We'll get you across the border undocumented at Juarez. From there you take the bus to Chihuahua. There's a motel near the Goat's Head that our friends operate out of. Kind of disgusting, looks like a hot-sheet place, but has a few apartments perfect for you; you'll get one. They have some tech stuff—a few mics and miniature cameras, plus a decent transmitter. Once you check in, your place will be discreetly wired up. Try to keep it as your base of operations, and we can watch and listen.

"Seems likely the Brillo brothers will find you, so you don't even have to look, which is good for us. Two of them have stayed close to Chihuahua. The Mexicans lost track of the third one after their one meeting at this cantina was picked up electronically last week. The surveillance is pretty passive, for obvious reasons—you know what that neighborhood is like—and the Mexicans apparently weren't watching the airports, trains, or buses. So the older twin, Felix, just vanished. He spends a lot of time in Matamoros still, even with the demise of the Butcher, but he's hard to track, they say. The Mexicans have some good troops in Matamoros, but they were really beat up and overwhelmed until last year. They'll need more time to get on top of what's left of the few nasty groups in that area.

"Once the Brillos contact you, you play it by ear. Unlike last time, you'll presumably be able to keep a cell phone, given the job they seem to want you for, so we can track you and keep in touch. As you get into and discover what they're up to, we will shape the mission as required. Your first priority—after your safety, of course—is trying to develop intelligence on the Butcher's old distribution network up here. That's one network we never did crack, and it seems to still be very active. That being the case, stands to reason that this Felix Brillo will want to keep on using it with whatever group he's trying to put together with his brothers.

"The beauty of this mission, which I don't have to explain to you, is that if what the Mexicans picked up is accurate and the Brillos want you as security chief, we have the best of all worlds. You can protect yourself with your duties and actions while getting us the information we need up here."

Ray had a very sober look on his face as Bennie finished up. "Question: Last time I went in, the only ones who knew about me were you and the DI," he said, referring to the director of intelligence. "That was reassuring and turned out to be crucial, but you keep mentioning the Mexicans. How many people are in on this from their side, and do you trust whoever is doing this eavesdropping?"

Bennie smiled, thinking that Ray never missed the details. "Good question, and yes, I trust them. Remember the ghost colonel who led the raid on the Condor, Vicente Portillo?"

Ray nodded his head yes slowly. "Yeah, a good guy, I think. We just spoke a little at the estate before they flew me out, but he was impressive."

"A very good guy, Ray," Bennie said. "He's a full colonel in the presidential guard now and is still running Los Pueblos Fantasmas."

This was news to Ray. The current president of Mexico, when commander of the National Police, had formed and funded out of pocket his own small private army in order to gain information on the old cartels and then be in a position to act, all the while keeping them concealed from his official government agencies, which were deeply penetrated by the cartels. This special force, known to only a very few as the People's Ghosts, conducted their operations in the interest of the Mexican people, but most often with methods that went contrary to the very constitution they were sworn to protect. Given the terrible situation that had been created by the cartels at the time, the only way possible to try to gain an upper hand was to fight fire with fire, and that was what President Rodriguez had done with his brother. His brother lost his life in the fight, and after the very successful raids a year ago that broke up the worst of the cartels and made Alberto Rodriguez president, Ray understood that the ghosts and their questionable tactics were simply going to disappear.

"I thought our friend was going to quietly dissolve those guys."

"Well, that was the plan, but he decided to make them part of his guard, with Portillo in command of what was designated as a highly classified counterterrorism branch. From what our friend tells me, Portillo knows about the surveillance and the take, as do the two members of his intelligence group who are actually running this cell. Vicente trusts his troops, and I trust Vicente, so there we have it."

"I'd like to know the names of the two who are running it, their backgrounds, and what they look like before I head south."

Bennie scratched is head, as if pondering Ray's request, but then said, "No problem there. I'll get that for you. I'd want to know that if it were me."

"It's more than that, Bennie. If I'm ever approached by anyone other than the Brillo brothers or the two you say are running this for the colonel, I'll know something's up, and I abort. If others know about this, which would be contrary to what you've been told, then this thing has gone bad before it gets started."

"Agreed."

Ray paused and looked at Bennie for a second before going on. "What's the timetable here? When do you want me south?"

"I've got your reassignment orders with me. Go home and pack a small bag—your oldest socks and underwear, preferably. Nothing fancy; basic white if you have it. Meet me back here before lunch. I'll have a word with the ASAC, then you and I will continue this conversation over some decent fish, and then we're off to El Paso and Fort Bliss, which President Rodriguez's American cousin still commands. I've got one of the agency Citations at my disposal, so it will be just the two of us and my pilots who know where we've gone. General Rodriguez was asking me about you the other day. It will be nice to catch up with him, but landing and operating out of his base keeps us off the local DEA radar."

Ray became very serious and quiet. "I'd like to see the general again. I'm afraid I wasn't the best of company last time I was down there. I seem to owe him a lot and have never properly thanked him."

"That's crap, Ray," Bennie said softly. "He knows what it's like coming out of a combat zone. I know personally that like his cousin down in Mexico, he admires the shit out of you, and so does his sergeant major. You made a friend for life out of that guy, and the sergeant major doesn't make friends easily. Fort Bliss gives us a place to light and then arrange for your transport south without getting my local office there involved. I agree with you it's enough that you, me, Portillo, and his two guys know about this. I don't want more.

"Our mission will be need to know with the general and his staff, and he'll be fine with that and anxious to help us any way he can. As to my initial thoughts on the operation itself, we'll transport you south in a delivery van from one of the shadow companies we operate out of Texas that trades with the Mexicans. We may even bag the bus idea and drive you straight on through to Chihuahua. I'll drop you off, and you get to the local bus station and from there to your motel. Once there, go have some of that green chili you like so much at the Goat's Head, and keep showing up until the Brillos make contact with you—not the other way around; that's key. Then we play it by ear from there. OK?"

"Sounds good, Bennie. I'm ready, and I won't let you down."

Bennie smiled at him again. "I don't know much, Ray, but I do know that. Now, get your ass out of here and be back by noon. I haven't had the plank-roasted salmon at Salty's in months."

8

The Beach House
Near Matamoros, Mexico
Late March; end of week two

Felix's flight from Houston landed in the late afternoon with the early spring temperatures of Monterrey already approaching ninety degrees. He took the shuttle to where one of his men had parked his car a week earlier; because he was wanted by the federals, he never landed at the same airport he had departed from. One could never be too careful. He threw his bag in the trunk and set out on the three-hour drive to Matamoros. He had a very nice townhouse in the upscale southwestern colony of San Raul Garza Garcia near Monterrey, where he would occasionally stay for long periods, especially when he didn't want to be found, but not this trip. He'd bought the luxury townhome in the gated community under one of the several aliases he maintained and came and went without attracting any attention. There was no mortgage, and his monthly association fees and utility costs were paid directly out of a checking account opened under the same alias. Those few neighbors who thought they knew him believed he was a legitimate importer/exporter of retail goods with interests all over the Western Hemisphere that kept him traveling constantly. Only his brothers knew of the townhouse, and they'd never tell a soul. And as much as he wanted to stop by and relax after his trip, he wouldn't. He had business with Diaz, and that took precedence over any thoughts of women and/or relaxation.

He thought the assignment Diaz had given him, driving the route where the Aguilars were ambushed or lost—a waste of time when he was handed it, but that all changed once he was there and did as he was instructed. To actually see the highway and do what Diaz had told him to do, drive the road both in the day and the night, had been illuminating, and he quietly admired the way Diaz's mind worked. While he hadn't given it a thought when Diaz said he also had a good mind and would have made a fine police officer, once doing as he was told, he discovered that Diaz's opinion maybe held some truth, and this surprised him. He wasn't sure he had accomplished anything meaningful, but he would pass what he did learn on and let Diaz be the judge.

He was never comfortable traveling in America, as well known to the authorities as he was, and each time he'd done so, he was very glad to get back safely. Always when going north, he had an altered appearance and decent papers. Even more so this time, what with the official government documents he was carrying. Along with the tickets, itinerary, and some traveling cash in American dollars Diaz had been thoughtful enough to include, there was a long note from his partner with small suggestions on a variety of subjects from how he should dress to the kinds of details he should look for when driving the Aguilar's route. He smiled when he discovered it, again amazed at the thoroughness and professionalism of his partner.

Once he'd finally arrived in the small southwest Colorado town of Durango by air, he settled in at his downtown hotel and then later walked around the quaint central business district, getting a feel for the place and trying to blend in until he found a nice restaurant for dinner. He was dressed casually but very nicely—the better to deflect the attention of the local police, he had thought when he changed into the clothes, but he needn't have bothered. There were a lot of Hispanics walking around, all dressed far worse than he was. And then he discovered that the town had a very nice small college, and there were lots of very casually dressed students on the streets too. If anything, he looked a bit overdressed, he decided, in his tailored slacks, black crew-neck sweater, and stylish black leather jacket.

The next morning he got into the very nondescript white Chevrolet Impala rental and drove the four hours east on the decent two-lane highway the Aguilars supposedly traveled until it ended at the federal highway near the small town of Walsenburg, Colorado. As he drove, trying to be mindful of what Diaz had said, nothing made an impression on him other than the nice scenery. He turned around and started to redrive the route, thinking more about how hungry he was and not where to look for a possible missing van. He followed some roadside signs to a nice hotel in the very small town of La Veta fifteen miles outside Walsenburg that advertised a nice restaurant, and he had a pleasant lunch. Once back on the road, he climbed up and over La Veta Pass, which was no more than a rise in the landscape, and tried to be more mindful of possible places a cargo van might crash yet go undiscovered, but seeing none. Little jumped out at him on the return drive, and by the time he got back to Durango, he thought the day had been a complete waste of time and that he was the wrong person for the job.

He spent the next day in Durango, mostly in his room, resting up for the evening and his first nighttime drive. According to Diaz, the Aguilars had called in from Durango at midnight and then headed east and disappeared, if Diaz's assumption was correct. He set out after dark driving the exact speed limit and simply drove and looked, but if anything, less came to him than during the daytime drive. It wasn't until he was passing over the one high mountain pass that he became aware of a detail he had not noticed the day before: on the way down the eastern side of the pass, there was a small construction project underway that seemed to be building short walls of stone at the road's edge. His grandfather had been a stonemason back in Chihuahua, and he and his brothers had hauled many a pile of stone for him as he did his exacting work. It was because of that connection that he even noticed the pallets of stone and what they were being used for. There were no workers now, as there had been during the day, but what stood out at night were the reflecting temporary signs that not only warned of construction and closed shoulders but also explained the nature of the project. His speaking English was decent and better than his writing or reading abilities, but he understood enough to get a basic understanding of the project. The low decorative stone walls were a safety measure, built to prevent cars from going off the road. He was a little disgusted with himself as he realized he had passed the construction area twice the day before and had not given it a thought, other than to be annoyed. The speed limit had been lowered, and what traffic there had been was bunched together more, impeding his progress.

He continued on in the darkness to Alamosa, the largest town in the farming valley on the east side of the great mountains, and decided to turn around. One conclusion he had reached the day before was that had the Aguilars crashed unseen between this valley town and where the two-lane road ended at the federal highway, any accident site would be easily seen from the road's edge. Immediately adjacent to the highway were either fields or native areas at about the same level as the road, but nothing that would conceal an accident. Even the shallow La Veta Pass could hardly be called a pass, and there were no dramatic falloffs that could conceal a crash. Any vehicle leaving the road would be easily seen, he judged.

That could not be said, however, for the drive between Alamosa and Durango. The more he thought about it, the more he thought there were several sections of the highway, the high mountain pass, and a stretch halfway between Durango and the pass where it might be possible for an accident to go unseen. There were places where the adjacent landscape was very rough, with either streams down embankments or deep forest and the associated native undergrowth immediately beside the road.

He returned to his hotel and tried to sleep for a few hours, disturbed with the realization that he had been going through the motions on his assignment. What had made him successful and kept him alive this past ten years was his attention to detail and his surroundings. Because he believed the missing money was a hijacking and nothing more, he had dismissed this assignment as a waste of his time and simply Diaz reaching for straws, but he knew now that had been a mistake. While he still believed one of their distributors or the Banker was behind the missing money, he now believed that a simple traffic accident going unseen was a possibility and that Diaz was right. That possibility had to be eliminated, if for no other reason than to return focus back to the real thieves.

He got up, dressed, and went down the street to a shop that sold cameras and purchased a small but decent digital camera. The college-aged clerk was happy to show him how to operate it, and once he was sure how to do it, he left and started driving the route again. But this time, for the first time on the trip, he felt he was in the frame of mind that Diaz had asked him to be in. He was still dressed nicely, but new clean Levis replaced the dress slacks, and new tennis shoes replaced the dress shoes he'd worn the first night. He set out on his drive once more, but this time, he really saw the kinds of features that he knew Diaz would have noticed from the beginning. When he arrived at the first of the several sections of road where you could not see far off to the side, either because of a steep drop-off or the dense natural foliage, he stopped in the nearest section of road where it was safe to do so and walked back to the point of interest and took pictures. He knew that in doing so he was attracting attention to himself, a pedestrian walking along the road in the middle of nowhere, but he decided to take the chance anyway. He looked like a turista, he believed, and that was what he would say if the state police stopped him.

In his half-assed frame of mind of the previous two days, the one thing he had noticed was the state police. Their cars were easily spotted, and their routine seemed to be the same, simply driving the road and stopping offenders. There were no checkpoints or roadblocks, as there were in many parts of Mexico, and there was no army. They seemed to be more interested in traffic safety and not much else, unlike the federals back home.

He stopped at a second section of road and photographed it before passing through the very quaint mountain town of Pagosa Springs, which sat at the foot of the one great pass he had to go over. The pass held his greatest interest because of the very dangerous-looking slopes at times on the steep downhill sides of the road. He drove up and over the pass and then retraced his route, this time stopping at the ski area near the summit. There were several pickup trucks and a trailer parked in the parking area, and they advertised the name of the company doing the construction work and also identified the trailer as the construction office. On an impulse, he decided to stop and ask about the project, his thought being that he needed to understand what had been completed when. He knocked on the office door, and a gruff voice loudly said, "Come in."

He opened the door, walked in, and found an older man dressed in warm but simple work clothes, standing and looking at plans on a large, high table. The old man looked him up and down and asked, "Help you with something?"

"Sorry to disturb you, sir," Felix said in slow but very clear English as he pulled out his police identification and handed it to the craggy-looking man. "I'm a Mexican Federal police officer on vacation. My name is Captain Martinez. My duties involve traffic safety back in my country, and I was curious about your safety project, so I thought I would stop and ask about it."

The old superintendent's wrinkled, worn face broke into a pleasant smile as he handed the ID back to Felix. "Sure, Captain. Name's Pete. Can I get you some coffee first?"

"That is very kind. Thank you, Pete."

Over their coffee, the longtime construction worker showed Felix the plans that had widened the road and what had been done and what was left to construct. Conveniently, there were start and finish dates noted in pencil on every small section of scenic wall constructed, so Felix could tell very quickly what areas had been completed several weeks ago or earlier, therefore eliminating those particular parts of the highway as possible crash sites. Felix asked Pete if the walls were necessary for safety or just scenic.

"Well, Captain, truth be told, most places they're nothing more than some engineer's idea of pretty edges to the new shoulders we've built over the last year. There are a couple of places—here at milepost 164 and here at 169, for example," he said while looking carefully at the large drawings, "where they are important as a guardrail. Nasty drop-offs at those two curves."

"Very interesting," Felix said as he noted the names Pete had given the spots, the mileposts. That was another small detail he had missed over the last two days—how the traffic engineers or the state police marked the highway.

He finished his coffee over small talk and then thanked the old superintendent and left. He continued east down the pass, for the first time noting the mileposts. The only point of interest he passed was marker number 169, where a crew was busy finishing up the scenic low stone wall in the tight curve. But the road and shoulder were so wide, he had a tough time seeing it as dangerous. As he passed slowly by the busy stonemasons, he thought of his grandfather and how he would probably think the work was well done.

When he reached the first crossroads at the base of the east side of the pass, he turned around, went back over, and stopped at a small roadside café on the outskirts of Pagosa Springs for an early lunch. After he settled into a booth adjacent to one of the large front windows, he saw a state police car pull in and park. A young officer about his age got out and walked in, greeting the waitress and several others he apparently knew, and took the booth next to him. Felix had been very uncomfortable when he'd first arrived in this part of America, having never been here before, but that had passed over the last several days. The local population was very friendly, as far as he could tell, and as a stranger, he didn't stand out at all. It wasn't like his old neighborhood in Chihuahua, or that in Matamoros, where every stranger was not only noticed but carefully watched. It was early in their tourist season, he discovered, and there really weren't many around. Yet his presence drew little or no attention; as a result, he had settled in and gained confidence. The pleasant and informative time he had spent with the old construction worker had bolstered his confidence further, and now, not only was he not uncomfortable in the presence of the state policeman, he actually found himself wanting to talk with him. Maybe there was something to be learned about how they investigated crashes. It was exactly the kind of thing he knew Diaz would do if he were here and what Diaz had meant when he said he would instinctively know what to do.

In what was for him an incredibly bold act, he made eye contact with the officer, smiled, and said, "Excuse me, Officer. May I interrupt you for a question before you receive your lunch?"

Colorado State Patrol trooper Larry McDermott had lunch at Lucy's every day about this time whenever he had the normal day shift. He hadn't noticed the man in the adjacent booth until he was casually looking around and the man had smiled at him and then asked his question. It didn't even register with Trooper McDermott that the man was Hispanic, because—and Felix didn't realize this—Hispanics had first settled in the area hundreds of years ago. A great many of the local Hispanic families were fourth- and fifth-generation residents of the state. A great many of his friends and fellow officers were Hispanic, so Felix was just one of thousands.

"Sure. How can I help you, sir?"

Felix had not yet received his lunch, so he got up and stepped to the officer's table, opened his police identification, and showed it to the officer. "My name is Felix Martinez. I am a captain in the Mexican Federal Police, passing through on vacation. I was recently promoted, and one of my new duties will involve traffic safety. I was curious about your procedures in such a difficult place."

Trooper McDermott broke into a smile, having never really even looked at Felix's false identification, simply believing what he said. "Have a seat, Captain. I'll tell you whatever you want to know."

Over the next hour, always being careful but casual in his questioning, Felix slowly began to understand what all the pleasant young trooper was telling him. When he was comfortable doing so, Felix asked, "Unlike most of the areas where I work, which are mostly flat and desert like, how do you manage in your mountains? You have explained clearly your accident investigation methods, but what I mean is, how is it possible for you to be everywhere at once? How do you even know an accident has happened, say at night on your high pass? As I was photographing some of the scenic areas, it seemed to me that a single-vehicle crash could go unnoticed."

Trooper McDermott nodded his head. "Well, it does happen. What I mean, Captain, is that we have plenty of single-vehicle wrecks, and I've even had a few that went unwitnessed and unreported for a time, but it was just hours. Two winters ago I had a bad one. Two local teenagers out of Durango headed to a party here in Pagosa. They obviously were speeding, missed a curve west of here down in the canyons, and wound up upside down in the creek bottom. It was snowing pretty hard, so there weren't any skid marks or other obvious signs. But within five hours, their parents had called in the fact they were missing. We located where they had been before they left town and when, so we got our helicopter up the next morning after the storm moved out and flew the highway. We found them on our second pass, once the sun got a little higher and a little of the snow had melted off. Sadly, they were killed in the wreck—just a couple of dumb kids not recognizing the dangers of speeding."

"So you could not see them from the roadway?"

"Yeah. I didn't really think about that at the time. It simply was quicker to use the chopper in case they were hurt and time was of the essence, but yeah, when I was directed to the accident site, I could not see them from the highway. The oak brush—that's the real tall kind of twisted stuff you see all along the road—was very thick, and they'd blasted over and through it and wound up right the hell in the creek bottom. Anyway, a sad event."

"Very sad," Felix said, nodding.

They finished their lunch and said their goodbyes. The trooper went east up the pass, and Felix headed west back to Durango and his hotel. Felix had learned two very interesting facts during his pleasant lunch with the trooper. First, the story about the two young men who had been killed in the traffic accident went a long way toward proving that it was in fact possible for an innocent accident to go unreported if there were no witnesses to the event. Unlike the two young men who had been killed, if the Aguilars had crashed at night unseen, there was no one to report the fact they were missing to the authorities. For all Felix knew, for the last two days, he might have been driving back and forth past them and was simply unaware.

From the trooper's story, it occurred to Felix that he had been too broad in his looking for possible accident sites. He had been noting every part of the road that had tall native foliage or steep drop-offs beside the road. Now it dawned on him he should have been concentrating just on curves. It seemed far more logical to assume that if the Aguilars were careless, they'd have crashed in a curve.

The second interesting fact that had come up casually in his discussions with the trooper was information he wasn't even looking for. It just came out in the trooper's careful and detailed explanations on their procedures. Every stop a trooper made during his patrol was called in to their headquarters and documented, both as a safety procedure for the officer and simply as a record of activity. Felix thought Diaz might well be able to find a record of every contact made by the state police on this road the night the Aguilars went missing. Perhaps such information would be helpful.

Felix spent another two days in the area rechecking the route and photographing the few places where he thought it would be possible to crash and not be seen. He bought a good map of the area in a shop near his hotel and marked the three or four places he thought an unseen crash was possible. He returned to the top of the pass to see his new friend Pete and asked him if it would be possible to walk some of the new construction with him, and Pete was very accommodating. Felix was able to see firsthand on foot the areas around mileposts 164 and 169, as these were the two areas that Pete had said most needed the guard walls. He saw for himself how dangerous the slopes were off the road, and in both cases, as he looked down the steep rocky slopes toward the forest, he could see that it was possible a van could go unnoticed if it somehow reached the trees, but reaching them in such a way as to be completely hidden seemed impossible to him. Surely the construction workers who had spent so much time in the area would have noticed a white van, because the trees would stop it, so how could they not? This thought put a damper on his building enthusiasm for the entire accident scenario, but it was still a viable possibility.

Satisfied that he had done all he could in the area, he decided it was time to go home. He returned to his hotel, packed, and then began the drive to Albuquerque, where he would then catch a plane to Houston and eventually to Matamoros.

Twenty-four house later, Felix opened the door to his Matamoros apartment, quickly disarmed the alarm system, and turned up the air conditioning. He was tired from the traveling and needed something to eat and drink and then some sleep. He kept prepaid cell phones in his car, so he had called Diaz on his drive into town. They had agreed to meet the next morning at the Beach House, where Diaz was anxious to hear his full report. When Diaz had asked him about the trip, all Felix told him was that what he suspected and had sent him to look into was possible. It was clear to Felix that Diaz took little comfort in knowing that he was right to look into this possibility—all it did was create more questions than it answered.

Felix was up early the next morning and organized his documentation and his thoughts for presentation to Diaz, and then he drove out to the house. It was hot and windy, but unlike his old neighborhood, where it always seemed the winds carried dirt and trash and was most unpleasant, here, close to the Gulf, the winds were hot but refreshing. Guards were visible all around the small house this time—at least a half dozen—and they all seemed on edge. He was recognized, of course, and he recognized all who were watching him as he walked in the front door and went directly to Diaz's office. He found his partner standing at the tall windows looking out over the dunes. Diaz turned when he heard him walk in and almost smiled. "Felix, welcome back."

Felix walked up, and they shook hands, and then he asked, "Why all the men? Has something happened?"

"Merely a precaution, my friend. Several of my police have noticed new faces around town, mostly in twos and threes. Call me old and paranoid, but I would not put it past the Banker to preposition some hired enforcers to do his dirty work against you and me. My men are carefully watching his, if they even turn out to be his. Whoever they are, I find them unwanted, so we watch and we stay prepared. Enough on that. Tell me what you discovered."

Felix simply nodded his head in acceptance, produced his map and camera, and made his detailed report to Diaz. When he finished, he looked up, and Diaz had a genuine smile on his face. "I am very impressed, Felix, very impressed. To speak with the state policeman was very courageous, and I commend you on your findings."

"My findings, Cesar? What have I really done? I only confirmed that your thinking was clever and that the Aguilars could have met with an unseen and therefore unreported accident. All I feel I have done is confirm that our money could be lost, never to be found."

"Do not think that way, Felix. You have done so much more. We have a new avenue to check, and you have given us the means to check it."

"What avenue, Cesar? You've lost me. How have I helped?"

"Think like a policeman, Felix. You have shown us it is possible that the Aguilars could have had an accident and that such an accident could go unreported—but perhaps their unfortunate accident did not go unseen."

Felix was staring at Diaz, a blank look on his face until his sharp but untrained mind started to understand. "I hadn't thought of that, Cesar. You think it possible someone may have seen them but after discovering our money did not report the accident. I will admit that never occurred to me. But how are we any closer to finding the truth?"

Diaz was smiling again. "The state police's methods of record keeping you discovered—it may well be nothing, but I am very curious as to what all happened on that part of the Aguilars' journey that night, aren't you? Perhaps in the small details of the normal and routine, there are answers. And there is a man I know who can get us the answers. We will not have to ask for ourselves, and therefore we remain in the shadows. No, you did very well my friend, very well.

"Lobo has seen and eliminated two of our distributors, and they appear innocent so far. Given his methods, had they been involved, they would have talked. But he has yet to meet with the two most powerful, and they are now aware, unfortunately, that he is in America and desires to speak with them. Word has gotten back to them despite his precautions. It will take him several weeks, maybe more, to finish his task and get us our answers.

"In the meantime, you have provided us another line of investigation to check out, and I'm grateful. I have a man in Brownsville, a district commander in the American ATF that I have owned for years. I will meet with him, and he will contact the officer in command of the state police in the area you just visited. We shall say that that the ATF was tracking a van full of weapons and lost contact with it, and one of the possible routes south was this highway. We will have him ask the good commander if he would provide us with all contact reports from that night and several others so that we may check for anomalies, and all very quietly. I am certain the state police would cooperate with such a simple and innocent request from another agency, aren't you? And then who knows what we may discover? Eh, my friend? In the very least, we will be able to eliminate a possible accident as the reason for our missing money."

"Whatever you say, Cesar," Felix said gloomily.

9

Jack looked at his watch and confirmed what the glow on the horizon to his left was telling him: it was after five thirty, and the sunrise was slowly approaching. Except for a short sleep break outside Saint Louis, he had been driving almost continuously for two full days. The two-thousand-mile drive turned out to be almost pleasant; this after a tense and busy two weeks of planning and worrying about it. Henry's suggestion that the first significant investment for their new company should be a used twenty-five-foot RV he had found online from a local dealership turned out to be inspired. As a transport vehicle for the boxes and boxes of dirty currency, the RV was perfect and unremarkable. And if he could not live on his new boat for any reason, the RV was a good backup and would help keep him off the grid, something that Henry kept insisting on.

It took Henry only a week to get a new judge to adjust his probation, allowing him to work out of state. While Henry worked on that and other details dealing with their start-up company, Jack talked with David Hammond and the owner of his apartment building about his need to start fresh. As Henry suggested, he simply told them he needed a change and to get closer to his girls, leaving both with the idea that he was headed to California. He gave Henry's office as a forwarding address for his mail so Henry could go through it and then forward anything of importance to him in Florida. He also set up automatic monthly withdrawals from his savings account to his ex-wife's bank for his child support as Henry suggested, so that was a nonissue and would be for the foreseeable future.

After he and Hank checked out the twenty-five-foot Holiday Rambler RV and bought it, he set about figuring out how to hide all the cash in the comfortable interior and quickly concluded it was simply not possible. While there were nice small storages spaces here and there, there were too much to hide. Henry suggested he hide the cash in plain sight using typical-looking packing boxes purchased from the local office of a nationally recognized mover. He agreed, and in all, it took twenty-four of the brightly colored corrugated boxes to pack the currency and Jack's few belongings. Henry came over the last day he was in town and helped him pack the money and label the boxes as standard items that would typically be moved. They loaded the RV late on Saturday evening and, as far as they could tell, drew little or no attention from the few tenants who drove by.

They met a final time over breakfast the next morning, and then Jack left Denver at noon, three weeks to the day after witnessing the crash. He felt strange, almost afraid. Until the past year, fear was something he had never really felt in his life; it wasn't in his makeup, he decided. He had never thought about it much until a marine officer he respected had made a point about his "cool" under fire and his "steely courage" in the face of a determined enemy during a medal presentation ceremony before the battalion years before. This was after one of his overseas deployments during which he and his spotter had operated in some badlands north of Baghdad for a month on their own. He remembered thinking about what the colonel was saying and decided they were kind words but simply not the case. In his mind he had not been cool or courageous, but neither had he been afraid. He was so confident in himself and his training that if anything, he felt bad, almost sorry for those he had been ordered to stalk and kill, as he had never been threatened, and killing them had been so easy at the distances he could shoot. It wasn't until his daughter was snatched that he felt real fear for the first time. She had been released before he was even notified of the near abduction, but his fear came later that night, when, after putting her to bed, he watched over her in the dark and the thought that she had almost been taken hit him hard. What he felt as he started east on Interstate 70, leaving Denver and his life there behind, wasn't nearly as complex or deep, but he was at a minimum anxious about what lay ahead; there was so much he didn't know and could not control.

He drove across eastern Colorado and all of Kansas and Missouri before finally stopping at a truck stop an hour past Saint Louis and the Mississippi River to sleep. He had covered the thousand miles in just sixteen hours, stopping only when he had to for gas, a quick meal, or a toilet break. He appreciated Henry's thinking about the RV being perfect for his trip whenever he grabbed a bite or hit the head, all of which took place at roadside rest stops in the privacy of his modern camper. The camper indeed met all his needs, as Henry had said it would, and once Jack was behind the wheel and on the open road, the anxiousness he had felt when first leaving Denver dissipated, and he began to feel almost normal again, even safe, as he noticed campers and RVs of all sizes and shapes in both directions on the highway. Like most people, he had never paid attention to RVs when driving before and therefore wasn't aware how common a sight they were on the interstates. He quickly realized he was simply one of thousands driving the highways of America, and the farther south he drove, the more RVs he saw.

On their last night together, when he had shared with Henry his anxiety about driving across the country with the boxes of cash simply stacked in the RV's interior, Henry told him to relax and gave him a quick lesson on illegal searches and seizures. As an ex-cop, he was familiar with the concept and the limitations of probable cause; he had just never imagined a scenario where it would apply to him. The rear part of the camper, where his queen-size bed was located, was stacked high with packing boxes with neat labels affixed identifying the contents within—everything from household goods, books, and business records to clothes. The familiar-looking storage space that extended out over the cab was jammed with the remaining boxes they could not squeeze into his sleeping space. As long as no one entered his camper, he was sure there would be no questions. If by chance someone did, they would see that he simply chosen to move all his belongings in the dry and secure space within his camper and not in some towed trailer. To a man unaccustomed to lying as he was, it seemed a plausible story.

The plan called for him to live in his camper or on the new boat while he was learning to sail. The boat was waiting for him at the Lake Park Marina north of Miami, halfway between West Palm Beach and Jupiter. After researching the area online, he and Henry had concluded that Lake Park would be the perfect community for him to live in when not in the Caribbean. It was small and typical, one of many similar, less affluent towns lining the east coast of Florida. After contacting the harbor master to arrange for continued dockage of the boat, Henry also arranged for him to park his RV in the large available trailer parking area of the marina if he wanted. He could live in the RV or on his new boat, his choice, as he worked out the logistics of keeping and hiding the boxes of cash in his new community.

Henry knew as little about sailing as he did, but he was an excellent researcher and perused the internet exhaustively until he was convinced he had found the best possible boat option for him. They got lucky when Henry learned during the negotiations that the broker he was using for the purchase was himself a dedicated sailor with a muddied personal past. Ed Harris was his name, and during his several telephone conversations with the man, Henry knew he liked him, especially after mentioning in general why Jack was relocating to the Caribbean. Ed lived in West Palm Beach, the more upscale enclave a few minutes south of the Lake Park Marina, where the boat was moored. After telling Henry about his own troubles with an ex-wife, Ed immediately offered his services as Jack's sailing instructor. He had been a very successful New York financial planner and investor when his wife of many years had unceremoniously dumped him for another man. Financially secure, even after having to split his fortune with his wife, he said goodbye to his old life and resettled in South Florida, where he set up a brokerage business for the buying and selling of sailboats and where he could also sail the Caribbean in peace whenever he felt like it.

The six-year-old fifty-three-foot Beneteau Ed brokered for them was a beautiful and elegant sloop. It was rigged for fast sailing and had been fully refurbished and refitted during its recent modernization for single-handed operation. All its running, rigging, and winch controls were fed to the rear cockpit, allowing for safe and simple operation of the boat. The graceful sloop had every modern convenience and was beautiful to look at. Ed told Henry that if he did not already own a bigger, newer version of a similar boat, he would grab the Beneteau for himself. As it was, he felt it would be the perfect boat for Jack. Henry bought the boat for the company and asked Ed to change the name to *Second Chance* before Jack arrived. Between the RV and the boat, various filing fees for their company, and the costs to set up Jack's several bank accounts, Henry had spent just over $300,000 of the start-up monies. He would gladly put up more cash if it came to that but was confident Jack could pay for whatever was needed in the future from his stash. He didn't have to tell Jack to be careful with his spending; his friend was all too aware of what was at stake and could be counted on to be cautious.

Jack drove into the near-empty trailer parking area of the marina just as the sun was starting to show over the horizon and pulled into an open parking space. It was only six, and he wasn't scheduled to meet Ed until eight. He needed to stretch his legs after sitting for so long, so he got out and locked up. Jack may have been born and raised in landlocked Colorado, but his days in the corps had seen him stationed near an ocean on many occasions. He realized, as he slowly walked out toward the docks and the beautiful orange sunrise, how much he loved and missed the ocean. The dynamic meeting of land and sea always stirred an emotion in him he never fully understood.

It was early, but there were a couple of young guys washing a boat, so he approached them, said good morning, and asked for directions to slip 60. They pointed across the channel separating the several rows of parallel docks, telling Jack he needed to go to the far side. As he walked, the breeze came up and felt great on his face. The slips were numbered, so he followed the signs until he reached slip 60, which turned out to be one of the larger ones located across the end of a dock for the bigger boats. The first thought that popped into his head as he walked up to the beautiful sailboat was, *Jesus Christ! How am I supposed to sail something that big by myself?*

He spent some time in the evenings before leaving Denver reading up on sailing, so he knew that single-handed sailing, as it was called, was a normal thing, but that didn't prepare him for the size of his boat; it was so much larger than he expected. He came up on his boat from the front—or the bow, as he reminded himself to call it—so he walked down the dock on its starboard side just admiring it, thinking the pictures in the internet brochure did not do it justice. The fiberglass hull had beautiful lines and was painted a deep blue from the gunwales to the waterline. Any part of the hull not painted blue was a glistening white. All deck surfaces were a light-gray weathered teak, and all the railings, lifeline stanchions, cleats, and winches were a brilliant polished stainless steel, all glistening in the early-morning light. When he got to the stern, he saw the name of the boat painted across the end just above a small deck or ledge that he knew from his reading was called the swimming platform. *Second Chance.* He knew the moment he saw the name that Henry's hand was in it. There was no way the boat could have coincidentally been called that, he reasoned, and he got a little emotional for a moment thinking about what his friend had obviously done and, more importantly, what the name foretold.

The solitude of the drive down had given him a lot of time to think about what he was doing, and he had come to realize that a second chance was something he desperately wanted and had not fully realized in the preceding year. He had "mourned" the loss of his marriage to the point that he now knew it had been keeping him from getting on with his life. In the tragic van crash and his attempt to be the Good Samaritan, serendipity, it seemed, had intervened, and his life was now forever changed. His one great hope was that somehow it would lead to a better life with his daughters. The tight schedule to get everything wrapped up in Denver and then get to Florida had made him miss his regularly scheduled weekend visit with them, but he intended to make it up this weekend. He would take the rest of the week to get settled into a routine in his new community, establish a good relationship, he hoped, with his sailing instructor, and then take the redeye from Miami to LA on Friday night.

He looked the boat over from bow to stern but decided not to go aboard until he hooked up with Ed at eight. He walked back to the parking area, past the RV, and crossed the street to a comfortable-looking diner located there and joined what looked like a local crowd for some breakfast. Afterward, he walked around the small downtown area for a while, killing time and working out the kinks from the long drive until it was time to return to the marina. When he got back to his boat, there was a slim, fit-looking, middle-aged, bald man with a tight gray beard standing in the cockpit looking over one of the controls. Jack walked up and said hello.

Ed Harris looked up and smiled. "Ahoy there. You Jack?"

"That's me," Jack said as he stepped from the dock to the small gangway and onto his boat for the very first time, his hand extended. The two smiling men sized each other up in a handshake, and each concluded that the other was a guy he could really like. Both had relied on first impressions their entire adult lives and nearly always trusted their instincts.

"I took the liberty of stocking your galley with a few basic provisions until you can get settled. I put some coffee on, and for later, there are a couple of cold six-packs in the reefer. How about a cup of coffee and I give you a tour of your boat?"

"Sounds great, Ed. Lead on."

When Ed said a tour of the boat, he wasn't kidding. He showed Jack every nook and cranny from the bilges to the mainmast; from the bow sail storage to the stern swim platform. After going over every inch of the main deck, where Ed pointed at every fixture and feature, telling him what it was and its use, they spent some time in the cockpit, where Ed showed him all the basic controls and navigation equipment. The boat was state of the art when it came to electronic or digital controls, right down to digital charts of the Florida coast and a great deal of the Caribbean. From the cockpit they descended into the boat's finely finished interior. The boat, or *she*, as Ed constantly referred to it, had a three-cabin layout, all with en suite baths, with the master cabin located in the bow and the two queen berths in the stern. The main living area, or salon, took up most of the below-deck spaces between the staterooms and included a living room with a built-in corner sofa arrangement, a very nice dining area for six, and the impressive-looking galley. All woodwork and cabinetry in the staterooms, the main salon, and the galley was done in beautiful cherry, and all the upholstery was a cream-colored leather. The galley had all new stainless-steel appliances and faux marble countertops. Jack had been very happy with the interior layout and finishes of his RV after they bought it, thinking at the time it was finished as nice as any place he'd lived in. The interior of the boat was so very much more. He couldn't help but visualize his girls, each in her own cabin on his boat. Wouldn't be a bad place to live, he thought. He only hoped that was something he could arrange for in the future.

The previous owners had sold the boat complete with fresh bedding and towels in the suites; and in the galley, all dishes, pots, pans, cutlery, and silverware were included, saving Jack the time and trouble of having to shop for any of it. All during their tour below, as Ed was showing him this or that, Jack was not only interested for interest's sake, but he was also looking for places to hide cash. Even though the boat was large and spacious, the closets and storage spaces were very tight, and if ever he was boarded, they would be the first places the authorities—or crooks, for that matter—would look. He knew he needed far more time on the boat to figure out how to hide the money. The thought put a damper on what was otherwise a great morning for him.

Touring the boat and listening to Ed's nonstop detailed explanations of all the spaces, equipment, and safety features was interesting and exciting to Jack, and the tour lasted several hours as a result. It was late morning, and the day was already hot and humid; they were taking a break, sitting in the open cockpit, each in front of one of the two identical helms with the onshore breeze washing over them, when Jack asked about his lesson schedule. Ed said, "Well, unless you have other plans or are just too bushed from the drive, we can start right now."

Jack was a little surprised. "Now, Ed? Didn't you say I need a license of some kind and a Coast Guard inspection?"

"Yeah, but that's so you can sail solo. With me on board, we can go anytime. It's a nice day, and we have a good breeze. What say we take her out for a little spin?"

Ed was dressed as you might expect the typical Palm Beach sailor to be dressed: an expensive polo shirt, tan khaki shorts, and a pair of L. L. Bean boat shoes. Jack, on the other hand, was wearing an old Colorado Rockies T-shirt and stained baseball cap, a pair of old cargo shorts with pockets everywhere, and his beat-up pair of everyday tennis shoes. Anytime he drove long distances, he dressed for comfort, not appearance. That, and it had been a long day since his last shower.

"Sure, Ed, but I should probably clean up some, maybe take a shower. That, and I should tell you I haven't had much time to check out the sailing websites you suggested to Hank I read up on. I thought I would be doing that the first few days."

"Don't worry about any of that. You might not think your attire is suited for this neighborhood, but the way you look will fit right in, in the Caribbean," Ed said, smiling broadly. "As to that other stuff, read it when you can, especially the definitions and sailing terms. That will help speed your education along some, but Jack, the best way to learn to sail is to sail."

With Ed at the starboard helm, they prepared the *Second Chance* for sailing. Ed produced a presail checklist from one of the cockpit storage bins and started going through it, checking gauges and flipping switches with Jack looking over his shoulder. After checking the bilges and allowing the engine to warm up, on Ed's command, Jack loosened the lines and stowed them as Ed instructed. He then swung the small gangway in and secured it as well, while Ed was busy calling up the proper digital chart onto their cockpit monitor and entered their GPS coordinates. Finished, Ed used what he called the bow thruster to push them clear of the dock. With the now-warm diesel engine purring smoothly beneath their feet, Ed slowly maneuvered them out of the marina, all the while explaining each and every step of the engine controls to Jack. They slowly motored past Singer Island, passing under the Jack Nicklaus Bridge as they eased toward the channel that led to the ocean. Once clear of the channel buoy and out into the two-foot seas and light breezes, Ed shut the engine off and started pushing the various controls that raised and lowered the sails, while simultaneously continuing his hands-on lessons.

When Ed finally had both the mainsail and the headsail up, they sailed parallel to the coast a mile to sea on a northerly heading, making good speed.

Jack was unabashedly happy, kind of like a kid with a new toy on Christmas morning, as he watched Ed and listened to his nonstop descriptions of each and every maneuver they made. *Second Chance* had beautiful lines and knifed through the water, throwing up spray that the breeze carried back to him and Ed in the cockpit. Ed told Jack how fast she was compared to other sloops, which made Jack chuckle, "fast" being a relative term, as they cut through the waves at maybe ten or twelve miles per hour. Ed also explained they were in the Gulf Stream current, which he described as a river in the ocean pushing them north, wind or no wind.

They sailed for thirty minutes, most of the time with the wind at their backs, sometimes running with the wind and other times gybing, as Ed called it. Ed then turned the *Second Chance* back into the breeze and started tacking into the wind, retracing their downwind course. The tone of Ed's lessons became more serious as they zigzagged the *Second Chance* back and forth on either side of their southerly course, making headway against both the prevailing wind and the current as Ed continued to explain what they were doing at any given moment and why.

Two hours later, after sailing back and forth outside the channel, the last hour with Jack at the helm and Ed watching and instructing, they reentered the marina, and Ed showed Jack how to dock the boat. In spite of the wonderful breezes that had cooled them during the day while they sailed, now, in port, Jack was dripping sweat from every pore. Ed showed him the outdoor shower on the swimming platform and how to operate it, so he stripped to his cargo shorts and took a good long cool rinse while Ed went to the galley to retrieve some of the beer he'd brought on board. Ed returned to the cockpit and handed one can to him as he was toweling off, kept one for himself, and tossed the rest of the six-pack into the cockpit cooler. They spent the next hour drinking and talking, getting to know each other, until the beer was gone and Ed decided to call it a day. As they shook hands, each in his own way knew they would be friends.

Ed's schedule was his own, and he and Jack sailed almost every day for the next two weeks. Each day they went out, Ed made him do more and more. Ed didn't believe there existed anyone who was what you could call a "natural sailor," but he became convinced Jack was close. Some people took to it; others never did. Anyone could sail a boat downwind. The reality was, however, most of the time, wherever it was you wanted to go always seemed to be upwind. The real trick or skill to sailing, Ed said, was mastering leeward or upwind sailing, and that was an art in three-dimensional relative geometry that some people never could grasp. Jack was one of the rare ones, as Ed thought he was, who could *see* the wind. Judging the wind direction and "beating" into it as close as you could to maximize the lift created by the wind passing over the very taut Kevlar sails, which acted like wings and actually moved the boat through the water, was the skill to be acquired, and Jack had it. The first time he was at the helm and tacking into the wind with Ed just watching, the wind direction had shifted ever so slightly, and Jack had sensed it or felt it and subtly changed course to keep his sails trimmed and tight. Rarely did his sails luff or flutter except when he was crossing the wind with a purpose.

As Jack's sailing lessons progressed, so did his plans. He was living on the boat and not in the RV, and he spent every night after Ed went home exploring ways to create concealed spaces for the money. It wouldn't be accurate to say he was becoming comfortable with the reality that he had $120 million cash in his possession, but he was worrying less about it. He concluded that for better or worse, at least half the cash would have to stay in the RV, or in some local storage place, and the other half would be with him on the boat. Once he could safely move the first half into a Caribbean bank, he would then empty the RV and probably sell it, but that was months, maybe even years away.

At the end of their second week together, late on a Friday afternoon, they motored south a mile down the inland waterway from the marina to the US Coast Guard station at Lake Worth Inlet to reregister the boat in his company name and get an updated safety inspection. The commanding officer of the station turned out to be a sailing and fishing friend of Ed's named Bill. They docked at the station and, after the introductions, filed all the necessary paperwork. When they were done, the commander climbed aboard with them, and while Ed motored toward Singer Island and one of his favorite restaurant and bars, the commander did a walkthrough of the *Second Chance* conducting his informal safety inspection. Because the boat had just been fully refitted and refinished, most of the inspection was reduced to the commander admiring his boat. Over cocktails before dinner, the commander innocently said, "She's a beautiful boat, Jack. I admit I'm a bit envious of your obvious success to be able to have her."

Jack glanced at Ed, then at the commander, and said, "Thanks, Bill, but it isn't what you think. What I mean is, except for being what I think was a good marine and then a good cop, success had nothing to do with my move down here and acquiring the *Second Chance*."

With that, as he had done with Ed, he gave him a short history of his background and how it was through the gratitude and generosity of his friend and partner Henry back in Denver that he was being given a second chance in life. Like most people who heard Jack's story directly from him, the commander was at first a little amazed, and then very understanding of Jack's situation, especially given the fact that he was the father of three kids himself. He felt bad that his innocent offhand remark on Jack's success had seemed to force Jack to open up about parts of his life he may have wanted to keep to himself. As Jack told his story, like any decent father, the commander couldn't help imagining what he would have done in the same circumstance, and killing a child molester didn't seem all that wrong, even to a regular church goer like him. Bill told Jack he didn't mean to pry, then immediately waved down their waitress and ordered another round of drinks on him.

Jack liked the Coast Guard commander, but for far different reasons than one would normally suspect. Having an acquaintance in the Coast Guard who could vouch for him if the time ever came he needed it would be a great asset.

When their drinks arrived, the commander turned to Jack and said, "Ed says you're a bit of a natural at sailing."

Jack smiled and glanced at Ed. "Is that right, Ed? Do I pass your test?"

Ed smiled back. "Not just yet, but real soon."

The next afternoon, as he and Ed were securing the boat to the dock following a long day of sailing, Ed said that he would be back at five thirty the next morning.

"Fine, Ed, but why so early? I know you old guys like your sleep," he said, smiling.

Ed simply smiled back and said, "It's time for your final exam, smart-ass. I'll tell you more in the morning."

The next morning, just before sunrise, there was Ed on the dock, along with a couple of sacks of groceries.

"What's all this?" Jack asked.

"Provisions. Let's get this stuff stowed below, and then I'll let you in on the plan."

The sacks contained good food, by the look of some of the packages—a couple of steaks, some fresh fish, and assorted premade side dishes, plus some decent whiskeys and wine. They returned to the cockpit and Ed said, "Jack, it's time for your final exam. And by that I mean it's high time you saw a bit of the Caribbean, especially since you intend to spend a great deal of the rest of your life there. So with me as your mate, simply watching and stepping and fetching to your orders, you're going to captain us out to Freeport and back with a one-night layover in Bimini. There's an old bar there where Hemingway drank away the better part of his life as an expat. Seems only fitting that part of your introduction as an expatriate yourself in the Caribbean should include such a historic watering hole; you'll fit right in. Besides, you're ready for some open-water sailing. I'm here if you screw something up, but I doubt that will happen; you're a good sailor, Jack, for a beginner. You know all the basics and then some, and you have a feel for the wind I don't see very often. Now it's time to apply them in deep water."

Jack smiled. "Jesus, Ed. You think I'm ready?"

"As ready as you'll ever be. Everyone's got to lose their deepwater cherry sometime; this is your time. Let's make sail, skipper."

Jack went through the presail check list like Ed had taught him and warmed up the engine while Ed went below and stowed the provisions he had brought aboard. As Jack finished up preparing to get underway, Ed came back topside and said, "If you're ready, how about I cast us off and we get going?"

"Fine, Ed. I'm set here. The bilge checklist is complete; just programming the navigation."

While Ed moved around the deck freeing their lines and stowing the gangway, he called up the proper digital chart from the navigation system and then set their current GPS location and their destination. Much like the GPS systems in cars, the navigation system plotted the most direct course to Freeport on Grand Bahama Island. Checking first to see that their lines were stowed properly, Jack used the bow thrusters, which he now knew about and how to control, to nudge them away from the dock and slowly motored to the channel, with just enough light from the coming iridescent dawn to see his way. Once clear of the channel buoy, he cut the engine, glanced about to get a feel for the wind, and then activated the controls for the mainsail. Freeport lay just over eighty miles beyond the eastern horizon on a compass heading of 103 degrees. The brisk morning breeze out of the southwest filled Jack's sail as he unfurled it and was favorable to their intended course. He pointed the sharp bow a few degrees south of east, tightened up his sail using one of his winch controls, and, when satisfied, ran up his headsail. Finally satisfied he had the *Second Chance* in good position to make best speed, he looked over at Ed, who was smiling and nodding while drinking his freshly brewed coffee.

As far as Ed was concerned, Jack had done everything just as he would have, only maybe a little slower or more deliberate, which was perfectly understandable. Ed noticed that Jack still had a serious, focused look on his face. He slapped him on the shoulder and said, "Jesus, loosen up and enjoy the moment, will you? You are way too serious. That was a good set on the sails; I couldn't have done better myself."

Jack's countenance relaxed as he momentarily took his eye of his course and smiled at Ed.

"That's the spirit, Jack. Keep an eye on things up here, and I'll go below and fix us some breakfast. I hope you like spicy omelets, because I fix a good one."

"I'm good here, Ed, and I'd love an omelet and some coffee, if you don't mind. Cream and sugar."

Ed nodded his head and said, "Coming right up." He went below as Jack quietly watched him, appreciating how the man had unknowingly helped him with his plans.

Ed couldn't know, but he had misread his serious look a moment earlier. Jack was very comfortable with the sailing; his look to the east and the coming sunrise was really a look into the future and what it held. At the moment Ed broke his concentration, he was not thinking about sailing, but rather about bankers and customs officials and Henry's concerns from several weeks earlier about staying in the shadows. Henry was far more worried about that aspect of his life change than he was, and that in and of itself was cause for concern. He didn't fully understand what Henry was so worried about, but he respected him enough not to dismiss it.

He had been a cop long enough to know that while appearances could be deceiving, more often than not, people believed what they saw. People would see him as the man in the picture he was creating; he could see it in Ed, and Ed was a very sharp guy. No one would look at him and suspect him of something more, especially if they learned of his background and his motives, and certainly no one would suspect that he was sitting on millions of dollars of cash and looking to launder it. He still had trouble believing it, and he was living it. As long as he was careful, no one would suspect a thing. That is, until he crossed the next big line, of course, which was involving others, such as a banker. But that step was down the road and would not be taken until he was sure of himself and the situation. For now he would enjoy the moment, as Ed suggested. He had made great strides so far; he could sail well enough to get himself around, and he had also managed to pick up his scuba certification in the last few weeks, so he could use that as well as part of his new business. He intended to buy all new scuba gear when they returned to port and he prepared to move into the Caribbean.

His plan was an evolving thing with nothing written down; rather, it was a mental list of milestones thought of and then, one by one, checked off. Their sail to Freeport and then Bimini and back would last three or four days, Ed said, which was fine with him. On their return, he would finish the modifications he needed to make to the *Second Chance* to safely conceal about $60 million cash, roughly half of what he had. Over the last two weeks, spending every night alone aboard his boat, he had searched out possible solutions— false panels in existing storage places, removable wall panels that could be hidden by the built-in furniture to access the void spaces between the outer hull and the finished walls of the interior, and then some waterproofed packages for some of the bilge spaces. He would need a few more days with a cabinet shop to get the final pieces he needed made from the sketches he'd prepared. With the finished pieces in hand, he would install them himself. He wasn't a finish carpenter by any means, but his dad had been. From his father he knew tools and woodworking well enough to get the job done. Maybe it was impossible in the real world to truly be objective, but he imagined himself as a cop again and having to conduct a thorough search of a boat—where would a cop look? As much as it was possible, he felt he had found a half dozen places no one would think to check for contraband, unless you were of a mind to simply take the boat apart.

As to the rest of the money, Henry helped again. He suggested Jack get some lockable storage boxes and repack what was left of the cash, labeling it as business and tax records and suitably backdating the boxes for the last five years, and then store them at a bonded warehouse, where there would be a much greater level of security and privacy, making the chance of discovery just that much less. Jack liked the idea of not storing the money in the RV and told Hank of his desire to keep it for the time being. There was an RV storage facility west of Jupiter, a few miles north of Lake Park, where he could store the RV in case he needed it again. Once all the carpentry modifications were complete and half the money was safely aboard, he could then provision the boat for a long haul and strike out again for Freeport. Henry's research on suitable banks had led him to the Bahamas. Nassau was the largest town by far, but after talking about it, they settled on a bank in Freeport as being potentially friendlier. He was a friendly person by nature whom people seemed drawn to, and a smaller town like Freeport seemed more conducive to relationship building.

After Ed's tasty omelet, taken in the open cockpit together as they sailed east-southeast at a brisk twelve knots, Jack shared with him his plans for returning to Freeport after their sail and establishing his security business there. Ed liked that, saying he had many friends in Nassau and Freeport whom he would be glad to introduce him to. His favorite bar and restaurant in the entire Caribbean, he said, was the Evening Shadows, located on the waterfront in Freeport and run by a friend of many years named Robbie Poitier; that was where the introductions would start. Robbie knew everyone in the Bahamas, Ed said, and once Jack was a friend of Robbie's, a lot of doors would open for him. Ed told him that Robbie was British educated, and after a successful start to his business career in London, he had resettled in his native Bahamas with his English wife, who sadly was killed accidently some years later in an apparent random and rare act of violence in the Bahamas. In his grief, he divested himself of most of his businesses, forever discarded his suits and ties, and bought the Evening Shadows and several other restaurants and bars scattered around the Bahamas. In addition, Robbie had a nice little charter fleet and could probably use the types of services Jack's new business would provide.

At the speed they were making, Ed said they would be there by midafternoon and would take dinner with Robbie that night. Jack was secretly very happy at the prospect of getting a few personal introductions like that in Freeport. This could only help him and make it easier to get to know others who could be of use, if and when the need arose.

The sun finally cleared the horizon, and the black of the ocean finished its transformation from indigo to a deep slate color as the reflected sky was passing through hues of orange and red before revealing a startling clear blue. Jack was overwhelmed for a few moments at the sheer majesty of the setting. Except for the sound of the wind in his sails and the unique melodic sound the hull of the *Second Chance* made as it knifed through the water, there was nothing to distract him. If anything, the setting brought a calm to him he had not felt in years, if ever. In his gut he was still uncomfortable with the deceptions and lies that his keeping of the illegal fortune was necessitating, and he hated the blurring of the lines that had always distinguished his life from the criminals he'd put away, but he could live with it, as he kept reminding himself it was all for the girls. He shook off the momentary ill feelings, and, with a fine breeze at his back, sitting in the cockpit of the *Second Chance* drinking his coffee, the bow of his beautiful boat pointed a few degrees south of east, he looked forward more than ever to his future and the great potential there, and maybe even the prospect of happiness. With the joy that came from being on the water, exposed to the great beauty and forces nature provided, he had experienced long moments over the last several weeks when the worst of what had happened to him was forgotten for a time. Whatever the future held, he knew it had to be better than his recent past, and as he made good speed toward Freeport, he was hopeful for the first time in a long time.

10

Ray stepped off the bus from Ciudad Juarez; at Bennie's suggestion he hadn't shaved or trimmed his beard in two weeks and not showered in a week. To put it politely, he was ripe, and despite whatever knowledge Bennie may have had about the lower classes of Mexico, he'd drawn a few stares and a number of wrinkled faces from others he sat near on the bus. He was wearing a badly faded pair of Levis, a T-shirt with a well-worn flannel shirt over, a pair of old Nike running shoes, and a dirty light cotton jacket. Where Bennie had come up with such clothes that fit him he didn't say; he had just told him to change. Ray had cringed some when putting the outfit on, knowing they had belonged to another man, probably someone swept up in another of Bennie's many operations, and nothing had been washed in a long time.

The last time he had entered Mexico undercover was after being incarcerated in an El Paso jail for three months and subject to the rules and regulations on personal hygiene of the detention facility. He had a very short and tight buzz hair cut then, was clean shaven, and could pass for a twenty-year-old and not the twenty-six he was at the time, and he didn't stink like he did now. He kept the short haircut look while undercover the first time, only growing his hair out some as his operation played out; now his unkempt hair was as long as he'd ever worn it, and he had a scraggly-looking beard and mustache and appeared nearer to his actual age. He was nearly unrecognizable, and he had not been kidding when he told Bennie the night before he didn't know who that was staring back at him from the mirror in the bathroom of their quarters on the large army base outside El Paso. The unrecognizable look was an important consideration to his safety and the success of this operation, because he was returning to Mexico as a wanted man.

His first operation had ended a year ago after he successfully infiltrated and exposed a cartel run by an enigmatic leader known as the Condor de Muerte, who turned out to be Mexico's most notorious trafficker, and powerful politician. He had gone under as Ray Espinoza, but the cartel had renamed him Ray Ortega. As Ortega, he was a known close confidante of the Condor, who unbelievably was elevated to the presidency of the country while also running one of the more sophisticated and powerful cartels. Anyone who could be considered a confidante of such a man and was still at large was a very wanted man indeed.

The night before, Bennie showed him a wanted poster with his name and face on it and said they were posted in every police station in Mexico, only the picture, taken from his Mexican driver's license photo of a year ago, was of a very young-looking, clean-shaven man. Ray remembered well when and where the picture was taken. He had been standing in the Condor's private study in the now-confiscated estate outside Monterrey, and it had been the Condor's intelligence and IT genius who had taken it. Even thinking about those times was still difficult for him, and he had spent a portion of the last year on Doctor Mercer's couch learning how to live with some of what had happened. But that was in his rearview mirror now, as Dr. Mercer would say. The doc often spoke in down-home little homilies like that, reducing complex emotional issues or events to their simplest form, and he liked the doc because of that.

He had been telling Bennie the truth when he said the bad dreams had stopped—most of them, anyway, but not all. You couldn't stab to death a man who had become a friend, however complicated or uncontrollable the events leading to such a horrific event may have been, and then blithely go on with your life as if it hadn't happened or didn't matter—not if you had a shred of humanity or a conscience, and he had both.

He was carrying a battered leather duffel bag with some additional clothes and personal effects, an old leather wallet containing some of the typical identification papers his cartel leader had provided him during his first mission, insurance cards, other such government-issued papers, and a fake driver's license that showed him as he looked now. All the identification was under the alias Ray Ortega and would be enough to get him past a run-in with one of the local cops if that happened. He had the look of one of the country's less fortunate citizens, but in his pockets he carried what appeared to be an older, well-used version of the iPhone and a few thousand pesos cash. He also had, stuffed down in his left sock, a bank card issued in his undercover identity, with which he could access an account in Mexico's largest bank chain at any of the thousand ATMs available countrywide if need be.

Then, there was his knife. He hadn't worn it in a year—in fact, he had sworn to himself he would never wear it again after his first mission, but Bennie insisted, as much to sell his undercover persona as for personal protection. The four-inch auto-opening Heckler and Koch switchblade still fit snuggly in the scabbard on his left wrist and lower arm, easily hidden by the loose-fitting flannel work shirt. The spring actuator in the bottom of the scabbard still worked and would propel the switchblade into his palm with a sudden flex if he needed it. He hoped he would not, but he had had that same hope a year ago, and two men died anyway.

The cell phone was more important to him than the knife was. A great many of the lower class had cell phones and were informers for the remaining cartels, under orders to call in anytime the local police or federal troops threatened in their areas. Despite appearances, his iPhone was anything but old and typical. Once it was turned on, if you knew how to find the secret log-in screen, it took a seven-digit pass code to access anything more than the basic functions and get to the more interesting parts of the internal programming. In the memory chip were encryption codes that could scramble any text message or email he sent if he wanted, and then the programming would store them where a random check of the phone would not reveal them. His findable call history was short; all innocent and actual telephone numbers to a few local restaurants in and around Juarez. Any calls he made to

Bennie would also not show up in any easily accessible record. As long as the phone was on, Bennie knew where he was through an encrypted GPS function. Unlike his first assignment, where things got a little dicey and Bennie lost track of him for a couple of months, he now had the ability to stay in touch with his boss, but never would such contact give him away if others demanded to check him out.

Bennie, dressed as a truck driver and driving a large panel truck with the logo of one of the DEA front companies they ran in the southwest splashed across the side, had dropped him off several blocks from the Juarez bus station the night before. They had no difficulties at the large and busy border crossing from El Paso to Juarez. Ray was safely hidden in the back, and Bennie's papers and manifest were top-shelf forgeries. The Mexican border guards, tired and bored so near the end of their shift, were not the least bit interested in a delivery truck going south or in doing their job well; all that was on their minds was the upcoming shift change at midnight and maybe a quick drink at a local cantina on the way home.

They had discussed driving him all the way to Chihuahua, but he'd suggested to Bennie that it would be better if he took the bus down. Part of his cover story was that he had hidden out in the border zone for the last year, most of the time near Juarez. Better if he showed up on the bus and had a used ticket as proof. Bennie agreed and, with a handshake, dropped him off in a dark, run-down residential area a short walk from the downtown station. He bought a ticket for the 6:00 a.m. bus to Chihuahua and spent an uncomfortable six hours at the station, sometimes faking sleep in the large waiting area, sometimes in the coffee shop, and always watching the local police and federal troops who made occasional rounds through the terminal. Except for the fact that he smelled worse than most of the others waiting, he decided that with the clothes Bennie had provided, he did more or less fit in; if anything, he was more ragged looking. The last thing he needed was to get pinched right at the beginning and to have to start all over.

It was only 210 miles from Ciudad Juarez on the border to Chihuahua, but it had taken five hours to drive, as the bus stopped in every small town along Federal Highway 45 as they made their way south. Ray walked out of the air-conditioned terminal into the breezy, dusty sunshine to get his bearings. It was already hot, easily over eighty, and he took off his light jacket and stuffed it through the handles of his duffel. He'd forgotten how hot and dry the place usually was. He spent a great deal of his time during his first undercover assignment in the foothills outside Chihuahua and was familiar with the city, but he had never been in the area around the new bus terminal. After a second or two to get his bearings, he knew the Hoyo del Infierno neighborhood was north, just this side of the central business and government district. There was a city bus stop at the main looping front drive of the terminal, so he followed a small crowd walking that way. After a quick check of the map and schedule mounted on the end wall of the minimal shelter, he waited fifteen minutes in the heat and dust until his local bus arrived. It was another twenty minutes before he got off at the stop nearest the motel where he was supposed to stay.

The Motel Matador was a run-down property on the main east-west commercial street that separated the Hoyo del Infierno neighborhood from another not much better. He realized when he saw the motel that the Goat's Head was only a couple of blocks south on the nearest cross street, deeper into the neighborhood, so the location was ideal for him. He walked into the small, messy office, where he found an older-looking desk clerk reading a paper behind a makeshift wire mesh security screen with a narrow slot in the bottom, as if the flimsy barrier could really protect him from the worst the neighborhood had to offer. The clerk looked up at him for a long second and then said, "What?"

Ray fixed the older clerk with a long stare, which clearly made the man nervous, and then asked, "The sign says apartments by the week."

"Do you have money?"

"Yes."

The clerk broke into a smile. "Well then, that is good, for I have one available, on the end. It is small but clean and has a small kitchen."

"How much?"

"For you, say a thousand pesos a week."

"I will give you eight hundred, and I sign no papers."

The old man started rubbing his chin and eyeballing Ray more seriously. "No registration could be difficult. I'm just the manager; I have records I must keep for the owner. How long will you rent it?"

"Several weeks at least. Maybe longer if I like it; I'm no trouble."

The clerk nodded his head, the prospect of renting the room out overcame any attention to rules and other details. That, and the young man carried himself well and spoke far better than he looked, and that was unnerving. "Ok, how about nine hundred a week? For that, we will wash and change your bedding once a week."

Ray watched the man, making the old clerk more nervous by the second, and then he reached into his pants pockets and counted out the nine hundred pesos and put the money on the counter in the slot. As the old man reached for it, Ray kept his hand on the cash and said, "As I said, I'm no trouble, but my business is my business. I would become very unhappy if I found out you spoke to others about me."

"Of course, of course, young man. What a man does is his own affair," the clerk said with a nervous laugh. "We are very discrete here, very discrete."

"For your sake, I hope so," Ray said as he removed his hand and the mousy old man quickly scooped up the money.

He turned to a makeshift wall-mounted board and removed a key. "Number ten, on the end. Enjoy your stay."

The old clerk was on the payroll of one of the local gangs and also, ironically, the metro police. Everyone, it seemed, wanted eyes on this area and any persons of interest reported. Normally, he would not have given the young man a second thought; he had seemed so typical for the area walking through the door, but there was something in his eyes and the way that he conducted himself that said there was more to him than the worn clothes. There were bonuses to be made sharing such information, but the young man had unnerved him with his calm confidence and his veiled threat. His instincts said this was a man to be respected, and he would hold his tongue. His life was worth far more than the few pesos he would be given for telling others of his new tenant.

Ray left the office and walked down the covered sidewalk to the end room nearest the street. He looked around casually, checking out the general area. Not seeing anything unusual, he turned and unlocked the door and entered the small apartment. To call it an apartment was, by any standard definition, a stretch. For all intents and purposes, it was a slightly larger motel room, and a run-down motel room at that, with a decorative half wall separating the small living space, which he entered from the bedroom. The so-called kitchen was a short linoleum-covered counter with a small two-burner stove and oven, with a small undercounter refrigerator against the side wall of the living room. Beyond the bedroom was a closet and the bathroom. The lights in both the hallway in front of the closet and the bathroom were pull-chain fixtures with exposed single light bulbs. The living area had two curtained windows, one adjacent to the front door looking to the parking area in front of the motel and another on the side overlooking the street. There was no telephone or television, but the front window had a through-wall air conditioner, its electrical plug dangling from the unit. He set his duffel down on the seedy couch and plugged in the air conditioner, which, to his surprise, actually worked. It was noisy, but with the sweltering heat in the apartment, he'd gladly trade the noise for the cooling. But he wondered how the noise might affect the listening devices that were going to be installed.

He'd passed the room the two agents of Los Pueblos Fantasmas were living in two doors down. He was curious how they had managed to keep their true job concealed from the nosy old desk clerk and the cleaning people. He would ask about that when he made contact with them, and he had better like their answer, he thought. He was to leave a small matchbook jammed in the door crack below the knob with the number of his room after he arrived. The matchbook would say "31," in case anyone else discovered it; only the agents would know to subtract 21 and understand the meaning. At some point the agents would make themselves known to him and do their work, wiring his rooms for sight and sound.

It was just after noon and too early to go to the Goat's Head, he thought, knowing immediately that was a lie. Point of fact, anytime was a good time to go, given what he was going to do, which was sit, drink, and be seen. The simple truth was that he wasn't fully in character yet mentally and he knew he needed some street time to settle in. He left the motel and walked down the busy commercial street, stopping at the first street vendor selling tacos al pastor, a style of street food he had come to love during his first assignment. The two young men operating the large steaming cart appeared to be brothers, which was typical for these small family-run operations. What was called tacos back home and what these guys were preparing were two different things. The meat was well-seasoned pork grilled on a vertical spit with a pineapple on top that was shaved off to order and placed on a warm tortilla with some fresh onion, salsa, and cilantro. He bought two and a can of Coke and sat on the curb enjoying his tasty lunch, the flavors bringing back all kinds of forgotten small memories of his first assignment.

The previous year, he had spent three months sharing a jail cell in El Paso with a big-time trafficker before Bennie orchestrated an escape that allowed his cellmate Carlo Vargas to take him to Mexico and into the man's cartel. The three months were time enough to get comfortable with what he was assigned to do. He now had experience from that mission to draw upon as he started this one. Except for the possibility of running into his onetime driver, Javier, he was in new and unknown territory, and the mission possibilities were very broad. The assignment could evolve and lead God knows where, and he was uncomfortable with that aspect. The only thing that made the unknown risks acceptable was that this time he'd be able to maintain contact with Bennie. And as long as he stayed in Chihuahua, there would always be backup nearby, and that was something, even if they were Mexican feds.

He wore a pair of cheap sunglasses when he was out and discreetly looked at a lot of faces in the unlikely event he might recognize someone. All the formally owned Vargas family businesses were in far better areas than this one, so he wasn't surprised he did not see one familiar face, despite the close proximity to their old family neighborhood. He returned to his room after appearing to walk aimlessly around the commercial area that ran up and down the major street and tried to nap, but sleeping here was going to be a chore. Between the noise of the air conditioner and the cycling of the compressor in his small refrigerator, there was a constant racket. He tossed and turned for a few hours, mostly thinking about the assignment and his initial introduction to the neighborhood.

He got up at five and left the room, walking casually but alertly south on the most active of residential streets. The Goat's Head was in a small retail area several blocks down. Whenever he and Carlo had stopped by the Goat's Head a year ago, they always arrived in a large armored SUV with an armed driver and, typically, a second guard. Often the driver had been Javier Brillo, whose brother, it seemed, was now looking for him if Bennie's intel was accurate. From a half a block away, he recognized the colorful awnings that made the small storefront stand out from the other local businesses, and he paused on the corner across the street watching as the occasional person came or went from the small cantina. It was still early, and there weren't a lot of people going in, so with a deep breath slowly exhaled, he walked the short distance to the entry and stepped inside, removing his sunglasses as he did due to the very low light level. There were a dozen small tables in the front, and then a bar across the back with a half dozen stools. Deeper into the room, past the end of the bar, were several larger round tables that most of the locals never went near.

He knew from past experience that any business of importance conducted in the cantina was conducted back there, usually by very important and dangerous people; there had been a short time a year ago when he was recognized as one of them. He stood for a moment just inside the front door letting his eyes adjust to the darkness, but he was also surveying the room and the few patrons already there. Not recognizing anyone, he walked to the bar and sat down. The bartender had his back to him, washing some glasses. There was a large mirror above the back counter, and the man was watching him closely. Ray immediately recognized the bartender's reflected image—his father had been the owner and a longtime friend of Carlo's. Always when they had been here before, Carlo would embrace the younger man and inquire of his family and then discreetly hand him an envelope stuffed with cash. He wondered how the man had managed in the last year with Carlo's death and the end of the informal gifts.

The bartender turned around and looked at him; Ray set a few pesos on the bar in front of him and said, "Una cerveza, por favor."

The bartender nodded, turned to a beer cooler, grabbed a bottle, opened it, and set it on the counter. Ray shoved the few pesos across the bar and picked up the cold beer. The bartender didn't reach for the money. Rather, he stood there for a moment before stepping closer, and then under his breath said, "Your money is no good here. You have been away too long, welcome." He nodded his head and moved down the empty bar, continuing with his chores, and then a few minutes later stepped away from the bar and went into the small rear kitchen briefly. When he came out, he was carrying a small tray, and he circulated to a few of the front tables, doing his job of delivering food or drinks and cleaning up. Ray had nearly finished his first beer when the man set a second in front of him, not saying a word.

The bartender's calm outward appearance belied his true feelings. He had watched the disheveled young man walk in, using the back mirror to do so, as he often did. Nothing struck him as unusual at first except he wasn't one of his regulars, which was all the more reason to keep an eye on him. Only after the young man sat down and he had watched him a few seconds more as he finished washing glasses did he realize who it was. The hair was longer and he now had a beard, but it was him, El Cuchillo. He knew immediately when he could see his eyes. You could always tell who the real dangerous ones were that way. There was a cold calm in their eyes, whereas most others who came in or lived in the neighborhood always showed fear or sadness. After serving him his beer, he stepped into the kitchen and quickly grabbed the prepaid cell phone that Guillermo Brillo had given him and speed dialed the number. He was not surprised when he heard Javier Brillo's voice answer. "Yes?"

"It's Angel. That package you wanted has arrived."

There was a momentary pause, and then Javier answered excitedly, "Is he there now?"

"Yes."

"Do nothing." And then he hung up.

Angel didn't need anyone to tell him to do nothing. The Brillos were up to something serious—that much was clear—and that made them more dangerous than usual. But as far as he knew, there was no more dangerous or ruthless man at large in the entire country than El Cuchillo. If even half the stories he had heard about him were true, this quiet young man had killed dozens of Vargas enemies, and he had done so up close with a knife. That thought alone chilled Angel.

⇢⇥◉ ◉⇤⇠

Javier and Guillermo were playing cards at their mother's kitchen table when the call came in. They quietly and quickly discussed it and then decided that Javier alone would go and try to meet the ghost that was El Cuchillo. It took Javier only a few minutes to briskly walk the two blocks to the cantina. He paused at the front door to catch his breath, and then he went in and slowly walked to the bar after verifying that none of the few men sitting at the front tables was El Cuchillo. The lone man sitting at the bar never turned as he came in, but there was something very familiar about him in the way he sat. Angel was standing in the kitchen door watching as he walked in. Javier sat down slowly on the stool next to the stranger and signaled Angel for a beer. Angel quickly got him his drink and walked off. Javier took a sip, and without looking at Ray, said, "It is good to see you, old friend."

Ray was sipping his beer and continued to do so, and then he set it down and turned his head slightly and looked at Javier. His expression never changed, but he was flabbergasted that it had taken less than thirty minutes to hook up with the Brillos, despite the Mexican feds' intelligence that the brothers were regulars at the Goat's Head. After a second, he smiled a small, tight smile and said, "Javier, you are alive. I'm glad; there are so few of us left."

Javier smiled back and suggested they move to one of the rear tables. Ray nodded, and they grabbed their beers and walked to the darker rear corner of the bar. The two young men sat there and looked over the front bar area but were being completely ignored. Angel walked quickly over with two fresh beers and a basket of fried pork chunks, salsa, and tortillas, set them on the table, and just as quickly went back to the bar.

"We thought you might never return to Chihuahua after what happened last year. I'm glad you did," Javier said quietly.

Ray looked at him for a second, a menacing look on his face, and said slowly, "Who is *we*?"

Just from the look on El Cuchillo's face, Javier realized he had made a mistake. He leaned in closer to Ray and said, "Excuse me, El Cuchillo. I should have told you that I have been reunited with my two older brothers. You shall meet them soon—tonight if you wish. We have been looking for you. I thought you had heard and that was why you returned."

"What do you mean looking for me? How? Who? I know nothing of this. Tell me everything you know and now," Ray hissed quietly.

Javier was suddenly panicked inside. He hadn't made clear at all what his brother Guillermo had done and had to fix it quickly. While he had spent a lot of time with the young killer when they were with the Vargases, it was wishful thinking for him to think they had been friends. That wasn't the case. Always El Cuchillo had been a favorite of the Vargases', first to Carlo and then his cousin, the Condor himself. This young killer had personally saved the Condor from assassination by knifing to death the assailant against great odds. All Javier had done was drive him around on occasion; they'd never run in the same circles.

"I am explaining this badly; I'm sorry. Only Angel and several more like him here in Chihuahua, and another two in Hermosillo who knew you, were asked to keep an eye out for you. They were instructed to call me or my brothers if you should ever show up. They are all trusted men who work in cantinas favored by you and Carlo. My two older brothers you have not met, but like you, they were very close to the Condor and trusted. Eleven years ago, Jefe sent Guillermo to Tijuana and Felix to Matamoros as spies, and they became important members of two of the other cartels, reporting back to Jefe. It was because of their sacrifices that the Condor was able to kill so many of his enemies last year before the federals got him. We are putting together our own family business here in Chihuahua to take over what is left of the Condor's. Guillermo discovered that you may have survived, and if so, he wanted you found so we could ask you to join us. I told them you should be in charge of our security; no one else knows you are alive."

Ray listened in silence, and when Javier was finished, he drank his beer and looked away as if in thought. He could sense the fear and tension building in Javier and, after a moment, turned back to him and asked, "What information did your brother receive that gave him the idea that I was alive, and from who?"

Javier explained how his brothers had arranged for legal services for some of the other surviving Vargas guards whom Ray knew and had lived with for months, and through them, he had heard the rumors about a possible escape route from the Chihuahua estate.

Ray nodded his head slowly as Javier nervously explained, and then he said, "OK, Javier, I understand. Relax; drink your beer."

Javier was immediately relieved and did as he was told.

Ray looked around and then back to Javier, and then he went on quietly. "There was an escape route from the Condor's rooms to one of the casitas at the wall. During the attack both the Condor and Eduardo were hurt badly. Raul and I could barely manage to get them to the secret tunnel beneath the casita. I was sent up first to clear the area of federals. They had not yet discovered our escape, but before I could return and help Raul with the others, they were attacked, and all were either killed or caught. I barely escaped. I've been on the run ever since, mostly near Juarez, surviving as a thief. I was running out of places to stay and becoming too well known, I think, so I came here last night. This is my first time back and the first time I have gone near one of our old cantinas. I am sure the federals must watch places like this. I probably should have stayed away, but I came anyway."

Javier was relieved that El Cuchillo was no longer angry with him, and it showed. "You are with friends now and safe. We have many reliable watchers in the neighborhood. Except for the occasional army or police patrol, we have seen nothing unusual. My brothers want to meet you. Guillermo is at our mother's now; she lives near here. Felix has been away. His life is very complicated right now, but he's due back tonight. Let me take you there; you can rest and clean up and even stay with us if you wish. Felix can protect you."

Ray looked at Javier, a neutral look on his face. "I have a room at the Matador. It is better I stay there, but I will meet your brothers."

"Whatever you wish, El Cuchillo. Come, let's go. Tonight you have dinner with us. My mother is a very good cook. You will meet my brothers and hear what they have planned; we all have a very good future ahead of us, believe me."

Ray looked down at his clothes and then up at Javier. "If I'm to meet your mother at her home, I must clean up first. I cannot go to her looking like this. I've been on the move for the last twenty-four hours. Let's go to my room first, and then you take me there."

After returning to his room, where Ray had a chance to shower up and change into the one clean shirt he had in his bag, they walked back to Javier's house. Guillermo and his mother were there, and the men talked and drank on the porch while she happily cooked dinner. It was after eight before Felix showed up. The brothers' mother fluttered around her small kitchen and dining room serving her sons and their guest until Felix quietly sent her to bed. Ray and the Brillo brothers sat at the kitchen table and filled each other in on what they had done in the Condor's cartel and what each had done over the last year. Even the very hardened Felix sat quietly and very interested as Ray recounted his time and responsibilities to the Condor. The brothers sat mesmerized as he told them of his part in saving the Condor from an assassination attempt by a traitor in his organization and then later helping him with the assassination of the country's preceding president. That story was mostly a lie for their benefit. He had had little to do with killing the sitting president. Mostly, given the circumstances, he had just stood by and not prevented it; not that he could have, another one of the events he'd processed and was now in his rearview mirror. But the Brillos didn't know that, and he could see that his involvement in such an important event in Mexico's recent history was having the desired effect on the older two brothers.

Felix was the most reserved during their talk, having missed the opportunity to get to know Ray better earlier. But it only took him an hour to believe that the stories Javier told of the young killer were most likely true. Felix had been relying on his instincts about people for a very long time to stay alive, and in many ways this young killer reminded him of El Lobo. That was both a reassuring thought and a scary one. After satisfying himself that

El Cuchillo was indeed a good choice for head of security, he shared with him the troubles he was having in Matamoros and how he needed his help as a guard and soldier for the immediate future. He also told Ray he would be safer in Matamoros than here.

After thinking about it for a second, and with a look around at the others, Ray agreed. How could he not, even if it meant deviating from the rough mission plan he and Bennie had talked about? Where better to discover information on a Matamoros distribution system than in Matamoros, even if it meant leaving his nominal Mexican backup behind?

After saying goodnight to the brothers, Ray returned to his motel, called Bennie, and updated him. Bennie was happy that he had hooked up with the Brillos so quickly but unhappy with the change in locale. He nevertheless reluctantly agreed with Ray's move and said he'd work on possible backup in the Matamoros area. Felix and Javier came by his apartment early the next morning to pick him up and take him to breakfast and then shopping. They first ran him by a good barber in the neighborhood to clean him up some, and then they bought him some good new clothes, shoes, and a nice travel bag to carry them in. They stopped by the motel so he could change and pack, then drove to the airport. There was a significant police presence at the airport that made Ray nervous, but now that he was dressed conservatively in a new suit and tie, none took special notice, and after checking their bags, he and Felix boarded their flight without incident. They flew a commuter airline direct to Matamoros, landed, and collected Felix's car. He drove them straight into town to what was considered a very nice downtown apartment and told Ray he would live there with him for the foreseeable future.

After unpacking, changing, and getting settled into his own room, he rejoined Felix in the living room, and Felix told him he needed to be armed. Ray nodded yes and said, "I am, but not with a handgun."

Felix nodded back, and as badly as he wanted to ask to see the knife that the great El Cuchillo carried and was apparently lethal with, he went to a locked cabinet and retrieved a new Glock 40 and shoulder holster, not unlike the agency-issued piece Bennie was holding for Ray back in DC. After checking to see if it was loaded, Ray holstered it and put the rig on as a dark feeling came over him that maybe this assignment wasn't going to be as easy as it had started out. He was fascinated to hear about the huge shipment of missing money, but that was just an interesting and dangerous sideshow. He knew there was nothing but trouble down that path because even rational people would do irrational things when it came to large sums of money. Nevertheless, to sustain his cover and keep his mission moving forward, he knew he had to help Brillo with the money nonsense, wherever that took him and however dangerous it might be.

11

Jack first noticed Madison when she served him his second Sands, a local Bahamian beer he liked. He knew her name only because she approached him from her side of the bar as he was turned away looking out toward the marina thinking about tomorrow's plane flights to LA to see his girls and asked him if he wanted another beer. A bit startled, and momentarily flustered in her presence as he spun around on his stool, he responded politely with a "Yes, ma'am," a reflex from his years in the corps.

She put her hand on her very well-defined hip and smirked, saying, "Listen, buddy, you can call me Madison, Maddy, or bartender, but never ma'am. Got it?"

He sheepishly muttered an apology and said, "Ah, sure, Madison. Sorry" as she smiled a dazzling smile, winked at him, and walked off toward the cooler. He'd been at the Evening Shadows every night since he arrived in Freeport; why he hadn't really noticed her before now was a mystery to him because she was gorgeous in a way only an older woman could be. He shook his head as if admitting *What an idiot* and wrote it off to being distracted by all the changes taking place so quickly in his life. She had a remarkable figure, was very fit, and because her skin was tanned and flawless, she could pass for thirty, but his cop's eye placed her nearer to forty. He thought she conducted herself with a bearing and confidence that could only have been borne of a maturity realized from more than a few life lessons, not that it mattered to him in his current state of mind. He thought she was the most beautiful woman he had ever laid eyes on.

As he watched her getting other patrons their drinks, all the while keeping up an almost nonstop banter with some of the locals, he was aware that he had not looked at another woman the way he was looking at this Madison since he first set eyes on his ex-wife almost twelve years earlier. Since his arrival, first in Florida and now in Freeport, he knew he was attracting the attention of women of all ages. Both areas were vacation hot spots where women as well as men were looking for a casual good time, so that was apt to occur. He was used to getting noticed by women, but now that he was tanned bronze by all the time in the sun, it was happening with greater frequency. Truth be told, however, he paid such adoration little attention. He'd been faithful to his ex-wife, and since the divorce, the wounds and doubts of his failed marriage simply were too raw to deal with possible new romantic relationships. But this woman stirred something in him, and he was surprised.

He had been in Freeport for only a week, but it had been busy and satisfying. His sailing test with Ed had gone off without a hitch, and he had proved his sailing worthiness to his thorough and detail-oriented instructor. It took another five days in Lake Park to make the necessary modifications to his boat and then move the money from the RV to the boat in a way that did not attract attention. Finally satisfied with his handiwork and with about half the cash he had left Denver with safely hidden aboard, he spent his last Friday in Lake Park for the foreseeable future provisioning the *Second Chance* for weeks of living in the islands. After a pleasant farewell dinner his last night with Ed, he set sail the next morning on his own. It was a now-familiar eighty miles to Freeport, and it took him only eight hours to transit, but doing it alone for the first time was very different—tranquil and truly awe inspiring on the one hand, but there was also a far greater awareness of how solitary and serious solo sailing was.

Henry arranged for twelve months of dockage at the beautiful Lucaya Marina on the south shore of Grand Bahama Island. The marina was surrounded by palm trees, always swaying, it seemed, from the constant sea breeze, and by several of the large full-service hotel resorts located on the island. Across the street was a wonderful open-air market that was resplendently painted in vibrant pastel shades of pink, yellow, and blue. The brightly canopied displays had everything he would need in the way of food and drink, and there was also a laundromat facility within walking distance. While he'd only been there a week, after sitting in the stern of his boat watching one beautiful sunset after another, he could see that living like this was something he could definitely get used to.

Jack had been a little worried about facing his customs inspection when he first arrived and had slowly entered the Bell Channel Inlet, which led to the marina and the customs station located there, but that ended up being a waste of energy. The polite Bahamian customs official, in his blinding white high-necked tunic, crisply creased Bermuda-length shorts, and knee-high white socks, took no more than ten minutes to walk his boat and ask his pro forma questions. Finished, and after glancing at Jack's registration papers and passport, he seemed interested only in collecting the $350 fee that covered his cruising permit and departure tax. After stamping his passport, the amiable official smiled, saluted, and welcomed him to Grand Bahama.

The money was always there in the back of his mind, but his thoughts about it were evolving. For the first time in his life, money for the bare essentials in life was no longer a worry, and that was a freedom he had never experienced before. It was all very liberating, and he was only human. He liked the feeling very much. He remembered reading news stories over the years how a great many lottery winners had their lives changed irrevocably for the worse after acquiring sudden fortunes, and he also remembered thinking they had to be stupid, weak, and foolish people to allow such a thing to happen. However, with his newfound wealth, he now thought he understood how so many could go off the deep end on spending binges, like some coked-out rock star, forgetting about everything that had once been central and important to who and what they were. Fortunately for him, he had two grounding companion thoughts always present whenever he thought about the money: his girls and the fact his money was dirty. If his new fortune was ever revealed, there was no doubt that would be dangerous, and perhaps even fatal.

During his last week in Lake Shore, Henry came down to Miami for a couple of days on other business and stayed aboard the *Second Chance*. He brought with him a new laptop and a new smart phone with international service for Jack. He showed Jack their impressive new web page offering charter security services and had him record a voice mail greeting for their new company's toll-free contact number. No one would ever get him directly except those who had his new cell phone number, and as of now, that was only Henry. In another example of Henry being very concerned about his profile, he suggested he rarely give out the new number. As to the business calls directed to the toll-free number or emails through the web page, Jack alone would decide what calls or emails to return, if and when he actually wanted to.

Over their last dinner together, Henry told him he had selected the Grand Bahama International Bank as their offshore bank and opened a numbered account with a $10,000 transfer from their bank in West Palm. All he would have to do was present himself and the PIN in person to access it. The morning after he arrived in Freeport, Jack made his first visit to his new bank as the managing partner of the business. On an impulse before going, he decided to take more cash than what Henry suggested, on the off chance that maybe a larger sum wouldn't matter. His new personal banker was a pleasant American-educated Bahamian named Oscar Wilson. Because his account was a numbered one, he didn't have to show his passport or introduce himself; he only had to fit the description that Henry had given the bank for the managing partner of their business and have the pin, and he did. He mentioned to the banker that he'd sold off a number of his possessions before relocating to the islands and had quite a bit of cash he was uncomfortable holding; were there any limits or rules on the size of cash deposits? The banker said yes, that any amount over one hundred thousand American was subject to added scrutiny under provisions of several international agreements to curb money laundering, but lesser amounts were not a problem and quite typical. Also, he took great pains, it seemed to Jack, stressing that the bank guarded its customers' privacy, even from foreign governmental inquiries, in spite of the international agreements.

Relieved, he gave the banker the entire $75,000 he had in his duffel bag and felt as though he was off to a good start. His future weekly deposits would be smaller and varied, but even at that rate, a million a year in deposits seemed possible. He made a mental note to ask Henry about opening other accounts at different banks around the Caribbean. He didn't know a thing about international banking laws, but if he could safely deposit around a hundred thousand a month in his Freeport Bank and not raise any suspicions, why couldn't he do that in, say, five banks and maybe get half a million a month safely deposited, all the while just sailing between islands and not doing any security business at all? At that rate, four to six million a year safely in offshore banks would mean that he need never involve others in his scheme, which was definitely worth considering.

Tomorrow afternoon he was flying from Freeport to Miami and then on to LA for his regularly scheduled weekend visit with his daughters. His flight out was at five, and given the time changes and quick layover in Miami, he would be in LA by ten Pacific time tomorrow night, giving him all day Saturday and Sunday with the girls. When money was tight and he was driving out, he always stayed in cheap hotels near the Burbank airport, but now that he had some cash, he was booked into a nice high-rise hotel near Burbank just minutes from his ex-wife's house. The return flight was a bit more brutal, as he'd be taking the Sunday-night redeye out of LAX to Miami, but he didn't mind; he would be back aboard his boat by noon local time Monday and could catch up on sleep then. Even though the distances were far greater, the flying in first class had the driving he used to do from Denver and back beat all to hell.

He was watching Madison without being too obvious about it when Robbie Poitier came by and slapped him on the shoulder and said hello, not missing Jack's gaze at his bartender. On his first visit to Freeport with Ed, they had had several meals and a bunch of drinks with Robbie and hit it off. His first week living in Freeport found him at the Evening Shadow every night, spending a lot of time with Robbie and his local friends. While he didn't yet feel like a regular, he was being treated as such and was grateful. Only Robbie was aware of some of the details of his life change—the killing and subsequent trial, his sacking, and, of course, the divorce—but Ed asked Robbie not to let Jack's history get around. It was enough to know that he was an ex-cop looking to start up a charter security business in the islands.

Robbie sat at the next stool and said, "Jack, my friend, I'm afraid some business has come up in Nassau, and I must back out of our dinner plans. Sorry."

Jack smiled warmly. "No problem, Robbie. I feel like I've been monopolizing all your time as it is and can't thank you enough. You've made this move a hell of a lot easier than I ever imagined it could be, and I'm grateful."

Robbie waved off Jack's sentiment. "Any friend of Ed's, eh, man? Listen, I cannot stand the idea of you eating alone," he said while turning and glancing at Madison at the other end of the bar. "And you are not the only friend I have who is beginning anew. I happen to know my bartender's shift is over at five, and she is free this evening. It would please me if I can help two of my friends at the same time."

Robbie was smiling now. Jack glanced past Robbie for a second and then said, "Thanks, Robbie. As much as I would like to get to know her, I'm on shaky ground here. You know how long it's been since I've had a real date with a woman other than my ex-wife?"

"Ed said a long time, man; I know. But you are in the islands now with a new life, eh? Best to get on with it."

Robbie turned toward Madison and said above the din in the bar, "Maddy!"

She looked up from washing glasses at the other end of the bar and smiled. "I'm a little busy here, Rob. Whatcha need?"

"A moment, girl, when you are free?"

She stopped what she was doing, grabbed a bar towel, and dried her hands as she strolled down the bar to them. To his surprise and some embarrassment, Jack was actually nervous; he'd never felt this way before, not even when he was really young and just beginning to notice girls and they him. He had never been a cocksman, but neither was he ever unsure of himself when it came to the opposite sex; things had always gone pretty smoothly and simply for him. But not now, and a part of him found that interesting if not a bit surprising. He suspected it was probably some psychobabble bullshit having to do with rejection after being dumped by his ex, but whatever it was, it was a new sensation.

"What can I get you boys?" she asked casually.

"Maddy girl, meet my friend Jack, a fellow recent expatriate from a place called Colorado on the mainland. Jack, this is Madison Taylor, Maddy to her friends. Maddy, we were to have dinner together, but I have business in Nassau and need a friend to take my place so Jack doesn't have to dine alone. Can you help me out?"

Maddy smiled her amazing smile, tossed the bar rag over her nicely tanned shoulder, and looked at Jack. "Well, Robbie, that depends."

Robbie asked, "On what, my dear?"

"On him," she said, gesturing with her thumb while looking at Jack with a twinkle of humor in her eye. "You going to call me ma'am again?"

"No ma'am," Jack blurted out in another old reflex, and then, realizing what had popped out of his mouth, he started stammering an apology as both Maddy and Robbie laughed.

"Oh, shut up, Jack. I'll have dinner with you. Might be fun to see if you can eventually talk to me without getting all tongue-tied. One condition, though. I get to pick the place."

Jack quickly regained some of his lost composure, realizing that Madison seemed as nice as she was beautiful. "Deal. I promise you I'm not nearly the idiot I appear to be."

"Well, I'll have to be the judge of that, won't I?" she said teasingly.

Robbie was still chuckling at Jack's clumsiness around his bartender, but he was also privately happy that he might be killing two birds with one stone. Madison he'd known and quietly loved like a father for years, but she had also gone through some tough times recently. Setting her up with a nice guy like Jack appealed to his sense of friendship. "Maddy, I know Harry is in the back. Why don't you go tell him you're leaving early and put him to work?"

Madison looked from Robbie to Jack, who seemed to have regrouped a bit. "Ten minutes, Jack. OK? Finish your beer."

Jack was blushing slightly and smiling, and he had no idea that he was having the same effect on her as she was having on him, only she was able to conceal her emotions, whereas Jack seemed to be wearing his on his sleeve. "Fine, Maddy. I'm in no hurry. I'm adjusting to island speed, and I like it."

She smiled and walked off. He watched the motion of her every step thinking, *Jesus, what a knockout.*

Robbie slapped Jack on the knee and stood up. "Good, I'm glad that's settled." Robbie's look turned more serious, and he leaned in to Jack and said, "A quiet word to the wise, Jack. She's been treated badly in the last few years—a real shit of a boyfriend she was in the chartering business with. He ran off and disappeared, breaking her heart in the process and leaving her alone to deal with many debts. She is very dear to me and has a good heart but terrible taste in men. I'm hoping you are the exception, so please, take care."

Jack's look also turned more thoughtful. "Thanks for the heads-up, Robbie. Believe me, I will."

"Be good, Jack," Robbie said, his normal and ever-present smile returning to his face.

Jack finished his beer and watched as Robbie slowly strolled through his bar, stopping here and there to say a few words to old friends and customers. Finished with her work, Madison came up on him from behind and put her hand on his shoulder, surprising him again. He turned quickly as she was saying, "Hi, I'm done. Shall we go?"

"Sure," he said as he slid off the stool. Once outside and away from the noisy activity of the popular watering hole, Jack asked, "Where would you like to go? This place is all I've really been to since I got here, but I'll take you anywhere you want."

She kept walking but said, "Let's go to the market. Unless you really hate the idea, what I'd like to do is shop for a few things and then cook you dinner, preferably in your galley and not at my crummy apartment. Robbie says you have a nice Beneteau."

Jack returned her look as they strolled toward the brightly painted marketplace. "Yeah, just got her as part of making my move here. A friend of Robbie's brokered the deal and then taught me to sail."

"Ed Harris, right?"

"You know Ed?"

"Only to say hi. I remember seeing you three together a couple of weeks ago when you first came in."

"You know boats?"

For the first time since he'd noticed her, Madison's countenance changed just a bit. She answered but was looking off toward the marina and not at him. "Yeah, I know boats. I was in the charter business here in the islands for many years, but I don't want to talk about that. Not right now, anyway. Maybe later, after dinner. Those days are over."

Her look turned cheerful again as she turned to him and smiled. "I do miss cooking in a galley, though, so how about it? Indulge me? I'm a mean chef when I put my mind to it."

Jack felt like a twenty-year-old again as he looked at her. Old feelings that he thought were long since dead, smothered by all that had happened to him, were coming back to him. How in the world was it possible that he had not noticed her before?

"My galley it is, Maddy. You pick out the groceries, I'll buy, and then you cook. Deal?"

"Deal," she said, smiling as she took his arm.

A woman can tolerate most anything from a man but indifference. Madison first noticed Jack when he walked in with Robbie's friend Ed two weeks earlier. She had been their bartender then and also when Jack arrived earlier in the week and was hanging out with Robbie. In all their brief previous encounters as she served up their drinks, she might as well have been another barstool for all the notice or attention Jack showed her. He simply looked by her or through her, but not in a hurtful or conceited way; he seemed terribly preoccupied or distracted. She was immediately attracted to him, and it was more than just his looks; there was a tenderness in his eyes she couldn't remember having seen in a man and an innate shyness she found compelling in one so good looking. It took her a week after Jack left the first time to weasel out of Robbie Jack's story, and only after he swore her to secrecy. She knew herself well enough to realize she was a bit on the rebound still, but Jack had an enormous impact on her.

She was the oldest of five children and was always the most adventurous and independent. She did the obligatory four years at the University of Wisconsin, as her parents had before her, receiving a hospitality management degree in the process. But she felt dissatisfied with the prospect of a life in the number-crunching side of the restaurant business. She wanted to get out of the Midwest, and she wanted to be a chef. Cooking was a passion for her and was what she really enjoyed, so she moved to New York City and enrolled in culinary school.

After graduating, she went to work as a line chef on big cruise ships for one of the major lines operating in the Caribbean and the Gulf of Mexico. She may have been born and raised in Wisconsin but was always attracted to the ocean and the tropics. What downtime she had between cruises was always spent on beaches and near the ocean, first in Miami and then the Caribbean. Based on her cooking skills, her looks, and her outgoing personality, she quickly worked her way out of the big galley and into the specialty restaurants the big ships always promoted, cooking in front of the vacation travelers and having contact with them.

At twenty-eight, she applied for an opening as a private chef for a yacht owner who turned out to be Robbie Poitier, got the job, and did charters for him the next few years, mostly based out of the Caribbean. She segued from motor yachts into sailing yachts based on nothing more than the appeal of the serenity of wind over diesel. She long held a romantic notion about sailing around the world, and doing it on a diesel-powered boat didn't fit the fantasy.

She had a number of relationships over the years, a few of them even serious. She finally settled down with a free-spirited Aussie she met while crewing as the chef on a vintage 150-foot schooner that Robbie owned and chartered out of Nassau. After working and sailing together for several more years, she and her Aussie set out on their own five years ago as owners of a 65-foot four-cabin sloop for charter. They were happy and almost profitable for a while, then the world economy staggered a little, and one morning her Aussie was just gone. The weak bastard left a typed note thanking her for some great memories but said he could no longer cope with all the pressures and needed a return to a simpler life. He simply disappeared, leaving her to clean up the financial mess and, to her great surprise, the emotional one as well, as she had not realized how much she had come to need him.

She lost her boat, but in the process of settling her debts, she regained some of her old independence and strength. Because Robbie was a friend of many years and comfortably wealthy despite appearances, he stepped in and bought her boat, giving her more for it than it was worth. The difference between what Robbie gave her and what she owed the bank and a few vendors about evened out, so while it had been a terrible experience to go through, it was in her past. Robbie then put her to work at his restaurant and bar, where she cooked for a while, but when she needed a break from the kitchen, he kindly made her the manager and head bartender. And over the last year and a half, she regained her old zing while avoiding romantic attachments like the plague. She knew it was in her nature to love and love hard; she felt more right when in a relationship, but over the last eighteen months as she regained her footing, she vowed to be more careful with her heart.

Then Jack walked into the bar a couple of weeks back, and all her newfound control and discipline went right out the jalousie windows of Robbie's bar. She knew if Jack gave her even the slightest chance, she'd be head over heels, especially after Robbie told her of his past. She quietly asked Robbie to introduce her when he returned to Freeport, and being the friend he was, Robbie orchestrated their introduction. Discovering that the handsome Jack was also shy just made him that much more desirable and was a welcome relief. She had always been able to attract great-looking guys, but she had to admit that every one of them at some point turned out to be a disappointment, more often than not shallow and self-centered. Jack seemed so different, and on so many levels.

As they strolled through the market together, her culinary mind was working overtime planning the perfect dinner; she very much wanted to impress this man. She found some fresh sea bass and some fresh mangos for a chutney she liked to pair with fish. With Jack walking alongside holding their shopping basket, she selected assorted fresh fruits and veggies for a Caribbean salad and some nice-looking shrimp she planned to serve up as a coconut shrimp appetizer. Satisfied with her menu and her selections, she suggested they also pick up some wines to accompany the dinner she had in mind. Jack said sure, pick out what she thought was best no matter the cost, as he was embarrassed to say he knew little about wine.

Jack paid for their groceries, and they walked back to the *Second Chance* making small talk about everyday life in the islands. Madison was very familiar with sailboats but was still impressed with the *Second Chance*. They climbed aboard and immediately went below so she could check out the impressive galley. Jack emptied the grocery bags, setting all that Madison had picked out on the galley counter as she rummaged through drawers looking for cooking pans and utensils she would need.

"How about you open the wine and pour me a glass, stash the rest in the fridge, and then get out of here and let me do my thing," she suggested.

Jack smiled and said sure. Then he did as he was told and went topside, carrying his own glass of the fine chilled white wine Maddy had picked out. The sun was still hot, even this late in the afternoon, so he rigged out the tentlike Bimini that covered the dining area portion of the cockpit and provided some welcome shade. He set up the cockpit table and then went quietly back below. There was a storage closet right at the foot of the stairs, and he located a white linen tablecloth he had seen there. In addition to everything else the previous owners had included in the boat sale, there was also some very nice china and flatware, and he grabbed that as well, wanting to set an elegant table on what was his first date in a dozen years. As he was quietly collecting the tablecloth and china, he paused and watched Maddy in the galley as she happily prepared their dinner. Her back was to him, and she was humming an old Crosby, Stills, and Nash song, by the sound of it, as she gracefully moved about the galley.

As he watched her, he thought back to when he first met his wife. He had been infatuated with her looks as well in the beginning, realizing now he should have been looking deeper. Maybe that oversight was just a function of age and maturity, he thought; maybe not. Intuitively he knew that Maddy was different, better. He shook his head and decided not to dwell on it any longer;

he'd done far too much of that already. He was living his life a day at a time now, smarter, especially in his relationships. But as he watched Madison in her element, stirring this or tasting that, he knew he was falling for her. He went back topside and set the table, pleased with himself when he finished, and then he sat down in the shade and drank his wine while Maddy finished her cooking. Thirty minutes passed before she announced from below that dinner was ready. He hustled below and helped carry the various dishes up, marveling at the great smells coming from the plates. She let out a soft whistle when she saw the table and said, "Very nice, Jack, but we're missing one thing."

She disappeared below but quickly returned with a large candle in a heavy glass holder Jack knew was from one of the end tables in the salon. She sat it in the middle of the table and lit it. Once everything was arranged to her satisfaction, Jack poured more wine, they said a quick toast, and then they ate. For him, it was the best meal he'd had in ages, and he said so, while she waved off his compliment with a smile, saying it was nothing special but that she had fun preparing it. The Bahamas are renowned for their beautiful sunsets, and this night was no different. They sat on deck eating, drinking, and talking as the shimmering red ball of a sun slipped under the horizon to the southwest. They talked for hours, like old friends who had known each other for years, when it had only been hours; never had Jack felt so close to another person so fast. She started it, wanting him to know everything about her past, even the moments she was least proud of. Jack wasn't aware of it, but she wanted there to be no secrets from him.

While it was unspoken, Jack felt the same way, but he kept the events of the last month to himself, not liking the way that made him feel but knowing for the moment it was necessary. Deep down he knew he wanted a relationship with Maddy, and he needed her to feel about him the way he was feeling about her before he told her he was a thief. He did tell her everything else, though, even things he hadn't shared with Henry. With all others, when discussing his time in the corps, it was all just superficial stuff such as duty stations, generalizations of his overseas deployments, what combat was like— never that he had killed men, and a lot of them. But he told her. He couldn't look at her when he did, and the stories came slowly, but something inside made him.

It started innocently enough when she tenderly asked him about the night with Henry's son and her comment that it must have been hard on him, even though the man he'd killed was so evil. For most people, the idea of killing someone was too horrific a thought, too abstract a concept, best left to storytellers in books and movies. Yet most people Jack met who knew something of his life, if from nothing more than the media reports during his trial, always wanted to ask *the* question. Even if they didn't, he could see the unasked question in their eyes: *What's it like to kill a man?* He told her it wasn't the actual killing of the pedophile that bothered him but, rather, the total lack of any feeling except relief. But there had been other times, other killings, when it had bothered him a great deal. There were still the occasional bad dreams, even though he never doubted for a second the righteousness of what he was ordered to do in the corps. He told her Sherry had forced him out of Recon and the snipers in her way, but as he looked at Madison, he admitted that it had been time. Some men could kill in war and not be affected; he wasn't one of them. If he had any other emotion beyond his initial relief that the pedophile he killed would never again harm another child he told her, it was a deep-seated anger that the bastard had made him kill again, and she seemed to understand.

Leveling with Henry as he had about all the mistakes he had made during his life, especially his marriage, was easy to do—simple bar chatter with an understanding close pal. With Madison it was much harder. He kept telling her he was over it, but he kept talking, and more and more of the angst of the last twelve years showed through. He realized, as he was slowly opening up, that with her, the talking about his past was so much more meaningful. For her part, she could see he was still vulnerable from what his first wife had put him through, and she knew she would need to give him time, certainly, and maybe space too, as their relationship grew. She was a patient person, and smart. She'd give Jack all the room he needed, knowing memories of his ex-wife would be little competition for her. The woman had been a first-class bitch, and she would never have to say so. She tried to answer his questions as a friend, but as she listened to him revealing his deepest vulnerabilities to her, she knew she desperately wanted to be more.

The hours simply dissolved away as they drank more wine and talked and talked, always in quiet tones, not all the conversation heavy. There were lighter moments, especially when Jack told her about the two loves of his life, Abbey, aged seven, and Molly, five. He beamed and laughed when he talked about his girls, their births, and stories from birthday parties and days at the beach when they were small, and now in California. The discussion got dark again momentarily when he told her how hard it was to leave them after every visit and, ironically, how it was his ex-wife's actions at the custody hearing that started him down the path of getting over her. He brightened up again when he told her that he was leaving the next afternoon for LA to go see them for the weekend, and Maddy was quick to offer to take him to the airport.

The sun had long since set, and Cassiopeia was prominent in the northern sky. They sat in silence for a few minutes, the first such silence in hours, both just looking into the night sky, the millions of stars pressing down on them, almost close enough to touch. Jack became conscious of the quiet, looked at Madison, and said what a beautiful night it was. Her face seemed to be glowing in the reflection of the flickering, diminishing candlelight, and she smiled and agreed. Then she got up and started gathering their few dishes from dinner. Jack got up to help, and they carried everything down to the galley.

"You cooked. I'll clean up, Maddy. Just sit down and relax. Finish off the wine."

He started to turn toward the sink, and she gently took his arm and stopped him. She stood there for a second, staring at him with a look on her face he couldn't decipher, and then she leaned in and tenderly gave him a short kiss, saying, "No, Jack. It's late. That can wait till morning; it's time for bed."

She took him by the hand and led him toward the bow and the master suite, closing the door behind him as he passed in. He turned toward her, trying to think of something to say in his awkwardness as he quickly tried to sort out his mixed feelings about what was happening. She stepped to him and slowly put her arms around his neck, pressed against him, and then kissed him very softly for what seemed like forever. When she stopped, she gently pushed him back onto the platform bed, and Jack pulled her tight as she lay down on him, kissing him softly again. He knew in that moment there would be no more talk, no more rehashing the mistakes he'd made in life or wondering about the decisions he'd made recently and whether they were the right choices. Those choices unbelievably had brought him to this idyllic island, onto this remarkable boat, and into the arms of this kind and beautiful woman. He was thirty-three years old, the divorced father of two, and had felt deeply at times over the last year that for whatever reason, the prospect of happiness was something this life was simply not going to allow him to have. But as he held Maddy close, his questions, doubts, and past were melting away, and he knew he was feeling true love for the first time. With that incredible realization, the prospect of a different and better future suddenly seemed possible, and he held her a little tighter.

12

Diaz paced back and forth behind his desk, the coffee he was holding in his hand growing cold. Brillo and El Lobo were on their way and due anytime. After five dangerous, unproductive weeks in America, Lobo was finally back in the country. He was glad his friend had survived the last month; many others had not.

Friend, he thought. *Are we really? I don't think so, but I'm still glad he lived.* Lobo's confrontations with the first two of the four distributors had not gone well, and after he had seen and violently dealt with them, the remaining two became aware that something bad was going down for reasons unknown and walled up. Getting to the well-protected distributors in Chicago and New Jersey had taken a great deal of time and proved dangerous and eventually deadly for a great many. It turned out that Lobo's efforts had been for nothing, as the distributors were innocent of any complicity in the theft. But they and their closest lieutenants were now dead nonetheless. Lobo had been very disappointed when he called from Houston last night to tell Diaz this, not knowing what all Diaz had accomplished in his absence. Diaz was anxious to talk with him face to face to tell him the search could now be focused on the true thief, for he was certain he knew who that was.

The information initially developed from the trip that Brillo had taken to southern Colorado four weeks earlier had ultimately led to his conclusion. He was certain now that his nephews had carelessly crashed with his money, somewhere on the one high mountain pass they had to drive over, and that a passing truck driver witnessed the crash and failed to report it. He ran the ATF scam he told Brillo about and was able to obtain the routine contact records of the state police activity for the night the Aguilars disappeared. From the computerized logs, there had been a total of four state police officers working the two hundred miles of highway the Aguilars were supposed to follow. From the look of the data, it had been a quiet night. There were no accidents reported, and all told, the four troopers made thirty-four contacts and wrote thirty citations for one infraction or another, most having to do with violations of the speed limits. Of the four contacts where no citations were issued, all were for assisting a stopped motorist.

The contact that most interested Diaz occurred on the high pass Brillo had described, near mile marker 169, which Felix made a point of saying in his report was at a particularly dangerous curve in the road. This to Diaz's trained mind seemed far too coincidental not to follow up. The contact was made by a lone trooper at 3:45 a.m., about the time the Aguilars could have been in the area, and involved a delivery truck that he was able to retrieve the motor vehicle information file on. Apparently, given the few details available, the contact involved nothing more than a quick investigation of why the delivery truck was parked alongside the highway at that time of night. There was nothing in the report to resolve that question, only that the contact had occurred. Within fifteen minutes the officer reported no further assistance was required, and he was patrolling once more.

To an experienced investigator like Diaz, there was much more to be learned. Why had the truck driver stopped at that particular spot at that time of night if not due to something? Had there been a mechanical failure or some other such routine event? Surely that would have been mentioned in the contact report, but it wasn't. Was it possible the driver did witness an accident? If so, he had not reported it to the officer, and that made him suspect and could only mean he must have found the wreck and the money. Was his money still there? Recovery of such a large amount without raising suspicions even by him, Lobo, and Brillo would be difficult at best. Brillo had reported that the area near this curve on this pass was very rugged indeed. How could anyone recover the money if it was there without being seen and questioned?

For the old police investigator, there was only one way to answer the questions he had, and that was to find the driver of the company truck and talk with him. To do so would mean the driver's death, but so be it. Lobo, in doing what he had to do to get answers from the distributors, had caused far too much of that already, but they had no other choice if in fact the passing truck driver had their money or knew where it was located. There were already a half dozen murder investigations underway in America because of Lobo; the only good news was they occurred over a wide area, and America was a large country. Lobo typically left few tracks, so it was highly unlikely that anyone would connect them. In any event, even if some of the distributors' surviving bodyguards could or even would identify El Lobo, it mattered little, for he was now safely back in Mexico.

Against Brillo's wishes, Diaz sent him north to America once more, this time to Denver, Colorado, where the company that owned the delivery truck was located. He would have liked to go himself, but that was impossible for him at this time, for there would be no explaining his movements. Instead, he gave Brillo explicit instructions as to how to proceed. Because they were dealing with a company that had its own delivery fleet, there would be a shipping yard or dock area. He instructed Brillo to observe only at first, without drawing attention to himself, and try to identify who was responsible for the drivers from a distance. Once such a person was identified, he was to follow this person when he or she left work. Eventually they would stop in a public place, a cantina or a restaurant; perhaps a marketplace. When that happened, he was to approach the shipping boss and identify himself as a Mexican federal officer working discreetly with the local police on a shared investigation. The idea was to try to talk a list of their drivers out of the shipping supervisor without him talking to his bosses. Diaz could do a lot with a list of names.

Brillo's experience talking with the state police officer on his first trip north served him well, and he was very successful in spite of his initial misgivings about the assignment. According to his verbal report when he returned earlier in the week, there was a visible dock area, and it was a busy place, but it didn't take long to identify the man in charge, as he was the only one dressed more formally and giving instructions to the others. At quitting time, the third day he watched the business, the supervisor got in his car, and instead of going right home as he had done the first two nights, he drove to a local restaurant that advertised takeout food, and Brillo had followed him. The supervisor was in the bar having a drink when Brillo did as he had been instructed. In his instructions before leaving for Denver, Diaz told him that if the truck driver they were looking for had witnessed the wreck, found the money, and not reported it to the police, that likely meant his character was suspect and he probably had previous trouble with the law. Based on that logical assumption, Diaz told him to start his inquiries by trying to determine if any of the company drivers had previous involvement with the police.

Brillo reported that after identifying himself to the dock supervisor as a Mexican federal policeman and telling him he was interested in one of his drivers who might have had a past involvement with the police, the supervisor suddenly nodded his head, as if he understood what he was asking about, and said something like, "Oh, I understand; you want to talk with Jack Williams, right? I mean, he was on the force, and you think I know where he moved. Is that it?"

Brillo had no idea who or what the man was talking about. But he recovered quickly, decided to go with it, and agreed that he was in fact looking for a Mr. Williams.

They spoke for another minute, and Brillo followed the conversation, not knowing at all what the supervisor was talking about and trying hard to remember everything he said. What he came away with and managed to tell Diaz was that this Williams had been the company driver responsible for deliveries back and forth from Colorado to Los Angeles. From his first trip north, Brillo knew the Aguilars' route was one of several possible ways to drive between the two points. It seemed that at the end of March, about the time their money went missing, this Williams suddenly picked up and moved to Los Angeles to be nearer his ex-wife and children. The supervisor said he was sorry, but he had no address or phone number for his former driver and was certain no one back at the company did either. The fact that the driver had picked up and moved so soon after being on the mountain pass the same night the Aguilars went missing, quitting his job suddenly and then disappearing with no forwarding address, could not be coincidental, thought Diaz. He didn't believe in such coincidence; this man either had his money or knew where it was on that mountain.

With the name, Diaz had found enough information to focus their investigation. From public records and news reports, he discovered the tainted history of the truck driver. He was a discredited former police officer whose wife had divorced him and left the state. And while he had no further contact information on this driver, he did have information on the ex-wife, and that was where Lobo would go next. He had to get from her the exact whereabouts of this Williams in LA, and once they had that, they would get their answers.

Lobo's truck came into view, and Diaz sighed with relief. He went to his desk and patiently waited for his enforcer to come in. When he did, he was limping slightly. Diaz stood up quickly, a look of concern on his face. "Lobo, my friend, you did not mention you are hurt."

Lobo grimaced as he walked up but waved off the question. "It is not serious, but with your permission, I will sit."

"Sit, sit, of course. Have you seen our doctor?"

"Yes, last night on my return, I went straight there. He has taken care of me, and I am much better. A simple flesh wound from four days ago; nothing serious. I was able to control the bleeding well enough to travel, and he has given me what I need for the pain and the infection."

Diaz went to a small built-in bar adjacent to his desk and poured two glasses of a fine tequila he knew Lobo favored and handed him a drink. Lobo took it, nodded his head thank you, and drank it down in one continuous gulp.

"Another, my friend, to help ease your pain?"

Lobo nodded again and said thank you. Diaz poured and handed him a second drink and then sat down at his desk.

"Our distributors were not involved, Cesar. I am sorry I could not be more invisible in my methods and so many had to be dealt with, but getting the truth is sometimes difficult."

Diaz was waving his hand in a dismissive way. "You did what you thought was necessary, my friend, and I am grateful."

Lobo took a drink of his tequila then asked, "Are you any closer to knowing the truth?"

"Yes. I believe I have discovered our thief."

"The Banker?" Lobo asked.

"No. Thankfully, he is not involved, but he has become an even bigger problem than when you left. Our banking partner has been on my back for weeks to ship more product north and get him something in return. I was able to put him off for a time, and then we got lucky and the American DEA announced a reasonably large raid last week in Los Angeles. I told him the point of distribution we were planning to use was also Los Angeles and that we either needed to change distribution points or wait until the DEA's attention was off before trying a shipment. This has bought us perhaps another month."

"Why not send me to the Bahamas and I simply get rid of him? We must do so anyway, is that not true?" Lobo asked.

"Yes, it is, it is, but you need to recover fully before I ask you to do that, and then only after I have thought of a way that ensures your success. We are sure he has some hired men in town, but they have not gone unnoticed, and they are unaware that we are watching them, as they seem to be watching us. It's as if the Banker is also trying to gather information around town to determine for himself if it is not we who have taken the money."

"We should eliminate them, yes?"

"In time, my friend; in time. For now they are merely watching and asking questions in places they shouldn't be and drawing attention to themselves, contrary, I'm sure, to the Banker's wishes. He was always a very capable financial man, well educated with interests in many areas that helped in distribution and, of course, the laundering, but he is as stupid on the street as he is brilliant in financial circles. This is to be expected, I suppose, of one raised in great comfort who has gained power and wealth without ever having to get his hands dirty. Given the way he now lives, while not simple, he can be killed when the time comes. I'm convinced he had no part in the theft, so we may eliminate him when it suits us. But for now, we must concentrate on finding our money, and Brillo has given us some hope."

Diaz explained to Lobo what had been learned from Brillo's trips to Colorado, and then he paused and looked at his enforcer. "It will be necessary for you to once again go north, to Los Angeles this time, and find this driver's wife, for only you will be able to get any answers quietly. Brillo is a surprisingly good man, but the next step falls to you, I'm afraid. I must say, however, that I am guilty of underestimating his abilities all these years. I usually do not make that mistake, but it seems I have in his case. He handled himself well in the north on our behalf."

Lobo was looking hard at Diaz as if making his mind up about something. "You know, Cesar, that he is planning something with his brothers, do you not?"

Diaz smiled slightly and nodded. "Yes, I know, and he has my support. He was very honest with me several months ago when we first decided to act together. How did you find out? I don't recall discussing this with you."

Lobo shrugged. "Simple. He spends a great deal of time in Chihuahua with his brother, and he's been trying to get his younger brother out of jail. With the Vargases no longer running that town, who better to try? It is his town."

Diaz smiled. "That's good reasoning, old friend. I'm sure he hoped that his actions were not quite so transparent. I only want to find our money and leave the country for good. A new, well-run organization out of Chihuahua might be a very good place for a man with your loyalties and skills."

"Yes, it would be. I do not dislike Brillo."

Diaz simply nodded his head in agreement. "I understand, and I admit I've come to like and respect him over the last few months. One more thing: Does the name El Cuchillo mean anything to you?"

Lobo looked at him for a few seconds and then said, "Yes, I have heard the name, and some of the gossip. A friend and enforcer to former President

Alvarez and the other Vargases, I understand, and if the stories are true, a dangerous enemy."

"That is what I also hear, and it is also true he is still one of the most wanted fugitives in Mexico, but apparently he is no enemy. You will soon be meeting the young man. He now works for Brillo."

Lobo raised an eyebrow but said nothing further.

Diaz went on. "Seems the youngest Brillo, Javier, and this El Cuchillo are friends. Whatever the Brillos are planning for their future, I take it this young man is to be in a position of importance. Given his skills, which Brillo has attested to, he has asked this El Cuchillo to be his principal bodyguard and also thought he might be useful to us with the Banker. We will need all the trusted help we can get, so I agreed. I've met him. Brillo brought him to me several weeks ago; he is living in town at his apartment. I do not know if his reputation is earned or deserved, but I tell you, old friend, it may well be. He presents himself well for one so young. But enough of that. After we meet with Brillo, I want you to go home and rest for a day. But then you must go north again."

"I'm fine, Cesar. I could go today. Do you want me to do anything about this El Cuchillo?"

Diaz shook his head slowly and then smiled. "Nothing, Adolpho. He appears loyal to Brillo, and like I say, we may need him."

As they were finishing up their discussion, the sounds of an arriving car could be heard out front, and shortly after, Brillo came in alone. Diaz was initially angry when Brillo told him that his new guard knew a little about their problem with the missing money, but he was mollified somewhat when Brillo also said that the young killer did not know how much was stolen. What was done was done, and he had enough to worry about without giving this El Cuchillo and what he now knew any more thought. The three partners sat down around Diaz's desk, and he took them through all the information he had been able to find from law enforcement and public records on this truck driver named Williams.

"My friends," he said, looking from Lobo to Brillo, "I have worked our problem through from every possible viewpoint, and as unbelievable as it seems, I have no doubts that we now know who has our money, or at the very least knows where it is located. I believe my idiot nephews carelessly crashed on that Sunday night, and I believe this truck driver witnessed the accident and stopped, maybe intending to simply do the right thing and help them. This driver either discovered my nephews injured or dead from the accident, or perhaps, after also discovering their cargo, maybe even killed them himself, for his record would indicate he is rash, maybe even unstable, and very capable of doing so. We must locate this truck driver, and we must do so through his family."

Diaz slid a folded piece of paper across his desk and then folded his hands together and leaned toward his longtime enforcer. "Lobo, there is the name and address in Los Angeles of this driver's ex-wife. She lives there with her two small daughters. You will have to talk with her and get from her the information we require. As she divorced and left this truck driver, apparently for his misdeeds, I do not want her or her children harmed. I simply want to know where in LA this driver now lives. If you must, you may use the family to get to the driver, but again, do not harm them. We may be traffickers and murderers, but we do not kill innocent women and children, understand?"

Lobo simply nodded his head; this wasn't the first time in their twenty years working together that Diaz had shown such a sentimental streak. Lobo knew with children involved, it would not be necessary to harm them to get the woman to talk. About the time he put his pistol to one of her children's heads, she would tell him everything she knew and then some.

Their meeting concluded, Lobo nodded his acceptance of the new orders, and he and Brillo stood up to leave.

Diaz handed Lobo more papers and said, "Here are your documents and tickets. Find the truck driver and get from him all he knows. You cannot kill him until we have a chance to check out whatever he tells you, so use caution, old friend."

Ray was sitting quietly outside on the porch, where Brillo told him to stay when they arrived together; he was anxious and impatient. He was spending all his time hanging around Matamoros but learning nothing. Brillo was consumed with his secret dealings concerning the missing money, and there were no discussions of networks or trafficking, nor were any shipments planned or discussed. Brillo had gone north to America for a week, leaving him alone to sit around Matamoros and the apartment. He had left only a few times, not wishing to draw attention to himself any more than was necessary—he was, after all, he reminded himself, one of the most wanted men in Mexico. He updated Bennie on his progress, or lack thereof, but what could he really tell him? This entire money chase Brillo and his partners were so focused on was secondary to his mission. He was only going along to gain Brillo's trust, but in the meantime, he was accomplishing nothing.

Brillo came out the front door followed by a very menacing-looking man with a limp, obviously the dangerous El Lobo Brillo had told him about. There were introductions but no handshakes, and then Lobo simply turned and walked with some difficulty off the porch and to his truck as Ray and Brillo stood and watched. As Lobo started to drive off, only then did Brillo look at him and say, "Let's go."

As they drove back to town, Ray's anxiety level was rising. He wanted to give Bennie a heads-up on this Lobo character, but doing so might tip off Diaz and Brillo to a traitor in their midst if a snatch and grab was handled poorly, and as the only new guy in town, he would be a logical suspect. For now, he had to stay silent, but even if he wanted to do more, he couldn't. All he had was the name Williams, an apparently corrupt ex-cop from Denver, and he had nothing on the ex-wife. He decided he would wait, listen, and watch.

Back in his office, Diaz stood before the tall windows and watched his man climb into his truck with some difficulty and then drive off. There was no question Lobo was hurt far worse than he let on, but to question him further would have been pointless. The man had great pride, and if he had needed him to go north today, he would have—a very formidable man indeed, thought Diaz. As unbelievable as it seemed six weeks ago, he was convinced that his stupid and careless nephews had killed themselves in a random car wreck, and the wreck was likely witnessed by this truck driver. The fact that the accident was still unreported could only mean that the driver had discovered the money and hoped to have it for himself. Nothing else fit or made sense. His last remaining hope was that the difficulties in recovering the money without being seen were too great for the lone driver to overcome, and the money was still sitting there on that rugged mountain. Once Lobo got them the necessary information and they confirmed it, the driver could be eliminated, and he and his partners could locate the accident site and recover their money at their leisure. Whatever the difficulties, that was a problem he would happily solve.

In the meantime, Lobo would be in LA by Saturday morning and might even have the driver as soon as the day after, if they were lucky. He would have Lobo sit on the man until Brillo and his young bodyguard could go north and find the money. Only then would the driver be eliminated. As to his nephews, the hell with them, he thought bitterly. If he found them, they'd stay where their own incompetence had led them, and his sister would just have to live with the fact her sons had gone missing.

13

Embassy Suites Hollywood
Glendale, California
End of April; week six

It was late when Jack checked into his hotel, tired from all the flying but excited and happy about the last two days with Maddy and the prospect of spending the weekend with his girls. Last night with Maddy was hard for him to put into words. He'd only just met her, but she seemed to complete him, and that was the sort of thought that had never occurred to him before. Every minute he spent around her seemed to bring greater clarity to what his marriage to Sherry had never been. He remembered reading somewhere that "you can't miss what you haven't known." After the last twenty-four hours with Maddy, he knew now the marriage he had mourned for over a year had never been right, and Sherry was incapable of being a loving partner. Be that as it may, she was still the mother of his children, and continued contact with her was unavoidable. But unlike his previous trips to California, he was no longer dreading seeing her. Without knowing it, in a short twenty-four hours, Maddy had helped put Sherry forever behind him.

They had spent the entire day together before Maddy dropped him off at the airport. Unlike last night, when he knew he'd been awkward and clumsy at the newness of her, waking up with her in his arms this morning seemed so natural, so right. She whipped up a great breakfast from the unremarkable foodstuffs he had onboard the boat, and then at her suggestion, they set sail for the west end of the island and a lovely lunch at her favorite seaside restaurant there. By the time they got back to the marina, he had just enough time to clean up and pack and for Maddy to drive him to the airport for his flight to Miami.

The flight across the country was long and typical, yet given his refreshed frame of mind and spirit and the fully reclining first-class seat, he almost enjoyed it. Sailing with Maddy intensified the newfound feelings he had for the open water. The more he thought about it on the flight, the more he was thinking about segueing from the charter security business that he was doing nothing with, despite the appearances created by Henry, and move into the actual charting business. He didn't know shit about that business either, but Maddy did. He couldn't help himself and started to imagine a life with her, sailing the Caribbean together, she the chef and he the captain. He knew she was coming off a bad experience of her own, and even he knew it was too early into their relationship to be talking about such things, no matter how wonderful the last twenty-four hours made him feel. Nevertheless, he thought about it a lot during the flight, and if their relationship continued to grow, it seemed a natural. As incredible as it was, after their long talk over dinner last night, with the exception of Henry and his old corps platoon leader and spotter Armie Armbruster, Maddy knew more about him than anyone. The fact they had known each other for such a brief period of time seemed unimportant. What did time really mean or matter when he knew without a doubt that he felt more in twenty-four hours with Maddy than he ever did the last ten years with Sherry? She seemed to genuinely understand him, and he knew a man could pass through a lifetime and never experience the closeness with another that he had felt last night.

The kinds of problems she had faced in her first venture with chartering—the unreliable partner and the debt and overhead—would not exist with him. He knew he would be a caring partner, and given his hidden wealth, there would be no such thing as debt. He made a mental note to talk to Robbie about the idea next time he ran into him before raising it with Maddy. He also wondered if Robbie still had her four-cabin sixty-five-footer and if so, if it was a finer boat than his Beneteau. In spite of the heartache and grief she had endured going through the abandonment by her old boyfriend and then having to give up her business and the boat, there were times at dinner last night when her eyes sparkled as she talked about her sloop; it sounded like a beauty.

As he made his way to his spacious room, he knew he couldn't get to bed and to sleep quickly enough and for the morning to come. He'd tried hard despite all the bad that had gone down over the last year to keep things positive whenever he was with his daughters, but he knew even they had seen through him at times. They were too young to really understand, and the most his seven-year-old Abbey had ever said when things were at their darkest and he was feeling his worst was to ask him one time if he was sad and needed a hug. He only hoped the happiness he now felt would be as transparent.

For the second straight night, he slept great. He was up at seven and went to the lobby for some breakfast and to kill some time. He found and browsed some of the touristy brochures from a display in the lobby, looking for new things to do with the girls. The visitation drill worked out with Sherry required him to call her before going over at ten. After picking the girls up, he had them until six on Sunday. After doing whatever he planned for Saturday, they always did a sleepover at his hotel with pizza and a movie in the room. That was their typical night and was what the girls wanted and always asked for. He was grateful because for him, it was more than just fun. It had also been cheap, and that had been a factor before the newfound money. He took them to the beach more often than not during the day, because they loved it and it didn't cost him anything. Now that money was no object and he was staying at a really nice high-rise hotel, they could have room service if they wanted, and he could plan more interesting outings to venues such as Disneyland or the huge Six Flags amusement park.

At eight, he couldn't help himself and called Maddy. It was eleven in the islands, and she would be starting her shift at the Evening Shadows at noon, so he caught her still on the boat. Her apartment was west of Freeport, in a poorer local neighborhood about five miles from the bar. As she was dropping him off at the airport last night, he handed her the keys to the boat and told her she was free to use it while he was gone, as it was just walking distance away from the bar. She hadn't hesitated, just smiled and snatched the keys and said thanks, she would; and while she was there, she said, she would do a little shopping for better provisions, and she gave him a hard time about what she had found in his refrigerator. Their call was all small talk—his flight, the weather, what he had planned for the day, silly stuff—and he enjoyed every minute. At 9:45 he rolled off the bed and called Sherry to let her know he was on his way, but he got her voice mail. He tried several more times and finally left a curt message, asking her to pick up. When he called back a minute later, she finally answered. "Hello?"

"Sherry, Jack. Just wanted to let you know I'm on my way over."

"I didn't recognize the number, Jack. You should really let me know when you do something like change your phone number. What if there had been an emergency with one of the girls?"

Jack ignored her attempt to suck him into an argument and smiled to himself. "I just got it, and now you know, so no problem. I'll be there in ten minutes."

"Not so fast. The girls were invited to a swim birthday party today for one of their classmates. I tried to call earlier in the week to let you know, in case you wanted to reschedule your trip, but you changed your phone. They're really looking forward to it, and it wouldn't be right for you to just take them off somewhere else."

Jack was immediately disappointed, but then he asked, "What time's the party?"

"Noon till four."

"No problem. Get them ready for the party and for our overnight. I'll be by in ten minutes. I've got some things planned and will have them wherever required by noon, and then I'll pick them up at four."

"Just what are you going to—"

Jack cut her off. "Stop, Sherry. Please, just have them ready." Then he hung up. He was determined not to let Sherry foul up his weekend. She had been unbelievably petty with him since the divorce, not making any attempt at civility despite the fact that she had initiated the divorce and then received everything she requested from the court. On every trip, especially when he was driving down from Denver, it was always the same. She picked at him, questioning every little thing he planned, and he had put up with it. But no more. She and her lawyer were responsible for the custody results, and she was as bound by the arrangement as he unfortunately was. And that arrangement said he had the girls from ten on Saturday until six on Sunday every other weekend. As long as he stayed within a hundred miles of her home, there wasn't a goddamn thing she could say or do.

By the time he got to Sherry's pleasant-looking house in the Burbank hills, he was over his mad. He was going to take the girls back to his fancy hotel and hang with them until noon, or take a drive with them in his rental Mustang convertible and then take them to the party; he knew they'd get a kick out of that. The party was actually a good thing, he decided; it was high time he and Sherry had a serious face-to-face talk without the girls around. He didn't want to rehash any of the past—Maddy had gotten him beyond all that. He wanted to talk about the future. She knew nothing about his move or the new business, and he wanted to tell her, and he also wanted to arrange for the girls to spend a chunk of their summer vacation with him. He discussed it with Henry when in Florida, and if necessary, he'd drag her nasty ass back to court and convince a judge that he should be able to see his daughters more often. He was not going to let it rest until he got them for half the summer.

Little Molly flew into his arms after Abbey opened the door. Sherry could be a bitch at times, but the past had shown that once he put his foot down, she'd go along until she could figure out how to deal with the changing circumstances. Jack's confidence and tone over the phone had unnerved her, and he could tell that when he saw her. Despite her obvious attempt to dig at him and not let him have the girls until after the party, ten minutes after their telephone call, here they were, all dressed and each carrying her own small decorated pink backpack. Even as she was trying to drag him into an argument, she already had the girls ready.

Sherry was holding a wrapped present and handed it to him after he sat Molly down and kissed Abbey. Sherry did a bit of a double take as she looked at him, not missing his Caribbean tan. "You've been in the sun, Jack. Here's the address; it's just a mile away. They'll eat nothing but junk at the party, so try to see they get a decent dinner and not more pizza."

"Sure, no problem. I'll see to it." he said pleasantly while smiling, as if their telephone call hadn't happened. "Come on, you monsters," Jack said, beaming at his two little girls. "Wait till you see my car!"

They both bolted out the door, squealing and running toward the red convertible.

He didn't say anything to Sherry, but he could tell she was a little off balance, what with his more confident demeanor, the expensive rental car, and the tan. He intended to exploit her discomfiture by just showing back up for the talk he wanted to have. With all his previous visits, there had been little talk between them other than her attempts to diminish his experience. Mostly he just picked up and dropped off, never getting past the entry hall. He intended to coolly and calmly keep hammering her until she realized that it was either amicably agree to the summer visitation or go back to court. It was amazing, he thought, how the last week had changed him. *Sherry, girl,* he thought as he backed out of her driveway with a determined look on his face, *you don't stand a chance.*

⭑

Adolpho Lobo's flight from Houston landed at LAX at 10:30 a.m. as scheduled and taxied to terminal seven. With his connections and the resources available to him, he was dressed very well and flew first class. He was a large man and needed the space and comfort; even more so today, as his leg was killing him. He cursed silently under his breath as he slowly lifted himself out of his seat and retrieved his one nice carry-on bag from the overhead. It had been a lucky shot that got him, an unaimed flyer by a panicked guard to the last of the distributors. The shot had been rushed, fired just a split second before his well-aimed shot dropped the last of the guards dead in his tracks. His wound was, luckily, a through and through, the doctor had said, and had missed both the artery and the bone of his upper thigh. Nevertheless, the muscle damage was significant and the pain damn near unbearable. Diaz's old sick doctor gave him plenty of pain pills, and they did the job—when he took them. Since getting up early this morning at the airport hotel in Houston, he hadn't touched the bottle; they dulled his senses as well as the pain. Today he would need to be sharp, and the pain focused him.

It always amazed him how easily deceived Americans were with appearances. If you looked prosperous and confident, others always assumed you were someone to respect and not question. His appearance, quality forged passport, and other identification papers provided by Diaz had easily gotten him through the border yesterday, and then through security at the airport this morning. He was traveling as a petrochemical security executive from Ciudad Victoria, the capital city of Tamaulipas, and had the business cards and a company brochure to support the cover. His travel bag was of the finest leather, as were his custom dress shoes, and his suit of clothes were clearly tailored and hung perfectly on his large frame. What made his shoes special was that they looked like typical expensive black dress shoes, but in lieu of leather soles, his were made of a durable but supple thin rubber. How long the soles lasted was of no concern to Lobo, but their nonslip characteristics and how quietly he could approach a target with them on was. He had his Federal Police identification safely tucked away in case he needed it, but with this assignment, he doubted it would be necessary. Women and children were never a bother, and a greedy truck driver would not be much more.

He walked off the flight into the gate area with only a slight limp and made his way to the street level, where he took the interterminal shuttle bus to terminal one. He found the locker area and removed the key he carried in his pocket and opened his locker. Inside was a brand-new brass-trimmed leather briefcase; he grabbed it and then caught the shuttle to the rental car center. As with his airline seats, Lobo always rented cars with room. Once in his silver Lincoln Town Car, only then did he open the briefcase and take out a complete third set of perfectly forged identification papers and the dull, flat-black-finished Sig Sauer P238 with the small accompanying sound suppressor. The handgun was the nine-millimeter variant, smaller and more compact than what he usually carried, but unlike most of those he was asked to deal with in the drug business, the more reliable knockdown power of the .45-caliber he had been forced to leave in Matamoros would not be needed on this trip. His five weeks in America on his last trip required him to be well armed and to travel by air. To avoid security problems, thanks to Diaz and his seemingly bottomless resources and connections, he had weapons and extra magazines stashed in several airport and bus terminal storage lockers around the country for when a need should arise. Like today.

He checked out the navigation monitor in the luxury dashboard of the Town Car and then punched in the address Diaz had provided. He hated driving in the LA area and knew from prior experience that it was anyone's guess as to how long the thirty-mile drive to the woman's house would take. Once he was in the neighborhood, there would be the additional time required to check out the general area and do a couple of drive-bys. While not formally educated, Lobo was also no fool; you could not do what he had been doing successfully for twenty years and not keep up with technology, be it in weapons, transportation, or information. From time to time he would hire younger, brighter men to show him what he needed to know, such as the GPS navigation in all the new cars. In addition to driving directions, you could also ask the system to find you a nearby hotel or restaurant, or more specifically to his needs, the nearest police station or hospital, and traffic conditions. What the local police looked like, where their offices were located, and how they operated was useful information to a man in his job, as were possible escape routes and their real-time driving conditions.

After the typically frustrating drive from the airport to the Burbank area, his first stop was to rent a room for several weeks at a run-down strip motel in North Hollywood he had found and used weeks before on his earlier trip. The rooms on the first floor of the neglected property fronted the parking lot, and he could park within a few feet of his door. He specifically picked a room on the less desirable backside of the motel, indicating the need for quiet with the uninterested clerk who checked him in and took the cash for the two-week stay. The back rooms were more private, and he would need that later on. They also came with kitchens, and he wouldn't be bothered with housekeeping for at least a week. His plan was fluid, but it generally required that he get to the woman and her children at the address Diaz had given him without raising any suspicions and sit on them until he could get the ex-wife to get the truck driver to show up. Once he had him, he didn't care much what the ex-wife did. He would make the usual threats about coming back for her or the children if she called the police, but whatever she did wouldn't matter. He would have the driver safely hidden away at his motel and would get the answers they required. While Diaz had Brillo and his new lapdog run up to Colorado and verify that they found the money, he would babysit the driver. After verification, he would kill him and leave him, suitably wrapped up in plastic that he would buy later to control the stench of decay. By the time the motel staff got around to finding the body, he would be safely back in Mexico.

The GPS said it was only a twenty-minute drive from the motel to the woman's house. Unlike his earlier business with the distributors, which required days of observation and planning before taking action due to armed guards and the secure locations, the woman and her children would require little advance planning to control. On the way, he drove by the police station nearest to the woman's house and the Burbank airport, and he noted potential escape routes and directions. He located the woman's street and drove slowly through the neighborhood, locating her house and checking out the general area. As he suspected, given the fact it was a Saturday, there were expensive-looking cars, minivans, and SUVs in many of the adjacent driveways and children playing in front yards, meaning there were many potential witnesses to any unusual activity. He would have preferred to be here on a weekday, as there would be less activity on the street at this time of day. But his target worked, so that meant taking her in the early evening, when neighbors were also home. But the night was an advantage. She would likely be home on a Saturday, but given the presence of so many on the street, that still meant coming back this evening.

To his good fortune, there was a home for sale two houses away and across the street from the target, so he pulled up in front and parked. A strange vehicle parked here for an extended length of time would not draw undue attention. There was a small plastic box attached to the sign with details on the home, so with some effort, he got out and took the available information flyer and returned to his car in case the authorities randomly came by and checked him out.

Lobo checked his watch. It was just before noon, and he had been parked for going on twenty minutes. There was quite a bit of traffic coming and going, but no one appeared to take any special interest in him. Nevertheless, he was conscious of how long he had been sitting. There was no car in the target's driveway and the garage door was closed, so there was no telling if the woman was home. There were two sidewalks leading away from the driveway, one to the front door and the other around the side of the house toward a backyard gate.

He was growing uncomfortable with the waiting and was about to drive off and circle the block and recheck the area when in his mirrors he saw a white minivan coming up the street. He glanced at the notes that Diaz had prepared, verifying that the target drove such a vehicle. He was in luck—it was her, as she slowly turned into the driveway and the garage door automatically opened. She pulled in but left the door open and clearly went into the house directly from the garage.

Lobo was a lucky man, and he knew it. You couldn't survive as long as he had doing his job and not have luck on your side; his present wound was such an example. Diaz had commented on how *unlucky* he was to have been shot when he told Diaz how he came to be wounded. But he didn't see it that way. Unlucky was to have the femur shattered and not be able to escape. Or worse, have the artery shot out and bleed to death where he fell. The random shot hadn't even knocked him down, as the panicked shooter was firing a nine-millimeter and not something heavier. No, despite Diaz's comment, he knew he had been lucky that day, and now he was lucky again.

He sat for ten more minutes, watching the house and the street. It was near lunchtime, and the neighborhood activity had slackened. He did not see the woman's two children as the minivan pulled in, but from Diaz's notes, he knew they were young, so they had to be there, he judged. He took the Sig out of the case and screwed in the suppressor and put it in his outside jacket pocket, then grabbed his Federal Police identification. What he liked about it was the large shiny gold badge; past experience proved that all he had to do was show the badge, and targets immediately allowed him to step close enough to control them without undue force. He started the car, slowly approached the house, pulled into the driveway, and parked as if he belonged or was expected. He got out and casually walked around the side of the house and slowly and quietly went in the gate, which to his surprise was unlocked.

The side and backyards were lush with blooming, well-kept shrubs and trees—all very attractive, but for Lobo, exactly the kind of visual screening from neighbors he required. For a large man he was light on his feet and naturally moved quietly, although less so with the limp. The backyard was mostly a swimming pool with decorative concrete decks all around, some lawn area, and then shrubs and trees against the six-foot-high perimeter wall for privacy. A covered patio extended from the rear of the house, and there was a wall of sliding glass doors leading to the interior.

Lying facedown on one of the lounge chairs near the pool was the woman. She was facing away from him, clad only in a very small bikini swimsuit and not wearing her top. He froze in place once he saw her as he came around the corner, and she clearly had not heard him, as she never moved. He carefully and quietly approached her, and still she did not move; it was as if she was dozing while sunning herself, oblivious to anything but the warm sun. He kept glancing all around as he approached, looking for the two children, but he didn't see or hear them. He took his Sig out as he got close—not to shoot, but merely to frighten and control her when the time came. He stood over her within touching distance for a full ten seconds, admiring her beauty, and then he dismissed the thought. He liked large women, and he hated rapists.

There was a large beach towel draped over the end of an adjacent lounge chair, so he picked it up and tossed it on her, startling her. She didn't scream or shriek—more like jumped and gasped—as she very quickly turned over, grabbing the towel and covering herself in the process. Lobo put his finger to his lips and calmly shushed her and then said in his decent but broken English, "Please, be silent. You will not be hurt if you do as I say and come inside with me now."

"Who, who, are you? What do you want?" Sherry spat out. From the look on her face, she was clearly frightened out of her mind.

Lobo took her by the elbow and helped her up as she struggled to keep her breasts covered with the towel.

"Get your swim top, please," Lobo said politely.

Sherry managed to grab her top and stay pretty much covered up as Lobo walked her onto the patio and through the sliding glass door leading to what was a large family room and dining area next to the open kitchen. "Please, dress yourself."

Sherry turned away from him and quickly put her top on but then picked up the towel and held it to her chest defensively once more. She was confused with the entire appearance and demeanor of the armed stranger, but not scared, as most others would be. He was too well dressed to be a thief, so she was pretty sure she was what he wanted, and she could survive a rape if that was what happened; she wouldn't fight it. She had grown up around guns, and of course in twelve years of marriage to Jack, there was always a handgun around the house; so the fact that the intruder had a gun was having less impact on her than it would on others.

She had learned Spanish as a second language over the years and was fluent. Switching to what she assumed was the intruder's native language, she asked, "Tell me what you want. My purse is on the table, but I don't have much cash, and I don't have anything else valuable. Just take what you came for and go, please."

She was standing within six or eight feet of him, and Lobo was impressed with her knowledge of his language and her courage. She was still startled and frightened, but not overly so.

"Ah, thank you," he said with a small smile in his deep but soft voice. "Your Spanish is so much better than my English, and we do not want any misunderstanding between us. Now, your children—where are they?"

Now he saw fear come to her eyes. "My...my children? What do you want with my children? They're not here, and I won't tell you where they are!" she said, her voice rising and breaking at the same time.

Lobo looked at her with what he thought of as his kind face. "I do not want to harm your children; I simply need to know where they are and that there will be no surprises. Now, where are your children?"

He could see she was still frightened, but there was also determination coming to her face—to be expected, he judged, by a mother protecting her own. "They're at a party, then a sleepover. They won't be back until tomorrow. Now tell me, what do you want? Why have you broken into my home? Why are you here?"

Sherry was finding her footing after being surprised by the intruder and was beginning to think, now that the initial fear and adrenaline rush was subsiding. Her intuition told her this wasn't rape, not after he told her to put her top on, but he was menacing looking despite the professional attire and the soft voice. What was really worrying her was that after weeks of flirtation, one of her lawyer bosses was coming by for a private swim party with her— or that had been the plan. She had not been intimate with anyone for months, and he definitely wanted her, and she was ready for him. A swim, some sex, and lunch afterward was her plan, and now it was all blown to hell with the stranger's presence. Her expectant lover was a real macho type, which she was attracted to for the potential sex it foretold, but not for the situation she was now in. She was very worried what might happen when he showed up, yet her instincts told her to keep quiet for the time being.

"I mean you no harm and will leave you as soon as you tell me what I need to know. You have a husband, a truck driver. I would like to know where he is."

Sherry was initially puzzled as to why anyone like this would want to know where Jack was, but as she thought about it, she knew he had crossed a lot of criminal types over the years, and it wasn't beyond the realm of possibility that someone had a past grudge. She really didn't like Jack at all, but neither did she want to give him up. "My ex-husband lives in Denver. Why don't you start there."

The intruder smiled at her, which she did not find comforting. "We both know that is no longer the case. He has moved to this area. We know this, and so do you. Now again, where is your husband?"

Sherry was more confused than ever. As far as she knew, Jack still lived in Denver, but there was the whole episode this morning concerning his changing his phone number. As she was thinking about that and what to say next, the man went on. "You are not good at deception. Your eyes betray you. We can keep this simple, just between us, or we wait until I have your children, and then you force me to make things more difficult. Now, where is your husband?"

Sherry was getting frightened again at the mention of her daughters and the incredibly calm and deliberate tone of the stranger. She was unsure what to say. Her mind was reeling when she suddenly saw her date, Josh, walk onto the patio. She had forgotten she'd told him she'd be at the pool and to come on back. The athletic-looking lawyer stopped immediately when his and Sherry's eyes locked. The anticipatory smile he was wearing at the thought of some afternoon romping with his very good-looking paralegal quickly vanished as he realized she was terrified, and there was a large man with a strange-looking handgun turning toward him.

Lobo was standing with his back to the patio door and did not see or hear her date silently walk up in his sweat suit and sneakers, but he did see her tense up and shift her eyes. Before she could say anything in warning, he spun around far more quickly than his size would have indicated possible just as the lawyer lunged at him through the open door.

For Lobo, everything about surviving his chosen work was founded on having good intelligence, good on-site reconnaissance, and total control of every situation. Rarely was he surprised as he now was. The leaping man gave him no choice, and he quickly fired a shot and then followed with a second. The moment he squeezed off the first round, a shoulder shot intended to wound and not kill—the last thing he wanted to do was kill her ex-husband if it was him attacking—he knew there was a chance it would miss. In a heartbeat, realizing the attacking man was not blond or tall enough, given the driver's license information Diaz had provided, Lobo aimed a second shot that caught the attacking man in the chest, and he collapsed facedown at Lobo's feet. Sherry started to scream. He stepped quickly to her, covered her mouth, and then pushed her into the nearby couch, where she sat breathing heavily.

Shit, he said to himself. He turned and quickly tried to judge the direction of the shot that had missed, checking for line-of-sight targets. His shot missed the attacker's shoulder just high, and unfortunately, the neighboring house to the rear was higher up the sloping hill. He knew there was a very good chance his miss had hit the house; no problem if there was no one home or the bullet struck some innocuous place, but dire trouble potentially if the neighbors were home and it struck nearby. That, and the woman had screamed. He knew he had to leave and leave now, and he also knew what he had to do with the woman. There was no taking her, not in broad daylight with so many neighbors out, and not with the possibility that the police could be responding to a reported gunshot. This was not Matamoros, where a gunshot or two was largely ignored; in a neighborhood such as this, the police would respond quickly.

He glanced first to Sherry, then looked down and shot the man at his feet in the back of his head to confirm the kill. He didn't like killing women, but she gave him no choice. Leaving a witness behind was not an option, and she was screaming again. He quickly aimed, right between her lovely breasts, and shot her, knowing from experience it was a kill shot and a second shot was not required. *What a waste*, he thought, shaking his head and then limping quickly for the door. *Such a fine body for a small woman.*

He moved quickly out the door and around the side of the house, pausing to check out the street from the screening landscaping before revealing himself. Seeing nothing unusual, he walked slowly to his car, got in, and started down the street, accelerating faster the farther he was from the scene. Diaz would not be happy, but he had been given no choice. He could not leave witnesses, and the unknown man had come out of nowhere. He had simply reacted, and in his current weakened state because of the leg wound, there was no fighting it out with the attacker. He had to shoot. Diaz would just have to get him some new information to follow up. There had to be more than one way to find the truck driver; surely he had other family or close friends. If he did, Diaz would identify them, and he would pay them a visit.

His mind was working rapidly, remembering possible escape routes, and he carelessly cut a corner at an intersection a block away too tightly and almost took the front off a red convertible. He swerved just in time and decided to make straight for the Burbank airport. He could be there in less than fifteen minutes and had the cash to buy a ticket on the very next flight out, whatever the cost and wherever it was going. There would be hundreds of cars in the airport parking lot, and his Town Car would be just one more; the gun he'd dispose of before he reached the terminal. With any luck, within an hour he would airborne and out of the city. He could then relax and decide on the best way to return to Mexico.

14

The Burbank Hills
Glendale, California
End of April; week six

Marsha Winston was in her kitchen rinsing off the kids' plates from lunch when Lobo's stray shot came through the high side of her kitchen window that overlooked her backyard and that of her lovely young neighbor, not that she could see anything more than her neighbor's roof with all the lush landscaping. There was a popping sound and glass shattering, and then the nine-millimeter parabellum slug blew her favorite copper stewing pot off its hook above the granite-covered kitchen island, creating a hell of a racket. Marsha was a crisis counselor at a women's shelter in one of the seedier parts of Reseda in the western part of the San Fernando Valley and no stranger to the occasional drive-by shooting by pissed-off boyfriends or husbands. She knew immediately that a gunshot had crashed through her kitchen. The kids, she knew, were either out front or downstairs playing Xbox, so she didn't panic, but she did duck down and grab her cell phone from her purse and punched in 911. The operator came on and asked her to state her emergency.

"Someone just shot out my kitchen window. We need help right now!" After giving the 911 operator her address, as requested, she stayed on the line but sat on the floor. She could hear her oldest daughter coming down the hall, obviously curious at the sound of copper pots hitting the floor, and Marsha yelled at her to stay down and get everyone in and downstairs.

Hours later, with police all over the neighborhood, her family safe, and with everything starting to get sorted out, the police were grateful to have such a cool, calm, knowledgeable eyewitness to talk with, but they were disappointed that she could shed little light on who had committed the gruesome double murder the police had discovered next door, or why. She said she thought she heard what could have been a scream but had not seen anything until her window shattered. The only potentially useful information she provided the investigating detectives was that her neighbor had two young daughters, both currently unaccounted for, and an ex-husband who showed up every other weekend from out of state for court-sanctioned visits. The investigating detective solemnly thanked Marsha and, after turning to his partner, raised an eyebrow and nodded. An ex-husband, a dead ex-wife in a skimpy swimsuit, and a new man, also dead but execution style—now that was a very promising lead. All they had to do was identify the ex, locate him, and most likely case solved. They'd seen it before.

⊷⊷ ⊶⊶

Earlier in the day, Jack had dropped the girls off at the swim party right at noon, met the birthday girl's parents, and then started for Sherry's place. She would hate it, him just showing up unannounced, but that was part of his tactics. It struck him as ironic as hell that in all his recent dealings with his ex-wife, he thought in military terms, similar to those he had used in the badlands as a sniper with his spotter. It was all strategy, planning, and tactics, and then reacting to the inevitable changing dynamics. A hell of a way to have to deal with someone you spent twelve years with and thought you loved.

He was thinking about how he was going to start their conversation when a speeding silver Town Car almost nailed him as he was approaching the turn to the street that led to Sherry's street. The driver of the Lincoln was so close he could almost reach out and grab him as he swerved from right to left around the front of Jack's rental. He instinctively took in the driver's appearance as he was stomping on the brakes, making a mental picture of the face out of habit as the large Town Car sped off down the street.

A little flustered with the near wreck, he pulled to a stop in front of her house, grateful to see the garage door open and her van there. She was in. That was perfect—he was feeling very determined about having the girls spend some extended time with him on the boat during the upcoming summer break. Sherry would be flabbergasted to learn that he was living on a fabulous sailboat in the Caribbean and ostensibly running a business; he could hear her already, saying how "unlike" him that was. This was his third trip to LA since leaving Denver, and he had not yet said anything, as their typical conversations were short and not all that civil, with him usually just standing at her front door. It had occurred to him during the last several years of their marriage that Sherry thought he was boring and uninteresting, given that she considered the jobs he chose to do mundane. She had zero appreciation for what police officers did; to her he seemed to always be slogging his way through reports and interviews, slowly piecing a case together and then finally making an unclimactic arrest with nothing more to show for the long hours away from the family than a pat on the back. With Maddy now on his mind more than ever, he really didn't give a shit what she thought, but a small part of him wanted to see her reaction to his recent changes. He was only human, and he was sure it would bother the hell out of her.

He rang the bell a couple of times, but there was no answer, and the door was locked. He figured she was out by the pool her daddy had insisted on having built for her, and he walked around the side, noticing the gate was already open. As he cleared the corner, he could see she wasn't around the pool, so he headed for the patio. He was under the patio roof and had taken a couple of steps toward the open sliding glass door when he froze, an icy ball forming in his gut. He smelled the very familiar acrid odor of gunshots before he saw the feet of the man lying on the floor just inside the door. The body was still but had an unnatural twist to it that he immediately knew was the result of horrible violence.

He intuitively started looking around, especially at the patio deck, glancing for evidence, and could clearly see several large partial bloody shoe prints leading away from the open door. That explained the open gate, he thought. Whoever had done this was gone, and in a hell of a hurry, no doubt, and careless.

His heart was pounding in his chest as he carefully walked around the bloody prints and stepped inside, and then it sank completely as he saw Sherry on the couch, head thrown back, eyes open, with an obvious fatal chest wound. The carpeting was a mess from the unknown man's wounds; whoever shot him did so at least twice from close range, the head shot execution style. He reached Sherry and realized tears were beginning to run down his cheeks. He checked her pulse. She was still warm but quite dead; the murders had happened within the last five or ten minutes, he judged.

He stood there, his head hanging, trying to suppress a sob, when a cold realization suddenly came to him that these murders were likely not random violence. Someone was looking for him. And then he thought of his daughters. The sudden adrenaline rush made him light headed, and nausea was coming on him fast. He had to get out and get to them before whoever had done this found them and did more. And he wondered if Sherry had told the killer where the girls were if it was him they were really after. He dismissed the thought as quickly as it occurred to him, ashamed and knowing better. Sherry may have hated him, but she loved the girls.

He managed to make it to the lawn without disturbing the obvious evidence before dropping to his knees and vomiting up his breakfast. He started to shake like never before, then staggered up and made his way to his car, wiping the spittle from his face as he did. He fumbled with the key for several seconds because of the shaking, then finally inserted it, glanced quickly around, and accelerated away from the curb. When he got to the next street, he barely stopped at the stop sign before gunning the ragtop Mustang around the corner and down the street.

That was when it hit him like a cold splash of water: *silver Town Car, silver Town Car,* the reckless silver Town Car. He realized it was likely he had seen the killer leaving the scene. That was why the guy was driving so fast and almost nailed him. Was it Diaz? If not, certainly someone who worked for him, as the face he'd made a mental picture of was a menacing-looking one and Hispanic. Something about the man—the darkness in his face, his size—screamed killer to Jack.

He throttled back the Mustang and started breathing closer to normal. He had to think. He couldn't get involved with an investigation—not if it was about the money. But he had to report to the local cops somehow what he knew, and quickly. But first he had to secure the girls, and then get them out of town, and fast. He kept breathing big, slow breaths to get his emotions and his body under control and clear his mind. If it was Diaz looking for him and not just a random and tragic coincidence, Diaz didn't know where to look. Why else had he been at Sherry's? Henry's continued insistence that he keep his profile low had evidently been necessary, but how did they find him? How in the hell did they zero in on him? He would think more about that one later.

He pulled up in front of the large home where the birthday party was being held and got out, straightening out his appearance as he walked to the door. The amiable father of the birthday girl answered the door and smiled at him. It had been less than thirty minutes since Jack had met him, dropped the girls off, and said his goodbyes.

"Jack, hi. Did you forget something?"

Jack tried to put a smile on his face but was certain it came off as forced. "Sorry to barge in like this, Ted, but I need to get my girls. There's been an… ah, an accident, with their mom, and regrettably we have to go, and quickly. I don't want to upset them or the party, and I no doubt will if I go out there. Could I get you to quietly go tell my girls there's a surprise for them inside and bring them here?"

"Jesus, Jack. Sure. I'm sorry to hear that; I hope it's not serious."

"Unfortunately, it is. I want to tell you more, Ted; I do, but I have to get the girls and go now."

"Sure, Jack, sure," the now very concerned father said. "Wait here. I'll be right back, and I promise, no fuss."

Jack had the girls' backpacks in the car. The plan had been to come back at four, have the girls change, and then leave for the hotel. A minute later they came rapidly tiptoeing into the living room wrapped in towels, big smiles on their faces at the expectation of some supersecret surprise.

"Daddy, Daddy," they squealed. "What's the surprise? What's the surprise?"

"Come on, you little monsters, and I'll show you," Jack said, his plastic smile still plastered across his face. "But first get in the car."

They seemed to be totally oblivious to the party they were leaving, focused entirely on his surprise. As the girls sprinted for the Mustang, Jack turned to Ted. "Ted, I can't tell you more about the accident, but I want you to know this: I just discovered it; I was not involved."

"I'm afraid I don't understand you, Jack. What are you saying?"

"You will, Ted, in time. Just remember what I said."

Jack went to the car, leaving the concerned and confused Ted standing in his doorway. After getting both girls seat belted into the front seat together, he started for the hotel, explaining what was in store for them, making the new lie up on the fly. He told them that he and mom had talked it over, and she wanted them to start their spring break a couple of weeks early, and the bigger surprise was, they were going to the airport and take a big jet on a long flight. He didn't have to say another word after mentioning the jet; they had only flown a couple of times in the last few years, to visit Sherry's parents in North Carolina, and it was always a special thrill for them.

They got to the hotel, changed, packed, and checked out in less than thirty minutes. It was now nearing two o'clock and the traffic for a Saturday not horrible, so they made LAX in another thirty. Jack had flown into LA on Virgin America, whose gates were in terminal three, so he took the rental car shuttle there, thinking that was as good a place as any to start looking for a flight. While on the shuttle, he decided on Orlando as their destination. Henry's warnings to stay off the grid were ringing in his ears, and until he could talk to him and get some perspective and advice, the last thing he wanted to do was potentially give Diaz a trail back to the Bahamas.

A very nice ticket agent for Virgin found him the next available flight to Orlando, an American flight leaving at three thirty from terminal four. A call over to the competitor confirmed there were three first-class seats available and that they would hold them for Jack until he got to their counter. After another short shuttle ride, Jack found the right agent and purchased the three incredibly expensive seats to Orlando with his company credit card after feeding the young agent a fascinating bullshit story about how he and the girls had suddenly decided to take a surprise quick trip to Disneyworld. He was watching the agent closely, worried the lie might raise undue suspicion, but this was LA; the young man had heard everything imaginable from the rich and famous who abounded in the area, and he found nothing the least bit unusual about the story as he processed the tickets. He was used to stupid people with too much money doing lots of ridiculous things. Jack was just one more.

They had about forty minutes before boarding; there was a Burger King near their gate and the girls were hungry, so they stopped in, and he bought them some lunch. They were happily sitting in their booth eating away when he got up, telling them he had to make a call to make sure their hotel in Disneyworld was all set up. They hardly noticed him leaving, so excited and engrossed were they in their animated conversation with each other, as he walked a few steps away to a relatively quiet spot near the entrance and called Henry. Henry's cell phone number was speed dial 1 on his new phone, and he answered on the first ring. "Jackson. How's California?"

"Sherry's dead, Henry. Dead. Shot. She and a male friend."

"What…what the hell? Say that again, Jack. Shot? Did I hear you right?"

"Yeah, Hank, shot. And it's all my goddamn fault. My fault."

A sudden sob came over Jack as he looked down and put his hand to his face, making sure the girls couldn't see him. "I as good as killed Sherry myself, Hank. I'm a fucking fool."

"Easy, Jack. Easy, pal. You don't know that. This could be just a horrible coincidence. Tell me what happened."

Jack took several deep breaths again, trying to hold it together. "You know as well as I do, Hank, this is no fucking coincidence. Somehow, that Diaz guy has found me—only not me, but a trail to me. Not knowing where I was hiding my worthless ass, he went after Sherry to get to me, and now she's dead." Jack's voice dropped almost to a whisper. "What do I tell my babies, Hank? How do I tell them something like this?"

A flight announcement came over the terminal sound system, loud enough for Henry to pick up in the background. "Jack, are you at the airport? What the fuck are you doing there?"

Jack tried clearing his throat. It felt tight. "What do you think, Henry? I'm getting lost, as fast as I can. I have to get the girls somewhere safe."

There was a long pause before Henry went on. "Jack, start from the beginning and tell me what happened and what you have done so far. And Jack, I need you to get your shit together and be clear and accurate."

Jack took several deep breaths again and settled down some with the help of the small rebuke from Henry. He told him everything in great detail, including what he had seen at the crime scene and a description of who he thought might be the killer and why. When he finished, there was silence on the other end as Henry was deciding what to say next, so Jack told him he was booked on the next flight to Orlando and asked him get him a rental car and a decent hotel where he could hide and figure out what to do next.

Henry finally spoke, clearly upset with the entire situation, but said he would. There was another pause, and then he said, "Jack, I'm contacting the Burbank police on your behalf with your eyewitness account and then telling them you grabbed the girls and split town for their safety."

"Jesus, Hank, I know it has to be done. I'm certain I saw the killer, but wait until we leave. If I were them, I'd consider me the prime suspect. I can see the reasoning: ex-husband, unhappy about losing the custody fight, kills wife and her new boyfriend and then skips town with the kids."

"Yeah, Jack, that's exactly what they'll think at first, but given your description of the crime scene, there's some decent evidence. Also, you've had a lot of run-ins with bad guys over the years. I'll tell them this is possible payback of some kind; there's some truth to that. When's your flight?"

"About thirty minutes. The girls are finishing their lunch; I'm about to grab them and head to the gate."

"I won't call for another hour. What size shoe do you wear?"

"My shoe size? What the fuck, Henry? A twelve medium. Why?"

"Think about it, Jack. Let's hope the bloody footprints you saw are not twelves."

"Oh, Christ, I'm sorry, Hank. I'm not thinking straight. The way my day's going, they'll probably match my Nikes to a tee."

"Don't say that kind of shit, Jack. And starting right now, I need you thinking clearly. Now, is there anything else I can do for you?"

"Yeah…yeah, there is. Somewhere Sherry has passports for the kids. Her parents took them all on that cruise last winter. If I take them into the Bahamas with me, they'll need them, won't they?"

"Not sure, Jack, but I'm thinking no. They'd be accompanied minors. But forget that. Do you want me to go out and get them?"

"Can you?"

There was another pause, and Jack knew Henry was thinking about something. "Yeah, I can. As a matter of fact, I was already thinking that going out there as your attorney and working with the cops would be a good idea, what with you gone. I'll get them looking for your big Mexican in the Town Car and then get to LA as soon as possible tonight. You take care of yourself and your girls for now, and I'll handle the rest. Check your phone for messages when you land. I'll have the hotel and car information by then."

Henry could hear Jack exhale a long, deep breath. "You didn't answer my earlier question, Hank. What do I say to my little girls? How do I tell them I killed their mother?"

Henry was as heartbroken as Jack was, and there was great emotion in his voice when he answered. "Stop it, Jack. Quit saying that. Don't tell them a thing—not yet, anyway. Give it some time, a lot of it, before you tell them their mother's gone. And if it were me, Jack, I'd never tell them why, other than to say there are evil people out there, and they do evil things. Let's get past the next forty-eight or seventy-two hours OK; let the dust settle a little bit. If Sherry didn't know anything about your life changes, this Diaz knows less now than he did, if he has indeed identified you. Your trail is clear, Jack, is what I'm saying."

There was more silence as Jack was thinking about what Henry had said. "Maybe, Hank, maybe, but they found me once. I'm sure of it, and I thought that would be impossible. I'll call later tonight. I'll never sleep until I hear from you what the local cops are thinking. You have to get them to focus on the Town Car, have them check on rentals at all the area airports. If the guy I saw was Diaz or someone working for him, he's from down south. He had to fly in, and I'm guessing he rented. Don't tell them why I think they should look for rentals, but tell them. I agree, Diaz probably doesn't know where I am. Sherry didn't know yet; that's what I was doing when I found her, going back to tell her. But it looks like he does know who I am and wanted to use her to get to me. Why he killed her makes no sense at all. Another thing, Hank: if this Diaz guy knows about Sherry, he probably knows about you and my parents. I want security on all of you. I'll cover the cost, but watch your ass."

Henry sighed. "You're right, Jack. Good idea. I'll take care of all of that. I know people, reliable people. Now settle down, and get to Florida. Let me handle things here and in California."

"I don't know what else to say, Henry. Thanks."

The flight to Orlando was long but smooth, with plenty for the girls to eat and movies to watch on their individual monitors until they fell asleep for the last several hours. It was near 11:00 p.m. eastern by the time they landed and midnight by the time they reached their very upscale extended-stay hotel near Disneyworld. The girls barely woke up during check-in, exhausted from all the excitement of the day. He got them into their apartment-like room, changed them, and tucked them into bed. Then he closed the door between the small living room and the bedroom and called Henry.

It was going on seven hours since they had last spoken, and Henry answered on the first ring and updated him. The chief of detectives was very unhappy when he first talked with him and told him whom he represented, but they settled down some when he passed on the description of the car and the driver Jack had seen leaving the area. As expected, he was their top suspect for most of the day until a trace of the few silver Lincoln Town Cars rented revealed one picked up at LAX earlier this morning and then found parked illegally in a handicap spot out at the Burbank airport. The individual renting used Mexican identification—that fact was confirmed—which might mean something, given that Jack was an old vice cop, and they had trace blood evidence on the floor mat of the Lincoln. A check of the airport security tapes gave them a Hispanic-looking individual matching Jack's general description buying a ticket for Salt Lake City on a Delta flight thirty minutes after the time of the shooting, which just happened to be the very first flight out when the cops factored in the time to reach the airport from the scene. And they had the gun. The bright young detective sent to Burbank by his chief to look for silver Lincolns got it in his head that the killer might have dumped the gun between the car and the terminal; a check of the three or four trash bins on the way got them the weapon.

"That's great news, Henry. So am I off the hook?"

"Yeah, now you are. They'd like you back for an official statement, but I nixed that. Told them we would get them what they need, all proper and legal, but under no circumstances were you bringing your daughters back until they got the killers. The chief of detectives is a father, Jack, and seems to be a good cop. He's read your file and appears to be getting on board the Jack bandwagon. For what it's worth, he told me he thought you got screwed last year. Your sharp observations got them the car and the weapon, and now the tape on the shooter. You're clear."

Jack exhaled a deep breath. "Thank God, Hank. Tell me about the weapon. Any evidence, prints, that sort of thing? Also, did they think to check the trash for documents or other evidence?"

"Jesus, Jack, you don't ever let up, do, you? Once a cop, always a cop... Christ, I don't know; I doubt it. The chief told me privately it was a cold piece, no serial number, and equipped with an illegal suppressor. Four shots fired. The gun won't help, and only you and I know where it came from. It was probably one of thousands the cartel keeps in their armory. Tomorrow the locals let me into the house, and I'll go through it for anything concerning the girls and send you the passports and whatever else I think you need."

There was a moment of silence, and then Henry went on. "Ah...listen, I spoke with Sherry's father and let him know what happened. I know he's an asshole, but he is her father. I felt like I had to tell him on your behalf. He's on his way out, and as if it was possible, you're even deeper on his shit list now. I told him that it appeared to be a random act of violence, most likely having to do with some case at the law practice where they both worked, but the fact that you took the girls and split has him really pissed off. He may make some custody noise, but I'm telling you, Jack, that's all it is—just noise. The wills are clear; you now have full custody. I'm speculating here, but given what you've told me about their social standing in the community, my guess is they'll have a big, splashy funeral for Sherry in Jacksonville within a week or so. Don't even think about going, Jack, OK?"

There was nothing but silence on the phone for a long few seconds, and then Jack said, "Yeah, I understand. I'll stay away. I wouldn't want to take the girls anywhere near their grandparents now anyway, and I can't just leave them here."

"Good. Sit tight for now. Under the circumstances, I know this may sound ridiculous, but you're in Orlando with your kids. Try to have a good time. I'll call you if anything comes up."

"What about the security for you and my parents?"

"It's a done deal, Jack. Real pros. We've used the agency before, rotating two-man teams on a twenty-four-hour basis. I'm using cash from my other safe deposit box to cover the cost, and there's plenty."

"It's all my responsibility, Henry. I'll transfer what I have in the Bahamas to the account in Florida as soon as I get back, or even fly a bunch up with me."

"Don't, Jack. I have all I need. We'll settle all that sometime way in the future. Just start working on getting your life back together with the girls."

There was a long pause before Jack said anything, and then his voice was barely above a whisper again. "I met a woman, Henry...in Freeport. I saw a glimpse of heaven through her I thought didn't exist for me. I saw hope; now this. I'm right back in hell, Henry, a hell I created...it's all my fault...it's all my fault..."

Henry became emotional as well, hearing the deep despair in his friend's voice. "Don't go there, Jack, please. What's done is done. You have to stay strong. Diaz is still out there, and you have a lot to protect. I'll try to figure out a way to get the information on this Diaz to the authorities anonymously somehow so you're not implicated. Maybe enough gets to the Mexicans so they can clean up their own goddamn house. You just stay out of sight and take care of your family. You'll make it through this, Jack. I swear."

Henry paused. There was nothing but silence on the other end, but he knew Jack was still there, fighting not to lose it. "Listen, my friend, there was a philosopher I read in college, a German named Nietzsche. What you just said made me think of something he wrote a long time ago. He said, 'Everyone who has ever built anywhere a new heaven, first found the power thereto in his own hell.' You've seen the hell, Jack. It doesn't get any worse. Now you have to find the power, the strength, to build that heaven you touched."

Henry could hear Jack breathing on the other end and listened until Jack finally said, "Thanks, Hank, for everything. Ah…listen…I've…ah…got to go check on the girls. Sorry to be such a mess. I swear I'll move on. See you."

Jack cut off the connection before Henry could say anything more, but Henry knew that he had broken down again. He hated what his friend was going through. And for his part in facilitating the whole scheme that had led to this tragedy, he deeply regretted not talking Jack out of keeping the cartel's money. That would be his own cross to bear. He wasn't Orthodox, but he did consider himself deeply religious, but at this moment, he could not understand a God that could hurt his friend as deeply as he had.

After hanging up, Jack sat unmoving on the couch for an hour, thinking. When he finally did move, he knew what he had to do, and Henry could not be a part of it. How to do what was necessary would take some time to figure out, but he knew what the first steps were. He dialed Maddy's number, and she answered on the second ring, very happy to hear from him, even at so late an hour. He slowly gave her an abridged version of the events of the long, horrible day, telling her the murders could be random, but also it was possible that one of the many real bad guys he had put away as a detective was tragically coming back to haunt him. He asked her if she would she come to Orlando, and she immediately agreed.

"Maddy, listen, and do as I ask, OK? I know you have to arrange for someone to cover for you at the bar. Tell Robbie that you have a family emergency and need a few days, maybe a week, on the mainland. Don't say anything more. OK?"

He sensed a slight pause, and then she said, "Sure, Jack, OK. Whatever you want." She had a good intuition about people, and she could tell there was more to Jack's troubles than he was letting on. But she trusted him and would do as he asked.

"I'll arrange all the flights first thing, Maddy. All you'll need to do is pack a bag and get to the airport. As soon as I know the flights, I'll call. I want you to meet my daughters and for them to meet you."

Jack didn't know it, but considering the circumstances, that was the nicest thing he could have said to her. She loved children, and a long time ago she had been heartbroken at the prospect of not being able to have any of her own, a victim since birth of her own physiology. Now that Jack had custody of his two young daughters, they would be living with him; she started to think about what that could mean as their relationship developed and how she might well be inheriting two daughters of her own. She stopped herself from thinking any more about it. After all, she had just met him, but despite the terrible news and her sense that Jack wasn't telling her the entire story for some reason, she went back to sleep with a very warm feeling inside.

Jack hung up and scrolled down through the few contacts on his new phone until he found the next number he needed to call. It was late, but Master Gunnery Sergeant Fred "Armie" Armbruster would take his call, no matter the hour. The phone rang four or five times before he heard his old sniper platoon sergeant and spotter's gruff voice. "What! There better be a fucking war."

"Master Gunny…it's Jack. Sorry to rattle your cage so late."

"Jack…Jack? Is that really you, shooter?"

"Yeah. Listen, partner, sorry to call out of the blue and in the middle of the night, but I've got troubles, bad troubles, and I need to see you. I'm in Florida and will be in Jacksonville in four or five days. Can I stay at your place on the down low?"

Armie was wide awake now, and Jack could hear him coughing and fumbling around for a smoke. In all the years he had known him, other than when they were hidden out in some tight spot in the badlands, Armie always had a smoke going. Jack always considered it a miracle his old spotter wasn't long since dead, another casualty from lung cancer.

"Jesus, Jack. More goddamn trouble? When the hell is this fucking world gonna lighten up and cut you some fucking slack?"

Jack was sitting slumped over on the couch, his eyes closed, rubbing his forehead at the growing headache he was feeling. Quietly he said, "I guess never, Armie. I need a friend, and I don't want anyone else to know I'm in town. Can I come up?"

"You know you can, shooter. Only I've moved since you were last here. Got tired of the fucking townies, so I'm living in the sticks out west, a lot quieter and plenty of shootin' room. Call me when you get to town, and we'll hook up someplace where no one knows you, and I'll lead you out. Gonna tell me what this is all about?"

"When I see you, Armie. Not over the phone…but it's huntin' season."

The line went dead quiet; Armie was the one who came up with the term "huntin' season" to describe their shoot-to-kill missions in Iraq and Afghanistan. Finally, now very serious, he said, "For fucking real, shooter?"

"For fucking real, Armie. I know I'm asking a lot, and I'll owe you big time, but you'll understand when we talk."

"Forget it. you don't owe me shit. Get your ass up here, and shooter, semper fucking fi."

Two thousand miles away in Las Vegas, Adolpho Lobo saw the flashing pink neon vacancy sign and pulled into the parking lot of the cheap motel. He limped to the office and checked in, paying with cash, and then went straight to his room and lay down. He was four blocks off the strip, and the area, while run down, was quiet and a part of town he was familiar with. The first flight out of Burbank had landed him in Salt Lake City, which was inconvenient, but it had him out of LA in under sixty minutes from the time of the shootings. He rented a large GMC Yukon with his third ID and headed south on I-15 toward Vegas. The normally six-and-a-half-hour drive took him ten, as he had to stop twice at rest stops and elevate his leg for extended periods. The swelling and pain were getting worse, and he needed to get back to Matamoros as fast as safety would allow and have Diaz's old addict of a doctor fix him up again. The drive was long and painful, but he knew it effectively killed his trail if by some misfortune the authorities were on to him.

Tomorrow he would park the SUV on the street nearby and take a cab to the airport; it would be days before anyone realized it was an abandoned rental. By the time anyone spotted it, he'd be long gone—there were plenty of possible destinations and flights to get him back to Mexico by tomorrow night. Diaz would not like his report, but he knew he would accept it. The one thing he could count on after all their years together was Diaz's acceptance that whatever action he was forced to take on an assignment was necessary. Diaz was brilliant; it wouldn't take him long to find another way to the truck driver, and when he did, he would finish the job.

15

Armie Armbruster's house
Rural North Carolina
Early May; week seven

Jack knew at twenty years old, after his first sniper deployment in Afghanistan, that it just wasn't in his makeup to kill people. Months of shooting at target silhouettes and attending lectures intended to prepare him psychologically for what he was going to be doing simply did not work in his case. He understood the live targets he was assigned were an enemy, some of them maybe even evil, and perhaps he would have been bothered less in a straight-up firefight, but they weren't straight up. He shot and killed target after target, some days ten or twenty men, from an average of five hundred yards or better, a quarter of a mile. The dead didn't hear his weapon, let alone see him, and had no idea as they were squatting before a campfire fixing their tea or smoking and talking with a friend that they were being acquired through his sophisticated optical scope. He watched them, waiting, and then, when the moment presented itself, ended them, the telltale pink mist his confirmation. If not for his spotter, the older and far tougher career marine Armie Armbruster, he would never have survived his first tour nor done two more.

Armie got him past his deep feelings by appealing to his patriotism and convincing him he was a machine, and a valuable and necessary one at that. "Leave the emotions back home, shooter," Armie would say. "Out here in the badlands, you have to be a machine with a heart of stone, or the bad guys win and we both die." So that was what he did—for four years and three tours, be the killing machine that his natural abilities and his corps training made him. That was until he was thinking about it so much in his downtime that he wasn't sleeping well, and then there were the long periods of silence, broken only by Sherry's constant complaining about his overseas tours. The time came when he had to finally face up to his personal feelings and the reality that he was a marine who wasn't cut out to kill. He had to get out and serve the corps in some other capacity, and his old friend, mentor, and spotter had understood, as only a true friend would. Armie said what he thought about Jack's decision only once in front of others, when at Jack's last platoon muster the day he transferred out, Armie shook his head and disappointedly said that Jack's leaving was the biggest waste of the best shootin' talent he ever saw.

The drive north to Jacksonville gave him needed solitude after four semi-wonderful days with Maddy and the kids to begin the process of corralling his emotions for what needed to be done. With the awful guilt from Sherry's death still haunting him, it was impossible to enjoy their time together, but he tried, putting up a believable false front around them. He so very badly wanted to tell Maddy the truth, but he desperately needed her help and was afraid, almost certain, that despite the strong feelings she clearly had for him, the terrible truth surrounding the money and the cartel's horrible response would kill all feelings she had for him forever, and he could not risk that, not now.

Following their brief vacation together in Orlando, he drove Maddy and the girls south to Fort Lauderdale and the airport there, and she and the girls were now safely back in Freeport. Always true to his word, Henry had overnighted a package of documents to him with the girls' passports included, and she was carrying those with her as well.

After saying goodbye to them at the airport, he first drove to the secure facility where the other half of the money was stored. His storage space was listed as a numbered account, accessed by entering an eight-digit unit identification into a keypad at the front desk with the facility's rent-a-cop watching. Once he had passed through security to the warehouse, there was an electronic keypad to access his specific unit, which required a second eight-digit code. Alone inside the small, dark space, he opened the nearest box, labeled Tax Records 2005, took out $250,000, placed the wrapped packs of cash in the duffel bag he brought with him, and left. He next dropped off the rental and took a cab to the RV storage lot where his camper was parked. He called ahead, and the lot attendants had the RV ready for him. After thanking and dismissing the attendants, he put the cash in one of the drawers beneath the bed and headed for Jacksonville. He told Maddy another lie when he said he had to go to his ex-wife's funeral and confront her parents about their threat regarding custody. He did stop by the funeral, though he skipped the service and only watched the interment from a distance, careful not to be seen, for he was in North Carolina for far different reasons.

He couldn't hear the graveside service from the small collection of moss-covered oaks near Sherry's grave. He watched, thinking how much he hated himself for her death and the liar he had become since discovering the money. He had never lied before that—not since he was a small child, and even then, he didn't do it much. But since the night of the wreck, starting with the state trooper, the lies had been pouring out of him at the drop of a hat whenever needed, all convincing, and all seemingly innocent enough. All because he had been weak and desperate following the trial and the dismissal from the force, and then the divorce and Sherry's taking the kids away. He knew now he had foolishly and impulsively acted on the discovery of the dirty cash, being so cocksure at the time that there was no way for the cartel to discover him. Not once did he really consider the potential repercussions if they did, and never, never did he weigh the potential devastating consequences if he was wrong. And was he ever wrong.

He told Maddy he wasn't sure when he would get back to Freeport, telling her after the funeral he had to fly to Denver and meet with his lawyer on both estate and business issues, another lie that had flowed easily off his tongue. She simply kissed him and told him not to worry about it. "I'm thirty-eight, Jack," she had said. "I think I can handle my job and two little girls at the same time. Take whatever time you need." With that he was planning, he really had no idea how long it would take. There were still so many unknowns, so much beyond his control, but several weeks was his best guess.

He called Armie from the cemetery after everyone left and he had placed the bouquet he was carrying on Sherry's grave. She had long since extinguished the love he once had for her, but she was still a part of so many of his early-adult memories. There would never come a time when he looked at one of his daughters and not see something of Sherry in them, her eyes in Abbey, the shape of her nose in Molly.

Armie had told him to pass through town on Highway 17 until he saw the Waffle House on the north side at Western Boulevard, then turn left and take it west. Two miles up there was a family-run convenience store and gas station on the right; that was where they'd meet. Armie said he would lead him to the house from there.

Forty minutes later he was sitting in Armie's rustic and comfortable kitchen, at his beat-up old kitchen table with a cold can of beer in front of him. Armie had had a dozen live-in girlfriends down through the years but had never married, and he was currently single again. He was fussing around the kitchen fixing them up some snacks, all the while telling Jack for maybe the thousandth time how their beloved corps was going to hell in a handbasket because the frigging brass didn't listen to him as often as they should. When finally finished with his scrounging, he produced a bowl of potato chips and some venison jerky he'd made himself, sat down, and lit a cigarette.

He stared at Jack through the wafting blue smoke for a long several seconds and then said, "OK, shooter, let's have it. Why is it huntin' season, and who the fuck do you want to shoot?"

Armie had been his best friend since he was nineteen, when he joined Armie's recon platoon and became his shooter. Armie saved his life twice in the badlands, and that was no bullshit. He wouldn't lie to him; he owed him far too much for that. He slowly told him the entire truth, witnessing the wreck, discovering the money, the plan worked out with Henry, and everything else that came after in great detail, right up to the present moment. He also told him what he wanted to do.

Armie blinked hard at the mention of the money but never said a word until Jack was through. He was on about his fourth cigarette, lighting the next one from the nearly spent previous one. He stubbed out his cigarette in the brass 20 mm shell casing a pal in the division machine shop had crafted into an ashtray for him before he finally spoke. "So…let me see if I got this straight. You're going to up and drive on down to Mexico, a country you have never been to and know fuckin' nothin' about, and somehow, based on the few shitty pieces of intel you managed to scrounge from the glove box of that fuckin' van, find and kill a big-time drug trafficker and his hired killer. Is that it?"

Jack looked at his old friend and then nodded his head. "Yeah, Armie, that's it. I have to. Only I need a weapon, and what I need I can't get anywhere except from your armory. I need my old M24 or the nearest thing to it, and some ammo. I also need something for close-in shooting just in case—small and light, but big magazine, high rate of fire, and a suppressor if possible. If I find them, I will likely need to do a detailed reconnoiter close in undetected, maybe set some wind streamers, and I need to be able to shoot my way out of a jam if I'm spotted. I also need some help creating hidden spaces in the camper so I can get past the border and back with the weapons and ammo. You're the division armorer master gunny; you're the only one who can get what I need and keep it quiet. If I'm asking too much here, just say so. If I have to, I'll buy me a new Remington 700 with one of the new tactical optic systems. But I have a lot to live for. I've been a fool, but I'm not foolish or suicidal. I need to kill these sons of bitches and survive this for my girls, especially now with their mother dead, and that means a long-range shot with absolutely certain results. I get one chance at this—one chance for tactical surprise, which means my M24."

Armie had lit a new cigarette as Jack was talking, the smoke fouling the air; he was sitting with his elbows on the table, his hands clasped together in front of him, his chin on his hands, listening carefully and looking at Jack. Finally he casually flicked his ashes into his ashtray and said, "Well, looks like I can stop worrying about my fucking pension being enough to live on." Then he smiled and took another drag.

Jack was watching Armie closely, expecting him to say something serious; probably an attempt to go along, or even an attempt to try to talk him out of it, but he hadn't expected the crack about his pension. He couldn't help himself; he laughed. It had to be the stress and tension of the last week, but Jack laughed until tears were streaming down his face and he couldn't catch his breath. Armie got up and walked to a cupboard and grabbed a bottle of Jack Daniels from a shelf. Good old JD—an old friend, Armie would often say, and his whiskey of choice.

He brought it back to the table and set it in front of Jack then sat back down. "Take a belt, shooter. You need to de-stress."

Jack did as he was told and the moment was over, but he was grateful. "Sorry, Gunny. I'm fucked up right now but working on getting my shit together."

Armie was lighting up another cigarette. He took a long drag and then shook his head slowly and said, "Anybody in your boots would be fucked up, shooter. You're a man, and a goddamned decent one, not a fucking fence post. Relax, and let's talk this through. First things first. I got me thirty days of unused leave on the books. So how soon after I get us some first-class hardware do we leave?"

Jack raised his hand. "There can be no *we*, Armie. This has to be a one-man show. I've messed up enough lives as it is. You're staying here. Thanks, but end of discussion."

Armie smiled at him again. "Ah, ain't you sweet, being all protective and everything. Next thing you know, you'll be wantin' to take warm showers together. Now, when do we go?"

Jack shook his head; he had known when he was driving up this would be the hardest part, convincing Armie he had to stay put. "Please, Armie, don't fight me on this. I go alone. I'll listen to anything you want to say about the mission. I want your input. I need it if I'm to survive this, but you stay."

Armie leaned back in his chair, eyeballing Jack, and then he leaned forward, took a healthy pull of JD, swallowed, and said, "I ain't promisin' you'll have the last word on this, but let's talk mission. When do you go and where? Give me a general overview and your idea of a plan."

Jack did as instructed, for under the gruff, foul-mouthed, country-hick exterior was a pure tactical genius with years of combat experience. Jack told him he had researched possible touristy reasons to go to the Mexican Gulf Coast and discovered some bird-shooting resorts south of Matamoros on the coast that he could reserve a spot for. Going to Mexico to hunt at one of their popular resorts would give him the cover and documentation he needed to be in Mexico if for any reason the authorities took an interest in him. He told him about the evidence he had taken from the van, the maps and the location of the beach house Diaz supposedly operated out of. There was a popular public beach on the Gulf about five miles north and east of the house. From the internet aerials, it looked as if many people camped out at the beach; there would be lots of overnight vehicles, and his RV would be just another one. He said the aerials online gave him the general lay of the land, and he would develop his plan in greater detail once he was on the ground in the area and completed a detailed reconnaissance.

Armie was slowly shaking his head. "Not good enough, shooter. Intel's too thin. We'll get you more. I've got a buddy, Gunny at Division Intelligence, owes me big time. I can get you hi-res aerials and decent topo maps, for starters. Military birds have been helpin' out drug enforcement for years. I'm bettin' none of the general overhead stuff near our southern border is classified, so we'll get it."

Jack had a concerned look on his face. "What do you have to tell him? How do we keep this quiet?"

"Don't worry about it; I own the fat bastard. I got more shit on him that would see him in the brig and run out of the corps than you can list. He's got alimony payments up the ass and needs to get his thirty in, so he'll play ball. I'll tell him I got an old pal who wants me to invest in a potential land deal on the Gulf Coast or some such shit, and I want to check it out. We'll get what we need, no questions asked. Once you're through with whatever I give you, fucking burn it, and it never existed.

"Next, you ain't going to Mexico with no fucking Remington 700—or an M24, which, truth be told, ain't no different. Shit, shooter, I got a Nosler 48 Trophy Grade with a tac optical scope right there in the closet that's better than both those pieces of shit, but you ain't taking my Nosler either. I can get you the latest variant of the M82 fifty cal if you want. You can kill the fuckers from a half mile."

Jack shook his head no again. "Too heavy, Gunny. And I want to get in closer. I need positive ID and a weapon more like what I used to shoot."

Armie smiled. "Then I got just the thing. We got us a new variant of the M110 SASS"—semiautomatic sniper system. "You were gone before we started shootin' the first 110s. The version I got ain't even in the field yet, and shooter, it's a fucking beauty. Best goddamn shootin' rifle I ever saw. Seems the corps values my opinion, so I'm evaluating it. We're doing our own testing down here while the rear-area motherfuckers do the official shit for the politicians and brass up at Pendleton. I've got my own personal weapon. Nobody fucks with it 'cept me—no log, nothin'. Comes and goes with me whenever and wherever I want. I shoot it up here all the time, and it's only twenty pounds fully loaded, and that counts the bipod and the badass new corps upgrade of the big Schmidt and Bender day scope. Ain't heavy, so even a soft civilian like you can hump it. Breaks down, too, so it's compact—concealable, which I'm guessing you'll need. I'll bring it back with me tomorrow, let you start running a few rounds through it, get it set up for the range you're thinking."

"What *is* the range, Gunny? I don't know squat about the 110."

"Eight hundred and fifty yards is the book range of the one I got, but a guy with your skills could probably hit what he's aimin' at out to a thousand yards with no more'n, say, a five-inch group."

"Not tight enough, Armie. I've got two targets, and at best, I'm guessing time for one shot each before all hell breaks loose and I get what I assume will be a shitload of pissed-off armed Mexican bodyguards beating the weeds trying to end me. I have to be perfect—two quick single kill shots. I need, say, two, three inches max MOA"—minute of angle—"at four hundred or five hundred yards. What's the MV"—muzzle velocity—"of this 110?"

"Shade over twenty-five hundred"—feet per second.

Jack was intensely focused on Armie as they went over the technical specs of the weapon. "That's good, very good. At a quarter mile, I can get the second shot off about the time the first shot finds the target. I can't have the second target ducking on me. I get one chance at this. At four hundred yards, under the right wind conditions, the hired guns I'm sure assholes like this surround themselves with won't even be able to tell where the shots came from, and they'll be looking close in for the shooter. I need to be close enough for a sure kill but need the distance edge to evade and withdraw."

"You ain't askin' for much, are you, shooter? The book MOA on the 110 is one point one inches at three hundred feet, or five inches at the range you're talking. Assuming you can still shoot like you used to, I'd guess your grouping with my weapon is closer to three inches out that far."

"Still no good, Armie. Three or four inches could mean hurt bad but not dead. I need dead with certainty with only one shot each. They've already murdered Sherry; if I miss, they'll be relentless trying to end me and my family."

Armie smiled, and then he chuckled.

Jack frowned and asked, "What's so funny, Master Gunny?"

"Just you and this one-shot bullshit. We ain't talkin' your old M24 bolt action here, shooter. The 110 I got is semiauto, with a fucking gas-operated rotating bolt and a ten- or twenty-round detachable box mag; your choice. With only two targets, ten will probably be enough, but nothing like havin' some extra rounds already loaded. With a little practice, I'm guessing you could get two, three shots on target one, switch to target two before the asshole has time to fucking flinch, and get two or three rounds on him, all inside three inches at four hundred yards. With the fucking kick and impact expansion of the hot 7.62 NATO 175-grain hollow-point round this bitch fires, close is all you'll need. Ain't nobody surviving two rounds center mass, let alone three or four. It'll look like a goddamn shotgun blast goin' out the other side."

Jack slowly nodded his head while rubbing his chin. "I didn't know all that, Gunny. Impressive, but what about recoil and time back on target?"

"Some, but nothing a former stud like you can't handle. You'll be back on target in time to see the first shot hit target one, get off a second, and then acquire the second mutt and do the same. Two rounds each ought to do the fucking trick; won't be much left of their lungs or tickers the way you shoot. I've got a meadow a full quarter mile long out back. We'll set up the shot here and give you enough rounds to get comfortable and see for yourself. And I need to be convinced you ain't lost it and can more than hit the broadside of a fucking barn if you're going alone. After I get you better intel, we'll go over it again and again till we have you a highly survivable action plan. I ain't about to let you go south alone unless I can see on paper you survive this. I ain't got that many friends, especially loaded ones."

Jack smiled for the first time since they'd sat down, and then Armie went on.

"Another thing or two you don't know: this 110 has a threaded barrel and flash and noise suppression. No one will hear or see shit at thirty yards, let alone three hundred. I want you closer to the targets; the closer you are, the deader they are. At eight or nine hundred feet, even the winds are no longer a factor. If the intel says there's a way to get you safely inside a thousand feet, with the weapon I'm givin' you and some practice, you can head shot the first piece of shit single shot if you want and center mass the second with a four- or five-round burst. Ain't a motherfucker on the planet surviving that, whatever size the group."

Jack smiled again at Armie's matter-of-fact confidence, feeling better about things and just to be hanging with him again; it had been a few years. "I'm beginning to think I may pull this off, Master Gunny," Jack said, reaching for the JD.

It required five days to get all the necessary weapons, ammo, field rations, and other equipment Armie insisted Jack would need. Also, there was the time necessary to obtain the better intel, do enough shooting practice to convince Armie he could still shoot, and lastly, to make the necessary modifications to the camper to hide everything Armie provided. Jack hated killing people but loved shooting, so it was very satisfying when, after Armie graded out his third practice session, he told him he was still the best goddamn shooter he had ever seen. True to Armie's word, his modified 110 was as good as advertised, and his groups at four hundred yards, just short of a quarter mile, were averaging 2.5 inches. He decided he could live with that with two shots each.

In addition to the sweetest M110 in the corps, Armie raided the confiscated-weapons locker at Jack's old CID company and came up with a brand-spanking-new Belgium-made FN-P90 compact urban assault submachine gun, complete with fifty-round magazine and a sound suppressor. At a rate of fire of nine hundred rounds per minute and only 6.5 pounds fully loaded, it was the perfect backup weapon in close if things got dicey. Armie threw in two extra quick-change magazines, just in case. He also secured a semiclassified new variant of the AN/PVS-10 Sniper Starlight scope for night shots that was spooky, it was so good, and a ghillie suit and blanket that would make Jack nearly invisible at several feet once he had secured some local vegetation to it. Somehow Armie had also been able to get his hands on the latest Gen III Night Vision (NV) gear, which amplified ambient light levels by forty thousand, also spooky. Jack realized the minute Armie pulled the NV headgear out of the box that when it became necessary to reconnoiter in close, he'd have a huge advantage over the locals, who would stand out in the dark like pale-green neon lights, especially when Armie pointed out that if he was on site within a week, he'd have low moonlight conditions.

The National Reconnaissance Office in Washington controlled all the military recon satellites in low Earth orbit and had been providing ultra-high-resolution aerial photographs of the border area between America and Mexico to other government agencies as needed for years. As the so-called drug war dragged on, more and more of the Mexican coast and areas around the key cartel strongholds such as Matamoros had been shot from 150 miles overhead by the NRO's classified satellites. The area Armie was requesting the shots for was not on any restricted access list, so once he gave the gunny he owned in Division Intelligence the GPS coordinates of the area he was interested in, they had excellent high-resolution overhead views that were many times sharper than what was available on the internet. Much of the area photographed had been translated to very accurate computer-generated topographic maps, so they got a very good general map of the area from the beach to Diaz's house and another of the area within a half mile of the easily discernible beach house to mark up for Jack's use as his in-country tactical map.

Every evening after dinner, they worked on the plan. Armie still treated Jack like a twenty-year-old boot as they pored over the aerials, challenging him time and again with questions and details. Jack was glad he had the master gunny on his side, because he could see details in a picture no one else but a pure tech weenie in Intelligence could. On their first night looking over the aerials, Armie's expertise showed. "Ah, now this is interestin'. Look right there, shooter. Tell me what you see."

"What am I looking for?" Jack asked as he took the 3D viewer from Armie.

"Ain't sayin'. Just look and tell me what *you* see. Right there." He pointed his stubby, thick finger at a specific spot on the aerial.

Jack looked but knew he was missing whatever it was that Armie wanted him to see. As sharp as the photos were, except for the obvious roads and structures and other man-made objects such as cars or trucks, it still was all just dunes, low native vegetation, and shadows that seemed to blend in together. "I know I'm missing it, Armie. What?"

"Are you fucking blind or somethin'? That fucking circular path right there, out about a hundred yards from the house."

Jack now saw what the gunny was pointing at. The "path" was nothing more than a thin, hazy, off-white, meandering line on the photograph that the house and several other small structures seemed to be more or less sitting dead center within. "OK, Gunny, I see it. Could be a path."

"You don't get it, do you, shooter? See what looks like two spokes radiating out from the rear of this small shack here near the main house? Them's the paths out to the perimeter one, and I'm guessing that shack is barracks for the close-in guards. This Diaz you're after ain't dumb. He's running a perimeter patrol, out about three hundred feet from the house. Now, look here. See the small, triangular-shaped shadows, here, here, and here?"

Jack looked closely, and the gunny was right. There were small, dark shadows among the low dunes. "I see them. So?"

"So they ain't natural. Too uniform; got straight sides."

Jack nodded his head. "So you're saying they're man made, Gunny?"

"That's right. What the fuck are most days like down there? Hotter than the hubs of hell, I'm guessing. So by day, the guards hike out to these shadows—I'm bettin' their lean-tos—and sit on their asses in the shade. By night, they walk that perimeter path. Look here. You can see the guard posts they want the opposition to see comin' up the lone access road. That's them shadows here and here, shacks. Look close, and you can count bodies lying around in the shade. They're the darker spots; looks like three or four at each shack. These perimeter positions is smart, real smart, for anticipating some action by another cartel or the local cops, but not us."

Jack now understood. "You mean not me, Gunny, because I'm coming from the east, the sea, and not up the road from the west."

"Now you're learnin', shooter. Their defensive orientation is all to the west for the one and only threat they understand, other bad guys fightin' up that road and trying to flank them. Those fixed positions out at a hundred yards makes for a nice surprise to those trying to do that. Look at these contour intervals, the elevation of these two dunes right here, and then look at this spot here in this mess of low dunes. This will be your principal nest—position A, your primary, about twelve hundred feet out. It's just about the highest point in the area, but you wouldn't know it to look at it. Ain't obvious, is what I'm sayin'. From there you have clear LOS"—line of sight—"to the front and east sides of the house, right through the cleavage of them two dunes. Then, by rotating your orientation a bit, you have LOS to two of the three lean-tos if need be and can also control any movement up the road. Listen, I know how you feel about killin', shooter, and I respect that, but after you take down the two mutts you're after, start takin' down guards. It'll be a fucking turkey shoot from the primary, especially if you end up doing a night shot. After you a drop a few guards, ain't no one raising their head for an hour, much less trying to find you. Gives you the edge to withdraw."

Jack nodded his head, knowing that what Armie said made sense, no matter his personal feelings about more killing.

"Shooter, I'd like to get you closer, but assuming you have LOS to the interior, the primary is fucking perfect for a lot of reasons. Also, I did some checking. Looks like the evening breezes are pretty regular onshore. That means your shots from the primary are mostly downwind, no more than thirty degrees across, meaning the fucking winds are not a factor. Just in case you've got lousy LOS, which, given your fucking luck I'd bet on, here and here are your alternate A and B positions to the front and side of the house. Alt A swings you closer to the road, which ain't ideal, but it's still survivable. But you have to take down the nearest guards at this shack after your primary shots, to give you time to evade. B is perfect for the side of the house and a rapid withdraw, but you can't see the front. Once you've done your recon and confirm target location and LOS, that's when you pick your firing point. But you know that."

"Yeah, I know it," Jack said, not taking his eyes off the map.

After three more days and nights, Jack had trained up to Armie's general satisfaction, and his plan was complete. It was all Armie's planning, and he eventually agreed with all of it. The one big stumbling block between them early on had to do with the timeline. Jack had it in his head that once he was at the beach within five miles of Diaz, he would hike out from the RV the first night after dark, do a detailed reconnoiter, set up a nest, and then wait it out until he got his shot. Armie had simply looked at him and asked, "So tell me, shooter, what happens if three, four days go by and your targets don't show up together? What then? You think these mutts are sitting around down there waitin' to get shot? With that fancy backpack you got, after weapons, ammo, rations, and the other stuff you'll need, like the ghillie suit and the night-vision gear, how much water will you be able to carry in one load?"

Jack blinked, seeing where Armie was going. "I don't know, Armie. Maybe five, ten gallons?"

Armie was shaking his head, as if annoyed by a child. "You got plenty of combat time in the sand, so think. Gallon of water weighs 8.35 pounds. Five gallons is 42 pounds, which is the most you'll be able to carry after the forty pounds of weapons and other shit. You need a gallon a day minimum, but double that in that heat and humidity to keep from getting the shakes. Don't know about you, but I ain't all that scared of a sniper who can't keep his fucking hands steady. Ten gallons minimum, shooter, if you're required to sit it out for three to five days. Do the arithmetic. I 'spose you could go back and

forth to the camper in the middle of the night to resupply, but all the movin'
around increases your chances of being spotted and erodes your energy.

"You need lots of water, and you need minimum movement. That means
two trips only out to the primary from the RV. First night you're just a pack
mule hauling as much water as you can carry, rations, and support gear. You
bury the water, hide the gear, and then conduct your close-in recon. Take only
the P90, 150 rounds, your map and GPS, and the night-vision gear. Now, you
might think you got lucky if you dummy into the targets when you're sniff-
ing around up close, but don't get trigger happy. Spraying them with that
Belgium pop gun and killing enough close-in guards to evade is too risky.
Look at the map. You approach from the primary along this line of dunes,
recon the general layout of the house and the sight lines to doors and windows, and then boogie straight back to the RV, heading east-northeast from
the house. You got the perimeter path to cross, but the lean-tos are all west of
you, and you'll be able to see in the dark and any guards will be night blind.

"Second night you take more water and all the weapons and ammo. Now
you're set for a week in the weeds. If you don't get your shot by then, you hike
out, regroup, and then go back with more water and rations and start over. If
that asshole is working out of that house like you suspect, all you're really doing
is waiting on the big guy who got your ex to show so you get them together."

Jack came around to Armie's reasoning and accepted the entire plan, realizing for the first time that maybe he'd have to settle for just Diaz—and he
had no idea what he looked like. His entire plan was predicated on identifying
Diaz by merely observing whom everyone else at the house was kowtowing
to. As to Sherry's killer, he did know what he looked like but had no idea
where the hell in Mexico he could be found, other than the beach house.
He was assuming the guy worked for Diaz and did more than just show up
occasionally. His entire brilliant plan was chock full of holes, and Armie
made him see them and face them. Jack knew he would need a shitload of
luck for his plan to work, and the way his life had been going recently, with
the exception of meeting Maddy, he seemed to be fresh out. But he couldn't
just wait around and worry about Diaz finding him or the kids. He needed
to end this now.

Their last night together, Jack went out to the camper after supper, brought in the duffel bag with the $250,000, took out $50,000 to keep just in case, and gave the rest to a stunned Armie. Like Jack, Armie had never seen more than his paycheck in cash ever. He told Armie the cash was his unless Henry needed it in Denver for the cost of the security. He would call Henry on the drive down to Mexico and let him know about the money. If it turned out Henry had what he needed, the money was Armie's to keep, a down payment on all his help. Jack started to explain to Armie the need to not attract attention by suddenly spending large sums of cash, but Armie raised his hand, stopping him, and said, "Save your breath, shooter. You're the dumb shit here. I'm the master gunny." Then he slid the bottle of JD sitting in front of him across the table and smiled as he reached for his pack of smokes.

They went over the plan once more and rechecked all the supplies in detail. Armie even remembered packages of backup batteries for the equipment that needed it. They packed the RV and then secured the false panels made in Armie's garage over the last four days, satisfied that even a very dedicated border guard would find nothing. It was Jack's call, but Armie persuaded him to do the sixteen-hundred-mile drive to Brownsville, Texas, near the border in two long days and not to go straight through like he wanted to do. Better to be somewhat rested going into the weeds, Armie pointed out.

Jack agreed. Tomorrow was Monday, and he'd go as far as Mobile, about halfway, and there were plenty of truck stops he could overnight in. Tuesday night he'd be in Brownsville, and then he'd cross the border on Wednesday morning. His resort reservation had him arriving on Saturday, but with any luck, he'd set up his primary on Wednesday night, be in position by Thursday night, and, hopefully, get his kills by Saturday.

They finished the last of the JD and hit the rack because Jack wanted to be on the road at six. When he walked into the kitchen at five the next morning, Armie was already working on breakfast. There wasn't much said while they ate, just the occasional reminder from Armie to remember to do this or do that.

As they walked out the back door to the RV and shook hands a final time, Armie said, "Be careful out there, shooter. Remember the plan and your trainin'. Don't go pissin' me off by gettin' yourself killed. And another thing: bring that goddamn hardware back so's I don't spend the next ten years in the brig."

As he drove off, Jack couldn't take his eyes off the big side mirror of the camper. Armie was standing there, arms akimbo, watching him. Jack knew he had no other choice but to do what he was trying to do, and as he fixed his eyes on the road ahead, because of his old friend, he felt he now had a chance. And he'd never forget.

16

The Gulf Coast
Forty miles south of Matamoros, Mexico
Early May; week seven

The drive to Brownsville was uneventful, as was the border crossing. It was only about a fifty-mile drive to the beach from the border after passing through the very windy and dusty Matamoros. Jack felt as if things might be going his way when he reached the several-mile-long public access beach on the Gulf and found maybe fifty other vehicles of all sizes and shapes and two or three hundred happy tourists and locals already camped out there and having a good time. He parked his RV as far south down the beach road from the other vehicles as was possible and then spent the rest of the day sitting in the shade of the camper watching the other vacationers and taking the occasional dip to cool off, all to kill time until nightfall. The temperature was easily in the nineties, and though there was a strong breeze, it was like a blowtorch coming off the low fescue and native grass-covered dunes; he could only hope the late-night onshore breeze would be cooler. It had been a long drive down, but he was sufficiently rested and was anxious for night to fall. He hated recalling his past as a sniper, but so much of the shooting he did in the corps had been done at night, the opposition at a huge disadvantage and no match for the sophisticated nightscopes and night-vision equipment the corps provided.

As dinnertime approached, a number of other nearby beachcombers dropped by from time to time with offers to join them for food and drink, but he turned them all down with a smile and a thanks, pleading the need to hit the sack early after the long drive down. He fixed his own dinner in the privacy of his small but efficient kitchen knowing the ten-mile hump round trip through the loose sand would be energy sucking. He lay down to rest, setting his alarm for midnight in case he dozed off, but he knew he wouldn't sleep a wink. Just getting off his feet for a few hours would have to do.

He was up at eleven and finished loading his backpack with the water, provisions, and equipment. It was well after midnight before the last of the nearest campfires finally died out, and he locked up the camper and silently made his way south and west, following the GPS coordinates of the very carefully laid-out route to his primary shooting point. He was dressed in a new pair of lightweight sand-colored camouflage utilities, another gift from Armie. The disruptive digital pattern of the utilities would make it very difficult for anyone to spot him during daylight even if he didn't have the ghillie suit. His boots were also Armie's, a broken-in pair of lightweight hot-weather combat boots that fit him perfectly. Armie was a full three inches shorter than he was, but thank God he had big feet because there simply wasn't enough time to break in a new pair of boots and get to Mexico during the low-moonlight period.

He was humping nearly a hundred pounds in his fancy pack, anchored by the two large plastic five-gallon jugs of water. He was carrying almost everything he would need for a week in the weeds except the M110, the ammo, and the extra water he would hump in tomorrow night. The five-mile hike took him two and a half hours, aided as he was by the night-vision headgear, which allowed him to see his path clearly. The last mile took the most time, as he shifted into a clear-and-move pattern of checking the area forward carefully and then moving up several hundred yards, only to stop and do it all over again. The last thing he wanted to do was give away his one shot at tactical surprise by accidentally tripping over some guards out for a late-night lizard shoot or something. Humping around and over one small dune after another was exhausting, and he collapsed to the ground the second his handheld GPS said he was finally at the coordinates of his primary. Armie was right—while there were the occasional higher solitary dunes around, the general ridge area he was in was, at thirty feet above sea level, the highest point between the ocean and Diaz's house.

As he was catching his breath, he took out his nightscope and did a careful check of the area, easily spotting any warm-blooded creatures moving. The few dim lights from the area around the small beach house—one pole-mounted yard light and another light on the porch—glowed like small suns in his scope.

It was approaching three by the time he had his nest set up, the packages of REMs (ready-to-eat meals) and water buried, and the rest of the equipment concealed by his ghillie blanket. He cussed himself for not thinking to buy another backpack before coming down. He needed the pack to haul tomorrow night's load but hated the idea of doing tonight's close-in recon carrying the now-empty pack. Not wanting to leave the pack here and backtrack to the primary after the recon, he put it on so he could boogie straight northeast from the house back to the RV. He would lose the darkness by five, and he needed to be safely back in his RV before that, so time was a factor.

He grabbed his nightscope and did a very thorough sighting of the guard positions he could see; to his surprise, there was very little activity. The nearest shack on the main road from the west was a good 1,500 feet away and appeared to have but one guard on duty outside, and from his posture, Jack was betting he was asleep in his chair. The two lean-tos he could see were dark, likely meaning that at night, these carefully positioned posts were empty. The beach house was a small one-story structure with a flat roof and a wide covered porch on the front or south side that wrapped around to the east side. On the porch he could make out two guards, one standing, one sitting, both smoking, the glow of their cigarettes bright as day in his scope. The guard shack near the house was on the north side, and he could not see it from his primary location.

Satisfied there was nothing between him and the house, he put on the NV headset and carefully and slowly made his silent approach. Carrying the backpack was not as awkward as he had thought it would be, so he stopped worrying about it as he moved in. He passed between the two lean-tos he had previously checked out, never nearer than several hundred feet, and could see they were vacant. Finally, after a controlled thirty minutes of closing in on the house, he knelt down in some sage-like brush well out of the dim glow of the pole-mounted yard light, no more than seventy feet from the front porch. He was just into the low native foliage that surrounded and defined the clearing the entry road from the west ended in. Across the clearing were two parked pickup trucks, both well off any of his sight lines to the house. There were no longer two guards on the porch, as during his approach he'd watched from several hundred yards out as one of them walked around to the side and disappeared toward the back, presumably to what Armie believed was the guards' barracks. He was just guessing, but given the slack security, one guard up the road to the west and one on duty at the porch, he suspected that neither Diaz nor anyone else of importance was here.

The minute he could clearly see details of the interior through the tall front windows, he could see there was an important main room that seemed to take up half the front and most of the east side. The tall windows looking out onto the porch on both sides were from the same room. He would have a shot from the primary and alternate A to the front windows and from alternate B to the east windows. The interior space seemed to be dominated by a large desk and credenza, identifying it as an office of some kind; he could only hope it was Diaz's.

Satisfied with all he could see, he attached small strips of cloth as wind streamers at several points along a fallen-down barbed-wire fence and then slowly retraced his path deeper into the dunes and out past the perimeter path. He checked the path carefully coming in and going out, but there were no guards doing perimeter duty. He then circled to the northeast, checking out the rear of the house and the guards' shack. After twenty minutes and a half mile of careful movement, he relaxed and started for the RV.

The hike back was far easier with the light load he was carrying, and in just over an hour, he was back at the camper. He sat at his small dining-room table and added notes to his tactical map. Then he went to bed and slept soundly, which, given what he was attempting, was surprising.

He knew he had slept hard when he realized the relentless knocking he thought he was dreaming about was really someone at his door. Startled, he quickly jumped up, dressed only in his gym shorts, and looked out the small window of the door. Standing there were two lovely young blondes in their twenties, clad in the skimpiest of bikinis, whom he recognized from a visit the day before—coeds from one of the Texas universities down on the Gulf for a long weekend with several guy friends along.

He opened the door, smiling, and said good morning. Both giggled and told him it was no longer morning and that they and their friends had prepared a nice lunch, and they asked him to join them. Wanting to fit into the beach scene and not raise any questions, he said sure, grabbed a T-shirt and his Nikes, and joined them up the beach for the rest of the afternoon. Toward the end of the day, after they asked him to stay for dinner, he thanked the young women and their friends but said he had some things to do and said goodnight, smiling and waving despite their attempts to get him to stay.

The campsite the coeds and their friends had set up was the closest one to his RV, and they partied around their campfire until after one o'clock before calling it a night. He had been ready to go for hours, forced to sit and watch the group out the darkened rear window of the camper, growing more and more impatient by the minute. Finally able to leave unseen, he felt his tension dissipate as he began his march. He was humping another eighty pounds of mostly water and ammo and carrying the fully assembled M110. At twenty pounds, it was very manageable, but even twenty pounds got heavy after a while trudging through mostly sand.

He reached his primary at three o'clock, grateful to be there, and set about organizing his nest. By daybreak, he was sacked out beneath his ghillie blanket, the nylon netting now stitched with the native grasses and rigged as a quasi tent. His nest blended in perfectly with the surrounding vegetation and provided him not only concealment, but shade. With the blanket propped up eighteen inches or so above the depression he was lying in, he was free to move around some beneath it to stretch his muscles and access water and rations while staying concealed. The ghillie blanket was large enough, and he had carefully set up his position, so not even the desert-tan-colored muzzle and sound suppressor of the M110 was sticking out from under his camouflage.

He fitted the rifle with his day scope and checked out the house. With the early-morning light peeking under the roof overhang of the porch, he could now see clearly into the office / living room space of the house, noticing that unlike the exterior, which appeared very run down, the interior appeared to be very nicely finished and modern. This confirmed in his mind that this could indeed be where an apparent drug kingpin such as Diaz might operate out of.

His shot from here would be through the tall front windows at about a thirty-degree angle to the glass. He considered what that might mean to his shot calculations and knew even a single pane of glass at that angle could alter a bullet's flight; he wished Armie were there because he would know for sure the ballistic characteristics of the rounds he was shooting. He decided he would have no choice but to shoot at the first target twice, counting on the first bullet to break the glass sufficiently to leave the second shot unaltered.

He was beginning to have doubts about being able to get eyes on the second target before he had a chance to react and protect himself. That raised the question, who would he shoot first if he was lucky enough to get Diaz and his hired killer together? As he thought about it, he decided if only one opportunity for a kill presented itself, he'd shoot Diaz. Killing him, if he was in fact the leader and he could identify him, seemed his best chance to end the threat to him and his family. He knew he was letting his emotions rule him, but he was also thinking he would not immediately bug out, but stay and try to get Sherry's killer. As concealed and as far away as he was, neither Diaz's killer nor the guards could ever spot him, and he was prepared to stay as long as it took. He could shoot up the pickup trucks, limiting their mobility, but he couldn't keep them from calling in reinforcements, and that could be a deadly problem if they brought in large numbers and someone with some sense of tactics started sending patrols out over the entire area. They'd be easy targets, but after a while it would become clear to them where he was, and numbers against him would be dangerous. He had eighty total rounds for the 110, four twenty-round magazines; every shot would have to count. If it came down to him having to use the Belgium P90, he was in real trouble.

Armie said time and again over their five days together that it was possible, maybe even likely, that Sherry's killer could be a contract one who never came out here, and maybe the instructions on the map were a onetime thing and no one of importance used this house. Deep down, he didn't believe that. He could tell from the handwriting that the instructions to the van's occupants were written by an educated man; it was too neat, too precise. At Armie's place he had gone back over the few internet stories he found when he Googled Diaz/Matamoros/cartel, and the only stories that came up were of the decorated Mexican National Police colonel from Matamoros and his fight *against* the cartels in the area. If the colonel and the cartel leader were one and the same person, it seemed reasonable to assume that he would operate out of a place far removed from his police offices, and this beach house fit that idea. As he lay there with the sun slowly climbing in the sky, he held on to that thought, for he didn't want to think about the possibility that neither Diaz nor the killer would show up and his trip was all for nothing. If that happened, he and his family would still be in grave danger.

Friday and Saturday in the nest came and went with little activity. There was a general changing of the guard once each morning as a new truck showed up with a half dozen men and replaced those who had been there overnight. Other than that, both days were a bust. Because there wasn't anyone of importance at the house, the guards' routine was lazy and unprofessional. No one walked the perimeter path, and none positioned themselves at the lean-tos. The six guards he'd accounted for each day could always be found in the shade of the porch, the shade of the one shack he could see, and, he assumed, the rear barracks shack he could not see from the nest. Despite their lack of attention and professionalism, he stayed vigilant and kept track of each one.

Both Friday and Saturday were brutally hot, with temperatures above ninety and a hot breeze blowing out to sea most of the day. The shade of his low tent was saving him, as was the sand, as he kept digging his depression deeper and deeper to find cooler sand until he had a full thirty inches of clearance beneath the ghillie blanket. After sunset, as the winds turned and came off the ocean, the temperatures dropped considerably, and he was almost comfortable. He had consumed two gallons of water exactly each twenty-four hours and catnapped from midnight to five each night, just enough to keep him sharp for the day.

One of the last hi-tech gizmos Armie had given him to take was an incredible battery-operated remote motion detection kit. There were eight small plastic detectors about the size of two cigarette packs taped together, with each detector mounted on a twelve-inch spike. Once the detectors were set in a wide arc around the approaches to his position out about a hundred feet, their invisible beams would detect anyone who entered their field of coverage. Having calibrated them to ignore small objects and go off only when a significant mass entered the beam area, if a signal was sent, he would hear a high-pitched pinging in the small headset that he wore when sleeping. As a team, he and Armie of course would alternate between resting and watching, but Armie wasn't here. So the old master gunny had insisted he take the system, because without it, sleep would be impossible for a lone shooter stuck out in the weeds for days.

Sunday morning broke hot and clear, just like the two previous dawns. He had fashioned a slit trench to the east of his position at the base of the ridge he was on, and when the need arose, he would slide out the back of his nest, go down the low dune, take care of business, and then return, never revealing himself to the targets.

As he was crawling back into the nest after his morning constitutional, he saw dust coming down the access road for the second time this morning. The regular guard change had already occurred, and there was too much dust for a single vehicle, so whatever vehicles were coming up the road were a significant change to the routine of the last two days. The small caravan consisted of a pickup truck hauling three armed men followed by what looked like an expensive Range Rover SUV. All the trucks he had seen so far were reasonably new, but nothing all that fancy beyond wider tires and shinier rims.

Jack scrambled back into position and sighted in on the clearing in front of the house as the new arrivals slowed and parked. His pulse rate jumped a few beats when he thought he recognized the passenger of the SUV as he climbed out. He was an older man, dressed far better than the guards and carrying himself with almost a military bearing. More importantly, he greatly resembled the one photograph included in the articles on the Colonel Diaz of Matamoros he had researched. His belief that this could be Diaz was confirmed in his mind when he watched the guards on the porch almost come to attention as he passed by them and entered the house, going right to the desk in the office that he could see clearly through the tall windows. The man casually sat down as if he belonged and started reading documents from a case he had carried in as one of the guards brought him a tall drink of some kind. It had to be Diaz, he thought, out on a Sunday away from Matamoros to conduct whatever illicit business he was conducting.

Jack watched with fascination for hours through his high-powered scope as the man seemed to work the rest of the morning and all afternoon, reading and writing, most of the time with his back to the desk as he sat in front of a now-open laptop computer on his credenza that Jack could easily see. At around five a plain white unmarked cargo van, not unlike the one that had crashed in Colorado, came up the road, and what looked like a delivery man got out and started carrying packages from the van to a picnic table in the shade of the porch on the east side. He'd noticed, of course, that the porch wrapped around to the side, but he didn't notice that the the side porch was bigger, like a covered patio, and as with a patio, it had a table. The delivery man set up a portable gas grill and a small side table just off the porch, and Jack could see that a Sunday meal was to be prepared by the delivery man, now turned cook, by the look of it.

Thirty minutes later a passenger car came up the road carrying two more men and parked in front. Both men were about his age, he judged, maybe a bit younger, and the driver was definitely showing deference to the passenger, who went straight in the front door as the driver took a seat on the front porch with the other guards posted there. Both the driver and the passenger were also better dressed than the typical guards, making them something other than just more guards.

Jack watched as the newly arrived young man entered Diaz's office. Diaz stood and shook his hand while also taking his arm and greeting him as if he was a friend or a close business associate. The two men then sat down, Diaz at his desk, the new arrival in a chair facing him, seeming to be talking.

Fifteen minutes later another pickup came down the road, this one nicer than the rest. He sighted the driver through his scope, and his pulse rate, which was already elevated, jumped again. His gamble and patience had paid off, as he saw the driver of the silver Town Car slowly park, get out of his truck, and then limp toward the house, neither acknowledging nor talking with anyone. Jack now knew for sure this was Sherry's killer as he also went to Diaz's office and was greeted warmly by Diaz but not the younger man, who simply shook his hand. Jack's intuition was telling him that the killer and the younger man knew each other but were not friends, as Diaz and the killer obviously were.

Unbelievably, he had his targets together, and knew he needed to collect himself and get his emotions and body under control and not rush the chance. As the three men in the office talked, he did a quick but detailed scan of the area, fixing everyone's positions. At the shack alongside the access road 1,500 feet to his west, there seemed to be four guards, either sitting or standing in the shade, not exactly vigilant but more attentive than they had been over the last three days. There were five guards on the porch, the four who had arrived with Diaz and the younger, better-dressed one who also had just arrived. At the back corner of the house, in the shade of the porch, were two from the regular detachment, more or less just peering around the back corner, as if waiting for the three principals to come out to the table. Lastly, there was the delivery man / cook, who was standing before the grill, busily preparing a meal.

Of the eleven total guards he believed were on site, he had eyes on all of them. It was clear to him that this Sunday meal was for the three principals, and he was going to get his shot. He thought about moving to his alternate B position; it was closer by a hundred yards and would allow him a straight-in shot to the east-side porch, but after thinking about it for a minute, he decided to stay put. The shot from here was only 1,200 feet, and his LOS was excellent. By staying put he also had access to all his water, rations, and equipment and was invisible in case he only got Diaz and had to stay for a longer period of time. A repositioning would also take him fifteen to twenty minutes, and he didn't want to risk missing a shot opportunity.

⋅⟿ ⟾⋅

Back at the front porch, Ray was very unhappy. Brillo had spent the last week back in Denver coordinating with some local hired thugs there on another reconnaissance mission, evidently trying to gather information on the friends and relatives of the mysterious truck driver who Brillo's partner, Diaz, was certain had stolen their money. The only thing of any value to his original mission that he had learned in the last several weeks was that the leader of what was left of the Butcher of Brownsville's cartel was none other than Colonel Diaz of the Federal Police. Brillo had mentioned Diaz's name often since they had first met and introduced him to the man when he first got here, but he had only just found out that he was also the commander of the Federal Police for the entire state of Tamaulipas. He had called Bennie and passed this nugget on as he sat around Brillo's apartment in town alone while Brillo was up north. In their subsequent conversations, Bennie passed on that their "friend" in the Mexican capital had taken the news very badly when Bennie told him of the traitor in his police, for apparently they were friends and had known each other for a very long time.

Since he had been recruited by Brillo, the information on Diaz was the only useful piece of intelligence he had generated. There were no shipments being planned, no discussions of distribution networks—nothing. It was all about finding their stolen money and then somehow taking on and eliminating their banking partner. He had wanted to bug out four days ago, when he easily could have with Brillo in America, and called it a mission, but Bennie wanted him to stay. Eventually, Bennie had said, Felix Brillo would do his part in the money nonsense and then return to Chihuahua and start setting up his organization. And when he did, there would have to be discussions about distribution in the north, and logically, that would mean tapping into the still-active Matamoros network. That network was what Bennie wanted,

223

so Ray was stuck and bored, and boredom dulled the senses, and that could get an undercover operative killed.

Today would be a little bit different because even though he was sitting on his ass on the porch uninvolved with whatever discussions were going on, he was invited to dinner with Brillo and his partners for some reason. From what little Brillo had told him since his return, he and his partners had suffered several setbacks in locating the truck driver. Apparently the brute killer El Lobo had gone to LA and, for reasons unknown, killed their best possible source to the location of the mystery driver. This was followed by the news that Brillo brought with him from Denver that as an apparent reaction to whatever had happened in LA, the other potential sources to the truck driver's whereabouts that Diaz had managed to run down were in fact now being protected, so the truck driver likely knew that he was being hunted. This dire revelation and what to do next was the subject of the important meeting now going on, for it appeared to Brillo that surprise had been lost, and with it the likelihood of finding their money.

Ray passed on to Bennie what he had learned from Brillo about the apparent murder in LA, but Bennie wasn't much interested. He said he did not want to get distracted or shift focus to whatever issues Diaz and Brillo were having about stolen money problems. Bennie reminded him that the five-county Greater Los Angeles basin had almost eighteen million inhabitants and said he wouldn't be surprised if there had been a dozen different homicides committed over the two- or three-day period Ray said Diaz's hired killer was in the area. He said he'd have the LA office generally look into the circumstances surrounding any murders but told him to keep his eye on the ball.

Ray sat in silence on the porch for the hour Brillo and the others met. The regular guards whom he was slowly starting to recognize had not warmed to him yet. Some knew of his El Cuchillo reputation and stayed distant; others just weren't friendly. Not that he cared; he preferred being left alone.

Brillo finally emerged from inside looking grim and said, "Sorry to leave you out here like this, but things are not going well for me and my partners, and we needed to talk in private. Come with me. Like I said earlier, Diaz wants you to join us for dinner."

Brillo led him to the side porch, where the rough wooden table was set nicely, and judging from the smells coming from the grill, the cook was very nearly finished with his preparations. Diaz and Lobo were already present, having obviously come out a side door directly from the office, and they were sitting at the table, their backs to the house, looking out over the dunes. Each had a drink in his hand as Ray and Brillo took the bench seat opposite them and Diaz offered them a drink, pointing to bottles of whiskey and tequila on the table and saying cold beer was available if they preferred; they both took the offered tequila. The cook started serving fully-dished-up plates that featured very nice-looking whole grilled fish as the main course.

Brillo had evidently spoken in detail to Diaz about some of Ray's history, because Diaz looked at him as he handed him a drink and asked if he would tell him about his time last year as an aide to the ex-president. The request struck him as genuine curiosity and not just some pro forma dinner chitchat request by a superior to a guard, so in between bites of the excellent fish, he did as he was asked.

Four hundred yards southeast, in the inhospitable-appearing dunes, Jack was set. Given the angle of the shot from his nest to the side porch, he could see both Diaz and the killer in his scope at the same time with them sitting side by side at the picnic table as they were. He was thinking he was lucky, but after the last year and a half, and especially the last week, he didn't really feel lucky about anything except for meeting Maddy. He swung his scope back toward the front of the house to find the small streamers he had set during his reconnoiter. He found both. They were fluttering, and he could tell the winds were beginning their normal shift from offshore to on as the sun began to set and evening approached, and while not calm, the light breeze was not a factor to his shot.

He did a reconfirmation of the guards and their positions. The one disadvantage with having his targets in the shade on the east side was that any guard with a nickel's worth of sense would quickly determine that the shots had to come from a very narrow quadrant to the southeast or east, as those directions had the only clear LOS to everyone on the porch. His nest location, while nearly perfect, as Armie had said it would be, required that he pass the house as he made his escape and headed back north to the RV, albeit at a distance of about five or six hundred yards to the east. Smart, dedicated guards would know to try to flank, or loop around the direction the shots came from, and that could mean guards moving out toward his intended path of escape. However, after two days, the guards he had observed simply did not appear sharp, and a big part of him doubted they would do anything more than just seek cover and perhaps fire wildly in every direction. He'd been going back and forth in his mind on the necessity of killing more than his two principal targets and reluctantly decided that he needed to heed Armie's advice and take some of them down, especially the two guards he could occasionally see toward the back and the four remaining on the front porch. They were the closest to his line of withdraw, if you could call being within four or five hundred yards of his intended course back north being close. There were also the two younger men invited to have dinner with Diaz; they were obviously special in some way, and that made them potentially knowledgeable about the money and him and therefore dangerous, so they also needed to be killed if possible.

He planned to take his backpack, which would hold the NV head-gear, his nightscope, the unspent ammo, and the FN P90, with him while carrying the 110. He had never used his ghillie suit and was leaving that, the water, and the rations behind, not caring if they were ever discovered. He decided he'd take the ghillie blanket and drape it over him in case he needed to make himself hard to find on the way out. The low ridge of dunes he was on ran more or less in a north-northeast direction and would effectively screen him from view from the house, but in turn, he would not be able to see or keep track of the guards' movements, if any, toward him. That was why Armie had been so insistent on him taking out as many guards as possible—so that even the most dedicated would stay down for a while. Escaping safely and returning to his daughters was the most important thing in his life at this moment, so as much as Jack hated the idea, Armie would get his wish.

He reacquired the group having dinner; Silver Town Car was the nearest target, Diaz was to his left, and the two younger men sat opposite them.

While he had planned to shoot Diaz first, the setup dictated otherwise. Given the shot angle, it would be faster to shoot the killer first and then shift slightly right to Diaz and not the other way around, so he accepted the situation. He would then acquire the nearest of the two younger men sitting opposite his primary targets and try to get them in order, knowing that with each shift in target, his chances for kill shots diminished as they reacted. He was lying in the textbook-perfect prone shooting position and started to breath slow and easy. He thumbed the safety from on to off and then began to exhale very slowly as he placed the thin intersecting crosshairs of his highly accurate scope on Silver Town Car's right eye.

Ray was sitting opposite Diaz, who seemed genuinely interested in the story he was telling about helping plan and execute the assassination of the corrupt president, when one of those incomprehensible somethings happened that your senses, and then your mind, can't at first identify or understand. There was almost a sound, something, as if there was a flashing whisper in the air, and out of the corner of his eye, he saw El Lobo's head silently explode. Diaz bore the brunt of the instant carnage and was starting to reactively flinch or cringe when he seemed to be hammered off the bench-like seat with two very rapid, powerful, invisible blows. It could not have been more than a second or two in real time, but it seemed much longer as the slow-moving gears in his brain finally comprehended what his eyes were seeing and screamed *shots*. He dived for the wood decking and rolled quickly off the porch. He heard Brillo scream and could see his left arm hanging strangely as he was knocked to the ground. Something in his mind told him that the shots—and that was what it had to be—had come from his left. So he gathered himself as he was rolling and dived back toward the end of the porch and what little protection it offered.

Two of the house guards were standing at the rear corner, eight or ten feet from where he had been sitting, watching the leaders eat and listening to his story when the shooting began. As he was diving for the end of the porch, he saw they were reacting much too slowly. The nearest guard suddenly flew backward, and the second ducked behind the corner as a huge chunk of the stucco-covered adobe block wall near his head was blown off.

The four guards on the front porch had no idea the house was under fire and that three men were already dead, including their powerful employer, until Brillo screamed. They were standing in a loose circle, smoking and talking in quiet tones while the bosses had their dinner, as one did not sit when the principals were around. Their reaction to what could have been a scream from around the corner was to simply stop talking and look in that direction. Without a sound the guard nearest the porch's front steps violently collapsed sideways. The setting sun was very low in the southwestern sky, and the intense late-afternoon light fell across the porch, the roof overhang no longer able to do its job. It took a fraction of a second for the other guards to realize that the brightly illuminated air around where their fallen friend had just been standing was filled with a reddish glow of suspended particles their slow-moving minds could not comprehend. The second and third guards were struck center mass no more than a second after the first, and the last, realizing too late they were being silently shot at somehow, was beginning to think about cover and starting his turn to dive clear of the porch when the 7.62 NATO hollow point passed from his right side to his left, the soft, heavy-grain projectile mushrooming and wreaking havoc, killing him instantly as it blew through his upper torso and lodged in the wood frame of the front door.

Jack shifted his sight line back to the rear corner of the house, but the one young man from dinner and the remaining guard there were out of sight. The one wounded target lying just off the porch, the older of the two who had arrived in the car together and had enough stature to meet with and then take dinner with Diaz, was trying to crawl to cover. Jack knew when he took the quick shot that it would miss high and to the right, a likely high shoulder wound and not the center-mass shot he'd hope to score, because the target, to his credit, had reacted far quicker than most to the surprising devastation occurring around him. Jack sighted him but knew he would never pull the trigger. Killing these men out of the necessity born from his rash and foolish behavior was bad enough, and he knew he would have to bear living with the memories, but to kill a wounded man was something he had never done in the corps and simply would not do now.

He shifted his attention to the guard shack up the road to the west. The four men there were smiling and talking, oblivious to what had happened over the last minute at the main house. They were a good quarter mile away and would not have heard screams of warning if there were any, even with the breezes now on shore out of the east. He centered up the nearest guard and watched him as he smiled and gestured expressively with his hands, making some point to the others, unable to pull on him. *That's enough*, he said quietly to himself. *That's enough.*

He slid out the rear of the nest, slowly pulling the ghillie blanket with him. His pack was already loaded and at the base of the dune, the submachine gun sitting on top. He hung the gun's sling around his neck so the weapon rode on his chest, making it quickly accessible in case there was a sudden fight, the extra clips already secure in the deep front pockets of his fatigues. He tossed the light pack that carried only the most sensitive of the gear he was returning to Armie over his shoulders and then pulled the native-grass-covered blanket over his head and pack and started north as quickly as he could. He was down sun, which was not good, the last brilliant rays of sunshine a beautiful sight, he was sure, to the tourists at the beach to the north, but nothing more than a harsh spotlight on him. He knew he had to move quickly for the first ten or fifteen minutes to take advantage of what would be the initial fear and confusion by the guards.

When he reached a position his dead reckoning told him was more or less east of his closer-in alternate B, he stopped, dropped the pack, and with only his 110 and the ghillie blanket, slowly crawled to the top of the low eight- or ten-foot-high dune he was behind, and reacquired the house. Twilight was upon him, and his day scope would only be good for another few minutes. The wounded man was gone, as were the two men who had taken refuge at the back of the house that he could now see clearly from his new position. A quick check of the guards down the road showed that they too were now gone, having apparently been warned by someone at the house.

He didn't panic, but his pulse rate jumped again as he realized he had no idea where at least six armed men were right at that moment. He started pushing sand around, improving his position. A large clump of high native grass was right in front of him, concealing him and his rifle. He decided to change to his nightscope and watch and wait for the nightfall that was rapidly descending on the area before moving again. He knew the human eye really wasn't very good at detecting objects in the daylight unless they moved, and he had looked in vain for a full five minutes as the daylight ebbed and had not seen a thing. The coming darkness, however, was a whole new ball game if you had the sophisticated night-vision equipment he had, for move or don't move, the human body radiated heat, and his scope and headgear would find you.

After a few minutes, as far as Ray could tell, the shooting had stopped. He wasn't really trained in military weapons or tactics but did have a solid police background, and that told him they had been attacked by a sniper, and a damn good one. During the frantic minute he knew for certain they were being fired upon, he never saw a shooter, and worse, never heard a shot; that meant professional weapons with sound suppressors, or scarier, a very good long-range shooter.

The surviving guard at the rear of the house was named Armando, and he was young and scared shitless. His cousin was lying facedown dead at their feet, a hole the size of a golf ball for an exit wound in his back; Ray recognized the horrific aftereffects of high-velocity hollow-point munitions. When he first thought the shooting had stopped, he heard some commotion at the front he was certain was the guards there taking fire. He hesitated for another minute, watching Felix slowly trying to crawl to safety, waiting for the assassin to finish him or shoot at anyone trying to help him. Despite his elevated survival instinct, he impulsively dashed from around the corner and half carried, half dragged Brillo to safety. Ray was experiencing a massive adrenaline rush with the effort; he totally expected to be shot at and didn't know for sure why he had even done it, but somehow he had survived.

As he returned to the here and now, his breathing slowly returning to normal. He ripped off his shirt and applied pressure to Felix's ghastly shoulder wound. Brillo's breathing was ragged and heavy, as he was in obvious pain, but he managed to clinch his teeth and say, "Thank you, Ray, thank you. The back door—get me inside, then help me with my phone."

Armando helped him get Brillo to a back screen door that led to a small kitchen, where Brillo managed to say through clinched teeth, "The couch. Get me to the couch in Diaz's office."

Ray stopped. "No, Felix, we stay here. Whoever is doing this is very good. There are too many windows. Lie down on the floor. Where's your phone?"

"My pocket, Ray...my pocket. Find Reyes's number; he's Diaz's doctor. You need to get me to him, or he comes to us. You must keep me alive. And Montoya—call Montoya, the first one on my phone. He's in charge of the guards on the road. We need men, more men. This is the Banker's work. Has to be, and there will be more assassins; we have been watching six or eight in Matamoros. We need Diaz's phone, the special one he always carries, not the others; and we...need...more...more..."

Brillo passed out from the shock or the blood loss; Ray wasn't sure which. He had the bleeding more or less under control, so he didn't think Brillo would die on him, but he did need help, and right now. He did as instructed and started calling people, getting the doctor and more men on their way to the house, knowing his mission was blown all to hell and gone, all because of some stolen money and now the apparent all-out fight between the partners, none of which was his business or in his mission. To the young, scared guard who was watching him take control, Ray knew he probably looked like a seasoned leader, but looks can be deceiving, as inside he was a wreck. In his six years in law enforcement, the last two doing undercover work with the DEA, he'd been in plenty of tight jams, but today was only the second time he'd ever been shot at. The first time was at close range and he suffered only a flesh wound, although the rib the bullet ricocheted off and snapped had caused him a great deal of pain.

Today was different. He was very lucky to have survived, and even though he'd made it through the terrible day without a scratch, his hands were shaking. Clearly Diaz and Lobo had been the principal targets, and only after they were expertly shot did the assassin start going for others. Brillo was unlucky, whereas he had been lucky on how they had randomly sat at the table; this unbelievably inconsequential fact was not lost on him. If not for the grace of the God he believed in but seldom worshipped, he'd be dead or badly wounded, and he couldn't shake that simple truth. The only good to come out of the horrible mess, besides the obvious fact that he wasn't dead or wounded, was that if Brillo survived and the mission went on somehow, he likely would be more trusted than ever after exposing himself to fire to save his wounded boss. It wasn't much, but it was something.

17

The Hilton Hotel
Shores of Lake Pontchartrain
Early May; week eight

It was a beautiful night on the Gulf Coast of Mexico. The onshore breeze had dropped the temperature ten degrees within an hour of sunset, and the star-filled night sky was awesome to behold absent any interference from man's intrusive background light. Jack lay in the dark for twenty minutes watching through his nightscope as the four guards from the shack at the entry road worked their way slowly and cautiously to the house and then position themselves defensively among the vehicles. Their movements and occasional looks in his general direction told him one of the survivors at the house had his shit together and had passed them the word on a shooter in the eastern dunes. He caught glimpses of the two rear guards now safely in the house but keeping well away from the large office windows, confirming in his mind that at least one of the two was experienced or intelligent.

No one was interested in finding him—that much was clear—so he pulled back, packed up, and set off for the RV. After an easy one-hour hike, he had to sit out in the dark dunes overlooking the beach for hours before things got quiet and he could safely move unseen to his RV. He'd left the kitchen light on to give the appearance he was there on the nights he was gone but would not have been the least bit surprised to find his camper broken into or just gone. However, the proximity to the college kids' camp must have saved him,

233

as he had hoped it would, for the camper appeared untouched. He carefully rehid the weapons and sensitive equipment, cleaned up, and then drove off the beach access and started west down the sandy road toward the highway. It was well after midnight, but he wanted out of Mexico. In an hour he could be back at the truck stop north of Brownsville on the highway to Corpus Christi where he'd stayed on the way down.

It was 1,600 miles back to Armie's, a full twenty-four-hour drive. He would overnight at the truck stop, knowing he needed some sleep first, and then would take off tomorrow whenever he woke up and drive until he couldn't. He did a lot of thinking as he sat in the dark, watching the beach, and thought he now understood how Diaz had found him. With the cooperation the Mexican Federal Police must have with American law enforcement, he had most likely identified him through the routine contact report he remembered the nice young state trooper saying he had to file that night on the pass. That was the only possible way, as other than Henry and Armie, the trooper was the only other human being who knew he was there that night, and that contact information had gone into a computer file somewhere. He had solved many a case himself back in the day by meticulously combing through such innocuous sources of information on the suspects he was pursuing. It bothered him that he had overlooked that possibility, but who could know that the trafficker he had stolen from was a senior police official with access to such information? He stopped dwelling on it, as it no longer mattered; it was clear from what he had observed that Diaz was the unquestioned leader and very likely the brains behind the cartel, and with his death, he felt certain the worst was now over and he was free of them, and most importantly, his family was safe.

Now he simply wanted to get back to his girls and Maddy and try to start living again. This meant telling his daughters their mother was dead and telling Maddy the hard truth. He would no longer live a life full of lies, and that meant risking losing her, but he saw no other choice. He knew that also meant turning the money in somehow, just giving it back and somehow not ending up in jail. He would ask Henry to come to Florida soon and help him figure out how. Otherwise, a clean start and a true new beginning simply wasn't possible.

He crossed back into the US uneventfully at 1:00 a.m., reached the truck stop thirty minutes later, and was in his bed five minutes after that. It was late morning before he woke up, still exhausted and emotionally drained by the last week. It was very hot in the camper, and he was dripping wet with sweat as he stepped into his small bathroom shower and took a cool rinse. He dressed for comfort in a beat-up old pair of denim cargo shorts, a T-shirt, and his old Nikes and walked across the large parking area to the diner, slid into a booth, and had a big breakfast. The strong bad coffee and typically greasy diner food actually made him feel better as he returned to the RV and started driving for North Carolina.

He checked his phone while at breakfast and had a half dozen short messages from Hank, each one testier than the last, and three messages from Maddy, all nothing urgent, just wondering where he was and if everything was OK. As he drove up the highway, he first called the resort he didn't make it to and after apologizing for not showing, explained he'd had mechanical troubles driving down and was fine with the loss of his deposit. He called Maddy next and told her another lie, saying he hoped that she would understand, but after the funeral he had driven rather than flown to California to take care of some business that needed tending to, and to meet with the local police regarding Sherry's murder. It was a cliché to say it, he told her, but he needed closure, and the road trip was giving him that. Remarkably, she said she did understand and to take the time he needed and then come back to her. Come back to her—such a simple phrase, but they were the perfect words, said at the perfect time, when she had no idea he needed them the most.

He swore to himself when they hung up that was the last lie he would ever tell her. He then called Henry to check in on the investigation and the protection on him and for his parents and could hear he was pissed off the second he started talking.

"Jack, I've been trying to reach you for days. Where in the hell are you, and why aren't you answering your goddamn phone?"

"Sorry, Hank. Uh, I've, uh been busy. Some urgent business that had to be taken care of."

"Why don't I like the sound of that? Seeing as I'm here at Sherry's with Sylvia, trying to wrestle all the girls' possessions away from your none-too-friendly ex-in-laws, what in the living hell can you be doing that's of any importance? I called your friend Armie trying to track you down, and he was like talking to a rock. Told me to, quote, lay the fuck off you for a while and that you'd call me back when you were goddamn good and ready, unquote. I know he's your closest friend, Jack, but I didn't appreciate the old son of a bitch chewing me out like I was one of his recruits."

He had last spoken to Henry as he was driving down to the border, telling him that despite his warning not to, he had gone to Sherry's funeral anyway, but only watched from a distance and that he was going to spend some time in North Carolina with his old corps partner. He gave Hank Armie's number, telling him only that Armie had resources for him if he needed them. Henry immediately understood that Jack had given the one other person he always said he could count on a pile of cash for protection expenses. Jack had never heard Henry mad before, and given the hell he must be going through dealing with his ex-father-in-law, he didn't blame him and owed him an explanation.

"Jesus, Hank, I'm sorry, really. I'm a jerk for not talking with you sooner and just dumping all this on you. I should be out there. Please don't blame Armie. I'm kind of like the son he never had, only I just realized that this past couple of weeks. He's only trying to protect me, like you are, and I'm grateful to you. A man could never ask for two better friends...I'm in Texas, Hank, on my way back to Armie's."

There was a long pause on the other end of the line before Henry spoke again, his tone completely different. "Jesus Christ, Jack, I'm sorry I jumped you. It's that ex-father-in-law of yours I'm pissed at, not you. Guess I'm not the friend I thought I was." His voice changed again, becoming even more quiet and serious. "Now...tell me, what in the hell are you doing in Texas?"

"I will Hank; I swear, but not over a cell phone."

"Oh, Jesus, that doesn't sound good...OK, where in Texas are you right now?"

"US 59, just north of Corpus Christi, heading to Houston."

"You're driving?"

"Yeah…I'm in the RV."

"What in the hell are…oh, screw it. Never mind. Tell me your route. What cities do you plan on passing through?"

Jack thought for a second. "Well…let's see. On the way down, I went through Mobile, Baton Rouge, and Houston. That's all I remember. Why?"

"I want to meet, as soon as we can make it happen, and I don't want to fly to fucking North Carolina. Where do you plan to stop?"

"I wasn't going to stop, but if you feel this is important, I will. Just tell me where."

"Let me look into flights from here and call you back. And Jack, please answer your damn phone."

It was an hour later, as Jack was passing through Houston, when Henry called him back and Jack updated him on his location. "OK, look. It's what… three central time where you're at. You have maybe six hours to New Orleans. I want you to meet me there, the Hilton at I-10 and the causeway. Remember that—the causeway. I've got us a room and will land around seven, so I'll beat you there."

"I didn't go through New Orleans, Hank. I said Baton Rouge."

"I don't give a shit. The nearest direct flight from here gets me to New Orleans, and it's not far out of your way. Humor me, please, and meet me there."

Jack knew he owed Henry a lot; he would not fight this. "Sure, Hank. The Hilton at the causeway in New Orleans. I'll find it. See you there in six hours."

It took the full six hours to get from Houston to New Orleans, and he was bushed as he carefully maneuvered the camper through the hotel parking lot. The preceding five days had sucked any reserve energy right out of him, and last night's fitful sleep didn't help that much. He called in as he was approaching New Orleans, and Hank gave him directions to the hotel and their suite number. Carrying only the small duffel bag holding the $50,000 cash, a change of clothes, and his shaving kit, he bypassed the desk, took the elevator to the top floor, and then walked down the corridor to their room. The door was partially open, so he let himself in. Henry was standing beside the small dining table in front of the large floor-to-ceiling window pulling boxes from a large paper sack advertising some restaurant and setting up what looked and smelled like a nice dinner.

Henry turned and looked over his shoulder as he walked in. "Jack, great. You made it. I thought you might be hungry, and the very good seafood restaurant next door delivers, so I got us some dinner and a couple of nice bottles of wine. Sit down. Take a load off."

Jack was surprised and grateful, and over their fine seafood and wine, he slowly and in great detail told his close friend what he had done and why. Most of the time, Henry sat wide eyed and silent, often shaking his head, but he never interrupted. When he finished, Henry shook his head again in obvious amazement and said, "Jack, that's either the bravest goddamn thing I've ever heard anyone do, or the most reckless. I simply can't imagine anyone else even trying to do what you just did, much less pulling it off. I salute you." He raised and tipped his glass, and then he went on. "I guess I can stop trying to figure out how to get the information on Diaz and the beach house to the Mexican cops. That was one of the things I wanted to discuss with you."

Jack had a grim look on his face, the retelling of the killings that he'd brought on himself depressing him, "Tell me what's happening in California, Hank."

Henry told him he figured the girls would need their belongings, so he told his wife he was going back out to LA and get their stuff, pack it, and send it to him. Sylvia had understood in a way only a mother could, apparently, and said she was going as well and there was no stopping her. Sherry's parents were already there when they arrived, doing much the same thing, and they refused them permission to enter the house. The old man was abrupt and uncooperative to a point, but after being threatened with legal action, he backed down, and they were able to finish the job. Henry also told him Sherry's very pissed-off father watched their every move and regularly demanded to know where his only granddaughters were.

Jack was staring at Henry, shaking his head slowly, sorry to have put his friend through that by not being there himself. The years had immunized him against his former father-in-law's hate, and he would not have been bothered by the grieving man's actions. "Did you manage to get everything?"

Henry sighed. "We think so. The place was pretty much cleaned out. The police have released the crime scene, and the old man is wasting no time removing all evidence of the murders and putting the house on the market. I just need to know where to send the boxes. There's a half dozen or so."

Henry paused and looked at him. "Jack, one other thing. I have to say this. Sooner or later you need to contact the old bastard and talk to him about the girls, even if it's to tell him to fuck off and quit bothering you. She was their only child, and the girls are their only grandchildren. Their grief was heartbreaking. You're my best friend and he's a prick, but I think I know how he feels. Call him, please."

Jack thought about it for a second and then slowly shook his head no. "I know you're right, but not now, or anytime soon. I want to get the girls settled into their new life first. Tell them somehow their mother's gone. I know its selfish on my part, especially since I'm certainly responsible for her death, but I need a little time to start putting my life back together too. He'll just have to wait. I realize I'm asking a lot, but call him for me, would you? Tell him I need to get the girls through the shock and the changes to their lives first but that he will see his granddaughters again. As to their things, how about you call Ed Harris and give him an abridged version of what happened and see if it would be OK if I picked the stuff up there? Once I get back to Florida, I'll figure out the best way to get their belongings to Freeport."

Henry looked at him for a second, then said, "Sure, Jack. I understand and will make both calls. Next thing, I don't want to alarm you unnecessarily, but there have been indications that some unsavory types have more than a passing interest in your folks and me and the family."

"Oh shit," Jack said, sitting up in his chair.

"Don't overreact. It was nothing more than our people taking notice of some Hispanic types cruising the neighborhood paying too close attention to our homes. Our guys are real pros and did nothing more than make their presence known, and the bad guys, if that was who they were, simply took off. We haven't seen a thing for several days. We'll keep the security on for a while, but I'm guessing you ended the financial source, so I'm not worried.

"As to the investigation, the local cops are sure the big Hispanic who rented the Lincoln is the killer. But the identification he used to rent the Town Car is a dead end, and they lost track of him after Salt Lake City. No one using the false name purchased a ticket or rented a car from there, so they're stumped on his location and motive. It's known the perp was a Mexican national, and they know he flew in from Houston first class the day of the murders, and no way could he have brought a weapon with him. Everyone believes he was a contract killer, given his access to a cold weapon here, his appearance, the execution-like murders, and what has to be multiple sets of identification, all real good paper. Just why someone wanted to execute the couple is the big mystery to the cops. The law firm they both worked at is a dead end; none of the other partners knows of any case that is so divisive that something this tragic could happen, but the police are combing their files just in case, for possible leads. They're going to waste hundreds of man-hours on this case, Jack. But I have no way of telling them not to without losing control of the situation, so I'm afraid we let that dog lie."

Jack was nodding his head in acceptance or understanding, and then he leaned in close to Henry, his elbows on his knees, his hands clasped together. "Tell me honestly, Hank. Do you think I'm clear of Diaz's organization with him dead? I can't live my life in fear and looking over my shoulder all the time, but…I don't know who else to kill."

Henry had an empty look on his face, and he sat back in his chair and rubbed his hand through his hair as he always subconsciously did when he was stumped or unsure about something. "Jesus, Jack. Honestly? Your guess is as good as mine, but I think so. I've researched the shit out of Matamoros cartels and gangs, and there isn't a whisper about this Diaz being anything more than a good, courageous cop. No connection whatever to the criminal side. That tells me one of two things is likely: either the man and his organization were fantastically good at controlling themselves and information to have remained off everyone's radar, or—and this is what I really think—his organization or gang, whatever you want to call it, was very small. According to all the articles I managed to find, there were half a dozen big-time gangs running amok in that area for years and one dominating cartel, and the Federal Police, ironically headed up by Diaz, with the army's help, rounded up or killed most of them. However, I did find a number of interesting articles on another aspect of the mess down there, having to do with how much of local law enforcement was in bed with the cartels purely for survival reasons. Poor bastards, they almost had no other recourse—the *silver or lead* choice, one article called it.

"I really think this colonel had to be cooperating with some of the bad guys all these years just to survive. It's not hard to imagine that with the decline in trafficking from that area, maybe he tried to fill a void and make a big score and failed, all because of a car wreck. You said it yourself when you first told me about the crash and the money—how you thought the cartels would be more sophisticated about getting their money back to Mexico. There was nothing sophisticated about a single van with two men transporting that kind of cash. The entire transportation scheme just screams small time to me, or inexperienced, so I'm back to thinking a small organization that you've rendered headless. I think you're clear, Jack."

Jack exhaled a deep breath, as if he had been holding it the entire time Henry was talking. "I think I agree, Hank. Call it intuition, but there was something about the way Diaz greeted and acted around the killer and the other guy meeting with him, a respect that one would have with someone like a partner or close friend. It makes sense that a high-profile cop like Diaz would have someone like the guy who killed Sherry around to do his dirty work. And the younger guy, for lack of a better word, looked smart. That also would make some sense. Maybe he handled the day-to-day stuff for him; I don't know. I want to believe what you just said and that I was looking at the whole of Diaz's group, but I guess the operative phrase there is 'I want to believe.' The young partner, if that is what he is or was, is still alive, I'm guessing. I winged him good but didn't kill him outright like the other two, so it's possible he is still a threat. But it strikes me that he wouldn't have the same access to information that a long-standing Federal Police colonel would. You have to figure whatever he knows all came from Diaz, so his access to information is likely cut off. The next several years probably won't be all that comfortable for me, always having to be watchful, alert, but if I ever saw the man or his driver again, I would recognize them. I agree with you about keeping the security people on you and my folks. If a month or two goes by and it's clear you're not being watched, hell, maybe the action I took, however reckless, worked."

Henry looked hard at Jack for several seconds and then asked, "And you're certain about Diaz and his killer?"

If it was possible, Jack's countenance became even sadder as his broad shoulders slumped, and he turned his head, looking out their fifth-floor window at the stream of headlights and taillights moving over the elevated causeway heading north out over Lake Pontchartrain. He nodded his head slowly as he turned back toward Henry. "Yeah, I'm certain. It's the pink mist… unlike me…it never lies."

18

The Townhouse
Monterey, Mexico
Early May; week eight

Ray's fast actions at the beach house had probably saved Brillo's life, and he knew it. Diaz's old addict doctor did what he could there, but he needed greater attention and couldn't go to a state hospital without getting the authorities involved. With Diaz dead, what protections from the authorities he once enjoyed were now gone. He had Ray drive them to his townhouse in Monterey. No one except his brothers knew of it, and now Ray and the old doctor did. Once he was recovered enough to do without the old addict, he would kill him; he couldn't be trusted. Ray, on the other hand, also now knew of this place, but he trusted him. Only a loyal man would have risked his life to drag him to safety before the assassin could finish him off.

Brillo was in great pain, but that confirmed he was alive. The doctor had returned to his room, and Ray was in the kitchen fixing dinner. The painkillers would start taking effect soon; until they did, he had to think. He felt trapped like never before, and his plans and dreams for himself and his brothers seemed all but lost, all because of the money and now the attack by his banking partner. He would gladly walk away and forget the money and start over some other way, but that wasn't possible now, with the Banker trying to kill him. What was most troubling was that it made no sense to kill off the people you believed had stolen from you unless you were willing to write off the forty million US that the Banker thought he was owed. He supposed it was possible the Banker could reach a point of frustration where he would do that; given what little he knew about Diaz's banking partner, he certainly sounded wealthy enough, but it still struck him as unlikely. Forty million was forty million.

In addition to being a place that few knew about, the townhouse was larger and far more comfortable than the apartment, and it was out of Matamoros. Brillo asked Ray to go back to the beach house and take charge of the recovery of Diaz's belongings, most importantly his computers and papers from his office, and also see to the disposing of the bodies. He sent the last of his most reliable and long-serving men from the Matamoros area to meet Ray there. They went armed to the teeth but hadn't seen a thing, nor had their hours-long search of the dunes to the east and the south that Ray ordered produced anything. Whoever shot them was a ghost, and the ghost left nothing for them to find. The men buried the seven bodies out in the dunes while Ray boxed up everything from Diaz's office and returned alone to Monterey.

After Ray returned, Brillo asked for a complete report, and the young killer said the most interesting thing, further confirming in Brillo's mind that El Cuchillo was special. Ray looked at him for a few seconds and then said there had only been one shooter, a professional, obviously, with a high-powered weapon. Surprised, Brillo asked Ray how he could possibly know this. Ray looked at him again as if he were a small child, shrugged, and said, "I looked."

He told him there was only one sign of a miss, and all the kills were highly accurate center-mass shots, except for Lobo and him, of course. Lobo, Ray said, for whatever reason, was head shot and also shot first, and of course, the shooter missed with the two of them because both he and Felix had started to protect themselves, though to Felix, it didn't feel like much of a miss. Felix asked him what he thought all this meant, and Ray said what he had said before: a very good professional assassin with a very accurate weapon.

Felix agreed with Ray's assessment. A man of the Banker's wealth and connections would hire only the best professional available, and he had the entire world to shop in. But there was one other thing Ray said that was interesting or even contradictory to the notion of a professional. Finished with his report, Ray stood and started to walk away and then stopped, turned to him, and said Lobo's killing was personal. For years Felix had been killing people on the orders of others. He'd never thought much about it. All the killings had been necessary to work his way up in the Butcher's organization and fulfill the mission given him by his mentor, the Condor. Never had the murders been personal to him, even when he knew those he was about to kill. The killings, even retribution, all had a purpose somehow tied to the business; the idea of a killing being personal was so foreign to his experiences.

He was puzzled, so he asked Ray why he believed that. Ray thought for a second, as if trying to find the right words, and then said, "You always kill the one you are after first. Once shots are fired, there is chaos, and you may not get another chance. A centered shot is more certain—a larger target, especially from a long distance, as was the case here. But this assassin shot Lobo first and in the head. Why do that, just to him? All the others were killed with a centered shot. That was good shooting, smart shooting. Why then the one head shot? Seems personal to me, like the assassin needed to see Lobo die brutally with his own eyes."

Ray's observation chilled Brillo and made him think. He had never told Ray about Diaz's plan to send Lobo into the Bahamas to kill the Banker, but if what Ray said was true—and to him it did make sense—it looked as if the Banker had found out about this somehow and had acted preemptively and killed the killer, further complicating the entire situation because no one but he, Diaz, and Lobo was supposed to know that. It made sense to him that while the assassin might be a professional with no personal interest in Lobo or Diaz, if the Banker found out somehow about all of their treachery, he certainly would take it personally and order the assassin to do what he did.

While the Banker was never far from his thoughts, he needed to find answers. He had been going through Diaz's personal effects and records for the last day in between doses of pain killers when the pain was the worst but his concentration the best, trying to find useful information. Other than some personal financial information that he would not be able to do a thing with, there was nothing of value except for Diaz's special personal cell phone, which Ray had recovered from his body. His official phone that he had used in his capacity as colonel of the police was of little interest to him, but the special one—that was different, for that was the way to contact the Banker. As strange as it seemed, over the last twenty-four hours, the more he thought about his situation, the more he believed the only way to end the attempts against his life was not to run and hide, but to somehow reach out and talk with the partner he had never spoken with or met personally. When he mentioned this thought to Ray, his bodyguard had looked back at him as if he'd grown a second head but said nothing. A cool, controlled young man, he thought.

Without his share of the money, he and his brothers had nothing to buy protection with, so there was no going up against the Banker. The Banker, with his vast resources, could put a large bounty on him that would mean his end eventually, or at the very least mean a terribly uncomfortable life always looking for the next assassin. After what he had just gone through, even looking wouldn't much matter if Ray's evaluation of the assassin was accurate, for they had never seen nor heard a thing before or during the attack. He'd just be dead one day.

He did have something to bargain with, however, and that was the identity of the truck driver. He didn't know where the driver was at this moment and didn't have anyone currently watching the parents or the lawyer, but he knew who they were and where they lived. The only reason he had gone to Diaz's on Sunday was to report on the surveillance and what he had done. Diaz wanted him to snatch the parents as soon as possible and force them to call their son and arrange a trade, the parents alive for the money, but that had proved undoable. Following the mess created by Lobo's killing of the ex-wife, the parents and the lawyer and his family were being protected. One of the teams of men he hired in Denver discovered this when they did a slow drive by the parents' house and realized they were being watched closely and photographed by another pair of men sitting in a car in front of their targets' home. His men left the area and never returned, and now he had to find new men to take their place.

A man with the Banker's resources could do far more than what he'd tried by hiring proven professionals and not the locals he had used. Felix wanted to make him aware there was 120 million missing, and not just forty, and he believed he had thought of a way to do that and get out from under a death sentence. Only Diaz and he knew of the very private partnership between them, and Diaz was now dead. The Banker knew nothing about him except what Diaz had told him—that he was a loyal lieutenant and, with the death of the Butcher, a minor partner well versed on the distribution side of the operation.

He would play dumb and innocent, explaining that when Diaz ordered him to move the entire inventory in one shipment, he assumed the Banker, as Diaz's partner, was in agreement. If he could get the Banker past wanting to kill him, he would suggest there was $100 million in it for him, not $60 million; all he wanted was his original $20 million share and to be left alone. The only problem was, he had no idea how to contact the man. There was no incoming call record on Diaz's personal phone, and it wouldn't have mattered if there was, for surely the Banker never used the same cell phone twice. His only option was to wait until the Banker called, which, according to Diaz, he did often. Over the simple dinner that Ray cooked, he told his bodyguard what he proposed to do. As with most conversations with the young, quiet killer, Ray listened, nodded his acceptance or agreement with the idea, and continued eating his food. He really didn't have his man completely figured out yet, but he owed him for exposing himself as he did and dragging him to safety. That was a debt he took seriously.

Another day passed with the only action being the doctor putting his shoulder, upper chest, and arm into a bulky, uncomfortable cast. Afterward the doctor had a quiet conversation with Ray in the kitchen before leaving the room. When Brillo asked Ray about it, he wasn't evasive at all. He looked him in the eye and told him the doctor said he doubted he would ever regain full use of his arm. There was far too much nerve damage in the shoulder, Ray said the doctor had told him, and he would probably not be able to lift it, let alone feel much. Brillo blinked hard at Ray's directness and the message, for the doctor kept telling him he would fully recover in time. But he was grateful for Ray's honesty. He would find a way to live with just one arm. He had survived, that was the important thing.

Ray was sitting at the kitchen table cleaning his weapon with Javier Brillo. The younger brother had arrived last night in response to Felix's summons and was watching and occasionally talking with his old friend. Felix told Javier of the setbacks to their plans, and later today Javier would carry the bad news back to Guillermo. The meet with the Butcher's Columbians had already been canceled for a lack of funds, and that connection was likely broken, as one did not contract for the amount of product they had and then not follow through. The one million US that he and Guillermo had put together between them as a gesture of their seriousness was forfeit, and it represented a huge hit to their resources for the future. All in all, he was in a foul mood given how badly everything was going, but he was snapped out of his funk by the sudden ringing of Diaz's special phone lying on the coffee table. He stared at the ringing phone for a moment and then picked it up. The screen indicated the number was blocked—not that it mattered; he would, of course, answer it.

He struggled to operate the phone one handed but managed it. "Yes?"

There was a long pause, and then a rich, deep, mature voice asked, "Diaz?"

"This is Brillo. Who is this?" he asked in his native Spanish.

There was another long pause, then the voice asked, "Brillo? Where is Diaz?" in English.

Felix assumed it was the Banker. He switched to English and said, "You know where he is. Quit playing games."

"This is the Banker. Get me Diaz, NOW!" the voice said angrily.

Something wasn't right. It was just a feeling, but Felix was certain the man he was talking to had no idea what had happened to Diaz. His anger was genuine. That, or he was a very good actor.

"I need confirmation of who this is."

There was another pause, and he thought he could hear whoever it was cursing him with his hand over the phone. "I will give you forty million clues as to who this is. Now, for the last time, where is Diaz?"

Felix was very confused. His confusion and tone alerted Ray and his brother, and they were now watching him closely. He was now certain it was the Banker, and also, unbelievably, he was very certain the man had no idea Diaz was dead. "Diaz is dead, assassinated at the beach house on Sunday."

"What? Say that again. Did I hear you correctly? Dead, you say?"

"Dead. He and six others. I was badly wounded."

The voice changed, no longer as angry, the words spoken more slowly. "Who did this? And more importantly, why?"

Felix finally exhaled and relaxed, for it now seemed they could have a civil conversation and he could implement his idea. "We have no idea. We thought it was you. I have a man who works for me, an expert in such things. He was there with me, and it is his belief we were shot from a distance so great we heard or saw nothing. Obviously a professional assassin, and therefore a highly paid one. We do not often see killing that skillful around here. That's why we suspected you. My apologies, Banker."

There was another long pause. "There is none required. How badly are you hurt?" The voice was almost sympathetic this time, sincere, and it sounded well educated, he thought, as a banker would be.

"My shoulder. I may never have use of my left arm again, but I'm alive."

"It is now I who must apologize for my earlier rudeness. I'm sorry you are hurt and that Diaz is dead, but we do have business to settle. I understand we have you to thank for the distribution of our products. Can you tell me where you are with the next shipment?"

Here was Felix's opening. He'd been trying to think of how to slip the 120 million into the conversation, and the Banker had done it for him. "What next shipment?" he asked innocently.

"The next shipment to secure me the forty million dollars I fronted. What do you mean what next shipment?" The Banker's voice was now angry again, and in no way faked, Felix thought.

"There is nothing more to send, Banker. Diaz said you two agreed on one large shipment, the first one, so we moved it all and collected not forty million but the entire 120 million US. That's what's missing. That's what we have been trying to find! How is it you do not know this? This is impossible!"

He hoped the Banker believed his outrage. The pain in his shoulder was likely responsible, but his tone had been sharp, angry, and to his way of thinking, genuine.

He could hear the Banker screaming at others or maybe to himself, a muffled string of violent curses about Diaz the traitor, then heavy breathing, then quiet again before the Banker went on. "Are you saying you knew nothing about this?"

"I knew about the entire shipment because that was what Diaz ordered me to do. I know we collected the money, for I was there, and I have been involved in trying to recover it. Beyond that, I know nothing. I took my orders from Diaz, and now he is dead." Felix paused for a second, listening. He knew the Banker was there, but he was also silent. Then he went on. "Banker, as we three were partners, until we find our money, I will honor my allegiance to you and follow your orders now."

After another considerable pause, a now clearly dejected Banker asked, "Where are you with finding our money?"

"There is progress, but the details should only be discussed face to face."

"Are you willing to come to me?" the Banker asked—clearly a test, Felix thought, but there was also something else in the voice. Hope, maybe.

He didn't hesitate. "Of course."

He heard a deep sigh on the other end, and then, "Very well. How soon?"

"The doctor has ordered me to rest for a week, but you tell me where and how, and we will be there Friday."

"We?"

"Me and the man who works for me that I mentioned earlier. My arm and shoulder are in a cast. I will need his help."

"Of course, of course. Forgive me; a thoughtless question on my part. Where are you?"

"Matamoros," Felix said, just in case he was misreading the entire conversation.

The Banker's voice changed again, more control now present. "I will make the necessary arrangements and call you tomorrow with instructions. Follow them exactly. I assume you have passports or can get them in time?"

"We have good passports."

"Excellent. Then we shall see you Friday. And Brillo, be careful. Whoever killed Diaz and wounded you is still out there. I assure you, it was not me. If I were you, I would try to determine as quickly as I can who my real enemies are." And then the phone went dead.

Ray and Javier came into the living room, having heard only half the conversation. "Tell me you are not going to meet him, Felix, on his ground. He probably killed Diaz," Javier pleaded.

Felix shook his head. "No…no, I don't think he was the one that attacked us. He didn't know Diaz was dead; I could hear it in his voice. He wants his money, and Diaz was his best chance at getting it. Now I am. And it is not just forty million. He knows that now and has a chance at so much more. He will not kill me or Ray, at least until he knows for certain where the money is. If we are able to recover it, that all may change, but we will have to let that play out. In the meantime, if I feel like we are threatened, we will try to kill him first."

Ray was very nervous and trying to conceal it. The last thing he wanted to do was to go off to who the hell knows where with a badly compromised Brillo and end up in a shooting scenario, all over some money he didn't give a good goddamn about. Keeping his face neutral despite his inner feelings he said, "He will be well protected, Felix. And we will be outnumbered. What do we do about weapons?"

Felix looked at him with understanding and then said, "Most of what you say is true, Ray, but I must convince him of our innocence first. Gain his trust. Going to him with only you to help me tells him I trust him, and therefore am trustworthy in return. As to weapons, do not worry. Diaz has already solved that for us. We will have our weapons, but if we are careful, they will not know this, and the advantage goes back to us. If at any time during our stay with the Banker we feel we are in real danger, we take our chances and try to kill him before he can kill us."

"I do not have a passport, Felix," Ray said flatly.

"That is also not a problem. I know the man who provided all of Diaz's false papers. We will return to Matamoros tomorrow and arrange it, and also pick up new luggage for each of us. Diaz had custom luggage made to pass weapons north to America. I know there were several pieces at the beach house; you will go get it."

Javier spoke up. "If it wasn't this banker trying to kill you, Felix, who is?"

Felix shook his head slowly. "Brother, I don't know. Ray thinks Lobo could have been the real target; I think Diaz. Both had many enemies, but none that I know of with the resources or intelligence to have hired such a clearly professional assassin. To answer such questions, we need money, and lots of it. With the resources the Banker has, if I can convince him of our innocence, we may be able to finish what we started as partners and find our money. And if we do find the money, I am betting my life we still get our share. And we need that money, Javier."

"And if you're wrong?"

Felix looked at his younger brother for a long several seconds, a sadness coming over him. "Then I am dead, and you will be the one who must tell our mother."

19

Interstate 95
South of Savannah, Georgia
Early May; week eight

Jack was having a déjà vu moment. It had only been five short weeks since he first found himself driving south down I-95 with a beautiful sunrise approaching to his left. So much had happened since then, and he knew he was no longer the same man. When he first became an MP in the corps, he pitied the mostly young men he escorted in irons to the naval prison up the coast near Charleston, wondering how they could have been so stupid as to end up facing years of incarceration and what he imagined was the resulting regret and eventual despair. He was on his way to Ed Harris's place and after an overnight stay in the upscale enclave of West Palm Beach was not headed to a brig but, rather, to the beautiful Caribbean. Yet he was feeling a similar despair, the same regret. A part of him wondered where the man he thought he knew had gone, and he couldn't help but think that people can believe about themselves what they wish, but it's the actions they take in life that reveal them for what they are.

His actions since that night on the pass eight weeks ago and the terrible consequences made him remember something his father told him the day he left for the corps. After giving him a final hug, his dad put his strong carpenter's hands on his shoulders and said, "Son, every man is born with just so much honor. It's like a piece of fine marble you carry deep inside, and throughout your life it will be tested, and others and circumstances will chip at it, trying to take it away from you, piece by piece. It's up to you to safeguard it and keep it whole." He didn't understand him at the time, but with his life experiences, and especially everything that had happened in the last eight weeks, he finally did. As he watched the iridescent sun begin to peek over the marshy coastline south of Savannah, transforming the open water of the wetlands from black to silver and then yellow, he wondered how much of his honor he still had left.

He had driven from New Orleans to Armie's place nonstop, and during the long drive, he couldn't stop thinking about the unknown men he had killed in Mexico. The momentary sight pictures of each one, framed in the crosshairs of his scope right before he pulled the trigger, were indelibly imprinted on his brain. He could live with the deaths of Diaz and his killer, even with the knowledge that he'd brought them into his life with his own reckless act, because they had killed Sherry. She was innocent, and her murder was cruel and senseless. He couldn't get the image of her on the couch out of his head, her young life over, his children's lives forever changed.

What made it impossible for him to remain a marine sniper was thinking what he did about the other five men he killed. It was almost a certainty that their deaths were completely unnecessary and nothing more than the turkey shoot Armie had said it would be. They were mostly young and certainly in bad company, but his thoughts kept drifting, thinking about them not as bodyguards or criminals in the employ of a corrupt cop and cartel leader, but as men, maybe even husbands, or worse, fathers, certainly sons or brothers. He had realized years before that his natural abilities and the corps made him an expert at killing, but nothing the corps or anyone else could do would help him live with it. That he had to do by himself, and he never did it well.

Over the last two days, following the detailed debrief he had conducted, Armie as usual became his backwoods therapist. Armie would not have lost a wink of sleep over the killings; they would have been processed in a single evening with his old friend JD, and that would have been the last of it. But Armie knew how the killings were affecting him, and he spent their time together trying to convince him not only that he was still a good man but had acted courageously in defense of his family, and his honor in all things that mattered was intact. Armie's opinions mattered to him and carried a lot of weight, and he was grateful. Despite his outwardly tough demeanor and foul mouth, Jack knew inside beat the heart of a good and decent man. Henry had told him much the same thing in New Orleans, and that also meant something to him. As different as Henry and Armie were, at their core, they were really cut from the same cloth, and their sincere words and friendship went a long way to keeping his head above water and moving forward.

He spoke with Maddy several times during the drive from New Orleans, and she said the girls were fine and the three of them were getting along famously. They were living on the boat together, which the girls loved, and whenever she had to work, the teenage daughter of her backup bartender stayed with them. He had called her last night before leaving Armie's and told her he would be there on Saturday and was bringing all the girls' belongings back with him without having to lie about how he managed to have it. She assumed that was why he had driven to California and back—he could hear it in her voice—but she never asked specifically, so he stayed silent. He realized that not correcting her assumption was virtually the same thing as lying to her, and he swore he wouldn't do that again, but this part of the truth was just so very hard. It was one thing to confess to trying to keep found money and quite another to tell her he had planned and then carried out the murders of seven people, however evil they might have been. How could he tell her when he still couldn't look himself in the mirror at the thought?

Maddy said she would tell the girls he was on his way, and as they were hanging up, he thought he heard her say, "Love you, Jack" or "I love you, Jack." He wasn't sure. She said it quickly and softly, as if afraid to be the first one to say it out loud to the other. But whatever she said, it brought a smile to his face, and his mood lifted greatly. He wanted to tell her he loved her as they were lying in bed their first morning together, but he didn't have the guts, thinking how crazy it probably was to feel that way after less than a day. He'd made a mess of his life for the most part over the last eight weeks, and others had been terribly hurt. He would have to learn to live with that, but with Maddy and his girls with him, he felt as if maybe he had a chance.

Over the master gunny's objections, he decided to leave at midnight and start for Ed's, anxious to get the last leg of the long drive from Mexico behind him. He was used to driving through the dead of night; one could even say he needed the solitude of the road to help him face his demons. Ed had been very sympathetic when Henry called him about shipping Jack's girls' belongings to him. Jack knew the seven large packing boxes had been delivered already, so all he had to do was get there. Ed had also solved his problem as to how to get the boxes to Freeport, telling him he had business in Nassau and was planning to sail there anyway, so a stopover in Freeport was on the way. Ed wanted to take him to dinner tonight and then set sail in the morning so he would be able to rejoin his family by late afternoon.

Once the sun cleared the horizon, it was another seven hours to West Palm. He first returned the RV to the storage lot and then took a cab to Ed's waterfront high-rise residence. Ed grabbed him after answering the door to his upscale townhouse and gave him a bear hug. "Jesus, Jack, get your ass in here and let me get you a drink."

He was a bit surprised by Ed's affectionate greeting but appreciated it and followed him to his large kitchen, where his bar was set up on the central island. Ed poured him a stiff Jack Daniels and handed it to him, then grabbed him by the shoulder and in a more somber voice said, "Goddammit, Jack, I was sorry as hell to hear about your ex. I know after a few belts I've said to you and others that if my ex got hit by a truck, I'd dance naked on her grave, but we both know that's bullshit. She was a shallow, unfaithful bitch, and I wouldn't cry alligator tears if she got the clap or something, but I never would truly wish her harm, and I'm sure you felt the same way. I'm so sorry for your loss."

Jack smiled, looked down, and shook his head. He did feel bad, but Ed just being Ed lightened the moment. "Thanks, Ed," he said, returning his look. "It would be easier if we didn't have kids. Looking at them will always remind me of her."

"Aw, hell, Jack. That'll go away in time; things are still too raw. Come on; let's knock these whiskies back and get your kids' stuff out of storage and down to the boat. The maintenance man has a pickup we can use."

Ed had a classic 1997 Swan 65 sloop he had lovingly restored to its original splendor and modernized so that he could sail it alone if he wanted. Jack had come to love his boat, but truth be told, Ed's was bigger and more beautiful. Between the two of them, they managed to carry the boxes from the dock down to the salon without losing any overboard and then spent the rest of the afternoon sitting in the shade of the cockpit bimini drinking the occasional beer and talking. As much as he wanted to, he couldn't tell Ed the entire truth, instead telling him the abridged version he had told Maddy. After that, they talked mostly about boats, but some about Maddy. Ed knew her only in passing but tipped his glass in salute and winked, telling him "Well done" when he told him they had become real serious real fast. Jack asked Ed about the chartering business, and Ed told him what he knew and suggested that if he was serious about getting into the business, to consider a bigger boat, something more like his Swan.

The hours drifted by as they talked, and it was nearing six when Ed said, "I've reserved us a table and two fantastic Bordeaux for tonight on the terrace over at the Palms. It's high time you start putting the past behind you. That's from Henry, by the way. He asked me to say that, and I agree. Good man, that Henry."

The two friends went back to Ed's place, cleaned up, walked the short distance to the restaurant, and had a fine dinner together. They drank entirely too much and stayed late into the evening as Jack watched Ed work the typically extroverted Friday-night crowd, flirting here and there, on the make for a new girlfriend. It was well after midnight before they staggered back to Ed's place and crashed. Unbelievably, Ed was standing over him at seven the next morning looking and acting perfectly normal, with a strong cup of coffee and a couple of aspirin in his hands. "Shag ass, Jack," he said. "We need to be on the water in an hour if you want to make Freeport by dinner."

Jack felt like shit. He wasn't much of a drinker but had done nothing but drink the first two nights with Armie and now last night with Ed. He realized it was a bad sign, but the drinking was therapeutic in a way, providing him a brief time out from his thoughts by dulling the strong emotions he was feeling. He took the aspirin and then a quick hot shower and was feeling almost human again by the time they shared a light breakfast and got to the dock.

With Ed at the helm and Jack acting as his mate, they were clearing the channel buoy by eight thirty, with *Ed's Swan,* as the sloop was named, pointed at the eastern horizon. With the strong breeze at their backs, Ed figured they'd make Freeport by six, just in time for Jack to have dinner with his two little girls. Jack tried calling Maddy to give her a heads-up on his arrival time, but there was no answer. So he hung up, thinking he would try again in an hour, and relaxed on the padded bench seat in the sunken cockpit beside Ed, enjoying being on the water again. He tried calling several more times over the next few hours, and still there was no answer, so he left her a voice mail about their arrival time. He only thought about it in passing as his attention returned to the wind and sails, but it was the first instance in their new relationship that he couldn't reach her when he called, and he couldn't help but wonder where she might be.

Devil's Cay
The Berry Islands, Bahamas
Friday

The Banker's instructions were simple and clear: be at the small airport in Reynosa forty-five miles west of Matamoros on Friday morning dressed casually but well, and make sure their papers were all in order. A private charter would be waiting to fly them directly to Freeport, with wheels up at eight. Once Felix and Ray arrived and cleared customs, they were to proceed to the heliport terminal at the airport, where transportation for the last leg would be waiting. Felix and Ray did as instructed and at seven thirty arrived at the small airport near Reynosa, where the two pilots of the small white business jet were waiting for them. There was far less traffic in both aircraft and people at Reynosa, and the security was lax, although it wouldn't have mattered, for their documents were flawless. Their flight left at eight central time exactly, and they covered the twelve hundred miles over nothing but water in just under two and a half hours, arriving in Freeport just before noon local time. The customs official who met their jet was polite and efficient, and after his brief luggage inspection and pro forma questions and answers, he stamped their passports and welcomed them to the Bahamas.

The day before, Ray had gone out to the now-vacant beach house as ordered and picked up two of the custom rolling suitcases. While neither one showed it, both he and Felix were quietly uneasy during the customs inspection and relieved when the official closed up their luggage and started stamping their passports. As they departed the customs area in the courtesy cart the polite official arranged for Felix, their personal weapons were now in the country with them. It was only a two-minute drive to the small adjacent terminal that served the heliport on the airport grounds. A native Bahamian-looking man, who apparently recognized them because of Felix's cast, walked up to them as they entered the air-conditioned terminal, introduced himself as their pilot, and asked them to come with him. They followed him out to the tarmac, where a small four-passenger helicopter was sitting. It was very sleek and modern appearing and painted a glossy white, the only color the word *Sikorsky S-434* in small blue letters on the side. There was room enough for two pilots and two passengers, but with Felix's bulky cast, there would be just enough room for the three of them. After getting Felix situated in the rear seat with his seat belt on, the pilot stored their bags in a small compartment and told Ray to join him in the front. Ray did as instructed, and as he was getting his own seatbelt on, the pilot climbed in, belted up, and put a set of headphones on. Then he pointed to a second pair hanging from the control panel in front of him and to a switch labeled Intercom, indicating he should put them on.

Ray, of course, had been in helicopters before, but none as small as this, and certainly had never flown over the open ocean in one. The pilot and Felix had no way of knowing this about him, but he hated flying in small aircraft and was not the least bit comfortable with the thought of the upcoming flight.

The pilot went professionally through his start-up procedures and, when satisfied, increased power and pulled back on the collective, and they were airborne. They climbed quickly, flying on a southeasterly heading passing over several resorts and a marina and quickly were out over the open ocean. The day was clear, but at the thousand-foot elevation they were flying, all he could see was water and a smudge on the eastern horizon that could have been low islands. Unlike the preflight information he remembered receiving on the few commercial flights he'd taken over water, the pilot had said nothing since takeoff, and he wasn't even certain they had life vests. As casually as he could, he turned, flipped the intercom switch, and asked the pilot where they were headed and how long to get there. The pilot never took his eyes off the horizon in front of him but did answer in his British clipped English, "The Berry Islands. Less than an hour."

The Berry Islands. Ray had never heard of them, and his anxiety level climbed that much more. He had far more to be nervous about than clearing customs with a hidden Glock and knife and then a flight over open ocean in a very small chopper. As far as he was concerned, he shouldn't even be in the Caribbean, but Bennie had convinced him he should go. The mission was completely off its rails, but the opportunity to identify and perhaps apprehend a longtime banker to the cartels would have repercussions throughout the hemisphere, Bennie said. There was the potential to get at hundreds of millions, perhaps even billions of dollars' worth of illicit investments, and Bennie told him that was important enough for him to stay close to Brillo and see the trip through to the end. Bennie was supposed to be tracking him through his special iPhone and was supposedly coordinating with reliable elements within the Bahamian police on getting some discrete backup near wherever he ended up. But as they flew farther south over miles and miles of nothing but deep blue water, the vast emptiness interrupted only occasionally by the random pleasure or fishing boat, he took little comfort that was actually happening.

There existed the very real possibility that the meeting they were heading for would end up in a shoot-out, and he knew nothing about their destination or the possible security a banker of this sort would surround himself with, but it was sure to be more than two. Brillo had told him they would no doubt be checked for weapons once they reached the Banker. With their weapons carefully hidden in the specially constructed bottoms of their custom luggage, they would appear clean. Their hope was that wherever they ended up, they would have their own room or rooms and then could arm themselves and conceal that fact from the Banker, just in case.

They had been airborne for fifty minutes when Ray saw low islands ahead and to their right. He glanced at the pilot and pointed, and the pilot said, "Great Harbor Cay." The island, or cay, as the pilot referred to it, was decently sized, and he could see an airport and what looked like a golf course cut out of the lush green blanket that covered most of the island. As they passed by, the pilot subtly banked the helicopter more southward, and ahead Ray could now see a long string of low islands extending all the way to the southern horizon in front of them. They passed just to the east of the first few small narrow islands, and then the pilot started slowly descending. Their destination appeared to be a small, almost rectangular-shaped island in the middle of the string. It was separated from several other smaller nearby islands with narrow straights and sandbars. The pilot pointed to their right front and said, "Devil's Cay."

Devil's Cay. The first thought he had after hearing the name was that the way the mission was going, it seemed entirely consistent that their destination would be called something ominous like Devil's Cay. The small island was covered with low dense trees and surrounded by a broken necklace of white-sand beaches. The pilot flew down the mile-long eastern side just out to sea and then banked hard, bringing them around to a wide-mouthed cove on the south end of the island, dominated by a picture-postcard pristine beach. Off the beach, just into the dense low trees on a sandy rise, he could see a low, modern bungalow-style house surrounding a clear blue swimming pool. There was a path leading from the widest part of the beach to the house, so he assumed they were headed to the bungalow and the pilot was going to land on the beach. The waters of the cove were an incredible pale-aqua color, and he could easily see the sandy bottom, the water was so shallow. Several hundred yards off the beach, where the water turned a deeper blue, was anchored a very large, sleek motor yacht, its three levels and brilliant white paint job reminding Ray of a tiered wedding cake, the many decks stacking upward as it glistened in the afternoon sun.

The pilot did fly toward the beach, but then he slowly banked back toward the open sea, the sharp nose of the small chopper pointing directly at the rear of the impressive yacht. As they slowly approached, Ray could now see the small white circle of a helipad painted on the light-gray decking on the very end of the topmost deck. Located on the handrails of a middle deck were several flag standards holding brightly colored flags, and he could see from the flapping that they were approaching the yacht into the onshore breeze. The pilot continued his slow, careful approach and then brought them to a stop, hovering in the buffeting breezes perhaps fifty feet above and behind the end of the yacht, where painted in flowing gold script were the words *Roberta's Dream.*

As the pilot hovered, apparently gauging the breezes, Ray carefully looked the large yacht over, trying to determine, if possible, how many armed guards there were waiting for him. The first thing he noticed was the main deck had a smaller lower platform just above the water, where four Jet Skis were lined up, ready to be launched. Tied up alongside the platform was a good-sized high-tech-looking speedboat or tender that he guessed was used to ferry people back and forth to the bungalow he had seen on the island. Up a half dozen steps from the platform was the large main deck area, with an expansive seating area for perhaps twelve people just visible beneath the overhanging second level. On the second level sat a man he immediately took for the Banker, relaxing in an overstuffed chair that was part of a smaller, fancier sitting area for another six or eight. The third or top deck, where they were about to land, while good sized, he thought, for a sun-bathing deck, looked entirely too small to be a landing platform for a helicopter.

Rising out of the middle of the upper deck, well forward of their intended landing spot, was an arcing superstructure from which a variety of radio masts, small white domes, and spinning antennas were congregated. This structure also supported a thin, flat, white cantilevered roof that covered the middle portion of the upper deck, providing shade for an extensive, brightly upholstered lounging area and what clearly was a fancy exterior bar with a half dozen polished metal barstools. Beyond the covered bar area, at the very forward end of the upper deck exposed once again to the sun, was a large raised Jacuzzi pool. Despite the great uncertainty and likely danger he was flying into, he couldn't help thinking that in addition to being a landing deck for the helicopter, it was this level where the more serious partying went on. He was very impressed with the sheer luxury and size of the magnificent yacht, thinking it was just the type of amenity a banker to the drug cartels would have.

While very nervous about what the pilot was doing during their approach and momentarily dazzled by the luxury yacht, Ray had bigger issues to deal with. The older man he took for the Banker was not alone. He was casually dressed in a flowing loose shirt and shorts and wearing a broad-brimmed hat and sunglasses, and even though they would be landing momentarily on the deck immediately above his head, despite the strong wind and obvious racket from their approaching helicopter, he seemed completely at ease. Not at ease were two hard-looking men standing in the shade near the Banker, whom he knew from experience were bodyguards. They just had the look; were not dressed as casually, wearing slacks, not shorts; and were watching the helicopter closely with very serious looks on their faces. In addition to the two with the Banker, waiting for them on the top deck were two more security types dressed similarly to the two guards below, their light, short-sleeve, tropical-weight shirts and slacks flapping in the strong downdraft of the approaching chopper. Ray could see they were armed with handguns in skeleton holsters that would be concealed on their hips when their loose-fitting shirts weren't flapping about. The pilot started to close the distance to the landing deck slowly. Ray could see the Banker was holding his hat in place with the same hand that was clutching a long black cigar and still holding a drink in the other. He finally lost sight of him as they made it to a point over the landing deck. The pilot hovered for a second as the chopper swayed gently from side to side and then planted them with a soft thump right in the middle of the small circle.

The pilot started flipping switches, killing the engine as the main rotor overhead slowly spun to a stop. The pilot motioned to Ray that he should get out, so he did as instructed and then opened the rear door and started helping Felix. The pilot retrieved their two bags from storage and then turned and walked off toward the guards, who were busy slipping a curved polished chrome handrail into slots that outlined a round hole through the deck where a small spiral stairway led to the deck below. Finished, the handrail once again in place to keep future partiers from falling through the hole to the next level, the guards approached Ray as he was helping Felix back out of the rear door. The older, more menacing-looking of the two said, "This way" and pointed to the stairway the pilot had just used. Ray went down the narrow spiral stairway first, with Felix awkwardly following him, turned sideways because of the size and angle of his bulky cast.

As Ray waited for him to come down the last several steps, he quickly checked out the large covered middeck area. To his immediate right, there was a wall of glass doors leading inside to a very elegant formal living room. They were still outside but beneath the uppermost deck they had landed on, which provided shade and shelter for a long, informal dining table surrounded by a dozen matching canvas-covered deck chairs. Beyond the dining table, toward the end of the deck, was the sitting area he had observed earlier and their likely host. If the man was indeed the infamous and dangerous Banker he had overheard so much discussion about, then his preconceptions of the man were way off. The Banker was still sitting in the casual furniture grouping smoking his long black cigar. As he turned toward Ray, who was helping Felix, the Banker smiled and waved, saying politely but loud enough in slightly British-accented English so his voice carried over the breeze that was washing the deck, "Gentlemen, welcome. Please come join me."

Ray let Felix take the lead and followed several steps behind, as a good aide or bodyguard would. The Banker stood, his broad smile turning to a look of concern as Felix walked up, and then he said, "Ah, Felix. How good to finally meet you. But the size of the cast. I did not fully appreciate just how seriously you had been wounded. You must be uncomfortable. Come, sit here on the couch near me, and let me get you and your young friend a drink."

The two men shook hands, and Felix said, "Thank you, Banker, for your concern. I have pills for the pain, but the cast does make moving difficult. I wish to also thank you for trusting me and arranging for us to see you."

"It is I who thank you for coming all this way in your condition. And please, my name is Robert, Robert Poitier. But all my friends call me Robbie."

20

Aboard Roberta's Dream
Devil's Cay, the Bahama Islands
Early May; week eight

As Ray and Felix joined the Banker, both had exactly the same thought: he wouldn't have told them his name unless he intended they never leave the Bahamas alive. He would use them as required to get his hands on the missing money and then dispose of them as he would the garbage generated from the galley of the luxurious yacht.

Felix looked at the Banker and said, "Robbie, allow me to introduce you to Ray Ortega. He is my most trusted of friends."

Ray leaned forward and took the Banker's extended hand just as several crew members came out the large glass doors of what Ray thought of as the living room. They were dressed in matching long white creased shorts, matching deck shoes, and colorful polos, the yacht's name emblazoned above their left breasts. An attractive young woman steward took their drink orders, and the three older men were introduced as the captain, the chef, and the chief engineer–second officer. The captain explained that the yacht maintained a permanent crew of six, and whenever they wished, any one of them would be happy to give them a tour of the boat. All they had to do was ask. They chatted for a brief minute until the steward returned with their drinks, and then she and the others all turned and disappeared again, as did all but one of the two guards who had been standing near the Banker during their approach.

The Banker smoked his cigar, exhaling slowly as if savoring the taste, and then looked at them. "Felix, this is Simon. I suspect he does for me what your Ray does for you. We have been associates for a great many years; feel free to say anything to him that you would say to me."

Simon acknowledged each of them with a look and a nod and then looked at his boss. It was warm, probably in the high eighties, but this Simon sent a shiver down Ray's spine. He was bald, dark skinned, and wiry, but he reminded him nonetheless of the recently killed El Lobo, a quietly menacing presence.

They sipped on their tall, cool cocktails while the Banker made small talk, the conversation mostly meaningless, having to do with the Caribbean in general, the yacht, and how *Roberta's Dream* was the centerpiece of a multicraft chartering business the Banker operated as his principal visible business. This information was worth remembering, Ray thought, as he knew that much of the transportation of the world's illicit drug products was done in high-end luxury vessels like this one. He would have Bennie to look into the dirty Mr. Poitier and his chartering business.

The Banker paused, took another long pull on his cigar, and then looked more seriously at Felix. "We have much business to discuss, but Chef has prepared a very fine luncheon for us. I think you'd be more comfortable at the table. Allow me to assist you so we may talk as we eat."

They moved to the large informal table, which was already set for four, and had no sooner sat down than the stewards began bringing out what looked like an incredible lunch. The chef arrived a few minutes after they began to eat and made sure all was satisfactory, and just as quickly, he and the stewards disappeared again, leaving the four of them to talk in private. At the Banker's urging, Felix told him everything from the beginning in great detail, the story carefully manipulated to conceal his involvement in the attempt to cheat the Banker of his share. Felix was telling him about the truck driver and how Diaz believed without question he was the thief when the Banker suddenly sat up a little straighter, a very queer look on his face, and interrupted Felix. "I'm sorry, Felix, but the driver—what did you say his name was?"

Ray had been observing people closely from within an undercover façade for several years now, and he knew instinctively that something was definitely amiss, given the Banker's very emotional reaction to the name.

Felix stopped and was momentarily puzzled, having been concentrating so hard on his story, making sure he kept fact and fiction straight, and then said, "The driver's name is Williams, Jack Williams. As I said, we have proof he was on the same road the night Diaz's nephews and the money disappeared. This truck driver has a questionable past. He was once a police officer but was removed for committing a crime, and now he has disappeared. Diaz did not feel this was a coincidence."

Ray had no doubts that the name had struck the Banker like a thunderclap for some unknown reason. It took several seconds, but then the Banker must have realized he was letting his emotions show in front of two strangers, because he seemed to regroup, slowly smoking his cigar to cover his emotional response to the name, and said, "Sorry to have interrupted. I once had a friend named Jack Williams. Forgive me, but recalling his name brings back unhappy memories. Please go on."

Ray wasn't buying it. Whatever the name meant to him, it wasn't past tense; he was sure of it. The next thought he had was maybe the Banker had enemies of his own, and this Jack Williams was one of them and not an innocent truck driver at all, and the entire theft was not what Diaz had believed. Given all that he had overheard regarding the theft and the truck driver, this seemed like a stretch, but anything was possible when you were talking about large sums of dirty money.

When Felix finished with his recap of where they were, the Banker stood up and glanced quickly at Simon and said, "Get Victor, please."

Simon went inside and quickly returned with the other guard who had been standing near the Banker during their approach.

"This is Victor. He will show you to your cabins. As the captain said, please feel free to go anywhere on the boat, see anything you wish. You will have to excuse Simon and me. We have prior business in Nassau that we must attend to this afternoon, but I will return in time for dinner. Rest and enjoy the day and all the hospitality we can offer. Chef has promised a special dinner tonight. Afterward, we shall see that you get a good night's rest. Felix, tomorrow over breakfast we will begin working on a plan to build on everything you have accomplished and find our money."

The Banker looked away for a second toward the island, as if thinking, puffed on his cigar again, and then returned his look to them. "Yes, the more I think on it, the more I am quite certain we will soon have our money. Until this evening, gentlemen."

The Banker turned to the second guard. "Victor, please show our guests to their cabins, and remind the captain that they are my very special guests and are to be treated accordingly."

The guard simply nodded and waited as Ray helped Felix out of his seat. They shook hands once more with the Banker and then followed Victor inside. It had taken Ray only a few seconds after the introductions to size up Victor and Simon. As old school refined, polite, and intelligent as the older Banker was, his two principal bodyguards were the opposite. They cleaned up nicely in their obviously expensive tropical attire, but not far beneath the surface were common uneducated street hoods on a tight leash. If it was possible, the much more heavyset and bearded Victor was even more menacing looking than the obviously valued Simon.

The good news, if there was any considering the circumstances, was that other than the four obvious guards and probably the pilot, there did not seem to be any armed security types. There was the possibility that the captain and second officer, and maybe the male steward, could also be part of the security, but his instincts said no. The six uniformed crew members all seemed to him to be just what they appeared to be—a professional yacht-chartering crew. If that was the case, if the shit hit the fan, it would be two against maybe six, and if they were successful in arming themselves and keeping their weapons concealed, they'd have the element of surprise on their side. And that would almost level the playing field. As beat-up as Felix looked with the large, bulky cast covering most of his left side, he was still right handed and had told Ray before leaving for the Bahamas that he could be useful with the small handgun they had brought for him. As Felix's bodyguard, he would be attracting the immediate attention of any shooters if things got ugly, and that would give Felix an advantage. He only hoped that if things got that far, Felix wouldn't hesitate and would know when to start shooting and whom, so he would have a chance of living through the first terrible few seconds of chaos.

They were passing through the living room space Ray had noticed earlier when Victor turned as he was walking and said, "This level is called the boat deck, and this room is the sky lounge. Through those doors to the front is where you will find the pilothouse and usually the captain. The deck above where you landed is the sun deck, the next level down is the main deck, and below that is the lower deck, where the guest cabins are located."

They entered a space that could only be called a foyer or lobby. There was a beautifully finished curving staircase going down, but Victor led Felix to a nicely paneled wall opposite the stairs and pushed a barely visible button in the molding, and a door slid open, revealing a small elevator. Victor turned to Ray. "Use the stairway and go two decks down. We will meet you there." He then turned and helped Felix into the small cab.

Ray did as he was instructed, realizing when he got to the main deck that this was the level that contained the truly remarkable interior spaces of the yacht, a fine large living room with multiple plush seating areas and a formal dining room with a small but elegant crystal chandelier over the highly polished table for twelve. He took a few seconds to check it out, shook his head in amazement at the sheer size and luxury of the rooms, and then continued down the curving main stairs to the lower level, where the stairs ended in a wide, finely finished hallway. The detailed wood panel concealing the elevator door on this level was already opening when he got there, so he stood and waited until Felix and Victor joined him.

Ray was making a great effort to keep his directions straight and committing as much of the boat's layout as was possible to memory for when he might need such information. Leading toward the rear of the boat was a narrower but still impressively finished hallway, the paneled walls decorated with several nice large photographs of the yacht under power. Toward the front of the boat from the main hall there was a very short corridor with a door on each side, one labeled C, the other D, and at the end a door labeled Crew Space in small polished brass letters.

269

Victor must have noticed him checking things out, because he said, "There are two guest cabins forward on this level and beyond that nothing but crew spaces. We ask that you do not enter their part of the boat. Mostly they are work spaces—the galley, laundry rooms, storage rooms—but their private cabins are also located there."

Victor turned to the side and said, "This way," indicating they should head down the hallway toward the rear. Halfway down, there was a single door on each side, one labeled nicely as A and the other B; at the end was another door labeled VIP. Victor stopped and opened door A and stood to one side, saying to Ray, "Your cabin." He shifted his look to Felix and said, "Robbie wants you to have the VIP suite."

Ray stepped into his cabin. His bag was already there, sitting upright on the thickly carpeted floor next to a king-sized bed. The cabin was an elegantly appointed bedroom with all built-in, highly lacquered wood furniture. In addition to the bed and two side tables, there was a desk and a bank of shelves and what Ray thought was probably an armoire or closet space. They were standing at the end of the large bed, and opposite them, above the bed's polished wood headboard, was a large oval curtained window—or porthole, as he thought it was probably called.

"Through there is the bathroom; you will find everything you need. If you want something, just pick up the phone on the end table or here on the desk. It will be answered immediately. If you want to see the boat, ask one of the crew, and they will help you." Victor turned to Felix. "This way."

Ray was amazed at the size and luxury of his room, and out of nothing but curiosity, followed Felix as Victor led them the few remaining feet to the end of the hall and opened the door to the VIP suite. Felix's cabin was a much bigger version of his, clearly spanning the width of the entire boat, with room for a sitting area with a sofa and chair in addition to the king-sized bed. Victor showed Felix his bathroom and other details, mostly having to do with the large flat-screen monitor mounted on the wall and the extensive lighting controls, and then, with a nod of his head to the both of them, turned and walked out, closing the door behind him.

Felix waited until the door was closed and turned to say something, but Ray quickly put his finger to his lips, as if silently shushing a child, and said out loud in what he hoped sounded like a normal voice, "A most impressive boat. Don't you think so, Felix?" He turned to the adjacent desk where in a tray was a pen and sheets of thick, creamy paper embossed with the logo of the yacht and quickly scribbled, "They are listening."

Felix's eyes got a little wider, as if he were realizing that without Ray's caution and quick reaction, he would have said something that would have given them away. But then he quickly gathered himself and said, "Yes, yes, very impressive, and the Banker is an impressive man. I'm glad we came." He took the pen from Ray as he was talking and quickly and silently wrote, "Should we arm ourselves now?"

Ray said, "He will be able to help in ways that idiot Diaz could not." He wrote, "Not yet. Let me look things over, and let's try to fit in first, make them comfortable with us."

"In the meantime, the Banker was right. You should take your pain pills and rest until dinner. I want to see the boat and will look in on you later. OK?"

"That's fine, Ray. I could use the rest. What time is it here?"

Ray glanced at the cheap watch he was wearing as Felix scribbled another note: "Be careful and smart." "Almost two, I think," he said, looking at Felix and nodding his head.

"Don't let me sleep past five, and then come help me with a shower. The doctor says I must not get the cast wet, and the shower, while nice, looked small to me."

"As you wish, Felix."

Ray nodded again, turned, and closed the door behind him as he left. He went back to his cabin, locked his door, put the small suitcase on the bed, and opened it. He noticed that while not easily detectable, someone had gone through their luggage and then took great pains to conceal that fact. He hoped the Banker and his guards were satisfied that they did not have weapons.

Felix had made him go shopping the day before for new, tropical-weight upscale clothing, and he began putting his few new belongings into the armoire while he passively checked for CCTV cameras, a thought that struck him after he and Felix started passing notes back and forth in Felix's cabin. He breathed a sigh of relief when he didn't spot any and assumed they were only being listened to, and not observed, but he would check out Felix's cabin at five.

He returned his attention to his typical-looking carry-on rolling suitcase; the hidden space was between the rear wheels in what he thought of as the "bottom" of the suitcase when it was standing up or being pulled through a terminal. The fabric lining was secured in place with Velcro, and after pulling it away, he used a thin Mexican ten-centavo coin from his pocket as a screwdriver and carefully removed the four small screws securing the thin metal plate concealing the inch-and-a-half-deep hidden space. He removed the cloth packing material and then the compact nine-millimeter Glock G26, the two extra ten-shot clips, and his sheathed H-K switch knife. Everyone wore short sleeved-shirts on the boat and so would he, so he could not strap his knife on and carry it as usual. He took the knife from its sheath and put it in the front left pocket of his lightweight dress slacks and went to the bathroom to check himself out in the mirror. Satisfied that the four-inch knife would go unnoticed, he returned to his room and picked up the compact Glock and stuck it in the rear waistband of his slacks, then went back to the bathroom and looked, again satisfied that as long as the wind didn't billow up his new Tommy Bahama silk shirt, the compact gun also would go undetected.

The new generation of "Baby Glocks," as they were called, offered lethal knockdown firepower in a subcompact package. Loaded, it weighed only twenty-six ounces, and at just a shade over six inches long was not uncomfortable stuck down the back of his pants. He tried putting it in his right front pocket and saw there was a bit of a small bulge, but as long as he kept his pants pulled up a little and his belt tightened, his long, loose shirt mostly covered it up. Getting to his front pocket in a hurry was a far better option than reaching to his back if everything went to hell in a hurry. He decided to keep his knife and returned the Glock and the clips to the hidden compartment, refastened the cover plate, closed the bag, and placed it in the small closet near the desk. Now that they had checked it, he felt certain they would not look again, and even if they did, it would appear empty. He went to the desk and picked up the phone. As he put the receiver to his ear, already there was a voice he was sure was the young female steward who had brought them their drinks earlier. "Yes, Mr. Ortega; may I help you sir?"

He was stressed because of the situation he was in, but he smiled at the professionalism she showed by addressing him by name and had the momentary renegade thought about her, thinking her British accent made her sound as cute over the phone as she had looked when serving them their drinks. He knew from past experience that from time to time while undercover, the need for normalcy could sneak up on you, and if you allowed your mind to drift, it was as if you subconsciously reacted normally to a situation when concealing your feelings was required. This was a young woman whom, if he were back in Seattle, he'd definitely be interested in, but he wasn't in Seattle. He needed to get his shit together. He shook his head at the stupidity of wasting a second of thought on her given the mess he was in, and he gathered himself. "It was mentioned that a tour of the boat could be arranged. Can you help me?"

"Oh, yes, of course, sir. If you will just return to the elevator lobby on your level, I will join you there promptly."

An English girl. Never been with one of those, Ray thought, smiling again as he said thank you and hung up the phone. By the time he walked the short distance to the lobby, the attractive young steward was already there, having come from the adjacent "Crew Space," he guessed.

"Hello again, Mr. Ortega," she said as she extended her hand. "My name is Stephanie, and it will be my pleasure to show you *Roberta's Dream.*"

She was about his age, he guessed, maybe a year or two younger. "My name is Ray," he said while taking her hand, thinking that *cute* was the wrong word to use to describe her. She was sexy as hell in a very understated way. *Jesus, Ray. Focus,* he thought.

"Yes, of course it is, Mr. Ortega," she said with a small laugh. "I'm afraid we are a bit more formal with our guests. Sorry about that, but Captain's rules."

"I understand," Ray said with a smile and a nod.

"Shall we begin your tour?"

"Please."

"This is the accommodation level, of course, and it is where our guest cabins are located. Forward, beyond that door, are the main galley and other such support spaces, as well as the principal crew quarters. In addition to our cabins, we have our own dining area and a small recreation space, all accessed from above by a separate utility stairway. If you will follow me, please, we shall go up one level to the truly magnificent main level of our yacht."

It was killing him to have to follow Stephanie up the main stairway, clad as she was in her nicely tailored white shorts, but he brushed the thought away again, thinking this mission could not end quickly enough for him, and when it did, maybe he'd take a little vacation back down here.

They toured the main salon, as she called it, with its large finely appointed living room and the formal dining room he had noticed earlier, and then went out onto the large, mostly covered main deck. They walked out to the very end and were looking out over the swim platform where the four Jet Skis were parked, and Stephanie explained to him the variety of recreational watercraft that was available to guests. Ray was listening, but he was more interested in the nearby island and was looking across the water at the just-visible roof of the bungalow he had seen on the flight in. Stephanie noticed and was starting to explain that Devil's Cay was Mr. Poitier's privately owned island, and the house there was his principal residence, when he heard the whining sound of the helicopter starting up. He knew what it was but asked Stephanie anyway, "What is that?"

"Oh, that's our helicopter. Mr. Poitier has business in Nassau. But don't worry; he will return later this evening."

"May we watch?"

"Of course. This way, please," Stephanie said, flashing her beautiful smile.

They went down a built-in stairway that led to the swim platform and were finally out from under the overhanging second level, exposed to the brilliant sunshine, and were immediately hit with the stiff downdraft of the main rotor three decks up as the pilot was throttling up for takeoff. Ray turned and looked to the top deck just as the chopper started to ascend straight up and twist to the left. He had a great sense of direction. If he could see the sun and knew the general time, he knew his directions. He was not at all familiar with the Bahamas. The only thing he knew for sure was that he wasn't all that far from the Florida coast. He knew they had flown southeast on the way here, and he also knew from the occasional glances he had stolen at the airspeed indicator that given the duration of the flight, they were eighty or ninety miles southeast of Freeport.

"Where is Nassau from here, Stephanie? I'm afraid I've never been to the Bahamas before and have no idea where we are."

"Oh, not far, Mr. Ortega. Only about forty miles from here, just to the south," she said while turning and pointing in a generally southerly direction.

He smiled at her, nodding his head thank you, and suggested they continue with the tour. She walked back up to the main deck, and he followed her, but not before he watched the chopper carrying the Banker as it picked up speed and altitude, heading straight north. His instincts told him that the mysterious Banker had not been planning to go anywhere this afternoon until Felix told him the truck driver's name. He then lied to them about having business in Nassau and was heading to who knows where in a big hurry, but nowhere near Nassau. The Banker had mentioned in their casual conversation over drinks that in addition to his chartering business, he had bars and restaurants all over the Bahamas, his favorite being the one on the waterfront in Freeport. Given the northerly heading, he could be going to Freeport, or Great Harbor Cay, the larger island they had passed on the way down.

OK, Mr. Poitier, where are you going in such a hurry, and why were you so disturbed by the name? Ray mused. His situation was already perilous; the last thing he needed was a mystery, but like it or not, that was what he had. His last thought on the matter as he rejoined the lovely Stephanie was that the Banker knew this Jack Williams, and if all the dots connected, this was the same man who had somehow stolen Felix's money. This fact had shocked the Banker. As to why, the possibilities were endless.

21

Ray had described the Banker's reaction upon hearing the name of the truck driver thief as a "thunderclap," and it had been, and very much more. As his pilot focused on their flight plan back to Freeport, Robbie stared out over the empty ocean, amazed at the coincidences that had occurred and overcome with a growing sadness at the sudden turn of events. The Bahamas had a population of over 350,000 inhabitants scattered over three thousand islands and cays and were visited each year by over two million tourists. What were the odds that the mysterious truck driver his partners had spent weeks searching for was his new friend Jack? He finally accepted the fact that the improbable had occurred because his various business interests put him in contact with a great many other business owners and investors throughout the Caribbean, and through his old acquaintance Ed Harris, Jack had become just one more. But as he came to know him, first through Ed's confidential retelling of Jack's history and then actually meeting and being around him, there was more to it. The similarities in their backgrounds that only he knew about were many. Each had suffered a great personal loss, and he had been drawn to him as a result.

Jack turned out to be a very good and decent man, and because of the turns his own life had taken to a darker side, he needed such decency in his life, if only to help him feel as he once did. He shook his head at the thought and at what he now had to do. From what he knew from Ed about Jack's background, there was no possible way the names were coincidental. The Jack his partners had been looking for and his new friend were, tragically, one and the same. Suddenly, everything had become so complicated.

Since his beloved Roberta had been killed twelve years earlier, the only woman who had made him feel anywhere close to the way Roberta did was Maddy. But he realized early on that their age difference was too great for her and they were destined to be only friends, and he accepted that. At least she was in his life, and that was enough for him. As much as he loved and admired Maddy, regrettably her judgment when it came to men and romance was poor, until Jack. He wanted her to be happy, especially after deeply hurting her with his part in making her Australian boyfriend and partner disappear. She had no idea how stupid her man had been, thinking that when he learned of a small part of his money-laundering operations, he could leverage him somehow. Her former lover and partner had not deserted her, as she believed, but, rather, was lying in a hundred fathoms of water off Devil's Cay with an anchor tied around his ankles thanks to an overzealous Simon. The cost to him for not anticipating Simon's actions had been to hurt the one woman who had shown him he could love again. The note he had typed and given to her to explain the Aussie's disappearance had been one of the hardest things he had ever done. And now, with the realization that he had unknowingly put her together with the man who had stolen his money, he knew he might have to hurt her again, and he despaired at the thought.

Felix was correct in his general assumption about him. He was very wealthy, but few people were aware of this. He had enough hidden away to last for several lifetimes in the banks he controlled by proxy on Antigua and in Belize. More importantly, he could live quite comfortably on the very nice income he generated and reported to the Bahamian government from his chartering business and the bars and restaurants, and not draw any attention to himself. Truth be known, the public persona he projected to his acquaintances who regularly frequented his establishments was very close to the man he believed he was, in spite of his dark secrets. He wished he could walk away from the stolen forty million, especially knowing what he now knew, but regrettably, he'd made his mistakes too, and getting involved with Russian traffickers had been his.

He had gotten involved with the laundering only as a means to take his revenge on those who had in some way been responsible for Roberta's death. The terrible truth had been that there was no way for the authorities to ever really know who was responsible. All that was known was the shoot-out that had accidentally killed her was drug related, and several of the dead at the scene were Mexicans. Not knowing how to kill, or even whom to kill, he used the only talent he had—his banking and investing experiences—and struck back. But unlike the Mexicans he had carefully manipulated and robbed for years, the Russians had proved far smarter and more ruthless, and they would not accept the losses he had created for them with his schemes.

The only good news, if there could be any, given the mess he had created, was they did not suspect deliberate acts on his part. Only poor advice and sloppy banking practices. Make them whole on their losses, and he would be clear of them. The ultimatum had been that simple. He needed a terrifying $100 million to get out from under the death sentence they had imposed, and he was gladly putting up half of it from his personal resources. But he needed the forty million the miserable crook Diaz owed him to help end his involvement. His hate initially, and his vanity eventually, had brought him to this point in life, and he wanted nothing more now than to be done with it. The great emotions that had pushed him to hate for so long had finally waned over the years, and he was tired. He loved literature and had a fine personal library at his home on Devil's Cay; he finally realized that Milton's words from *Paradise Lost* summed up revenge the best: "Revenge, at first though sweet, Bitter ere long back on itself recoils."

Getting into the laundering business had been easy. The getting out was proving difficult, dangerous, and now complicated. He knew well from his own actions over the years that honor among thieves was the rarest of commodities, and now Diaz's detestable actions had led to the inexplicable payback—or recoil, to use Milton's word—he was now faced with. He wasn't sure what he was going to do. He liked Jack, and he liked that Jack made

Maddy happy. Making her happy was important to him, especially since he had broken her heart over the worthless Australian, but with this new development, he was deeply torn. The thought of having to eliminate Jack once he forced him to give back his money sickened him, but on first reflection, he could see no other alternative. Not so complicated was what he would do with his wounded partner and his bodyguard. Simon already had his instructions, and they would be dealt with when the time came, a necessary tying up of loose ends that no one would miss.

With what Brillo had told him earlier this afternoon, he now knew that his dead partner's killer was responsible for killing Jack's wife. He had been very curious when Maddy returned from the mainland with Jack's two little girls in tow, but she said only that they were to live with Jack for a while, and he'd thought little more about it, except in the context of perhaps Maddy finally having some children in her life, as she had always wanted.

As they approached Freeport, he still didn't have a complete plan put together in his head. All he knew was that he needed to control Maddy and Jack's two little girls in order to control Jack and get his money back. The hard part was somehow keeping the truth about what he was doing and why from Maddy. He knew that how she saw him was an illusion, but for his own deeply personal reasons, he wanted the illusion maintained.

He called ahead and had his jeep waiting for him when they landed. He ordered his pilot to stay at the airport and prepare for their return flight later in the afternoon and headed for the marina with Simon. Simon had no idea what was bothering him, and he had to tell him something, and what his part would be in his evolving plan.

As Simon drove them, he started to explain. "When we get to the marina, you are to take Maddy and the two children she is watching and sail for the cay on the boat she is living on. Once there, keep them at the house and treat them as my guests, but keep the crew and my other guests away from them. I will be explaining to her that for reasons she does not know and I cannot share with her, her life is in danger and that this movement is for her and the little girls' protection. Get them there safe, Simon." Robbie paused and then looked sternly at Simon. "And Simon, the girls are young and may get frightened on the open ocean for the first time. Smile occasionally, and reassure them and Maddy that they are safe and you are a friend."

Simon nodded his acceptance of the order. His boss was upset and acting strangely, and he didn't know why, and as long as he didn't know, he would worry. Clearly something his Mexican partners said had upset him, but he hadn't been listening as closely as he should have during the lunch, and he had no idea what it was. He would do as ordered but liked the idea of being around the good-looking bartender; he'd have had her, one way or the other by now, if he didn't know how Robbie felt about her. As ruthless as his boss could be, the woman was his one great weakness, and he could not allow that weakness to expose them. He'd been in and out of Fox Hill, the one terrible and overcrowded prison in the Bahamas, and the last stiff old judge he faced said if there was a next time, he'd be classified a habitual criminal and never released. Robbie had helped to keep him out of jail for the last ten years, and he had money, women, and a life because of him. There was nothing he would not do to keep his life, and that sometimes meant having to do what Robbie didn't have the stomach for. The Russians he was dealing with behind his boss's back didn't seem to have his weaknesses, and their pockets were just as deep.

When they arrived at the marina, Simon walked off toward the boat where the bartender was living temporarily as Robbie went in the back door of the Evening Shadow. He had called Maddy's backup bartender from the helicopter on the way in and ordered him to meet him at his office and to stay out of sight as he did so. Just inside the back door was a stairway leading to the second floor of the bar, where his office and small apartment were located. As he walked in, Harry was there waiting for him. "I need you to work all of Maddy's shifts for the foreseeable future. Call around and get some relief help from the list. You'll be managing things for a few days, as I have urgent business to attend to in Nassau. Any questions?"

Harry shook his head no.

"Go downstairs and tell Maddy I'm here and need to speak with her right now."

Harry, like Maddy, was an expatriate from the States and had worked for Robbie for years and liked him, but he was also scared shitless of him. Not many bar owners would have employed an obvious alcoholic like him. Yet Robbie did, and he tried to help him with his addiction, and he was grateful. After all their years together, Harry suspected the man was into other businesses that were likely illegal. He just didn't know what they were and didn't want to know, but a nice guy like Robbie wouldn't have men like that Simon and Victor discreetly following him everywhere if he didn't need them. He scurried out of the office and went downstairs to get Maddy as quickly as he could.

Maddy was busy serving drinks to the Friday-afternoon crowd and was surprised to see Harry when he came out the door from the kitchen a couple of hours earlier than expected. Harry had a bar towel already thrown over his shoulder and his typical cigarette hanging from his lips as he quickly walked up, but as Maddy smiled at him and was about to ask him why he was early, she stopped, given the unusually serious look he had on his face. "Hi, Harry. What gives?"

"Robbie's here, upstairs. Says he needs to see you, pronto."

Maddy frowned as she was wiping her hands on her towel. "He say what's on his mind?"

"Nope. Just that he needed to see you."

She tossed her towel onto the back counter and walked through the kitchen and then up the stairs. Robbie was sitting at his desk, his hands folded together in front of him, looking at them as she entered. He looked up, and she was immediately worried. The last time he had looked at her the way he was now had been when he delivered her the note from her old boyfriend.

"My God, Rob. You look awful. What is it?"

He looked at her for a very long few seconds, causing her anxiety level to rise even higher. "Jack called me. I do not want to alarm you unnecessarily, but he has troubles. It seems there are men from his past bent on retribution, and they are trying to find him. He fears they have been monitoring his cell phone calls, tracking him somehow. He has asked that I get you and his daughters someplace safe until he returns."

Maddy put her hands to her face, her eyes wide. "Oh my God. That explains…" She stopped and looked at Robbie.

Now he was confused. "Explains what, Maddy? What are you saying?"

Maddy had a stricken look on her face, the color gone. "If Jack called you, you need to know. Jack's girls are not here just visiting. His ex-wife was murdered several weeks ago, in Los Angeles. That's why he has them. He didn't know why she was killed, but this explains it. How does he know they are following him, whoever they are, and why did he call you and not me? He called me just last night and said he was driving to Ed Harris's place in Florida and then sailing here tomorrow. He sounded tired but fine, and said nothing about more trouble."

"Obviously the trouble must have become known to him today. I do not know how he knows what he does, but clearly he is trying to protect you. That's why he called me. He figures I will be able to defend myself better if his call leads those seeking him to me, and he is right. Now we need to get you to safety. I have sent Simon to Jack's boat; he's there now. I want him to take you and the children to Devil's Cay, my house there. Few people know of it, and you will be well protected."

The color was starting to return to Maddy's face as she listened to him, but her countenance changed again at the mention of Simon. "I don't like that man, Rob. He scares me. I've never understood why you keep him around."

Robbie's look also became sadder as he listened to her, understanding. "I know how you feel, and I do not blame you. You know of his past, his troubles with the police, but he is loyal and helped me at a time when I needed it. You will have to trust me on this, Maddy. Now please, go to the boat and get to Devil's Cay. Simon has many talents, but I'm afraid sailing is not one of them; he's there for your protection. I assume you know how to sail Jack's boat?"

She was looking at him wide eyed and scared, but she nodded her head. "Yes, I do. Did Jack say when he will be coming back? Is he still going to be here tomorrow?"

Robbie had no idea and needed that information. "We didn't discuss that. It was a short call. He sounded as if he was on the move, though, but from where to where, I have no idea. Do not worry about that. I will find out and will be here to meet him once it's arranged, and then I will get him to you. Do you have your cell phone with you? The one he called you on?"

Maddy looked at him, confused. Then understanding began to come to her face, and she reached into the pocket of her shorts. "Here."

He took her phone and set it on the desk. "I do not know the capabilities of those looking to do Jack harm, but he seemed worried about their ability to track calls. I've got a new prepaid one for you."

Robbie opened a desk drawer and came out with a package containing a new phone. The one he was giving her was only good for local calls on the island, but she would not know that. He couldn't take the chance that despite his warning on the tracking, she would still attempt to call Jack. If she did, all she'd get was a busy signal. "Take this and call me once you're on the boat so I have a way of calling you back. I'll hold your phone until Jack says it's safe and then give it him to return to you."

The worried look returned to Maddy's face. "Robbie, if Jack's right and somehow these bad people find out you're involved, I need to know that you will not be hurt because you're helping us."

Robbie smiled a fake smile, hoping Maddy would believe it. "Do not worry yourself, Maddy girl. I have protection and connections in the police. We will be watching the marinas and the airport closely. Even though I do not know who is after Jack, I'm sure we will be able to spot the type that would want to do harm to others, and we shall deal with them. Jack will be here by tomorrow night, by the sound of it. We will both learn more, and I will bring him to you. You both will be very safe at my house until Jack can determine how to resolve this threat. Now go, while you have the tide."

Maddy stood and came around the desk, leaned over and hugged Robbie, and then kissed him on the top of his nearly bald head. "Thanks, Rob. I'll call you shortly. Please tell Jack to call me when you can. I need to hear his voice."

Robbie could see the tears welling up in the corners of her eyes, just before she quickly turned and headed for the door and the stairs. He clasped his hands together once again, placing them on his desk, and then slowly leaned forward until his forehead was resting on them, the terrible emptiness he had been feeling earlier returning to him. After Maddy had entered his life and his grief over losing Roberta waned, he realized Maddy could never truly fill the void created by her death. As a result, his affections over the years had changed. What he felt for her was still beyond simple friendship—that hadn't changed—but now he thought of her more as the daughter he and Roberta never had. He was certainly old enough to be her father, and it was something they had never discussed, but it was the way he felt. He was sure Maddy was unaware that his feelings had evolved from friend to surrogate father. To her he was just a good friend—one of her best friends, she had often said—and he could live with that; a father and daughter should be best friends, he thought.

Breaking her heart over the Aussie had, in a way, broken his again. To see her suffer as she had, knowing that he was responsible, was hard on him. He had really never wanted the Aussie dead, even though he knew that Simon was right and that was the answer to the attempted blackmail. He wanted to believe that when he sent Simon to talk to him in the way only Simon could, the threat would be enough and the Aussie would get in line and stay silent about the illicit parts of his business he had discovered. But deep inside he knew that belief had been fantasy. Simon being Simon, he had done what was necessary and presented the fait accompli to him, and he remembered weeping when he sat at this desk typing the false note explaining her partner's disappearance that he and he alone would have to deliver to her. Now she was clearly in love again, and with a much finer man, or so he had thought until he learned what he did today.

If the Jack he thought he knew was an innocent, he could understand him taking the chance he did. From the sound of it, Diaz's nephews were careless and wrecked, and Jack must have seen it and then discovered the money and tried to keep it. When he thought about it, his first impulse was that that didn't make Jack bad; it actually made some sense. From what Ed had told him, Jack's life had been difficult; he'd lost his job, his wife, and his children, all very quickly. He considered himself an excellent judge of character, and Jack had it, and he also sensed that Jack could be very emotional. Losing his family the way he did, and the resulting loss he must have felt, was something he could understand, as he also had felt such loss. As an ex–police officer, once Jack discovered the money, he would have known it was dirty. And if no one else had seen the wreck and the wreck was as hard to discover as his partner had inferred, it seemed simple human nature to try to keep it. He couldn't fault him for that. When he heard Jack's life story from Ed, he remembered his first thought being that the man was good and decent but very unlucky, and now, with the inexplicable crossing of their secret paths over the money he desperately needed, it looked as if Jack's bad luck would continue.

He was at his wits end. He could not see his way through the maze that would be created by revealing his situation to Jack, forcing him to tell him where the money was and collecting it, and somehow keeping his secret life from Maddy. He was certain that Maddy knew nothing about Jack's secrets and what he had done. Was Jack the type of man who could know and keep their shared secrets from Maddy and allow their friendship to grow? He had no idea, but a part of him wanted to find out. Another part of him knew the old threat created by the Aussie two years ago was back, and he also knew what Simon's reaction would be when he learned of Jack's involvement. He could not bear the thought of putting Maddy through the pain of loss again. But it was likely necessary, and he doubted his ability to keep Simon under control, another troubling thought.

He raised his head and glanced at his watch; he had dinner guests for this evening and needed to get back to Roberta's boat. He stood and went to the small round window he enjoyed looking out of and peered over the low rusted metal roof of the bar toward the marina and could see Maddy in the cockpit of Jack's boat, getting it ready to sail. Beside her were the two excited lovely little girls trussed up in their bright-orange life preservers watching her as she prepared the boat for the trip. Simon was there, obeying her orders, by the look of it, getting the gangway taken in and their lines freed up. He watched her as the boat moved slowly under power toward the channel. His phone rang, and it was her, telling him they were underway and would make the near ninety-mile trip in about six hours. She told him she had full tanks and planned on motoring, not sailing, in order to maintain at least fifteen knots all the way there.

After they hung up, Robbie glanced again at his watch. It was half past five. If the crossing went as planned, Maddy would be at Devil's Cay before midnight. She was an experienced sailor and knew the waters around his island well; she would make it. He would have dinner with his guests and then go to the island, wait until she arrived, and personally make sure she and the little girls felt safe and comfortable. He could not call Jack and ask when he would arrive but felt certain Jack would call Maddy. If only he would, and then leave a voice mail with details so Robbie would at least know when to expect him.

As he watched Maddy sail out the channel, a feeling of dread came over him. He wasn't looking forward to the next conversation he must have, and what he was likely going to have to do. A month ago he thought he was regaining control of his life, but that turned out to be as great an illusion as Maddy's perception of him. He was no longer controlling events, but, rather, with the startling revelation that Jack was the one who had his money, uncertain events were now controlling them both.

Aboard Ed's Swan
Saturday, late afternoon

Jack was feeling better than he had in weeks. Just the sight of the channel buoy rocking in the shallow swells and the marina now in sight lifted a great weight that had been sitting on his heart since Los Angeles.

"I'm making for the customs dock, Jack. We need to get your girls' stuff inspected. I'll take care of that and the entry paperwork while you go check in with the family."

Jack turned from his spot in the cockpit and smiled at Ed. "Thanks, buddy. I appreciate that. It's been a long couple of weeks." He couldn't wait to see the girls. That was foremost on his mind, but the thought of embracing Maddy again was not far behind. Ed was a master sailor, and he enjoyed watching him as he maneuvered the *Swan* expertly through the entry channel and made the turn toward customs. Their route would take them right past his berth, so he turned to Ed again. "Hey, Ed, any chance you can drop me off at my boat as we go by?"

"Jesus, you're not too anxious to see your daughters, are you? Or is it something else?" Ed said as he smiled and winked. Jack had been in the sun all day and had a little extra color, but Ed could swear he was also blushing.

"Not a problem, Romeo. Just let me bring her alongside first so you don't go in the drink. I'll square things with customs if they see you jumping ship and get excited."

"Aye aye, Captain," Jack said mockingly, and then, more seriously, "Thanks for understanding, Ed."

"My pleasure, Jack. Move forward and guide me to her, would you? Before we lose the light."

Jack did as instructed and moved to the forward part of the cockpit, where he could see over the raised portion of the salon and past the mast. He looked toward what he thought was his berth area but didn't see his boat, so he did a quick check of his bearings. His was the eighth berth down, right against the main dock after making the turn into the main marina, but the *Second Chance* was nowhere to be seen, his berth empty. Jack's intuition got the better of him, and he said without thinking, "Something's not right."

"What's that Jack?" Ed asked, a quizzical look on his face, not missing the sudden change in Jack's demeanor.

"My boat's gone, Ed. The berth is empty." He grabbed his cell phone and punched Maddy's speed-dial number but got her voice mail again. Under normal conditions, given the sailor that she was, the first and most logical assumption would be that she had taken the boat out for an afternoon sail and simply was not back yet. But his life was far from normal, and there was no explaining her not answering her phone this morning, or now.

"Something's happened, Ed. I know it."

Because Ed didn't know the full story, he simply could not see or under-stand Jack's boat being gone as all that ominous. "Easy, Jack. She's probably on the water. It's near dark. Money says she follows us in. I must have seen a dozen sloops rigged liked yours as we were coming in."

Jack's lips were pursed, his look grave. "Get us docked, Ed. I'll run up to the bar and ask. Someone there will know."

Ed nodded his head and made for the customs dock as quickly as was allowed, confused by the urgency and the worry Jack was exuding. Jack had the bumpers over the side and was tossing lines to the dock hands when the boat was still several feet off the dock, and then he jumped from the *Swan* to the dock and took off for the Evening Shadows at a sprint, drawing a serious look from the customs official who had come out of the small building as they approached.

"Ahoy there," Ed said loudly, drawing the attention of the official to him. "That's Jack Williams. He's berthed here on an annual basis. Don't mind him; come aboard."

It only took Jack a minute to run to the restaurant. Given the time of day, the place was packed, as usual, and he had to work his way through the crowd to get to the bar. Maddy's backup bartender Harry was working, as was another bartender he couldn't recall having seen before. He got the attention of Harry, who nodded when he saw Jack and motioned to him that he should go to the end of the bar. Once they were standing close enough to hear each other over the din of the other patrons, and before he could ask Harry about Maddy, Harry leaned in to him and said, "Robbie's upstairs. Said I was to tell you he needs to see you the minute you came in. Through the kitchen, then make a left and up the stairs."

Jack nodded and made for the door. Harry never looked all that happy, even in the best of times, but he looked more serious than usual to Jack, and that only increased his rising anxiety levels as he raced through the kitchen, startling the cook and his two helpers, and then took the stairs up two at a time. Robbie's office was right in front of him as he reached the second floor, the door open. He saw Robbie standing, looking out a small round window that must have looked out over the marina. When Robbie heard Jack coming in, he looked at him, then slowly turned and walked to his desk and sat down. The grim look on Robbie's face was unsettling to Jack and sent a cold chill down his back. Given everything that had happened in the last couple of weeks, Robbie's look put the fear of God in him, and he expected the worst. "Robbie, what's wrong? Where's my boat? Where's Maddy and the kids?"

Robbie was looking at him, his look changing, becoming more troubled, as if he didn't know what to say.

"For Christ's sake, Rob, tell me. Where are Maddy and my girls?"

"Sit down, Jack. They…are safe."

Jack stared at him. The words were welcome but not what he was expecting to hear, and the way Robbie said it confused him. It had been a statement of fact, totally devoid of warmth or caring. Just, *they are safe.*

The words were said so flat, so cold, he was knocked off balance. "They're safe? Jesus, Robbie, what the hell does that mean? Safe from what? What's happened?"

Jack was still standing, leaning forward, his hands on the desk. Robbie was looking up at him, his face frozen and pained. "Sit down, Jack," he said softly and sadly. "I'm afraid we have much to talk about."

22

Hearing from Robbie that Maddy and the girls were safe was reassuring as far as it went, but Robbie's entire manner was so strange, so distant. Nothing like the warm, ebullient man he had come to know. He slowly sat down, but his senses were suddenly heightened. Something was very wrong here, and he had no idea what it could be.

Robbie's next words came more slowly, and with great melancholy, it seemed. "We are so much alike, Jack. So much more than you know. Ed has told me some about your past, all the terrible misfortune you have experienced, and now…the mother of your children is dead, and in such a violent and tragic way. My Roberta was also killed tragically by those associated with the trafficking, but I'm guessing you and I are the only ones who know that."

Jack was stunned. There was no way Robbie could know about his ex-wife, but he seemed to. Robbie swiveled his chair slightly and seemed to be looking up through the small round window in the wall adjacent to his desk. All that could be seen without standing up were some passing clouds, vibrantly brushed in hues of orange and red with the approaching sunset. He turned back to Jack and slowly started talking again in his rich, deep voice, but softer, as if reminiscing or telling a child a bedtime story.

"I met Roberta in London, at the School of Economics during our first year. I was so full of myself back then, so vain. I thought myself the brightest among a very bright group, yet she eclipsed me, and in so many ways. She made me a better student, and we became fast friends, which, given the great differences in our backgrounds, was a surprise to me. Early in our second year, when she told me she felt as strongly about me as I did about her, we moved in together and became a real couple. The day after we graduated, we married in a small civil ceremony in London with only our few closest friends about us. It seems even in a liberal-minded nation such as England, the aristocracy her family was a part of could not accept her marrying someone like me. She did so against their wishes and then compounded their opposition and resentment by moving with me back to Nassau. She sacrificed everything to be with me, and not only did she not have any regrets, she gave me the greatest gift of all by showing me through her kindness how I could be a better man."

Robbie paused, clearly moved emotionally by the retelling of the memories. He looked at Jack for a long few seconds, composing himself, and then went on. "I've never known such love, such happiness, Jack. With what has happened to you, perhaps you alone are in the unique position to really understand what I felt when she was struck down twelve years ago…she was shopping, just one of hundreds on a crowded street. The two local drug gangs that opened fire on each other were two blocks away. I doubt she even heard the gunfire. We will never know what it was they were fighting over. All the official record says is that the shoot-out occurred, and two blocks away, three innocent bystanders were struck by stray shots, and one, tragically, was killed—my Roberta."

Jack felt genuine pain for Robbie as he talked; looking at him, he could see the great sorrow that still existed in him at the simple retelling of the events. But his feelings of sympathy were overcome by a rising feeling of dread and a basic question: *Why is he telling me this, and how on earth does he know how Sherry was killed?*

"I had no idea, Robbie. No one has ever said a word to me about your past, and I am sorry. I think I do know how you must have felt, but why are you telling me this now? What's this have to do with Maddy and the kids? What are they safe from?"

If it was at all possible, Robbie's look became even graver than it had been during the telling of his recent past.

"We both have our secrets, Jack. It is why I said we are so much alike. I also believe that we are much alike as men, in our basic decency and honor. Yet somehow, destiny has taken over our lives, and we no longer control the paths we are on. And as remarkable as it seems, those paths have crossed, our secrets merging. I think I know everything now and still have trouble believing it, but it has happened."

Jack's intuition was telling him he was about to be blindsided, exposed to the light as Henry once warned him was possible. "Robbie, I'm very confused, and I'm afraid I don't understand. What's happened? What in the hell are you talking about?"

"You are here, Jack, and not in your Colorado, where you ought to be. And it seems you have something of mine, and sadly, as a result, I have something of yours."

Jack couldn't believe what he was hearing, and his confusion was rapidly turning to anger at what was clearly a veiled threat. "Robbie, I don't know what you're thinking or what you think you know, but if you're saying you have my kids…"

Robbie slowly raised his hand, as if telling Jack silently to calm down. "Your children are safe and will remain so, and I'm disappointed that you think I could ever harm them. My secrets are as dark as yours, Jack. Perhaps darker, and like your life, mine has not turned out as I wished. I want nothing more than to unite you with Maddy and your children, just as soon as you return to me the money that is not yours."

Jack sat back in his chair, his rising anger snuffed out by the tidal wave of words that had just washed over him. *Jesus Christ, how in the hell does he know? Am I never to be done with this!* He was flabbergasted and couldn't speak, and Robbie could easily tell.

Robbie looked away from him again toward the small window, as if lost in thought, and then, in his soothing voice, continued with his story. "I believe

I can imagine what happened. You were alone, driving a deserted mountain road late at night, no doubt thinking about your daughters, if I know you like I think I do, saddened at having left them in California with the mother who so unfairly took them from you. The night was dark, the traffic light perhaps nonexistent in such a place, and there was an accident."

Robbie turned back to him, their eyes locking, his soft and understanding, Jack's full of apprehension and fear. Then Robbie went on. "I have no doubt that you were trying to do the right and good thing, because that is the kind of man you are. You stopped, didn't you? Your only thought being to help the poor unfortunate victims, the true and good Samaritan. But, I'm guessing, given the rugged area, the accident was catastrophic, and you found Diaz's nephews dead. And, of course, you then found the money. I've spent a lot of time in the last twenty-four hours trying to put myself in your shoes. For the same reasons I think you can understand my grief, I believe I can understand your actions. I know what desperation feels like, Jack, the wishing that you can change events that seem so beyond your reach or control. You were feeling such desperation that night, I would guess, and then suddenly, fate steps in, and there it is—a path out. In your shoes I would have done the same thing. You took a chance and tried to change your path for the better, but what have you found down that path, Jack? Is there happiness? Is the desperation gone? I suspect not, for I have been traveling a similar path for twelve years now, and despite my wishes and my best intentions, there exists nothing but more loss, more despair."

Robbie leaned in toward him, his entire manner that of a friend or confidant sharing a private moment. "In many ways my path is so much worse than yours, for where you took a chance with a serendipitous event and were propelled almost innocently down yours, I consciously, and with malice, planned mine. My reasons were perhaps more noble than yours, the avenging of my beloved Roberta's death, but who's to say what is noble in these times and circumstances and what is not?

"Let me save you more heartbreak, Jack. Down that path you've chosen lies nothing but sadness and your eventual destruction. I know. The wounds never heal, and they ultimately lead only to one's own unhappy end. Our fates are, sadly, the same. We are once again both ruled by forces we cannot control, and happiness, I fear, is forever beyond our reach. You are a good man, I think, and have been so very unlucky, it seems to me. I suppose one could say that I also was unlucky, that my wife was struck down as she was, but the truth is that luck had nothing to do with where I find myself today. With Roberta's death, and without her love and guidance, I desired only revenge, and I once again became vain and thought myself so much smarter than those I sought out to do business with and wished to destroy. I was bitter and wrong, where you truly are just unlucky."

Jack was still flabbergasted that Robbie knew everything, and he had a thousand questions. But his mind was spinning, and he'd lost all spit, his mouth as dry as the Mexican beach he had camped at. All he could manage to say in his distraught state was, "How, Robbie?"

Robbie sat back and smiled a small smile. Jack had no idea what made him do this. There was nothing funny about the conversation or the situation. Maybe it was the look on his face or the stupid simplicity of his question.

"Ah...such a simple question; I only wish there were a simple answer, Jack. But what is it you are really asking? I wonder. How do I know what I know about you and your secrets? Or are you asking about my secrets? How is it that the money is mine, and how did I come to be where I am today? Do you feel enough friendship or compassion for me in the short time we have known each other to ask such a meaningful question? Sadly...for both of us...I think not.

"There's more I must tell you Jack, none of it good, I'm afraid. Unfortunately for you, I required Mexican partners to help free me of the Russians I unwisely involved myself with, and we seem to have those Mexicans in common. Several of those looking for you and the money were responsible for your wife's murder, but you know this. Now...they too are dead, and the timing of their deaths and your recent travels seems too coincidental to me, so I ask myself, Where have you been, Jack? And more importantly, what have you done?

"Ed mentioned you were a member of your corps of marines for a very long time before becoming a police officer. I'm curious. What is it you did for those years in your military's elite service? Such service would suggest that you are capable of killing men. Is there blood on your hands, Jack? If so, one would never guess this after getting to know you. Another of your dark secrets, I presume? Are you in league with others, I asked myself rhetorically last night, guiding events somehow, or are you simply reacting? It didn't take much thought to realize that in the short time we have known each other, I feel I know with certainty you are simply not the type of man who indiscriminately plots, steals, and kills. I suspect that after your wife's murder, you realized that my Mexican partners had discovered you, and you only did what you felt you had to do to protect yourself and the rest of your family. Ironically, I admire you for what you have done. That took great courage. One might even say it was noble—good overcoming evil—even if what you did is contrary to civilized behavior. That being the case, can you not see that my actions over the last dozen years were not so unlike yours, and therefore no less noble?"

Robbie leaned in toward Jack and said with emphasis, "I…don't…know… how…to kill, Jack."

He leaned back and seemed to sigh, the look of despair returning to his face, and was lost in thought again before adding, "In honesty, I should amend my last comment and say, at least not with my own hands, but that is another part of my sad story that I shall keep to myself.

"You, on the other hand, I'm guessing know how to kill, but I understand why. Faced with my own terrible tragedy and not having your skills, I had to try to exact my revenge in the only way I knew. So I became a banker to the filth that traffics, laundering the only thing they care about—their dirty money. Only I did it in ways that cost them dearly. I cheated and manipulated them out of tens of millions, steered them to worthless investments, charged them outrageous transaction fees, anything I could get away with to hurt them. As a result, in Roberta's name, so much good has been funded here in the islands with what I have stolen. Schools and hospitals that would not exist. Scholarships for our best students, programs for the needy. But as someone once said, Jack, revenge is a bitter pill. I have lost my appetite for it and find that I simply want out and to have a chance to live again.

"In the last few years, with the demise at the hands of the Mexican authorities of so many of my clients, the opportunity seemed right for stopping and putting that terrible life and my terrible secrets behind me. But I let my vanity rule me again and made a fatal mistake, cheating those not so easily fooled by my manipulations. I can still get out. The Russians suspect only that I gave them bad advice and handled their money poorly, and they will accept reimbursement for my actions in exchange for my life. I understand your desperation, Jack, for I too am desperate. The money you stole is part of what I must pay to get my life back. So you must tell me where it is, and as distasteful as it is for me to have to say this, until I have it, I am going to have to ask you to accompany me to a place where we will wait until I have confirmed it. Once I have the money, you will have your daughters. I am sorrier than you can know that circumstance has brought us to such a moment."

Jack's anger was slowly rising with the threats to him and his daughters, but so were his feelings of desperation that Robbie seemed to know so well.

"I don't even want the money anymore, Robbie. Thinking I could take it and somehow my life would be better was the greatest mistake I've ever made. I just want my life back, my girls, and Maddy. But what guarantees do I have that after I tell you where it is, you don't kill me and my family? I've done some dumb things in the last couple of months, but I'm not stupid or naive. How can I possibly trust a man who has kidnapped two little girls to use as leverage? What the fuck kind of man does that, Robbie? Tell me. Noble? Any thoughts on nobility you ever had went out the window when you took my girls!"

Jack had lost his temper, something he seldom did. He was breathing heavily, was red in the face, and had risen out of his chair and was leaning very menacingly into Robbie.

Robbie's expression never changed. He'd leaned back in his chair as Jack had stood, his hands folded on his stomach, listening, as if their conversation were a normal one. He then simply raised his hand again, as if silently with a gesture telling a child to quiet down. In his soft and calm voice, he went on. "I deserved that outburst, Jack, and would have acted similarly, I think, if our positions were reversed. You are an honorable man. I know this, in spite of the actions you were forced to take recently. I don't blame you at all for having tried to keep the found money and change your life, and I don't blame you for the revenge you exacted from my former partners in defending your family. You made some hard choices in the last several months. Can you not see that I am not so different, my choices no less difficult?

"As to your lovely daughters, I would never harm a child and would certainly never harm Maddy. She is as dear to me as your daughters are to you, and I love her very much. She is in love with you, Jack. I can see it in her, and I'm happy for her and would never want to see her happiness destroyed. Surely for her sake we can work this out as men of honor. I assume the money is still on the mainland. If that's the case, you or I, depending on how you wish to do this, will have to arrange to get it here safely. Can we not reason our way through this and trust each other? If you wish, get the money here yourself, and when you return, your girls will be here waiting for you.

"There has been enough blood spilling, Jack. I need that money, and I want my secrets to stay concealed, especially from Maddy. Do you not wish for the same thing? And if so, cannot this be the foundation for how we resolve this—a shared destiny from this moment forward? Can we not be friends and help each other out of the darkness that is ruling our lives?"

As Robbie was talking, Jack knew in his heart that he was going to tell Maddy everything. If they were to have a life, it would not be built on lies, but he also knew that was the last thing he would tell Robbie as long as he had the kids. He had settled down some and was trying to get control of his emotions. He had to buy some time and think. He thought it likely that Robbie was telling him the truth—some truth, anyway, the parts about Maddy and the girls not being harmed. He, on the other hand, was in the deep shit. Despite glimpses of what he thought was sincerity from Robbie, he could see and hear it in him that keeping all this from Maddy was very important to him for some reason, and the only way Robbie could be certain his secrets would always be safe was if Jack was dead. He had to just play along until he could see his way through this mess, and until he could, he realized his life was hanging by a thread.

"The money is in packing boxes in a secure storage facility near Miami. There's so much of it that it's hard to move without drawing attention. I'll tell you which storage business and the access codes after I see for myself that Maddy and the girls are OK. I must see them, Robbie. You want the money, you send someone to go get it and bring it safely here. I'm through with it. But from this moment on, you and I stay together until we each have what we want. I insist on that. Once your people call you, my girls and Maddy and I leave together. I don't know if we can ever be friends after this, Robbie, but I'll keep your secrets if you'll keep mine. Our own devil's bargain."

Robbie knew a subtle threat when he heard one, but again understood where Jack was coming from and accepted it. He slowly stood up and then extended his hand toward Jack. "Trust, Jack. That is the key. I want you to have your life, just as I wish to have my own. Please accept my hand in trust."

Jack stood, and they shook hands. All he saw in Robbie's eyes was sadness, but sadness about what was the big question.

For Robbie's part, what he saw in Jack's eyes was determination, or perhaps calculation. He couldn't decide which. And like Jack, he had no idea what that meant. But if Jack was responsible for the recent killings in Mexico—and he believed he was—that could only mean danger, and that would force his hand.

Robbie called down to the bar and told Harry to keep an eye out for Ed Harris and tell him that some trouble had come up from Jack's past, and Jack would call him later. They left together out the back door and took Robbie's jeep to the airport. Robbie called ahead and told someone named Charles that they were on their way and to prepare the helicopter. Once they arrived at the small terminal building, Robbie led him out to the small helicopter sitting on the tarmac, where the pilot Robbie had talked with was waiting for them. They both got in the backseat and belted in. As the pilot climbed in, Jack's police eye detected the subtle bulging of a shoulder holster under the light windbreaker he was wearing. The sun was just setting by the time they took off; they flew south over the now-lit-up marina and then quickly were out over the black ocean. Robbie leaned in close to him after takeoff and told him their flight would last about an hour. After that, neither one said another word, each wrestling with his own thoughts and emotions.

They were airborne for no more than forty-five minutes, and except for a few lights on an island they flew past, Jack saw nothing but blackness. He could feel the chopper beginning to descend but couldn't tell how far they were above the black water. Off to his right was a different shade of black and the ghostly irregular shape of an island. There seemed to be a growing yellow glow there as well, and suddenly, as they banked around the end of the now more visible island, he could see a large, brightly illuminated motor yacht sitting just offshore. As the pilot maneuvered them slowly and carefully for the few minutes it took to set them down on the well-lit top deck of the large yacht, Jack was closely watching the two men waiting there, hunched over against the strong downdraft of the main rotor. As he and Robbie waited a few seconds for the main rotor to a stop, Robbie turned to him and said, "You will join me in my suite, Jack. There we will talk more in private."

Robbie must have seen him checking out the two guards and went on. "You've noticed my men. Let answer the questions you must be thinking. They are part of my personal guard, and they are armed. Not because of you or your presence, but rather as a precaution against those I owe so much money to. That is God's truth, Jack."

Jack nodded his head as if he accepted the explanation, opened the door of the helicopter, and got out. He had been arresting bad guys for many years and could tell in a second what kind of lowlifes Robbie's guards were. As to the plan he was evolving in his head on the fly, he now had three possible shooters to keep track of and deal with.

With one of the two guards leading the way and the other following, Robbie led them down a small spiral stairway to the next deck, where a sliding glass door was already open and the first guard was standing in such a way that the only direction Jack could go was inside. As he was descending the last few steps, he glanced toward the stern and a plush seating area located there. Two men were seated, casually drinking and watching the small parade coming down the stairs. Both were young, and one was in a bulky cast. He immediately remembered the faces and had a sudden adrenaline rush as the sight picture of the man he had wounded in Mexico popped into his head. The other younger man was certainly the driver he had missed entirely, who had also been taking the final meal with Diaz. He now understood more fully how Robbie knew what he had done, and he silently cursed his luck that the men he'd ripped off had Robbie as their money launderer. As he stepped into the plush interior, his mental list of shooters to keep track of went from three to five.

They passed through a large informal space that Robbie identified as the sky lounge, then down a highly finished curving stairway to the main deck below. The owner's suite was also on the main level, forward of the formal dining room. The suite was large and truly magnificent. Robbie stood to one side to let Jack enter first and then closed the double-door entry behind him while the two guards took up positions outside. Jack stood in the middle of the room taking it all in, his mind still in a state of shock at seeing two of the men he had tried to kill in Mexico sitting and drinking on the same boat he was now on. It was clear from looking at them that while he knew who they were, they had no idea who he was. Curiosity only registered on their faces as he had briefly passed from the stairway to the interior, but nothing more.

"Please, Jack, sit here and make yourself comfortable," Robbie said as he pointed to a comfortable-looking seating area. "May I get you a drink? Something cool, perhaps refreshing?"

Jack was between a rock and a hard spot. He wanted Robbie and his shooters relaxed as if he was cooperating, but knew he was lousy at concealing his feelings. Trying to play along as if he and Robbie had a true bargain was simply beyond him. "No drink, Robbie. Where are my kids? Are they aboard?"

Robbie looked momentarily disappointed with Jack's terse tone, then said, "Nearby, Jack, as is Maddy and your boat. She sailed it here last night. She of course knows nothing about what exists between us. I told her you had troubles from your past and called me yesterday and asked that I get her and your girls to safety. What I propose, with your acceptance, is that you tell me where the money is, I have my people go verify it, and then we part as friends and get on with our lives. If your journey is to continue here in the islands, it is my hope we truly will be friends."

"I need to see them, Robbie."

Robbie looked at him and then picked up a TV remote sitting on the coffee table in front of them and pointed it at the large flat-screen monitor mounted on the exquisitely paneled wall. The screen came up blue. Then a computerlike menu appeared, and Robbie scrolled from one topic to another until he clicked on what he was searching for. The screen was now split into four very sharp black-and-white images, obviously CCTV views of four different rooms. The brighter, lower-left image was of a large family-room space with a kitchen in the background. Sitting on the couch watching television was Maddy, with one of his girls on each side, her arms around them.

"Closed-circuit security camera views of my home on the island, Jack. As you can see, all is well, just as I said it would be."

Jack's heart was heavy as he emotionally watched the silent scene for a full minute. Robbie, for his part, seemed to understand and also stayed silent, watching him. Finally, Jack turned and looked at him. "Get something to write on."

Robbie's hope that somehow this could all end without Jack's death was fading fast. Jack was so angry with him—Robbie could see it plainly, and the rift between them seemed too large to overcome.

"As you wish, Jack," Robbie said sadly.

Robbie went to an adjacent desk and returned to the couch with a pen and paper. Jack closed his eyes for a second and then said slowly from memory, "Gold Coast Secure Storage, West Palm Beach. The space is a numbered account, security pass code, 091515. That will get your men past the manned entry security and into the warehouse. The unit number is A-3000; the keypad code is 032516. The money is in banker's boxes labeled as business and tax records. There must be twenty or thirty of them. Send someone, confirm it however you want, but when you get that call, I leave immediately with Maddy and my kids. We go our way, you go yours."

Robbie realized he was genuinely disappointed with Jack's continuing hard tone, but it made letting Simon solve the problem of Jack and then living with it easier in a way. He was sincere in his offer to him and did hope that somehow out of this mess they could be friends, at least for Maddy's sake, but Jack's attitude was making that wish impossible. What Jack didn't realize about him and the situation was how strongly he felt about Maddy. As much as he hated the idea of Jack's death, what was worse was the thought of losing Maddy, and that was what would happen if Jack took her and left for good or told her the truth. If there was a Hobson's choice in this, he'd take Maddy and deal with her grief over Jack's death as best he could.

As all this was going through his head, he had a sudden thought that hadn't occurred to him before. Maybe there was a way for Maddy to raise Jack's girls. He knew she always wanted to be a mother, but, like Roberta, was not able to have children of her own. Having the little girls would help her get over Jack, he thought. Perhaps there was a ray of hope in this after all. As he wrestled with the awful possibilities facing him, he came to the conclusion that it probably wouldn't matter what he wanted once Simon was told who Jack was and what he was doing here. Keeping Simon from killing Jack would be like trying to keep the sun from rising.

Lynden Pindling International Airport
Nassau, the Bahamas
Saturday, early evening

The light private jet taxied from the main runway to the smaller air charter terminal of the airport and came to a stop, the engines whining down. Bennie glanced out the small oval window to see if his liaison officer from the Royal Bahamian Police Force was waiting as promised, then gathered his two bags and headed for the main door. His copilot was waiting, the door already open, and then he smiled and said goodbye. Bennie nodded his head, ducked through the low opening, and walked down the stairway built into the door and then toward the Range Rover sitting on the tarmac adjacent to his agency jet.

He had flown from DC to Miami and then to Nassau. He was bushed from all the traveling and pissed that the technology he was counting on to keep track of Ray didn't seem to work for shit. He knew his agent had arrived safely in Freeport yesterday at noon, but within an hour of that event, all contact had been lost, and he had no idea where Ray was or what was happening. To a control freak like Bennie, that was unacceptable. On a more personal note, it was the second time in just over a year that he'd sent Ray into a situation undercover and then lost track of him. His young agent and friend had barely survived the first time, and he had sworn it wouldn't happen again, but it had.

The back door of the Range Rover opened, and a casually dressed Bahamian about his age stepped out and smiled. "Mr. Santiago? I'm Commander Owens of the RBPF. Welcome to the Bahamas."

Bennie set his small travel bag down and took the commander's extend hand. "Thanks, commander, but please, call me Bennie."

The senior police commander smiled. "I'm Oliver. Allow me to help with your bags."

The bags were thrown in the back, and Bennie joined the commander in the rear seat as the driver bodyguard closed the rear door, got in, and carefully maneuvered the large SUV past the terminal and toward the main airport drive.

Commander Owens turned to Bennie. "Your director called mine and said only that you were on your way here and that an important operation you are running has somehow found its way to our islands. I've been instructed to provide you with whatever assistance you require. What can you tell me?"

Bennie nodded his head thanks and then gave the friendly senior police official a quick thumbnail sketch of the original operation in Mexico and how the mission had evolved into trying to identify and apprehend a long-time banker to the cartels. Bennie told the commander that the most recent information his undercover agent had passed to him was that the banker was likely a native and resided here in the Bahamas. He didn't have to say more to the Cambridge-educated commander for him to understand the significance of the new direction.

"That is most interesting, Bennie, and most welcome news. As chief of our Drug Enforcement Unit and concurrent commander of our Counter Narcotics Strike Force, I've been working hard for some years now with our bank fraud branch to eliminate our islands as a safe haven to those wishing to launder their profits here. I will do everything within my power to assist you. Tell me, where is your agent now, and more importantly, who is he with?"

Bennie had a frown on his face and was silent for a second. "Well, you see, Oliver, that's our first problem. As of this moment, I don't have a fucking clue where my man is. And according to the briefing papers I was reading on the way down here, apparently the Bahamas are made up of several thousand islands."

The commander's serious look turned to a wry smile. "Indeed we are, Bennie. Unless we get more information, that makes finding and assisting your man a bit difficult, I'm afraid."

Bennie looked at the commander. "Don't I know it, Oliver. Back home we'd call it looking for a needle in a haystack."

23

Jack glanced at his watch as Robbie was writing down the information on the storage space. It was seven thirty. Robbie folded the piece of paper and stuck it in his front shirt pocket. "I will send Charles and one of my men to Florida as soon as he says the helicopter is ready to fly. They will need to refuel at Great Harbor Cay and then will fly on to Florida. I have no doubts you are sincere about giving up the money, but as we discussed, they will confirm the money is there and then call. After they do, I will have you taken to the island, where you may collect Maddy and your lovely daughters and set sail on your boat. Is that acceptable?"

Jack nodded his head. He was unhappy and angry, and unless he could figure a way to get the upper hand and soon, this was all going to end badly for him. No way could Robbie count on him not to tell Maddy the entire truth, and Robbie would figure that out himself if he already hadn't.

"One other thing, Jack, as a demonstration of my feelings for Maddy. At a bank on Antigua I control, I have set up a trust for her, a little something to ensure she never has to worry again about her financial future. I did this several years ago, but she has not yet been told. My managing partner there is an old and reliable friend well removed from all my other businesses, protected from scrutiny, and very trustworthy. From the beginning I have realized that this business with the Russians could go badly for me, and as a result, I have taken several other steps for Maddy. I've transferred ownership of my restaurant on Freeport and the sloop she lost to her, through my banking partner on Antigua. She is to inherit both, either at my death or, more happily, at such time as she marries—my gifts to her. It is my hope that I can put my current troubles behind me and that we will all be friends for a great many more years, but I am also thirty years older than the two of you, and death comes for us all eventually. When my time comes, if she hasn't married, I want her to have both, so it is a done thing."

Robbie stepped closer to Jack, his expression one of pain or melancholy, and said softly, "Maddy loves you, and it is clear to me that you love her. For reasons that are important to me, her happiness matters. I do not have any idea what your future together holds, but after she was…ah…abandoned, I think she found real happiness in Freeport at the Evening Shadows, and I thought you should know this. I think in the short time you have been in the islands, you know Freeport would be a fine place to raise a family."

Robbie turned, walked to the desk, put the pen down, and then turned and faced him. "Once I have the money and have settled my debt with the Russians, I will have much more remaining than my needs require and will be making a generous deposit in her account for you both. Knowing you like I think I do, after everything that has happened between us, I'm certain you would never accept such a gift of thanks and gratitude directly from me, but it will be there in Maddy's name. It saddens me deeply, but I can see in your face that you loathe me now, and I understand and do not blame you. But time passes, Jack, and as it does, I hope there will come a time when you can understand and accept my actions as I have yours, and that we can be friends once more. But whatever happens, wherever you go, you and your family will be able to live comfortably on the trust. Perhaps in our mutual gestures to each other, there can be happiness for each of us down our separate paths."

As he listened to Robbie, he wanted to believe him in the worst way, but he suspected that was wishful thinking. Also on the boat with him were men he had attempted to kill. How was Robbie going to deal with them? He hadn't said a word about them or that part of it yet. He wasn't sure what the relationship had been like between the two young Mexicans and Diaz, but surely they would learn that he was the one who had killed Diaz and his killer. Then what? Robbie might indeed be sincere, but it didn't seem to matter much, for surely the Mexicans would want their pound of flesh in return. Unless...

Jack suddenly wanted to smack himself for his stupidity and for over-thinking the entire situation. He didn't have to worry about the Mexicans because the only thing that made sense was for Robbie to kill them too. They were dead men and didn't know it yet. What other answer could there be? Robbie couldn't let them leave, not if he wanted his secrets kept. And if he didn't have to share the money with them, naturally there was more for him. There was also one other important consideration. The Mexicans were in some small way still a part of Robbie's past and, by association, a part of the culture responsible for killing his wife. He'd seen the grief there at the simple retelling of his story. No way the Mexicans survived this.

Robbie really had not shown himself to be greedy, but he had been ruthless in his own way, by taking his kids as he had. The only question in Jack's mind down this particular train of thought was, Would Robbie have them killed first, or him? If he killed the Mexicans first, maybe there was a chance Robbie wanted him to live. His mind was spinning, and he couldn't keep all the possibilities straight, but he would proceed on the premise that he was to be eliminated soon after the money was verified and plan accordingly. He was at a distinct disadvantage, unarmed and outnumbered. He had a sick feeling in the pit of his stomach as he watched Robbie pick up the phone on the credenza and order his pilot to join him in his suite. He couldn't see a survivable path forward, and for a terrible fleeting second wondered who would take care of his girls.

Robbie replaced the phone and turned, his look changing again; Jack could tell the man was struggling with many emotions but couldn't decipher whether that was good for him or fatal.

"Jack...I wish you were simply my guest and I could show you all the hospitality we have available here on *Roberta's Dream*, but under the circumstances, that doesn't seem possible. I want you to be comfortable, but until we conclude our distasteful business, prudence, it seems, dictates that I keep you secured, just until we can complete our agreement. To that end, I'm going to have to ask you to accompany my men to the lazarette in the stern. I'll send for you once my men have confirmed the money is there."

Jack suspected that he would be detained, and asked out of curiosity, "The lazarette?"

"It is a sort of workshop for our chief engineer. It's below the main deck, accessed from a hatch on the stern swim platform. There are quarters there also, with a bathroom and a bunk for a second engineer, but as we do not carry one full time. That will be your cabin until our business is concluded. I'm afraid I must also ask that you relinquish your cell phone until we are through."

Jack stared at Robbie but didn't argue; he simply reached into his pocket and slid the device over. Given the situation, there was only one person he would want to call, or could call, to help get him out of this jam, but North Carolina might as well be the moon. Robbie went to the double-door entry to his private suite and opened the door and gestured to one of the men still standing there. "Take my guest to the lazarette."

Jack got up and walked to the door just as the pilot showed up and walked in. The pilot had cold, almost lifeless eyes, and as they looked at each other as they passed, both saw danger in the eyes of the other. With one guard in the lead and the other following, they walked through the large formal spaces of the yacht, passed through a wall of glass doors, and walked out onto the large covered aft main deck. The deck was lit up by dozens of small recessed lights in the finely detailed coffered ceiling. At the end of the main deck on the left side was a built-in teak-planked stairway leading to the darkened swim platform. As they descended to the platform, he couldn't help himself and paused, looking up. The only ceiling here was the incredible star-filled Caribbean sky, a sight that always moved him. What little man-made light there was simply spilled over from the deck above.

Because of the low light level on the swim platform, the lead guard was fumbling with the key to the lock that secured the small vertical hatch. Jack tried to look disinterested, checking out the Jet Skis parked on the platform, until a glow above him caught his eye. Still sitting on the midlevel deck he had passed quickly by after landing were the two Mexicans, visible in the seating area through the polished decorative guardrail that defined and enclosed the end of the deck two levels up. The one he had wounded was getting his cigar lit by the younger one, and that was what caught his attention. They seemed to be watching him and the guards with detached interest, still not sure of who he was or why he was being placed in his cell.

Robbie's guard finally managed to get the hatch open, the opening about half the size of a regular door. Instead of going through it, the guard reached in, turned on a light switch, and then stood to one side. Jack looked inside and saw there was a short, steep ship's ladder just inside the opening. With a quick look at the two hard men, he ducked his head, stepped through the small opening, and started down the steps as they closed and locked the hatch behind him.

He descended into what he thought of as his cell, noticing that like everything else he had seen so far on the yacht, the space was finished nicely, especially for a work area or shop. It was a decently large area spanning the width of the stern, at least fifteen or sixteen feet wide, he judged, and was about eight feet deep. The headroom was a little low but was greater than his height, and he didn't have to duck at all. There was a door in the wall opposite the short entry stairway that he assumed led to the engine room of the yacht, but it was locked, as was a full-height stainless-steel storage cabinet to the right of the engine room door. There was a spotlessly clean stainless-steel workbench on each side of the stairs he had come down, and in the left corner of the room through a narrow door, he could see a toilet and a sink, similar to what one would find on a commercial airliner, and a small shower. To his right, underneath a sloping ceiling he figured was the underside of the stairway they had used from the main deck to the swim platform, was a narrow bunk nicely made up.

He walked around the space checking things out in general, but he was really looking for a weapon. He reached into his front pocket and took out the Swiss Army knife he always carried and started working on the storage bin lock. Why Robbie didn't have his men pat him down was a mystery but one he was thankful for. By the sound of it, he was stuck for several hours, maybe even until morning, and by the time they came for him, he intended to be armed with something more than just his pocketknife.

⊷⊨◉ ◉⊨⊷

As Jack went to work on the storage bin lock, two decks up in the plush seating area of the middeck, Ray was trying to appear bored watching the Banker's men lock up the stranger who had arrived, but inside, he was in knots. The day had been a complete bust in paradise despite the efforts of the yacht's crew. The Banker and his two key men had been gone almost the entire day. The Banker and his primary thug, Simon, were off somewhere in the chopper, while Victor came and went all day, apparently keeping an eye on things on the island. Always there were at least two guards on board, but he was never sure of their location, as they remained mostly out of sight.

He became convinced during the day that with the exception of the second officer, the crew of the yacht was not involved with the intrigue going on and was oblivious to the mounting tensions. The second officer / engineer was aloof and seemed to silently watch him and Felix a great deal more than seemed natural, making him suspicious. The rest of the crew, especially Stephanie, were warm and friendly and went out of their way to make the day as enjoyable as they could, including making water toys and even scuba lessons available to him. He had declined, only taking several brief dips in the waters off the swim platform when he got really hot. He asked Stephanie about going to the island but was told that couldn't be arranged, as Robbie was entertaining some other guests there who required privacy. Ray supposed that explained the nice sailboat, now anchored near them but closer to shore, that had arrived sometime last night. Several times during the day he saw a woman and two kids walking the beach as if looking for shells, with Victor or one of the other guards watching them from a discreet distance, but then they would disappear. As to who they were and what they were doing there, that information was not available to him, nor was the whereabouts of the Banker and Simon. He hated mysteries anytime, but especially when undercover and out of touch with Bennie.

He was out of touch because his supposedly fancy encrypted satellite iPhone was turned off and had been most of the time since he had arrived. To his disappointment, he discovered first thing this morning that he was low on battery, and the charger he had brought didn't seem to be working. He wasn't sure if it was the type of power available aboard the large boat or just a faulty charger, but he was in no position to ask someone for assistance, for all the obvious reasons, so he was keeping his phone turned off until he really needed it. He had tried texting a couple of quick updates to Bennie from his room, but there had been no response, so he wasn't even sure if Bennie had received them. His phone had been on when he arrived in Freeport yesterday and during the chopper ride down to here, and he hoped that had given Bennie the fix he needed to keep track of him. Even if he did know where he was, as he looked at the setting around him, while glorious if you were a tourist seeking solitude in paradise, there was no possible way for the Bahamian backup Bennie had promised to get anywhere near him and not be easily spotted. With the exception of the yacht and the recently arrived sailboat, the waters in and around the island were empty, another fuckup with the mission plan as far as he was concerned.

Felix was sitting as casually as his cast and inner feelings allowed, smoking his Cuban cigar, lost in his own thoughts. They had been quietly discussing when they thought the Banker would make his move to eliminate them when the stranger who had arrived with the Banker an hour ago was paraded down to the swim platform and locked up. Felix didn't recognize the man, but his sense was that the stranger was formidable.

It was clear to Ray that Felix was bothered by the recent events and wanted to ask him what he thought was going on, but before he could, one of the sliding glass doors from the sky lounge opened, and the Banker and Simon came out on deck and walked toward them. Ray had been looking past Felix at that moment, toward the southwestern horizon where dark storm clouds were gathering, silent flashes of lightning punctuating the otherwise perfect night. The breezes were soft, the air comfortable, but as the Banker joined them in the seating area, Ray couldn't help but feel that the approaching spring thunderstorm was a harbinger of the impending chaos and death that he was certain was also fast approaching this night.

Ray had no way of knowing, but he and Felix were not alone in their anxiety. Robbie's relaxed outward demeanor as he sat down also belied what he was really feeling. In spite of all the good fortune that had fallen in his lap in the last twenty-four hours, he knew fully that as events unfolded this evening, men were going to die, and he also was anxious and afraid. In the twelve years he had been involved with the cartels, laundering their illicit money and stealing them blind, with the exception of Maddy's Aussie, he had never been involved with any direct or indirect violence. Tonight, however, would be different. Killing was a bad business, and until the Aussie was disposed of two years earlier, it had been about as far removed from his life as the stars overhead. But before joining the Mexicans, he and Simon had briefly discussed what was to happen later in general terms, and the discussion had not gone well, as far as he was concerned. The way things actually went down would depend on many variables, according to the experienced Simon, not the least of which was how they were to deal with the yacht's crew. Except for one confidant he had in the crew to watch and listen for him, they knew nothing about his illicit businesses, and he wanted that status quo maintained. Simon, on the other hand, said that there was only one way to ensure this, and that was when their conversation became uncomfortable for him. He had tried to keep his feelings concealed, for it was clear from Simon's look and demeanor that he wanted all loose ends tied up tonight—the Mexicans, the crew, and no doubt Maddy, even though her name was never mentioned.

He'd been absolutely honest with Jack when he said he didn't know how to kill, but he had excused himself briefly from Simon before they came out on deck and returned to his suite and now was armed, something he had never done before, knowing that not under any circumstances could he let Simon hurt Maddy, or his crew, for that matter. Simon was a killer and he was not, so Simon would probably instinctively know how to deal with unplanned or chaotic events as the evening progressed, but Simon also knew he was never armed. He hoped if the time came, Simon would remember this fact, for he would need surprise on his side if Simon had to be dealt with.

The part of their discussion they had both agreed to was that they needed Felix and his young guard to be comfortable and relaxed this evening. Simon wanted to separate them somehow and deal with each one individually, for reasons only Simon knew. Victor, having thoroughly searched their luggage when they arrived, assured them they had no weapons, so according to Simon, disposing of them when the time came was likely not too dangerous. But both knew any man when put into a corner would fight for his life, and Felix's young bodyguard had a hard look to him.

Stephanie silently showed up a few seconds after they joined the Mexicans with a snifter of Cognac for him and a dark rum drink for Simon and then, just as silently, was gone again. He looked at Felix and asked, "Gentlemen, I trust you have everything you need. Another drink, perhaps?"

Felix glanced at Ray and answered for them both. "Thank you, no. We're fine."

Robbie leaned forward and took a fine black Cuban from the hand-carved wooden cigar box sitting on the low coffee table of the sitting area and slowly and carefully lit it. Finally satisfied it was burning properly, he looked at Felix. "My apologies for abandoning you today and most of this evening, but I am pleased to be able to report that we shall have our money located within the next few hours."

Felix was surprised, Ray expressionless.

Robbie puffed some on his cigar, clearly relishing the flavors, and then went on. "You've seen my new guest, I trust? His name is Jack Williams... your mysterious truck driver, Felix."

Felix's mouth dropped open. He was stunned. He looked again to Ray, who could not hide his surprise, and then to the Banker. "My God, how can this be? How have you done this so quickly, and from here in the Bahamas?"

Robbie looked at him through the blue smoke as he exhaled. "It is a long story. The short version is that this man recently relocated down here with a new business, and we were introduced. He was supposedly into chartering security, and as I was an owner of numerous vessels for charter, the mutual acquaintance who put us together thought our businesses were a good fit. It is purely coincidental he turned out to be your truck driver and I your partner. It seems, Felix, that providence wants us to have our money. After you mentioned his name yesterday and I realized who he was, I took and am holding his family. As a result, he had no choice but to admit his actions and has told me where the money is currently stored. As soon as Charles can have the helicopter ready, he will fly to South Florida with one of Victor's men and verify it is where he says it is. I'm confident he is telling the truth, but until we do confirm it, we will hold him. I am also pleased to be able to tell you that you can stop wondering which of your enemies in Mexico tried to have you killed."

Felix was stunned again, and he struggled against the bulk of his cast to lean more forward in his large, soft lounge chair. When he managed, he asked, "You have discovered who hired the assassin who tried to kill us?"

Robbie was working on his cigar some more, but Ray saw him subtly glance at Simon before he answered. "No assassin, Felix. The truck driver, personally. I am as of yet unsure exactly how he managed to do this, but I have learned he is capable of such an act, and he was the one who killed Diaz and his dreadful killer—vengeance for the murder of his wife, I believe. I have told him that any actions he may have taken in Mexico are of no consequence to me and that once we have verified the money is there, he is free to take his family, who are currently houseguests on my island, and sail off. That is his boat you see in the cove. But, of course, between us, his leaving is out of the question."

"You're goddamned right that is out of the question," Felix spit out angrily, surprising Ray. "I want to kill him myself for what he did to Diaz, and to me. I insist upon it, Robbie. I'm crippled for the rest of my life because of him!"

Robbie was nodding his head as if he understood and was sympathetic, his outward countenance calm, but inside, his anxiety level spiked. He knew from Simon's harsh reaction during their private discussions before joining the Mexicans that any thoughts he had on somehow letting Jack live were impossible. Even if he ordered Simon not to, Jack wouldn't live to see the morning once they had the money. Now there was this eruption from Felix, which was the first serious emotion he had shown since arriving. The outburst would not sit well with Simon, and he needed Simon under his control until the time was right to kill Felix and his bodyguard.

As coolly as possible, he said, "Of course, Felix. I understand your feelings. We will work this out between the two of us. My business arrangement with Simon and Victor pays them significant bonuses for…how should I say this…dealing resolutely with certain problems. As long as they get their bonus, I'm certain it will not matter to them who actually pulls the trigger. Isn't that right, Simon?"

Simon was drinking his rum concoction, watching and listening carefully, but to the others, he seemed almost disinterested. He casually put his drink down, looked around the gathering, and said, "Fine. What do I care? And the others?"

Robbie puffed on his cigar to hide his growing fears at Simon's direct question. They had discussed only Jack and the two Mexicans and what must be done and when. Maddy, the little girls, and the crew were never mentioned, and he had hoped it would not be necessary to even bring them up, but here it was, out there for everyone to hear.

"The others?" Robbie said as he tilted his head back, as if enjoying his smoke and not understanding the question.

"On the island. The woman and the children. What's to be done about them?"

Ray was beside himself watching the unexpected dynamic being played out between the Banker and his killer and the dangerous direction the entire situation was taking. The Banker was going out of his way to be obtuse, it seemed to him, whereas the killer couldn't be more transparent. For whatever reason, maybe just out of common decency, it was clear the Banker did not want to harm the truck driver's children or the woman mentioned, whereas there could be no mistaking what this Simon wanted.

The evening was growing more and more complex, and Ray knew he needed time to figure out how to survive the night, but he also suspected he wasn't going to get it. He had assumed that finding the truck driver and therefore the money was going to take a while, giving him all the time he would need, but with the unbelievable revelations from the Banker and the seemingly suddenly developing friction he was watching, he was out of time. There was clearly a rift of some kind between the Banker and his killer, and there was no doubt in his mind that the shit was going to hit the fan soon, and in a big way. No doubt Simon, a professional, was aware of the friction as well, and Ray could not help but think that if he were in his shoes, that meant getting rid of excess baggage such as him and Felix sooner rather than later.

Felix was not yet armed, but he was. Earlier, after he and Felix had their dinner together alone, he had gone back to his cabin and tried using some of his precious remaining battery to call Bennie, but he couldn't make contact, given what he assumed was interference from the deck upon deck of steel around him. He had to try again, but from somewhere higher and outside, and that could prove dangerous, as he would be out in the open. His instincts told him it was time to arm himself, even at the risk of being discovered, so he took the Baby Glock from his luggage and put it in his front pocket. When he returned to the middeck, where Felix was still lounging alone, he walked up to him and asked Felix how he looked as he did a slow full turn. After looking at him with a puzzled expression for a second, Felix smiled with understanding and looked him over closely. "Good, Ray. Good. I can't see a thing. What about me?"

He had intended to go back below and retrieve Felix's weapon for him, but before he could, they both heard the rapidly approaching helicopter, and he was stuck carrying his piece and Felix was unarmed. With the unexpected scene between the Banker and Simon playing out in front of him, he knew he had done the right thing. An unarmed Felix would be a liability if things got out of control, but a liability he had little feeling for under the circumstances. He hated that he could think so callously about another human being, but the man was a trafficker, and push come to shove, he really didn't care about him.

Back in the moment, there was an uncomfortable silence as the Banker looked at Simon, slowly smoking his cigar, and then said in a voice possessed with more authority, "Maddy knows nothing, and of course the children are innocent. She believes what I have told her, about Jack being off dealing with enemies from his past. Sadly, she will be told those enemies unfortunately got the best of him, and that will be the end of this, Simon. They and the crew are not to be harmed. Is that clear?"

As he and Felix watched the mini drama unfolding, both unknowingly had the same thought. If this Simon could so openly discuss the murder of an innocent woman and two kids, what had been discussed about them? They were as good as dead; that was confirmed. Ray stole a quick glance at Felix just as Felix glanced at him while taking a drink. It was clear from his look that Felix wanted him to act and shoot them now, but Ray's gut was telling him not yet. They were exposed sitting where they were. He had no idea where Victor, the pilot, and the two other guards were at that moment. For all he knew, they were just inside watching. If he started blasting people, there was nowhere to hide, sitting as they were on the end of the deck, if they were attacked from the interior. As casually as he could, he reached for his drink and subtlety shook his head no to Felix, hoping no one would notice the small tremors of his shaking hand.

Simon sat back in his chair and drank his rum, nodded yes, and then said, "I just wanted to be clear, Robbie. What do you want me to do with the truck driver?"

Ray could see that the worst of the moment had passed, and everyone seemed to be relaxing a bit. Robbie slowly glanced at each of them and said, "We will deal with him later this evening. He tells me our money is in a secure storage business in West Palm Beach. Charles is preparing the helicopter for the flight to Florida at this moment and will take one of Victor's men with him."

Robbie glanced at his watch. "They should be there before ten. We should have our confirmation soon after."

Simon spoke up again. "Victor is supposed to take over watch on the island at ten."

The Banker was making every effort to appear relaxed and unbothered by the tensions earlier, but Ray could see it in him. He wondered if any of the others could also, or if the Banker could see it in him.

As for Robbie, he was certain he was losing control of Simon, but what to do? He decided that as dangerous as it could be for Maddy, he needed to get Simon off the boat before he did anything stupid and deal with him through Victor, whose loyalties he felt he still controlled. He had suspected for years that a moment such as this would arise and it would become necessary to deal with Simon. Of all those who had been in some way a part of Roberta's death, whether directly or indirectly, as Simon had been, he had elected to help Simon with his legal defense years ago in an attempt to buy his loyalty. He knew back then he would require help in taking his revenge in a world he knew nothing about. His idea had worked to a point, but the characteristics that had made him choose Simon in the first place—more intelligence, the power to reason, and not just be a hired gun—almost made it inevitable that one day an independent-thinking Simon's interests would run contrary to his own. He had cultivated his relationship with the intellectually devoid Victor, whom Simon had brought on board, for just such an occurrence, and his thickheaded but dangerous associate was about to get the bonus of a lifetime.

He was rolling his cigar in his fingers casually, looking like a man enjoying his smoke, and then looked at Simon and said, "You go to the island. I will have Victor bring the truck driver to you after we get our confirmation, as if we are releasing him as agreed. Finish him there and see that the body is buried where it will never be found. Do it silently, Simon, and then the two of you come back here. I will deal with the woman and the children personally."

Ray was watching the discussion closely and could tell that Simon was not happy, but he seemed to be going along with the Banker's orders. Simon stood up, nodded his acceptance to the Banker, and walked to the stairway that led from their deck to the main deck below. Why the Banker was sending this sociopath to the island where the innocents were was beyond him, but Ray said nothing and sipped at his drink.

As they were watching Simon ready the hi-tech tender to ferry himself to the island, Charles came on deck with Victor and one of his men. The pilot and the guard were dressed better than usual, probably in anticipation of being greeted by US customs, Ray thought. The Banker got up, walked over to them, put his arm around his pilot's shoulder as if he were a friend, spoke to him privately, and then handed him a slip of paper. The pilot and the unnamed guard went up the spiral stairway, and the Banker then had a private word with Victor.

Ray was watching them closely, trying not to appear overly interested, and was glad he was, because whatever the Banker said to Victor surprised him in some way. There was a definite reaction, as his look and body language visibly changed, and then he nodded his head and disappeared again inside.

Ray was trying to interpret that new ominous input when he and everyone else heard the helicopter spinning up. The Banker returned to the seating area as if all was normal and blissful in the Caribbean. "Well, gentlemen, Charles tells me he will be in South Florida within two hours. I've verified that the storage facility is available to clients on a twenty-four-hour basis, so we will get our confirmation this evening."

The Banker glanced at his gold wristwatch and went on. "It is now eight o'clock. I suggest we avail ourselves of the many amenities *Roberta's Dream* can offer her guests to pass the next several hours."

Ray was glad that Simon, the pilot, and Victor were now gone, giving him three fewer guns to deal with, and that the tension in the air was dissipating. But then Felix spoke up again and poisoned the entire atmosphere, as far as he was concerned, by leaning forward as best he could and asking in a none-too-friendly tone, "I thought we agreed that the truck driver was mine to deal with, Robbie."

The Banker didn't seem to be bothered by the directness or the tone of Felix's question, but simply nodded as if sympathetic or in agreement. "I understand your strong feelings, Felix, and am sympathetic. But there are other considerations—your wounds, for one, and the need to keep such necessary but distasteful activity from my crew. Having said that, however, I would be agreeable to any suggestions you have with those considerations in mind."

Felix looked from the Banker to Ray, and then he settled back in his chair and said, "If Ray were allowed to go with Victor and kill the bastard for me, I would accept that."

Ironically, the Banker, Felix, and Ray all had the same thought at the same moment. Letting Ray be involved and getting him off the boat was, from their individual points of view, to their advantage. The Banker, of course, was thinking that he would have Victor kill young Ray after taking care of Jack and Simon. Felix saw it as an opportunity for Ray to kill the others and then return to the yacht and take care of the Banker at his leisure. And for Ray, anything that would get him off the boat and give him a chance to contact Bennie and maybe give him the opportunity to surprise Simon and Victor without having to worry about the others was the break he needed, absent time to think of anything better.

The Banker puffed on his cigar and then smiled at Felix. "A very good idea, Felix. I will arrange it. Until then, we have several hours together. What is your pleasure?"

To Ray's great relief, Felix saw the same opportunity he did, the chance to arm himself. "Robbie, with thanks, if it is all the same to you, I need to take some of my pain medication and lie down in my cabin for an hour or so. My shoulder is bothering me."

Ray thought the Banker looked genuinely concerned, which didn't seem possible or likely, really, as he replied, "Of course, of course, Felix. I will call you when I hear something if you choose to remain below. If you get to feeling better, please rejoin us here or in the sky lounge."

Felix nodded his head and then looked at Ray. "Ray, if you would, please help me to my cabin."

Ray stood and did as ordered, noting that the Banker seemed to be fine with what was happening. Ray only hoped that Felix would remember that their cabins were likely bugged, and that was probably why the Banker was not concerned about them. After taking the elevator to the accommodation deck, as they were walking down the narrow entry corridor to their cabins, he made eye contact with Felix and silently put his finger to his lips again as a reminder, and Felix nodded his understanding. Once in Felix's suite, they made casual and expected conversation about the general events, finding the truck driver and how lucky they were that the search for the money had ended so well, as Felix pretended to take meds and Ray quietly retrieved his Glock from his luggage.

Because of the large cast, in the several days before leaving Mexico, Felix had his tailor make him several custom silk shirts with snaps that worked with the cast. As a result, they were large and easily concealed Felix's Glock from view, even when in his front waistband, which made it more accessible. Felix did lie down, telling Ray to come by for him at nine thirty. Ray said he would, and then he went to his cabin, quickly pocketed his cell phone, and then went back to the small elevator lobby down the hall from his cabin.

He punched the button for the top level, the sun deck, his rationale for doing so simple. Since he had been on board, the only times the top deck had been used were when the helicopter was coming and going. For whatever reason, the Banker seemed to enjoy the lounge area of the midlevel or boat deck over all the others, so that was where they hung out most of the time.

The elevator stopped, and the door slid open. Ray stepped out onto the top deck, where there was nothing but the sky overhead and therefore unimpeded cell coverage. What roof area there was provided shade only for the mostly open-air bar and lounge area. He moved toward the front of the deck to where the platform-mounted Jacuzzi was located and looked around. He was alone, and all he had to do to remain so was watch the small spiral stairway on the far aft end near the helipad and listen for the elevator. He determined it was not possible for one of the other guards or a crew member to surprise him.

He took his phone out, took a deep breath, and then turned it on, seeing immediately that he had good reception, but the battery was dangerously low. He punched in zero one, Bennie's speed-dial number, and to his great relief, the phone rang only once before Bennie gruffly answered. "Well, it's about goddamned time you called. Where in the living hell are you, Ray?"

24

T he night was dark and getting darker. A cool breeze was freshening out of the southwest, and on the horizon, the dark storm clouds were slowly rolling in. There were flashes of lightning putting on a beautiful natural light show for anyone interested in watching, although the distant rumbles of thunder were still too muted to attract much attention. On board the magnificent yacht at anchor in the pristine cove, as he watched the rapidly approaching storm from his position on the uppermost desk, the hairs on the back of Ray's neck stiffened, and not because of the sudden drop in temperature or the nasty tone of his boss's voice. Rather, it was from the certain knowledge that people were going to die this night, and as a law enforcement officer, he could see no way to prevent it. The much more disturbing reality was that given the circumstances, he wasn't even sure he could defend himself and survive. As for most of the others involved, considering their crimes, he wondered if he should even try to stop the coming carnage.

Despite Bennie's nasty attitude, when he heard his voice, he felt a sense of relief he had not felt since returning from his first undercover mission a year ago after he had been out of contact with him for months. In this case it had been only a few days, but knowing there was going to be deadly violence, and soon, his feelings were intensified.

He shrugged off Bennie's pissed-off tone, glad he was finally in contact. "Nice to hear your voice, too, boss," he said quietly and sarcastically. "You're the one who's supposed to have all the high-tech shit keeping tabs on me. You tell *me* where I'm at. All I know for sure is the island we're anchored off is called Devil's Cay."

Ray could hear Bennie talking to someone else, saying, "My agent, Oliver—he's on something called Devil's Cay." He could hear the other man talking but could not make out what was being said. Then Bennie returned his focus to him, and in a far more sympathetic tone said, "Sorry if it sounded like I was jumping you. I've been worried. What's your status?"

"I'm not on the island, Bennie. I'm on a large yacht called *Roberta's Dream,* a couple hundred yards offshore."

He could hear Bennie passing on what he had just said to the other person again, and an excited voice or voices responding. "OK, Ray, that's good intel, real good. That's what we needed to know. I'm in Nassau with the island cops. We're like forty miles away, and the top cop I'm with is working on a way to get us there quickly without blowing your cover. He wants to know if you know who chartered the yacht."

"No charter, Bennie. The Banker is the owner. It's his boat."

Bennie was again talking to the top island cop, by the sound of it, and while he couldn't understand all that was being said, he could tell that the information had struck a chord.

"Ray, the commander wants confirmation. Are you saying the yacht owner is our guy, our cartel banker?"

"Affirmative, Bennie. He's the man, and in about two hours, he's going to try to have me killed. Don't worry about blowing my cover, boss. I'm in the deep kimchi and need the cavalry right the fuck now!"

There was more of Bennie talking to the Bahamian commander, and then he was talking to Ray again. "OK, OK, Ray, settle down a little. The Royal Police have high-speed patrol boats, I'm told. We'll be en route within thirty minutes, ETA your locale about an hour after that. Once we're close, their air assets will be timed in to that Devil's Island or whatever the hell you called it. Sit tight. Backup is on the way."

Ray glanced at his watch. Ninety minutes until help arrived. That was cutting it close, and he didn't like it, but he still had the element of surprise on his side. That would have to do.

"OK, Bennie, listen. One other important thing. The yacht has a chopper, and it's on the way to the West Palm Beach area. Check the nearest airports for arrivals. Two of the Banker's men are headed there to confirm that the stolen cartel cash that's been driving this train wreck is being kept in a public storage place in the area. I don't have a business name, but it is a secure public facility, special somehow. Check the phone book or something. You're the brains here, but we should nab these guys. The shit won't hit the fan on my end until they've confirmed the cash is there. That buys me time until you and the local cops get here."

"Say no more, Ray. I'm on it. Now, sit tight and don't do anything stupid like getting your ass shot off. See you in an hour or so."

The phone went dead, so he pocketed it. The breeze was picking up even more, and the storm was closing in. *Shit,* he thought as he glanced at the sky, the black clouds and lightning looking more and more ominous with each passing minute. *This is going to fuck things up, or my name isn't Ray Cruz.*

⟶▭ ▭⟵

Even though *Roberta's Dream* was a modern, fully air-conditioned yacht, the air in the lazarette was warm and sticky, and the sweat was rolling off Jack. He managed to force the lock of the storage bin at the cost of the principal blade of his Swiss Army knife. As he suspected, the bin was a tool locker with tools of all sizes and shapes designed to work on the yacht's diesel engines and other onboard equipment. The closest things to weapons were an assortment of polished stainless-steel screwdrivers and a glistening ball-peen hammer. He'd spent a bad ten or fifteen minutes trying to determine the best place to be when the guards returned and eventually decided that sitting on his bed and looking nonconfrontational was his best option. He hid the hammer beneath his pillow and the screwdriver he selected was tight to his right side as he sat.

He remembered something Armie had tried to pound into his head when they were in the field, about all situations having a tactical solution. You just had to find it. Recalling those lessons, he was trying to think in tactical terms now and find a solution within the lazarette that would allow him to live. There would likely be two guards when they returned to get him, and they would be armed, but he started seeing how the situation and the lazarette could work for him. He doubted they would outright kill him on the boat, not with the island so close. It seemed far more likely that Robbie would have them continue the charade of letting him go and reuniting him with his family, and then kill him when they got there—better place to conceal the body. He would know one way or the other when they came for him; if their weapons were out, he was in immediate trouble. However, if their weapons were holstered, then it was to be the island, or at least that was what he hoped.

He paused and smiled to himself when the word *hope* crossed his mind. Back in the day, the first time he was with Armie in the badlands and things got tight, he remembered looking at his spotter and squad leader and saying he *hoped* they would get out of the mess they were in. Armie, being Armie, looked back, took a drag on his ever-present cigarette, and then told him to *hope* in one hand and shit in the other and see which one filled up faster. Such were Armie's views on hope.

The recollection forced him to focus on the real and now and what he was going to do, but in a way, it calmed him. The second tactical advantage he had was the lazarette's entry. However many men came for him, they could enter the space only one at a time through the small hatch and descend only one at a time down the short but steep ship's ladder. Then there was the element of surprise. Most thugs were bullies and had been their entire lives. They only messed with people and situations if through size, numbers, or weapons they could dominate. They did not often find themselves faced with a strong, determined, motivated adversary with skills, and he was all those things. So he did have advantages, he decided, but he couldn't see how to use them just yet and live. His first impulse had been to attack whoever entered first, stabbing him with the screwdriver, maybe disabling him and gaining his weapon in the process, all while the next guard was still descending the ship's ladder. It wouldn't be easy in the narrow confines of the ship's ladder, trapped, so to speak, between the stainless-steel handrails, to cleanly produce a weapon. That would buy him a precious few seconds and maybe the edge he needed.

However, as he sat on the bunk, glancing at his watch often and waiting, doubts began to permeate his thinking on that plan. What if Robbie did intend to let him go, and the guards were only there to escort him? If that was the case, any action he took would obviously screw that up, and of course, the outcome of an all-out fight in the lazarette was very much in doubt. A second concern growing in his mind was that even if he did achieve surprise, there would undoubtedly be shots fired between him and a second guard, and if those shots were heard, he had no idea who would be waiting for him if he managed to make it to the swim platform. He might make it off the yacht by making a swim for it, but the other guards would have the tender or the Jet Skis and could cut him off or beat him to shore. Certainly they could get to his family and Maddy before he could, so that was out. There was no planning in advance for what was coming, he finally decided. He'd have to play it by ear, and getting to the island alive was the imperative.

As he sat, now gloomier than ever at his prospects, he could hear and feel that the weather had changed for the worse. Like the engine compartment on his boat, the lazarette was sound insulated to save the well-heeled guests of such a yacht from hearing the noisy and gritty work often required to keep such complex pieces of machinery operating, but he could still hear muted rumbles of thunder, and even with the yacht's great size, he felt some wave action.

He looked at the time again. It had been over ninety minutes since he had heard the helicopter depart; Robbie would get his call anytime now, he judged. Another lesson from Armie came to him as he was sitting and sweating, only this one made him feel worse, not better: "Shooter," he would say, "expect the clusterfuck, and always have a back door." Well, he was in a dangerous clusterfuck now, right up to his eyeballs, but for the life of him, he could see no back door.

Two decks up, in the cool and finely appointed sky lounge, Ray spent most of the two hours the chopper was gone in the comfortable seating area talking with the Banker as Victor and one of his men sat at the nearby bar watching silently. It was nerve racking just sitting there, three against one the entire time, even knowing intuitively that they probably wouldn't kill him or Felix on the boat. But sitting with the Banker as he was left him exposed to the two at the bar, and there wasn't a damn thing he could do about it.

With Felix resting in his cabin below decks, this was really the first occasion since he had arrived that he was alone with the Banker. The man was very pleasant, even charming, asking him questions about his past, as if he really was interested, and how he came to be involved with Felix. As had happened at Diaz's, he told him about meeting Felix's younger brother in the Chihuahuan cartel, which then led to the story from last year about having been a bodyguard and confidant to the corrupt former Mexican president. It never failed, it seemed to him—whatever kind of shit was going down, tell that story, and people were just interested. He acted if he were enjoying the conversation in an effort to keep the guards especially more relaxed, but in reality, all he was doing was counting the seconds until Bennie arrived and worrying about what the building storm outside was doing to his timetable.

At nine fifteen, he excused himself from the Banker and went below to get Felix. Felix was up and silently waiting for him, and during some perfunctory chitchat for any microphones, they checked out each other's appearance to make sure their weapons were concealed. As a rule, Ray never carried around an unsafed weapon, but tonight would be the exception, and he whispered to Felix to do the same. He traded the switchblade in his left front pocket for a second ten-shot clip, knowing that he might need it. And then, satisfied, he and Felix walked to the elevator. As they did, he whispered to Felix, "Let me be the one to start shooting. I will know when."

Felix looked at him and simply nodded his head in agreement, deferring to the young killer's instincts, which by now he trusted completely. As they reached the middeck and Felix stepped off the elevator, they could see that the weather had worsened, and the large yacht was being pounded by the spring thunderstorm. Felix glanced at him, a worried look in his eyes, and then put a smile on his face and walked toward the Banker, still sitting where Ray had left him. Earlier, as the storm was approaching, the Banker had told the crew to take the night off, so they were in their quarters below decks. Victor was nowhere in sight, but his goon was still sitting at the bar, so Ray went there and started making Felix a drink. But he was really looking for a place from which he could control the situation when the time came. He had sized up everyone's positioning as he followed Felix into the large room. It was clear to him that the Banker was not going to initiate any action on the boat where the crew would learn of it. Ray, on the other hand, was not governed by such a condition. As it stood, once Victor showed himself, it would be Ray and Felix against three, and that was manageable, especially when they had surprise on their side. And he doubted the Banker was even armed, tilting a potential fight just that much more in their favor. He wondered if this was the time to take control of the situation, but something in him said no, wait for backup.

As he was making Felix his drink, he couldn't help but notice that, like his father, apparently the Banker was a classical jazz fan, because in the background, the great Miles Davis's masterpiece recording *Kind of Blue* was playing, triggering instant memories in him of Sunday afternoons spent in his dad's study after their family dinner, listening to his collection of jazz greats. The memory only heightened his need to survive.

Once they were seated, Felix with the Banker and Ray at the bar near Victor's goon, the Banker gave them an update on events and also filled them in on his suggested plan for the evening. Charles and his guard had landed safely in West Palm Beach, just ahead of the line of storms passing over Southern Florida and the near Caribbean. They were already through customs without difficulty and on their way to the storage facility in a rented car. Charles would be calling with the confirmation on their money within the half hour. Once the money was confirmed, Victor and Ray would then go get the truck driver and take him to the island in the tender, where Simon would meet them, and Ray could finish the driver off. The three of them would then take care of the body, and the night's dirty work would be finished. Robbie looked at Felix. "Will this be acceptable to you, Felix?"

Felix looked from Robbie to Ray and back, nodded his head, and said, "Yes, fine," thinking that if Ray decided not to take out the Banker and his guard in the next thirty minutes, he was putting himself in a tough spot, going up against the Banker's top two men on the island. His young bodyguard would still have surprise on his side, and darkness, and if that was how he wanted to play it, Felix was confident he would pull it off.

There was no possible way that Felix could know Ray was getting more and more tense by the minute, as he appeared to be his usual cool and aloof self sitting at the bar. Ray knew Bennie, and with what he had passed on to him, certainly the Banker's men in Florida were in custody by now, or would be very soon, so they wouldn't be able to call. He was sure the Banker wouldn't take action until he received his confirmation, therefore allowing Bennie and the Bahamian cops time to get here, but he was worried the storm was wrecking that part of his plan. If it delayed Bennie too long, how would the Banker react? Ray hadn't thought about that possibility. What would the smart bastard infer from the delay? Would he try to contact his men after a point, and what would his reaction be if he couldn't reach them?

As Ray sat on the barstool listening to the Banker going on with his thoughts, occasionally glancing out the large side windows at the storm buffeting the large yacht, all he could think was, *Unintended consequences; Jesus, if it's not one thing, it's another. When will something go as planned with this lousy mission?*

Robbie continued with his thoughts by telling them the broad outlines of how and when he planned on getting the money back to Devil's Cay. Once the money was back here, he suggested two possible courses for handling Felix's share. One, he could leave it here in the islands, where Robbie said he would set up new accounts for them and launder their share of the cash back to the Mexican bank of their choosing, or if they wished, he would arrange for them to take it to Mexico with them. He told Felix that he had a very nice fifty-foot two-suite motor yacht in his charter fleet and had already ordered it to the cay with the idea of taking him and Ray directly back to Mexico in style and comfort. They would simply move their share of the money to the smaller yacht, and once they reached Mexico, Felix could decide how best to smuggle it ashore.

Felix smiled and nodded his thanks and said, "Thank you, Robbie. That's what I'd like to do. I have the means and the place where we can get it safely back into the country. This is excellent. Thank you again."

Ray was watching the friendly little masquerade with dismay, thinking he had not heard so much friendly bullshit in a long time. He knew there was no smaller yacht headed their way, and he knew Felix and the Banker also knew this, each believing that within the hour, the other would be dead.

As he was thinking about this, the Banker's cell phone, sitting on the seating area coffee table, started ringing and vibrating, getting everyone's attention. Robbie picked it up and said, "Yes?" There was nothing but silence for a minute; even the storm outside seemed to abate as Robbie listened. Finally, he said, "Excellent, excellent. No, get a decent room and a meal; let the storm pass, and return in the morning. And Charles, well done."

Robbie sat his phone down and seemed to sigh a deep sigh of relief as he looked to Felix. "Our search is over, my friend. The money is there. Charles sounded in awe at the sight. There is so much, he says, it will require a day or two to safely arrange for its confidential transport back here. I'm afraid you and Ray will have to be my guests for a few days longer."

Ray could see Felix forcing a smile as he reached for his drink. "My thanks, Robbie, and a toast to your remarkable efforts. Salute."

The others were drinking and there was a forced celebratory feeling to the air, but Ray was thinking, *What in the hell happened with Bennie? Why weren't the Banker's men picked up! Jesus, this is about to get way out of control!*

The menacing-looking Victor walked back into the room from wherever he had been. Felix broke the collegial spell of the moment when he sat his drink down and said to Robbie, "Now, what about the thief?"

Ray was watching closely as the Banker's smile turned to a frown, and he glanced quickly to his man Victor and then back to Felix. "Yes, of course, it is time. Victor, take Ray with you and get the driver. Take him to the island; I'll alert Simon. And Victor, try to appear relaxed, even friendly. Here, take his cell phone and return it to him. Tell him the money has been confirmed, and he and his family are free to sail out this evening. And make sure he's buried away from the house where he can never be discovered."

Ray spoke up. "I will need a weapon."

That had been an unasked question since Felix first posed that he should kill the truck driver for him; he was curious what the response would be. Victor surprised him by speaking up before the Banker, whom he always seemed to defer to, had the chance. "I have a weapon for you. We will get it on our way to get the driver."

Ray nodded his head in acceptance as Robbie spoke again. "Right, then. Victor, it is time."

Only Ray was in a position to see the look that the Banker gave Victor, and it was an unsettling one, as it seemed to convey far more than just *It's time to take care of the driver.* He thought, *This is it. From this moment on, Victor will look for an opportunity to kill me.*

As he stood to follow Victor from the room, he knew it was only a matter of when and where Victor would try to kill him. He could feel the weight of the Baby Glock in his front pocket and had another impulse to start shooting, but the setup was wrong, the players too dispersed, and Felix was holding his drink and not prepared to shoot. He focused once again on the present. Victor would want him alone, maybe on the swim platform, or even in the lazarette with the truck driver, killing two birds at once. Deep down he still believed that they'd make the island before Victor made his move, but he would assume nothing of the kind.

They went out onto the middeck and down the stairs leading to the main deck below. Left and right of the wall of glass doors leading to the posh main interior spaces of the main level were some locked storage closets. Victor went to the port-side storage, took a key from his pocket, unlocked the door, took out a handgun, and handed it to him. Ray recognized the type as a full-size Beretta nine-millimeter, a model he had always avoided due to the excessive weight. But as he took it, something wasn't quite right. It just didn't feel like similar Berettas he'd shot on the range in Seattle. It was a bit lighter. That was when the obvious occurred to him: it was likely the magazine was empty, so he had his answer to the weapons question.

While Ray was dealing with this new revelation, the mostly silent and sullen Victor was deeply immersed in his own world, adjusting to the many surprises of the evening with the limited intellectual capacity he possessed. He had been dumbfounded when his boss took him aside earlier in the evening and told him what he wanted done once they had confirmation of the money. He had known and worked for Simon for years, but they were hardly what you could call friends. It mattered little, however, for his loyalties always were with whoever was paying him, and the Banker was paying him well. The Banker's instructions were simple: Simon was getting out of control, and he was not to leave the island alive. This was necessary, the Banker explained, to keep him from killing the woman, the children, and maybe even the yacht's crew, which undoubtedly would draw the attention of the police and endanger them all.

That was unacceptable, and even Victor realized that the killing of all the others was possible if Simon was allowed to be Simon. The Banker would call Simon and have him waiting on the beach. Victor knew how professional Simon was; surprising him would not be easy, and he would have to take him as soon as possible after they arrived. The driver and the Mexican he could kill whenever he wished, and he decided he would do so as they transferred from the yacht to the tender, always an awkward movement, especially in the dark and with unsettled waters. He had his personal weapon in his waistband, not a holster. After he had screwed on a sound suppressor, it was the only way he could carry it concealed. The Banker was worried that the driver might resist and had ordered the suppressor in case action became necessary in the lazarette.

Victor wasn't worried. He would have the young Mexican move to the tender first, then the driver. They would be defenseless, and he would shoot them both from the swim platform. He would then take the tender to the beach, and once there, he'd let Simon know that he had already killed them both. This would surprise and please Simon, as they had already agreed to split any bonuses. Once Simon got close enough to see for himself, he'd shoot him, and that would be the end of it. Considering the considerable dangers, the Banker had said he'd pay him a half-million-dollar bonus for tonight's work. Victor wasn't sure what the Banker's plans were for the future, but whatever they were, he would be his number-one man now, and that would mean even more money. Satisfied and thinking his plan was simple and fool-proof, he was actually looking forward to it.

⋖⋗ ⋖⋗

Jack was sitting on the bunk in the lazarette when he heard footsteps coming down the stairway above his head. From the sound, it was two men, just as he had expected. He glanced at his watch for perhaps the hundredth time but knew before he did that enough time had passed for Robbie to get his confirmation. The last thirty minutes had been hell. He had been in some tight places before, but nothing like this. He was anxious and frustrated, and he had been thinking about his daughters for much of the time. That only made the situation worse at first, but then, in a way, it seemed to focus him, as the need to survive for their sakes overcame all other thoughts and feelings. Only briefly did the horrible thought that they and Maddy might already be dead flash through his mind. He refused to believe it—not after what Robbie had said and how he had said it. They were alive, and he needed to get to them.

He could hear someone fumbling with the hatch lock and made an intuitive decision to stand, turned slightly sideways, and palmed the screwdriver, holding it tight to his leg, his posture concealing it from view. He was as ready as he could be.

The hatch opened, and a rush of cooler air hit him as the shorter and thicker of Robbie's two principal guards looked in, and then they came slowly down the ship's ladder. He was watching the man closely when he saw the young Mexican he had missed entirely with his lone shot at him at the Beach House look in and then closely follow the stout Bahamian. So he was to participate in his execution as well. Only at some point, he had to be a target too, but who could know for sure? Jack was still amazed that that the two younger Mexicans having dinner with Diaz had survived. Unlike the four guards at the front porch of the Beach House, who all seemed to freeze when he shot the first one, giving him ample time to sight and shoot the others in rapid succession, both the young man coming down the steps and the one he had seriously wounded had somehow understood intuitively what was happening and saved themselves with their fast reactions. Admirable, he thought, but a damned bad break for him, as things turned out.

The Bahamian forced a smile, as if trying to reassure him, and said, "The money is confirmed. You are free to go. The storm is passing; we will take you to the island, where you may get your family and leave. Robbie said to give you this."

The smile and the sentiments were phony, and Jack could easily tell. Why an intelligent man like Robbie would surround himself with such obviously flawed lowlifes was a mystery to him. He'd seen plenty of criminals in his time, and many had been polished, even intelligent, but not Robbie's men. They appeared to him like the bottom of the human barrel, flawed to their core, blunt tools to be used when necessary.

Unfortunately, Jack's assessment of the brute Victor was correct. The characteristics in Simon's and Victor's makeup that Robbie had sought out years ago out of necessity to help him navigate and survive the trafficking circles he knew nothing about, but so very much wanted to destroy, eventually could lead only to disaster. Despite Robbie's clear instructions to put the truck driver at ease, Victor saw determination in the man's eyes, not fear, so he defaulted to the only course of action he knew well. As he extended his left hand, holding Jack's cell phone toward him, he also started to reach for the bulky silenced nine-millimeter in his rear waistband with the other, and Jack recognized the move and was ready. With Victor's premature and badly-thought-out action, he set off the terrible chain of events that had been slowly building.

25

Jack was on autopilot. After all the time he had spent worrying and wondering what he should do when the time came, as Victor went for a weapon, he just instinctively reacted. It had been years since he had gone through the hand-to-hand combat course all recon marines were required to excel in. He struck suddenly and lethally, he thought, aiming his rapid upward thrust for the small area above the large man's stomach yet below his ribs, trying for a lucky but fatal heart wound. Jack knew immediately he had missed his initial chance as the thick man reacted far quicker than most and partially deflected the thrust lower. He could tell with the resistance from the puncture wound that he was into far more mass and muscle, and while excruciatingly painful, no doubt, the wound would not be instantly debilitating. The one positive from his attack was that Victor tried to defend himself with both hands and did not get his weapon free.

Victor had one hand at his throat and the other powerful hand on his arm, trying to keep Jack from striking again. Jack was taller than the Bahamian, but the man had the weight advantage and was forcing him back toward the bunk as he tried with all his strength to extract the screwdriver and strike again. The death struggle in real time was measured in seconds, but for Jack, it seemed to be going in slow motion. He managed to pull the screwdriver out and get his arm free enough to strike again toward the man's neck just as a now-desperate Victor struck at his head with his clenched fist. Out of the corner of his eye, he saw the young Mexican, now fully in the room, pulling a small pistol from his pants, but—strangely, it seemed to Jack—not immediately opening fire. The man instead took the added second to drop into the classic and universally taught standard two-handed firing position all police officers were trained to use in order to shoot accurately. Jack was poised to stab the attacker again but was fixated on the Mexican and his unexpected action, and he knew in that instant he would never again see his children.

The loud reports from the two rapid shots of the baby nine-millimeter were greatly intensified given the tight confines and hard metal surfaces of the lazarette, but those same surfaces contained the deadly noise within. The Bahamian violently lurched forward and Jack was off balance, so there was no preventing them both from falling hard toward the bunk. His ears were ringing, and the air was thick with the terrible acrid odor of the burnt sulfur of the spent rounds, triggering an instant memory in him of walking onto Sherry's patio. Unbelievably he wasn't hit, but he knew his attacker had been as blood and matter from the man's catastrophic head and chest wounds were all over him. He knew he had just seconds to reach the Bahamian's gun and defend himself before the Mexican finished him, and he tried in vain to push the badly wounded or dead man off him, but he was spent from the quick, intense fight and the passing adrenaline rush.

He suddenly felt weak, and the man was just too heavy. The Mexican was cautiously approaching and seemed to be saying something to him, but he didn't hear him; his ears were still ringing, and his focus was inward as he sank into own thoughts. His body relaxed as he closed his eyes, expecting the inevitable. He read somewhere that at the moment of death, a person's life passes before his or her eyes, but he had no such moment. All he felt was a deep sadness that his impulsive actions two months earlier had made his girls orphans.

His hearing was returning, and he more heard than saw the Mexican do the strangest thing, and he opened his eyes. Instead of walking up and shooting him, the Mexican instead quickly jumped up a few steps of the ship's ladder, looked out, and then closed the hatch. He came toward Jack, saying in perfect English, "I said, let me see those hands!"

Jack's head was spinning, and he struggled to understand what was happening as the Mexican repeated his command. He didn't know how, but he was still alive and slowly regaining some of his reasoning powers. "My...my hands?" he repeated back.

"I'm undercover DEA. Don't fuck with me. I want to see those hands, NOW!"

Jack closed his eyes again, thinking, *DEA? Can this be for real?* He opened them, realizing he was blinking hard, as if trying to wake from a deep sleep. "Are you real? DEA, here? But I saw you, in Mexico. You were with Diaz. You're one of them."

"I was undercover in Mexico, you dumb shit, and ended up here because of you and the fucking money chase. Now the hands—let's see them. I've got to know who and what I'm dealing with here."

"What...what do you mean?"

"What I mean...Jack, is it? What I mean, Jack, are you really just some dumb-shit ex-cop who stumbled on some cartel cash, or are you something else? You admitted you were in Mexico, so was that really you doing the shooting? Explain that to me, and quick. We haven't got much time, and I'd better like what I hear."

Jack relaxed again and closed his eyes. He couldn't believe what was happening. He was going to live, at least for the moment. The relief was palpable.

The DEA guy came close enough to take the silenced nine-millimeter from the dead man's pants and then stepped back again.

Jack was struggling to move the heavy man off him. "Could you help get this guy off?"

"No. Manage it, and I'm waiting."

Jack's strength was returning, and he managed to push the now-obviously-dead Bahamian to the floor and sit up. He tossed the screwdriver to the floor also, looked down at himself, and, without thinking, started trying to wipe the blood off.

"Forget that, Jack. Talk. What kind of man are you? Help me understand what I'm dealing with here. Convince me you can be trusted."

Jack looked at him, and then a small but genuine smile came to his face. "Thank you," he said softly.

"Thank you?" Ray asked, perplexed and still slightly pissed. "For what?"

"For saving my life. What's your name?"

Ray was a bit confused with the change in tone and substance of the conversation, and he had the distinct feeling that he had lost control of the questioning—and he was the one holding the gun! But there was something about the guy—his eyes, maybe. They were sincere, nonthreatening.

"Ray, Ray Cruz. We're out of time; we're expected on the island. Quickly, tell me about Mexico and the money, your involvement."

Jack nodded. He too would want to know who he was dealing with if the situation was reversed.

"Short answer...it was me in Mexico. I did the shooting. I was a marine sniper in another life. After they killed my ex-wife, I had no other choice. I felt I had to kill them before they killed me or my little girls."

"How did you know about the Beach House?"

"The crash site, in the glove box. The two stupid guys in the van were Diaz's nephews. They had maps and instructions to be at that house on a certain day. That kind of stuff. It was a stab in the dark. I went down and waited and watched, and then you all showed up on that Sunday. As to the money, I was simply driving home from California when the van passed me and missed a curve. I stopped and grabbed a first-aid kit and climbed down to them, to help. The driver was dead, the other one just hanging on. He asked me to tell someone named Diaz in Matamoros and then died in my arms. Then I found the money."

Jack looked at Ray, a great sadness evident on his face. "I know this will sound like an empty excuse, but I was in a bad way at the time, Ray, and I knew it was dirty. Given how they crashed, I realized only I knew where the money ended up, so I tried to take it. It's turned out to be the worst mistake of my life. I was a good marine and a good cop, I've never done anything like that before and wish I'd never tried to keep it. I told Robbie where it is. I don't even want it anymore."

Ray was looking at him and clearly digesting what he had heard. Then he smiled, pocketed his handgun, and extended his hand to him. "Ok, Jack, I believe you. That pretty much sounds like what the bad guys were thinking about you. And you get your wish about the money. If I know my boss, it's already in federal custody. I'm just glad you didn't shoot at me in Mexico. You're a hell of a shot with a rifle. Can you use one of these?" he asked, handing Jack Victor's silenced nine-millimeter.

Jack smiled back and stood up with Ray's help. "Yeah, I can, and thank God you're quick. I must have missed you by a good four inches high. An unfamiliar weapon—the recoil got me."

The look on Ray's face changed from relief that Jack was a good guy to one of surprise. "You missed? You bastard! You mean you actually shot at me?"

Jack shrugged and took a deep breath and exhaled slowly, and then he said, "Yeah, sorry about that, Ray. Who knew? What happens now?"

Ray was still feeling a great sense of relief at having survived Jack's attack when so many others had not. He shook his head in amazement and then got back to the here and now. "Get that windbreaker off Victor, and we gotta find you a hat or something to cover the blond hair. We're expected on the beach about now. That psychopath Simon is there with your kids and the woman, and if my guesses are correct, he'll try to take us both out about the time we hit shore. We've got to make him think you're Victor until we get close enough I can shoot the son of a bitch first. That's how I see it."

Jack nodded and started rolling the badly-shot-up Victor over and removing his dark windbreaker. He remembered seeing a dark baseball hat with the yacht's logo on it hanging from a hook in the small bathroom. "In there, Ray. There's a hat."

It only took them a minute to transform Jack as best they could under the circumstances, and then Ray went up the ship's ladder, opened the hatch, and went out. A second later he whispered down, "We're clear. Move it!"

Jack climbed up the steps and stepped out onto the swim platform. The night was still very dark and almost silent, disrupted only by the occasional distant lighting strike and rumbles of thunder. The rain had stopped and the winds had died; the worst of the storm was well past. He stole a glance up toward the yacht's deck upon deck of superstructure; the only interior lights on were from the middeck spaces, and there didn't appear to be any activity whatever outside on any of the decks. He exhaled a deep breath, thankful that it seemed they had not been heard or seen during the fight and the shooting.

Ray was already on the tender, fumbling with the controls. "Shit!" he hissed. "Jack, get your ass in here. See if you can figure this out."

Jack had become generally familiar with tenders during his time in Freeport, as the customs officials there used them to motor around the marina. The tender tied alongside the yacht was a sixteen-foot rigid inflatable type with a center console, similar to what they used, only this one was black or gray and hard to see in the night. He took a quick look from the platform and then said, "Give me a second, Ray. There's a flashlight in the lazarette. That'll help us."

Ray was impatient but knew what Jack was suggesting made sense. "Fine. Just make it quick."

It took only a few seconds to dash back down into the lazarette, find the flashlight in the tool cabinet, and get back topside. He climbed into the tender, where Ray already was standing, holding on to the sides due to the light wave action, and then, carefully shielding the light, looked the console over. Satisfied it was not unlike the engine controls of his boat and that he knew how it worked, he turned the key he located hanging from a switch on the console, and the tender's inboard motor instantly purred.

"Cast off that line, Ray," he ordered, and then, when Ray had done as he was told, he advanced the throttles slightly and steered them away from the yacht at a very slow speed.

They were both silent at first as Jack slowly turned the tender toward the beach, but then Ray, who was sitting behind him, whispered, "Whoa, slow us down, Jack. You need to see this if it's what I think it is."

Jack turned and looked. Ray was unrolling what appeared to be a beach towel or a small blanket, and then he looked up at Jack and said with a smile, "Well...what do we have here?"

He was holding a small black assault rifle, and fortunately for them, Jack recognized the type. It was the second time since he had found the money that he had seen such a rifle in the possession of bad guys.

"That's a Belgian-made FAL, Ray. The 50.63, with the folding stock and the paratrooper's shorter barrel." He put the tender in neutral, and it started rocking with the shallow swells. "Let me have that."

Ray watched as Jack expertly folded out the stock and checked the magazine and the chamber. "Change of plan, Ray," Jack whispered. "Get over here. You drive the boat."

"Didn't you hear me a minute ago?" Ray whispered back. "I don't know how."

"Yeah, but you can be taught. It's easy; look."

They stood side by side, and Jack took him through the basic controls until Ray nodded his head in understanding.

"I'm moving to the front. I'm a shitload better with one of these than that pistol. If that Simon's on the beach, I'll get him before he ever sees me. If he's not, you run us up on the beach, then get out but stay close, like you're waiting for him, until he shows himself."

Ray was immediately concerned he'd be a sitting duck standing on the beach if Simon stayed in the undergrowth that covered the island, and he really wanted to live through this, especially after surviving the lazarette. In low, hushed tones he asked, "What if he shoots from cover?"

Jack was looking the newly found assault rifle over almost affectionately and then looked up. "He won't. He can't. Must be forty or fifty feet of beach where we're landing. In this light, it would be a miracle shot if he hit a barn with a handgun. Didn't you say this guy was a pro?"

"I said he was a psychopath, but he struck me as an experienced killer."

"You said he was expecting us—or you and Victor, I should say. He's thinking that he has the edge. He knows he's going to be killing whoever Victor shows up with, and he also thinks he has a second shooter in his friend. We still have surprise, but not for long, especially when he doesn't see his friend. No offense, but you're too small and I'm too tall to pass for Victor, even in this light from very far. You drive this thing slow and straight, and I'll take him before we hit the beach. If he's not there, you get out but stay close and I stay hidden, and we wait until he shows himself. He's probably looking for us now, only thank God the night sucks."

Ray decided that Jack was probably right and then slowly advanced the throttles, heading for the spot Jack pointed out to him. They were a good hundred feet off the beach when Jack's assessment of the situation proved to be correct. From the general area where Jack told him the path from the beach to the house was located, he thought he saw movement, and then a shadowy figure stepped out of the low tangled trees and walked about half-way down the beach and then stopped, his hands on his hips. Ray had to alter course only a few degrees to keep the tender's bow, where Jack was lying low, aimed right at him. Jack had the small assault rifle resting on the top surface of the inflatable pontoon, his head and shoulders barely visible, the baseball hat on backward, the bill on the back and pulled down tight. The wind had died down to nothing, and the air was heavy with humidity from the passing storm. Ray kept glancing at Simon and then at Jack as they drew closer and closer, waiting for him to shoot, thinking that at any time, Simon would clearly see something wasn't right.

The waters were getting calmer the shallower it became as they approached the shore. Ray couldn't stand it. They were only about fifty feet from shore, and he was about to say something. It wouldn't be long before he could start to make out features in the dark.

Then, without warning, there were several sharp cracks, and Simon dropped where he was standing. The shots startled Ray, and he jumped, even though he had known they were imminent. He shoved the throttles forward and ran the tender up on the beach and hit the kill switch as Jack had instructed. Before he could do anything more, Jack suddenly jumped up and out of the boat and rolled off to the right in the sand, almost as if he were evading fire. He sprang to his feet, rifle in hand, aimed, and made straight for Simon in a low crouched posture. Ray followed his lead and jumped out of the other side of the boat, his Baby Glock in his hand, and ran at Simon from the opposite side, just in case.

Before he could get near the fallen man, Jack stopped, dropped to a knee, and fired off two quick shots, but the body didn't move. Jack beat him to the fallen Simon and was already checking him over. Then Jack looked up at him and shrugged. "Sorry about those last two shots. Just wanted to make sure, but looks like they weren't necessary."

Simon was staring straight up with wide eyes, a frozen surprised look on his face. Ray could see for himself that Jack's first two shots, even from a slightly rocking and moving small boat, were clustered dead center in his chest within a few inches of each other. He looked at Jack, who was still looking at him, and said, "Man, remind me to never piss you off. That's some shooting, Jack. Well done."

Ray was pumped, and his face showed it. The worst of the night was over. The Banker's two most dangerous men were dead, they were still alive, and Bennie and the cops couldn't be far off. He was smiling, but Jack's look was still grim. Before he could say anything, Jack jumped up, slinging the rifle over his shoulder as he did so, and jogged to the water and cleaned himself up some. Then he turned and ran past him toward the trailhead, so Ray followed.

The trail led to a gate in a tall wall, and through it was a luxurious pool and patio area. Jack crossed the patio, went through the nearest sliding glass door into the darkened house, and checked out the main rooms. Ray caught up with Jack, who had stopped rushing around and was now walking quietly and slowly toward a hallway where the bedrooms were no doubt located. Jack turned to him and whispered, "My kids are small. I don't want to scare them by barging in out of the dark. We need to find my girlfriend, Maddy, first."

Ray nodded his understanding and followed Jack to what looked like the master bedroom. The door was closed, but there was some light showing from under the door. Jack slowly opened it and peeked in, and then he gasped and darted in. Ray followed and wished he hadn't. The woman was sitting on the floor naked, her legs demurely to one side, her hands tied behind her to one of the corners of the large four-poster bed by pieces of shredded sheets.

Jack was throwing a blanket over her as Ray stepped in, and then he bent down to her and removed a gag from her mouth and started untying the knots binding her hands as she started to sob.

Ray stepped back into the hall and took a few deep breaths, hoping she hadn't been traumatized and that the kids hadn't been hurt. He said quietly from his side of the semiopen door, "Jack, you help her. I'll locate your kids."

He could hear muffled sobs and then warm endearments, and then Jack said, "Thanks, Ray, thanks. We need a minute."

He found the little girls sleeping peacefully and soundly together in a bed in the second bedroom he checked. He went back to the master and knocked quietly on the door. "Can I come in, Jack?"

He heard a quiet yes and went in and found the two of them sitting on the bed's edge, the woman now wrapped in a blanket, their arms around each other. They both had been crying, and he hated to interrupt the moment, but there were still things to do.

"Sorry to interrupt, Jack. The kids are fine, sleeping peacefully down the hall. Your friend needs to get dressed, and we have to get out of here."

Jack didn't understand what Ray was saying or why, but he turned to Maddy and told her gently to dress and gather her things; they had to go. Then he went to the hallway with Ray.

"What's going on, Ray? What happens now?"

Ray seemed pensive and was silent for a moment, looking at the floor, and then he looked up. "Listen, my boss and the island cops are on their way. They should be here anytime now. I've been thinking about things, and I think you should grab your family and we get you guys to your boat and get you out of here before they arrive. Fewer questions that way. If they get here and you're still here, you're just a family that sought shelter in this cove because of the storm."

There was gratitude in Jack's eyes. "What about what I did? The money, and...the murders, in Mexico?"

Ray stared at him and then said, "I'm not sure what I think about that yet. There's a part of me that would like to believe that if our situations were reversed, I would have done what you did. I don't know. But I was in deep shit until you gave me the chance to take Victor out. I need to think this through, but we don't have the time, not now. For the moment, let's say we're square. Now, can we please get the hell out of here?"

Jack was grateful, but then his look changed and became harder. "What are you going to do about the Mexican? And Robbie?"

"Don't worry about me or them. With the cops on the way, both will be in custody within the hour. Head back to Freeport and wait for me there, and we'll figure out the endgame."

Maddy walked into the hallway as they were talking and had no idea what was going on. She was looking from Jack to the kind young stranger when Jack said, "OK, whatever you say, Ray. We'll be in Freeport waiting if we make it out of here. And Ray…thank you."

Jack got Maddy moving, and they finished gathering her belongings and then the girls and their things. Only then did Jack wake them. They were sleepy but very quickly grew excited at seeing him again; it had been too long. Ray watched as Jack hugged his little girls and then started getting them organized, telling them that they were beginning an adventure and had to move quickly and quietly because they needed to get back to the boat and go.

Maddy walked up to him as Jack was dealing with his daughters and said in a very shaky voice, "I'm Maddy. I know your name is Ray, but who are you? Where is Si…Simon?"

Ray took her by the hand and led her into the family room. "I'm with the DEA. Simon is dead, on the beach. Are you OK? Did he…ah, hurt you?"

Maddy stepped toward him and buried her face in his shoulder and began to sob quietly again, then took a deep breath and calmed herself some. Without looking up, she said, "No…no, he was about to. He had a gun…and told me to remove my clothes or he would hurt Molly. But…but then he got a call—from Robbie, I think—and tied me up and left, I guess to the beach. I don't know what's going on or what you're doing here, but thank you."

All Ray could think to say was "Come on. Time to get you guys out of here."

Maddy grabbed him again by the arm. "One more thing. It may be important. Simon was very angry before he came after me. In between watching me and the girls this evening, he spent all his time looking for something, mostly in Robbie's office. After I put the girls down, I quietly looked in. That's when I overheard him talking on his phone to someone he called Borisov, or Borimov, something like that. He was telling him he didn't have it yet, whatever it is, and then he said he'd get it out of Robbie. I got scared and turned to go to my room, and I must have made a sound, because that's when…when…he came for me…and…made me take my clothes off."

Ray nodded. "Thanks, Maddy. I don't know what it means, but thanks for telling me."

Jack was finished getting the girls organized, so Ray patted Maddy on the arm gently and then went into the bedroom to help him. He carried the younger daughter, and Jack carried his older one, and they walked the path to the beach and managed to get the girls on the tender without them seeing the body. Maddy simply stared at it as she slowly walked by, and then, quickly, at Jack's urging, she got in the boat with the little girls.

Ray was still standing on the beach and said quietly, "Jack, come here a sec."

He walked a short distance down the beach. Jack followed, a curious look on his face.

"What is it, Ray?"

Ray looked troubled. "Did that Robbie ever mention anything about Russians?"

Now Jack was surprised because Robbie had, earlier that evening, back at the Evening Shadows. Only with everything else going on, he simply had forgotten about it. Why was Ray asking him? he wondered. He nodded yes. "Yeah, he did. He said something about getting crosswise with some Russians and owing them a bunch of money. What made you ask? What do you know?"

Ray was glancing at the boat, where Maddy was watching them closely, and then looked back to Jack. "Maddy said that Simon character was looking for something in the house and talking to Russians about it over his phone. Sounds like Simon was working for them. Come on, let's get the hell out of here. We have enough to worry about without worrying about some Russians too."

Jack took the controls. Ray pushed them off the beach and then jumped in as Jack accelerated away and made for the sailboat a hundred yards into the cove. Jack maneuvered the tender alongside the nice-looking sailboat to where an accommodation ladder was hanging over the side. "Maddy, climb aboard. Ray, toss her that line. Get us secured."

Both did as Jack instructed, and then they transferred the girls and the few bags they had aboard. Jack looked up at Maddy. "Sweetheart, get the girls below and then get the boat fired up and ready to go. I'll be back as soon as I can."

Maddy's look of sadness, which had remained unchanged since they found her, turned to desperation. "No, Jack. No, you get on this boat, right now!"

Jack looked at Maddy with real tenderness and said softly, "I can't leave Ray, Maddy. I have to help him. I swear, I'll be back soon."

Maddy broke into tears again and was about to plead with him, but she didn't have to, as Ray spoke up. "Give me that windbreaker and the hat, Jack, and get out of the boat, now. I can handle the other two and the last guard."

Jack looked at him, determination in his eyes. "I can't, Ray, after what you've done. I couldn't live with myself if this all goes to shit somehow. Two guns are better than one."

"Out of the boat, Jack. I don't intend to get into another shoot-out. All I have to do is watch over things until my boss and the cops get here. I'll meet you in Freeport in a couple of days. Now go, now!"

Jack hesitated, and then he took the dark windbreaker and hat off and handed them to Ray. Then he grabbed his shoulder and squeezed. He moved to the accommodation ladder, joined Maddy on board the *Second Chance*, untied the line, looked down at Ray, and forced a small smile as he tossed the line into the tender. "Don't piss me off, Ray, and go and get yourself shot. You know how I can get. See you in a couple of days."

Ray smiled back, appreciating the small inside joke, and advanced the throttles, steering the tender away, his smile disappearing the moment he did.

As he headed to the yacht, he wasn't sure what he was going to do. If Felix and the Banker were still in the sky lounge and he walked in, the Banker would know immediately his plans had gone to shit somehow, and it was more than likely that he or the remaining guard would do something stupid. He'd had enough action for one night and knew he had been lucky to survive it. He hadn't been bullshitting Jack when he said he had no intention of getting onto another fight, but if he did anything other than just stay out of sight, that was exactly what would happen.

26

Aboard an RBPF Patrol Boat and Roberta's Dream
Devil's Cay, the Bahama Islands
Saturday night

Bennie hated boats, always had. It was his opinion that if man were meant to spend time on the water, God would have given him webbed feet. He was as sick as dog from all the bouncing around the small RBPF patrol boat had done during the storm, and they were over an hour late getting to Ray. At least now that the rain had stopped, he could station himself on the exterior flying bridge of the police boat, where the wind actually felt good despite the humidity in the air. If necessary, he could lose it over the gunwale in private and end the humiliation of having to run to the toilet every ten minutes with the disgusted patrol boat captain watching. Commander Owens was sympathetic. For whatever reason, he just didn't get seasick, but he had often seen it in others and knew how miserable it made them feel.

The door from the pilothouse slid open, and Oliver stepped out. "GPS puts us fifteen miles out, Bennie. We shall have them on radar in a few minutes. The swells are lessening, and the captain can start putting on some speed. No more than twenty minutes."

Oliver was a helluva cop if first impressions meant anything, and to Bennie, they did. But the commander could not flatten the ocean, and he couldn't make the goddamned storm pass faster. He worked his way over to the very civil and decent senior commander, holding on to the guard rail with

349

both hands the entire time. "Thanks, Oliver. My apologies for being such an unmitigated pain in the ass. Me and the water just don't mix."

"Not to worry, my friend. My helicopter left Nassau five minutes ago; ETA the Cay about fifteen minutes. I have my best six-man squad from my counternarcotics branch on board. They are heavily armed and quite good at what they do."

Bennie was feeling desperate about Ray. Somewhere in his communications with the Miami office, his instructions had gotten screwed up, and his men had not apprehended the chopper pilot and his associate until they were coming out of the secure warehouse. A check of the pilot's cell phone indicated he had made his confirmation call a few minutes before being grabbed. That was almost an hour ago, which meant if Ray's gut instincts were right, the shit had probably hit the fan on the yacht, and for the second time since he had begun running Ray in undercover operations, he'd let him down.

"How do you suggest we use them, Oliver?"

"We are flexible. We don't have to land them on the cay to use them. We can have them hover and do a direct rappel to the yacht if that's where you think they'd be most useful."

Bennie was nodding his head as if yes, but then said, "Thing is, Oliver, I don't know where my man is or will be unless he calls me back. I've tried reaching him, but that's a no-go. Let's not deploy them until we're sure where he needs us. But in the meantime, get them in the area, and if necessary, fly them in circles out a safe distance until we can call them in."

The commander nodded his head in the affirmative and went back into the pilothouse and made the necessary call with his orders.

Fifteen miles to the northwest, the skies were rapidly clearing, and more and more stars were becoming visible as the last vestiges of the storm passed over. Ray didn't notice them as he slowly approached the yacht in the darkness, carefully looking for sentries. As far as he could see, nothing had changed in the short time he'd been gone. The only interior lights on were from the middeck, as usual, and the few overhead lights always left on at night to partially illuminate the covered main decks. He eased up to the swim platform, cut the engine, and quietly jumped to the yacht with the tie-off line in his hand. Once he had the tender secured, he crouched down and carefully went halfway up the steps to the main deck, far enough to check the area. Seeing no one, he sat down and pulled out his cell phone to call Bennie, but it was as dead as Simon and Victor. He was blind again, but he knew Bennie was close; he had to be. As much as he wanted to stay where he was and wait for the good guys to get there, he knew he couldn't. He needed to confirm everyone's positions to eliminate possible resistance when Bennie and the cops arrived.

He cautiously got up and moved quickly over the main deck until he was back in the shadows adjacent to the main sliding glass doors. He peeked in and the formal salon was dark and vacant, as he suspected it would be. Since he had arrived, the more formal spaces had never been used. He slowly climbed the starboard side exterior stairs from the main deck to the middeck and paused near the top, squatted down, and carefully checked out the empty seating area where he'd spent so much time. From the darkened stairs, he could see into a portion of the sky lounge through the wide sliding glass doors. The Banker and Felix were still seated there and appeared to be relaxed and talking. From his sight angle, he could not see the bar area, where the one remaining guard he was aware of had been sitting, so he couldn't be sure he was even there. He quickly moved from the stairs and darted past the spiral stairs from the helipad above and ducked into the shadows on the narrow starboard perimeter deck.

On the midlevel, the perimeter deck went completely around the large yacht. It was how the crew got to the pilothouse up front without having to disturb guests who might be in the sky lounge. The lounge had three large picture windows on each side, and if he was careful, he'd be able to look in and confirm whether the guard was still at the bar. Spill light from the interior and the pilothouse farther forward shed some light on the narrow perimeter deck, but where there were no windows, the shadows were deep. As he was moving down the narrow deck to the first window, he heard something behind him and turned and froze, dropping to a knee to lessen his profile. Thankfully, Victor's large dark windbreaker effectively covered his light-colored slacks, making him difficult to see in the shadows. The hairs on the back of his neck stood up for the second time this evening as the armed guard he was hoping to locate suddenly appeared at the starboard coaming of the deck he had just passed through, looked out over the small cove, casually took a cigarette out, and lit it.

There were so many thoughts going through his head at the sudden turn of events that it was impossible to do anything but stay frozen like a statue. The man was no more than ten or fifteen feet away. Once the guard's eyes adjusted to the low light levels, if he simply glanced Ray's way, he would easily be seen and be at an enormous disadvantage, for there was no place to hide in the narrow confines of the perimeter deck. A desperate feeling came over him as he tried to focus. His only options if the guard noticed him would be to go over the side or hope he could win a quick draw down with the guard. Like a dummy, he had stuck his Baby Glock in his pocket as he was moving about, and there was no going for it now. Any movement on his part would only attract the guard's attention.

He was trapped but kept telling himself over and over to stay cool and let the guard have his smoke, and maybe he'd go back inside. As he was thinking that things couldn't possibly get any worse, he heard a second noise, this one from the direction of the pilothouse behind him, and he knew immediately without looking it had to be the captain or the second officer coming out the pilothouse door. The guard heard it too and turned and looked casually to his left, but his night vision must have been affected when lighting his cigarette, because he seemed to look past the shadows and wasn't surprised or alarmed that someone was coming out of the pilothouse farther forward. But what little luck Ray possessed ran out when whoever it was coming up the narrow deck behind him ended any illusions he had that somehow the entire situation wasn't about to turn to shit by asking in a challenging voice, "You—what are you doing there?"

The guard seemed puzzled at first by the challenge, thinking that the crew member was speaking to him. But Ray saw his eyes shift and finally take notice of the darkened lump low in the shadows, and he started to reach for his weapon. Instinctively, Ray did also, knowing whoever got to his gun the fastest and shot the straightest was maybe going to survive this evening.

Everything was happening in a blur; he rolled out flat as fast as he could, trying to jam his body into the base of the steel coaming where it met the teak decking as he reached for his handgun. But in his panic, the Baby Glock got hung up in his pocket lining, and he frantically tried to pull it free. His feelings of desperation became far more intense, as he knew in that instant that he was going to lose the draw and the guard would get off the first shots. His eyes never left the guard as the now-startled thug quickly leveled his weapon at him and Ray continued to struggle with his own. Suddenly, there were several loud shots, and he recoiled and ducked, thinking the guard had shot. But that wasn't the case. Ray glanced up and saw the man lurching face forward toward him and then falling in a heap to the deck.

In his surprise and the developing chaos, a part of his mind was trying to tell him there was something different about the sounds of the two shots, but suddenly, there were multiple handgun shots from behind him. He felt several hard, painful kicks to his leg, the teak deck next to his head splintered, and the air became filled with the whine of ricochets off steel plating. He finally freed his Glock and threw himself over on his back against the other side of the narrow space, taking the Glock in both hands as he did so, to shoot at who he now recognized was the engineer / second officer rushing toward him, still firing wildly. As he started to return fire, there was the definite deeper cracking sound of what he realized was rifle fire, and the crewman tumbled down hard to the deck not twenty feet from him and was then still.

Ray was breathing hard and was dazed by the sudden shoot-out. He tried to get to his feet as quickly as he could. But his body wouldn't obey his mind, and in that instant he knew he had been shot at least twice in his lower leg. As he was struggling to get to his feet, out of the darkness near the stairwell a low voice hissed, "Ray, you OK?"

Before he could answer, several more shots rang out, this time from inside, then several more. But again the sound of the second shots was different, as if from a second weapon. He felt light headed, likely from the onset of shock, but also with the realization that the dangerous situation was not yet over. At the same time, however, he also felt a ray of hope. By some miracle he was not alone, and the voice from the dark had to have shot the guard and maybe even the charging crewman and saved him. He shook his head to try to clear it and keep from passing out, and then he grabbed the top of the perimeter coaming and pulled himself up. That was when he saw Jack quickly rise out of the dark stairwell from the main deck below, the Belgian assault rifle in his hands, looking and aiming toward the interior of the yacht but moving quickly toward him in a low crouch. Jack seemed out of breath as he got to him, and then, in a quiet, concerned voice, he asked, "Are you hit? Who's shooting inside?"

Ray grabbed Jack to hold himself up. "Has to be Felix. He was armed. Maybe the Banker too, I didn't know about him, but I heard different shooters. Come on, give me a hand. We need to find out quick."

With the powerful Jack holding on to him and helping him to the sliding glass doors, they looked inside. It was suddenly very quiet. Felix was still in his lounge chair, his right arm dangling to the side, the Baby Glock on the floor close by, his head snapped back, clearly dead from an obvious nasty wound to his forehead. Robbie was on the floor, badly wounded, it appeared, given all the blood, slowly trying to pull himself up off the floor and back onto the couch. At first glance, it looked as if Felix had opened up on Robbie when the shooting outside started, wounding him in the gut, but then Robbie, who was also armed, it turned out, returned fire and managed to take Felix out with a head shot. He was about to step in but then stopped and looked at Jack. "Not that I'm not glad to see you, but how'd you get here?"

Jack pointed, and Ray could see the tall mast and supporting guy lines of his sailboat close alongside the port side of the yacht but slowly angling away.

"I convinced Maddy we should swing by and get you and the tender and get you out away from here. I thought I'd find you on the swim platform keeping an eye on things, and when you weren't, I figured you were doing something stupid and might need help."

Ray was really hurting now but forced a smile through the pain. "I was stupid, but I couldn't just stay down there, not knowing where everyone was. I happen to like my boss, and I'd never be able to forgive myself if I let him get shot. I'm grateful, though. You no doubt saved my ass, but you have to get off the boat right the hell now, or you'll be up to your ears in this shit with way too much to explain. Now go, please. I can handle it from here."

Jack looked grim. "What about the rest of the crew? That guy shooting at you was one of them."

"I'll take my chances. I was never really sure about that one. He mostly kept to himself, and he just had that look to him, if you know what I mean. The captain and the chef are the only guys left, and the rest are women. I really doubt the others are involved. Now go. The island cops will be here any second. But one last favor on your way out."

"Anything, Ray. Name it."

Ray motioned to the dead guard lying a few feet from them. "Flip that guy around before you go and leave me the rifle."

Jack looked at him and then nodded his immediate understanding of what Ray was doing and why. He handed over the rifle and then patted him on the back. "Get that wound compressed quick before you pass out from blood loss, and get some sugar in you to combat the shock. See you in Freeport. And Ray, save Robbie if you can. He's not all bad. He's done a lot of good, if you give him a chance to tell you."

Jack quickly went to the fallen guard and moved him around to make it look as if Ray had shot him, then sprinted for the stairwell and was gone. As Ray watched him disappear, he was puzzled by his comment about the Banker, and then shook his head again, trying to clear it. He forced the heavy glass door farther open and slowly limped in, the blood from his leg wounds staining the fancy flooring.

As he entered, Stephanie, another of the women stewards, and the captain rushed into the large room from the elevator lobby at the other end. They stopped when they saw Felix, and then Stephanie started screaming as the captain eyed Ray, clearly scared out of his mind. Ray was holding his Glock pointed at the floor, with the rifle hanging from his shoulder. Firmly he said, "Undercover US DEA, Captain. This is a police action; stay where you are."

The captain froze, and Stephanie put her hand to her mouth, stifling her scream, her eyes wide, terrified, as the remaining members of the crew came rushing up the main stairway behind them.

"Captain, slowly back up, and everyone, put your hands on your heads where I can see them, and keep them there until I can get this mess sorted out."

Robbie didn't seem to hear any of his commands and had continued to slowly struggle up on the couch. He managed to get himself into a sitting position, still clutching his handgun in his right hand, and then he grabbed one of the decorative throw cushions from the couch and held it against his obviously serious gut wounds with the other, as if trying to stem the flow of blood. He slowly turned toward him, as if noticing him for the first time, and said with difficulty, "Ah...young Ray...you are a hard man...to kill. I understand now...why Felix...valued you so much. Are you truly an American... policeman?"

It was clear from his labored speech he was in terrible pain, and Ray knew he wasn't going to last much longer unless his wounds were treated very soon.

"That's right, Robbie. Felix didn't know. Now please, put the gun down. Help is on the way."

Robbie looked at him. He was ashen and had a very sad look on his face. Slowly he asked, "The money?"

"We have it, and your men."

Robbie sank back into the couch, his head falling back, his eyes staring at the ceiling. He then slowly returned his glassy gaze to him. "Then I'm afraid...there can be...no help for me. It is far too late...far too late for that... my time is done. Do me...a last kindness...and finish me, please...don't leave me to the Russians...or make me...do it myself."

Robbie started coughing and was having difficulty getting his wind, so Ray slowly tried moving toward him, his Glock pointed at the grievously wounded but still-armed man, thinking about what Jack had told him, not wanting to shoot, and wondering what the truth was.

"No, Robbie. Put the gun down. It doesn't have to end like this."

Robbie seemed to gather himself as the coughing stopped, and then he looked at him with more determination in his eyes. "Two...two things Ray. Please tell my Maddy...I'm so sorry about her Aussie. A better man would... would have stopped Simon."

He paused, struggling again to find the strength to speak, and then went on. "My library...the bookshelves, a hidden door there...my records. Find them, use them...Roberta's death...must not be in vain."

Ray was still lightheaded and dizzy, trying to remember everything being said, knowing he needed to sit down before he fell down. He was also thinking about what Maddy had said about Simon's search and the Russians when suddenly, with a quickness that startled him, Robbie jerked the gun up under his chin and shot himself before Ray could do anything more than flinch. He quickly looked away, stunned, then lost his balance and fell to the floor as a terrible sick sensation came over him. Stephanie and one of the other women started screaming hysterically again. The pistol report was still reverberating through the room, mixed now with the screams and shouts from the crew when the cacophony of chaotic sounds was slowly drowned out by the loud, high-pitched whining of twin turbine engines as a large Sikorsky helicopter moved to a hover overhead.

27

Freeport, Grand Bahama Island
Thursday, late afternoon
May; week nine

I t took the local authorities a few hectic days to get everything sorted out and for Commander Owens and Bennie to get Ray debriefed. The days were hard on him. Between his short stay in the hospital, the long debriefing sessions, and the pain from his wounds, he'd managed very little sleep. Despite what he'd learned about himself in the past year from his shrink, Dr. Mercer, he was finding the events of Saturday night hard to process, and the worst of the bad dreams he thought he'd put behind him returned.

The Royal Bahamian Police Force patrol boat with Bennie aboard arrived fifteen minutes after the counternarcotics team rappelled to the yacht from the hovering chopper. Ray learned during the debriefs that the pilot had seen multiple gun flashes in the darkness from a half mile away through his night-vision gear as they were orbiting and waiting for instructions. When the pilot relayed the information on the shooting to the commander, they received the go command to assault the yacht and made directly for it.

The senior lieutenant in charge of the counternarc troops had been briefed to the fact that there was an undercover US DEA agent aboard and to proceed with caution. By the time the lieutenant and his squad made their way down to the middeck, they found Ray sitting bent over in a lounge chair, his head in his hands, staring at the floor, two dead men with catastrophic head wounds also sitting nearby. After securing the area and moving the shocked and frightened crew to the pilothouse at the forward end of the mid-deck and putting them under guard, the preliminary investigation began as the lieutenant and his troops did a careful but quick search of the yacht. The lieutenant's men found the dead second officer on the outer deck and Victor in the lazarette, in addition to the guard they had seen lying on the mid-deck when entering the lounge. The lieutenant called his commander aboard the approaching patrol boat and reported the yacht and crew secured, but five men were dead from a shoot-out, and the American agent was alive but wounded. This report caused Bennie several minutes of great distress until he arrived and actually saw Ray for himself.

The squad's medic did what he could to treat Ray's wounds, but in the depression that had engulfed him, Ray was uncooperative, answering only a few simple medical-related questions and ignoring everyone else, especially the self-important lieutenant. It wasn't until Bennie came aboard that he came out of his sullen state and slowly began filling Bennie and the commander in on what had happened.

Commander Owens ordered a second helicopter with the necessary forensic and technical specialists aboard to the cay and then offered Bennie his assault chopper to fly Ray directly to Nassau and the hospital. Over the following several days, as he recovered from his wounds and the prelimi-nary investigation progressed on the yacht and the cay, he went over and over everything he had learned in the last forty-eight hours in the Banker's company, and then everything he had learned in Mexico associated with the case.

All Ray wanted was for the questioning to stop so he could go to Freeport. He hadn't really been sure what he was going to do about Jack when he first put him and Maddy and Jack's little girls on their sailboat. But that was now an answered question in his mind, and he didn't want to leave Jack and Maddy hanging, worrying about what he intended to do. He knew that if Jack hadn't taken the chance he did and come back, he wouldn't have survived the night; the situation couldn't be any clearer. How much was his life worth? At what cost would he protect Jack in return? It was all he could think about.

Preliminary ballistics reports from Commander Owens's team indicated that both the guard and the second officer were killed with rifle fire, and very accurate rifle fire at that, for which Ray was commended. His descriptions of the various shoot-out scenes matched up with the physical evidence, and the only story he had some difficulty explaining was what had happened in the lazarette. There was no way to say there had not been another man being held there, because no doubt the yacht's crew was aware of him. He said he didn't know why the unknown man was being held, for he had just been brought aboard. Ray went on to say the only thing he knew was that he was ordered by the Banker and Felix to help Victor take the man to the island, where his wife and kids were supposedly being held. Once there, he was to help Victor and Simon kill them all and then bury the bodies. He said he also knew that was when Victor would try to kill him. He told the commander and Bennie he was certain the family were innocents who had sailed into the cove seeking shelter from the oncoming storm and were simply in the wrong place at the wrong time.

He believed in honesty and considered himself an honest man, but he had already lied to Bennie once on this mission, at the beginning, when he told him the nightmares from last year's mission had stopped. He really didn't think of it as a lie at the time, rationalizing the whole thing because he knew he was getting better and the few dreams he did have wouldn't affect his performance. But there was no rationalizing the lies mixed with truth he was telling Bennie and the commander now. He told them he knew Victor was going to try to kill him at some point, so when they got to the lazarette and the unknown prisoner defended himself, he shot Victor, but in the ensuing chaos, the prisoner escaped and made a swim for it in the dark. Ray went on to say he then made the decision to take the tender to the island in an effort to locate and save the woman and the children supposedly being held there. When the armed Simon showed himself on the beach, again believing he had no other choice, Ray shot him first and then made a quick search of the house but found no one. He returned to the yacht with the intention of waiting for help to arrive, but then one thing led to another, and he found himself trapped between two more shooters with no choice but to defend himself again.

Commander Owens was easily satisfied with his explanation and very complimentary about his actions and courage, telling Bennie that he intended to see that Ray received his department's highest award for valor. It was the rare and gifted agent, the commander noted, who could single-handedly take on a half dozen armed men and live to tell the story.

After the commander left and Ray and Bennie were finally alone, Bennie looked long and hard at him and then asked, "So, whoever this mystery man is, you're saying he had no part in this, and you're sticking with that fairytale?"

His look was no less hard in return. "That's right, Bennie. No part."

Bennie knew intuitively that there was more to it than that, but for whatever reason, Ray wanted it dropped. Given the cache of information Oliver's troops were discovering in the small hidden safe room at the island bungalow and because he trusted Ray implicitly, he decided to give Ray a pass. They had a hugely successful operation that was going to put a serious several-billion-dollar crimp in a bunch of cartel-connected laundered US businesses by the time this thing was through. The US attorneys office was going to be busy for years investigating and prosecuting the many tentacles of what was being discovered. He could live with that, and Ray could keep his secrets. As far as Bennie was concerned, he'd earned them.

The worst part of the last few days for Ray had been last night. In addition to the many meticulous records the highly organized and educated Robbie Poitier had kept, they also found a video library of tapes in the hidden records room, each one more or less a personal video letter to his dead wife. He would set up his camera and then sit in his favorite chair in his large library with a drink in one hand and a fine cigar in the other and talk to her in long, affectionate personal conversations as if she were in the room with him, telling her what he was doing, the good and the bad, and why. It was as if he needed her blessing or something, and by his sharing with her everything he was doing, she was giving him tacit permission to continue. The tapes wouldn't be of any use in court but would help the investigation.

For Ray, they were maybe the saddest thing he had ever seen. The few tapes he watched in Bennie's suite when Commander Owens brought them over only deepened his depression. The only good was that he now understood what Jack had been trying to tell him about the Banker, especially after Commander Owens told them the sad story of Roberta Poitier's tragic death.

Last night he'd had enough. They were in the middle of one of the videos when without a word he stood and left a surprised Bennie and Commander Owens to watch the rest without him and went back to his room with decidedly mixed emotions about himself and his future. Several hours later, when his perceptive boss came by to check in on him, he told Bennie he was through. Bennie was startled at first, and then he sat down beside him and asked why.

It was difficult to look Bennie in the eye, and he got very emotional, but when he managed to compose himself, he said, "I don't see where I'm doing a damn bit of good, Bennie. Nothing I ever do seems to matter. I...control... nothing, and as a result, good men keep dying. And the circumstances seem to always end up forcing me to do things I would never do, all in the name of survival. I stare in the mirror and hardly recognize myself anymore, Bennie. I need to get away from this before I lose myself completely."

Bennie was shaking his head no, to accepting his resignation. "I've been where you are more than once in my career, Ray, and you're wrong, dead wrong. You've done more good in your work than any dozen agents I have working other investigations. Listen, son, our world is a hard place, a real place, and bad shit happens. Are you bothered that you couldn't save Poitier? Is that it? If it is, don't be, Ray. He was a decent man. I see that now, and I feel bad too, after what we've learned, but he was a misguided fool, and in way over his head. You did what you could. His own actions led him to his own end. His suicide just shortened the timeline. Don't beat yourself up because you couldn't keep him from pulling the trigger."

Ray stared at Bennie, not knowing what to say that he hadn't said already. Bennie's intuition had served him well his entire career, and he knew what he had to do.

"Listen, Ray, take some time. As of this minute, the agency has just loaned you out to Commander Owens for coordination and follow-up. You are to stay here at the hotel for the next month, to be paid for out of the director's confidential fund. In a month, come see me up in DC. If you still want out, maybe then I'll accept it. But not now, not when you're all shot up and raw."

Bennie got up and went to the door and then turned back to him. "I'm out of here tomorrow morning after breakfast with Oliver. I'll tell him you'll be around but that I would appreciate it if he left you alone. A month, Ray, in Washington. I'll be looking for you." Then he went out the door, closing it behind him.

In spite of all that was bothering him, somehow after Bennie left, he managed the first decent night's sleep he'd had in weeks and woke up in the morning feeling a little better. He spent the morning alone by the pool, thinking about everything, and some of what Bennie had said made sense. The prospect of spending a month in the Bahamas also helped. With the agency picking up the tab for his room and any meals he had in the hotel, it wouldn't even cost him much. He'd been shot through his calf and also had a flesh wound in his lower thigh. Neither shot had hit bones or an artery, so he'd recover relatively quickly. The Bahamian doc treating him gave him different pain killers yesterday, and they were an improvement over his initial meds. There were fewer side effects, and he wasn't all that uncomfortable anymore, contributing to his change in spirit. He was on crutches for a week or two, and that was a pain in the ass, but he could live with it.

There were two important things he had to do before becoming just a tourist: go see Jack in Freeport and tell him how this was going to end, and then try to find Stephanie. The last time he had seen her, she was in shock and thought he was a murderer. He knew the crew had all been interviewed and cleared, but he also knew that for security reasons, they knew very little about him and his truth. There had been something about her as she toured him around the yacht, something beyond the instant physical attraction he knew he felt. As they talked afterward, there was a connection between them that he could tell she felt too. He couldn't help feel she might be the one for him, and he had to find her and find out and then persuade her to give him a second chance. The look on her face when he last saw her was not something he could live with.

He booked an early-afternoon interisland flight to Freeport with a return later this evening and took a shuttle to the airport. He was airborne an hour later, and after the short flight, he took a cab to the Evening Shadows, knowing that the marina where Jack kept his boat moored was located close by. He really hadn't taken particular notice of Jack's boat when it was anchored off the cay, so he hobbled off to the customs office to ask where he would find a Jack Williams berthed.

⋯⟫══◉ ◉══⟨⋯

Jack was sitting in the shade of the cockpit bimini and did not notice Ray when he went from the bar to customs. He was lost in his own thoughts, not knowing if he would ever be able to put behind him the events of the last several months, and not just because of what Ray may or may not tell him about his future when he showed up. After he had taken the yacht's tender and caught Maddy, they sailed directly from Devil's Cay to here, and little was said during the night passage. Mostly Maddy had been below with the girls, finally getting some sleep after several terrorizing days. Early the next morning, after they arrived in port and with the girls still sleeping below, they sat down together in the cockpit, and he told her if they were ever going to have a future together, she needed to know the entire truth about him and the last several months. Maddy knew intuitively that Jack had secrets, and she had frightened eyes as she silently nodded her head and then said, "Tell me, darling."

He was holding her hand tightly but staring out over the water, wondering how to begin, when the words just started. "It was late, must have been around three in the morning. I was returning to Colorado from California, where I was visiting the girls, when this van passed me on Wolf Creek Pass…" He stopped and turned to her, a very hurt look on his face, and then said, "No…no…I have to go back farther."

He cleared his throat as if it was difficult for him to speak, and then, in a softer voice, went on. "Abbey was walking home from school the day she was grabbed..."

Maddy knew some of his history from their talk the first night they were together but sat stunned, yet supportive initially, by the complete story. When he told her about Armie and why he went there, and then what he did in Mexico, her countenance changed for the worse as she blinked hard, removed her hand from his, and held both of hers clasped together in her lap. When he finished, the look on her face was heartbreaking to him, and without a word, she went to their cabin and closed and locked the door and stayed there for the better part of the next four days. The local internet and papers were full of the shocking story about one of the island's better-known philanthropists and prominent businessmen being killed in a police raid because it turned out he was also a big-time banker to the drug cartels.

There was no keeping the news from Maddy, and that sent her even deeper into her personal tailspin. She only came out of their cabin for the occasional meal, always eaten alone back in their cabin, and hadn't said ten words to him over the last four days. He wasn't sure what she was thinking about but knew his only path to happiness was hanging in the balance, because a future without her in it could never truly be happy.

As he sat alone with his thoughts, it was another perfect afternoon in paradise, but worrying about what Maddy was going to do was preventing him from enjoying it. Earlier, out of a feeling of desperation, he'd talked to Henry, and that had helped him some, and Henry hadn't hesitated at all when Jack told him he could use a friend and asked him if he could come down for a few days. He would arrive tomorrow.

Jack was nursing a cold beer and thinking about some of what Robbie had told him about his banking partner on Antigua and how he could be trusted when he saw Ray on his crutches approaching the boat from the direction of the customs shack. He stood and waved and then smiled a nervous smile as Ray smiled back and asked, "Permission to come aboard?"

"Permission granted, but only if you have a beer," Jack said, his smile and friendly tone forced.

"Done," Ray said. "Now, if you would be so kind, Captain, as to tell me how I do this without going overboard."

Jack helped Ray across the narrow gangway and got him settled on the padded bench seating of the cockpit and handed him a cold Bahamian beer from the cockpit cooler. Ray thanked him and was starting to fill him in on the case when Maddy suddenly came up from below. She looked as if she had just showered. Her hair was wet and combed straight back and her face was serious and drawn, but she managed a small smile for Ray. Then she sat down beside Jack without a word. Ray knew something was amiss between them and was a bit embarrassed. He wasn't sure what he should do, but Jack solved that for him.

"Maddy knows everything, Ray. Everything. Please, go on with what you were saying."

Ray nodded and then told them what he had learned in general terms, why Robbie had done what he had done, and about the secret room and all the records. The detail was amazing, his personal legal accounts clear and separated from the illicit accounts, and every illicit dollar he'd stolen or collected accounted for. After swearing both of them to secrecy, he told them that the Bahamian government at the highest levels had been brought into the case, because so much good in the islands was being funded by monies purposefully stolen from the cartels and wisely invested by Robbie, all in the name of revenge. No one wanted the good work to be stopped, so the muck-a-mucks at Government House in Nassau were hard at work trying to craft a legal solution with the US authorities to keep the funding coming.

He then told them about the tapes and the conversations Robbie would have with his wife. He paused and took a long drink of his beer and then looked at Maddy, whose eyes were glistening with tears that seemed to refuse to run down her cheeks.

"Maddy, there's one other thing. Before he died, Robbie asked me to tell you he was sorry about your Aussie. I didn't understand at the time what he was saying, but on one of the tapes, he explained it all to his wife, Roberta, and then broke down and begged for your forgiveness. It seems your old partner found out about some aspect of Robbie's illicit business and tried to blackmail him. Robbie sent his thug Simon to make him an offer to contain it and to keep you from finding out, but Simon killed him instead."

Maddy reached over and grabbed Jack's hand and nodded, and then she put her face in his shoulder and softly sobbed. Jack held her for a minute, the silence awkward, and then he looked at him and asked, "What about us, Ray? How does this end?"

Ray took another pull on his beer and then looked at Jack as Maddy also looked up, a desperate look in her eyes, waiting to hear the answer.

Ray smiled. "That's easy, Jack. I owe you. The agency and the island cops are all happier than pigs in shit with the results of this case, the records, and everything. We have the sixty million in cartel cash in Florida that you found, although that little sideshow was never a part of my mission. All the money chase did is get my ass dragged to the Bahamas and damned near killed. But it also gave me the opportunity to meet you two, and that almost makes getting my ass shot off worthwhile."

He smiled at his own humor, then grew more serious. "As far as I'm concerned, with respect to the money, you did nothing wrong. Besides, you gave it up, and there's no evidence you ever were involved. You're a good man, Jack. You tried to be a Good Samaritan, stumbled onto the cash, and ended up doing what I think anyone would have tried doing in the same circumstances. You couldn't know about Diaz's corruption or reach, or his ruthlessness."

He paused and glanced at Maddy and then back to Jack. "Your children's mother is dead; you and your daughters have paid a terrible price already. If some sort of punishment was ever called for, that's punishment enough."

Ray's serious look turned back to a wry smile. "One piece of advice—from a friend, though, not a cop. I'd maybe think twice, Jack, if I were you about stopping the next time you witness a wreck, no matter how much you may want to help."

Maddy smiled a bit, and Jack did too. Then Jack raised his beer in a toast and said, "Good advice, Ray. Thanks. Here's to the last good Samaritan."

He and Ray clinked beers, and Ray nodded his head yes and took another swig of his beer. Ray's look then changed back, the smile disappearing, his more serious look returning. Once again he glanced at Maddy first and then back to Jack. "As to Mexico and what happened down there...well, I really don't know shit, do I? Last Saturday night is a blur, frankly, and I don't remember much, if anything, of what you told me in the lazarette. I never saw the shooter or shooters down in Mexico, and the last time I checked, the dunes south of Matamoros are just a bit out of my jurisdiction. From what I hear, the Mexican cops are now wise to Colonel Diaz's criminal life and aren't losing any sleep over his recent disappearance. This probably sounds callous, and I apologize in advance for saying it, Maddy, but except for Robbie and your ex-wife and her friend, Jack, it seems to me that everyone who was killed in this mess deserved it. The locals and my agency don't know anything more about the mystery man who was on board *Roberta's Dream* the other night other than it looks like he and his family simply took shelter from a storm and ended up in the wrong place at the wrong time. It happens, and that's the end of it. All I ask is if I can convince a certain young Englishwoman that she should give me a second chance and feel about me like I'm feeling about her, maybe you'll give me the family rate on a week's charter and show us the more romantic parts of the Caribbean—give me a chance to work on her."

Jack smiled, as did Maddy, for the first time in days, and then Jack said, "Done deal, Ray. Anytime you want for however long you want. Our boat is your boat. You will always be welcome here. That's what second chances and this boat are all about."

They finished their beer, and Maddy finally spoke up, her voice quiet and weak. "Will you stay for dinner, Ray? I'm a pretty fair cook."

He glanced at his watch. "Thanks for the offer, Maddy. Another time— soon, hopefully. I've got a seat on the six thirty puddle jumper back to Nassau. Commander Owens says he has a phone number and an address for me on Stephanie. I need to find her, and then I need to change her mind about me. If I'm lucky, maybe in a couple of weeks I'll be back with her and can take you up on that offer. Wish me luck."

Maddy and Jack both did, and after Maddy hugged him and kissed him on the cheek, Jack helped Ray to the pier. They shook hands for a final time, and then Ray surprised Jack by quickly leaning in closer, taking him by the arm, and saying in a voice suddenly husky with deep emotion, "Thank you for my life, Jack. I'll never forget you."

Ray turned away quickly and hobbled back toward the Evening Shadow. Jack watched him for a minute, amazed and deeply moved by the generosity of the young man and thinking there were now four people in this messed-up world he could count on and who in turn could always count on him.

Jack turned to board the boat and saw Maddy still standing there, gazing at him, her arms tightly hugging herself. He went to her and slowly took her hands as she looked up at him, and he asked, "Are we OK, Maddy? Are we going to make it?"

She smiled tenderly and reached up, touching his face lightly, and then kissed him gently. "Yes...yes we are. Some of it is ugly, Jack, but as I thought about it, I realized I know you and always have somehow. I'm sorry it took me so long to remember."

She paused and looked deeply into his eyes. "You...are a gentle spirit, and I've known that since the first moment we spoke. A woman doesn't find that in a man very often. I know now how very hard it was for you to do what you felt you had to. I also know that everything you did, you did for us, to protect us. I can live with that, if you can."

Jack couldn't find the strength to do anything more than just pull her close and embrace her. She then leaned back and looked up at him. "So where do we go from here? I'm not sure, but I don't think I have a job anymore."

Jack pulled her hands to his lips and kissed them, more grateful to her for her understanding than she could ever know. "Well...I know you have some bad memories about the chartering business, sweetheart, but if you're up for it, that's what I'd like to do. There's something about the water...I don't think I want to be very far from it ever again."

Her smile faded as she turned and looked off across the marina for a few seconds, but then she turned back to him. "It's a hard business, Jack. We'll have more tough times than good as we build a following. And there are the girls to think of—we'd be on the water a lot. We can keep them with us and homeschool them somehow, but that limits the number of cabins we can offer and the types of charters we can do. If we put them in the private school here, or in Nassau or Florida, they could live on a campus and have friends their age and a bit of normalcy, which may be better for them in some respects. But we wouldn't see them much, and the cost is terrible."

"We could get a bigger boat, Maddy, one with more cabins like Ed's. His has some crew berths up front, which would be fine for us and the girls, and there would still be three guest cabins. Why couldn't we make that work, and keep the girls with us?"

Maddy smiled at him tolerantly. "Well, that could work, in time, but we need to start small and work up to that. Bigger boats are expensive to buy and to keep. I've been down that path before, Jack, and lost everything because of the debt. I can't do that again. We have time. Let's start with what we have. Together, we'll make it."

Jack had a funny look on his face that Maddy couldn't read. She tilted her head quizzically and asked, "What is it, Jack? Why such a strange look?"

He started rubbing his chin, looking down at his feet and then back to her, as if afraid to go on. "Ah...sweetheart, you know I've been honest with you, but I, ah, haven't told you everything yet. There are...uh...a couple of other things I was trying to find a way and the right time to tell you about. Stuff about...our boat...and the bar, and your old sloop. You see, it wasn't just $60 million I found, sweetheart. And Robbie had made plans for you. He told me about this close banking friend he has down in Antigua...at a bank he owned..."

Ray was standing near the entrance of the Evening Shadows waiting for his cab and looking back down toward the marina. He really liked Jack, and he'd only known him for a few hours, really. He liked Maddy too but was worried about her, and he wondered if she could ever really understand what Jack had done and why and then truly forgive him. It wasn't just any man who would risk his life for those he loved as Jack had. As he watched them talking and holding each other close, his thoughts returned to Stephanie and what he was going to say to her if he got the chance.

Suddenly Maddy jumped back, and her hands went to her face, and she screamed what sounded from a distance like "Oh...my...God!" Then, just as quickly, she jumped back into Jack's open arms, holding his face and kissing him over and over.

Ray's cab pulled up as he was watching the strange and unexpected scene. He turned, struggled in, and sat down, pulling the door closed behind him. He needed to make sure he made his plane, and then, once back in Nassau, try to reach Stephanie, and then, somehow, change her feelings about him. As the cab started for the airport, he glanced back to the *Second Chance* and smiled, thoughts of how to approach Stephanie ever present in his mind, and he said quietly, "Damn, I wish I knew what Jack said to her to make her so happy."

The cab driver looked in the rearview mirror and said, "Sorry; what you say, mon?"

"Nothing," Ray said with a sly smile on his face as he met the driver's eyes. "Nothing. Just talking to myself. The airport, please, as fast as you can make it. There's this girl I need to see…"

About the Author

Photo by Desmond Boylan

Chris Thomas successfully practiced architecture after graduating from the University of Colorado in 1977. However, from the time he was thirty he felt he should be writing stories. What began as an unrealized dream finally became a reality when at fifty-five he semiretired from his architectural practice and fully committed himself to writing his novels, *Until Philosophers Become Kings; Book One*, and *The Kingdom Shall Fall, Book Two. The Last Good Samaritan* is his third novel.

Thomas, a third-generation Coloradan, resides in Denver. He invites you to visit his website, booksbychristhomas.com, and his Facebook page, @chrisbthomasauthor, for more information about his work.

Made in the USA
Las Vegas, NV
10 December 2022

61365994R00213